Their eyes n   pulse
to be soothi   buble
was she ap   That
morning, after the milking, when she and Stephen had
stood in the mowie and kissed until their mouths ached,
her innards had turned over and over with her longing
for him. And yet moments later, when, to test herself,
she had thought of Mark and all the wonderful times
they had known together, she had felt that same
hollowing-out, that same almost infinite yearning. It
made her wonder if she weren't more in love with love
itself than with any actual man in her life.

Also by Malcolm Ross

The Dukes
On a Far Wild Shore
A Notorious Woman
An Innocent Woman

A Woman Alone

Malcolm Ross

HEADLINE

Copyright © 1990 Malcolm Ross Macdonald

The right of Malcolm Ross to be identified as the Author of the
Work has been asserted by him in accordance with the
Copyright, Designs and Patents Act 1988.

First published in 1990
by Judy Piatkus (Publishers) Ltd

First published in paperback in 1991
by HEADLINE BOOK PUBLISHING PLC

10 9 8 7 6 5 4 3 2 1

ISBN 0 7472 3576 7

Typeset by Medcalf Type Ltd, Bicester

Printed and bound by
Collins Manufacturing, Glasgow

HEADLINE BOOK PUBLISHING PLC
Headline House
79 Great Titchfield Street
London W1P 7FN

For Marlis and Cliff

PART ONE

THREE'S A CROWD

1

Stephen was watching the two girls, though they were not aware of it. Nor was *he* aware that his young sister, Annette, was watching him. He had found an old theodolite in the attic at Skyburriowe and had taken it out in a half-hearted attempt to survey the fields between Breage and Trequean. Since they would all be his one day, it seemed a worthwhile occupation for an idle late-summer afternoon. But the moment he had spotted Roseanne Kitto and her friend Mary whatsername through its telescope, he had dropped the intention completely – and doubled his pretence at taking it seriously.

They were still a good half-mile away, but he would know Miss Kitto among a thousand. It was not just her bonny figure, her pale green eyes, and flaxen hair, but something altogether more mysterious and special that seemed to cling about her. For more than two years now he had loved her from a distance – that unbridgeable distance which separates the squire's son and the stonemason's daughter.

In the next field, her eyes glued to the binoculars her father had given her three years ago on her fourteenth birthday, Annette chuckled. For she had also spied the two village girls, picking blackberries and working their way slowly along the schoolhouse lane toward Trequean. Knowing very well what one of them meant

3

to Stephen, she settled to enjoy what she felt sure would be one of the more interesting encounters she and her binoculars had witnessed.

Roseanne Kitto and Maria Curnow were discussing their respective beaux: Mark Bodilly and Johnny Tregear. All four of them had attended the same village school — and so, indeed, had Stephen and his sister in their infant years. The girls had passed the place half a mile back; in fact, the sight of it had started their present conversation — for Roseanne and Mark had been more or less promised to each other from those times, when she was fourteen and he a year or so older. Now, seven years on, he had just embarked on a rather precarious career as cattle dealer and auctioneer, having squandered his life so far in various menial posts only to see advancement go to the sons of the owners or their chief clerks.

Maria plucked a dandelion from the hedgerow and blew at its down to see whether anyone loved her or loved her not.

'Mark do have a nice smile when he remembers it,' Roseanne said. 'You got to allow that.'

Maria paused between puffs. 'Johnny don't have to remember. He's always smiling.'

'Call that a smile?' Roseanne chuckled. 'More a vacant grin, if you ask me. You still see him, do 'ee?'

'In and out.' Maria gave a casual little toss of her head to show it meant little. 'He's gone to live down Falmouth. He's doing very well by all accounts.' She threw the denuded seed head away. 'He loves me. But I'm sure I don't know who.'

'Last I heard, Johnny was working in Rosewarne's Export Brewery there.' Roseanne eyed a cluster of blackberries, huge and ripe. 'We should ought to pick

4

they,' she said. 'They'll kill we if us don't bring home a pint at least.'

'A pint each,' Maria agreed glumly.

They paused and reached among the thorns for the glistening black fruit. Some were so ripe that they fell when a neighbour was plucked. Maria squatted to find them among the long grass at the foot of the hedge.

'Gusson! Leave they,' Roseanne chided. 'There's millions down Trequean.'

Her friend rose reluctantly. 'It do seem so wasteful, somehow,' she complained.

The moment they set off again, Roseanne picked up the earlier thread of their conversation: 'At least Johnny haven't fallen in a vat of ale and drowned hisself.'

Maria made no reply.

'Like in they stinging nettles!' She dissolved in fits of laughter.

'I know very well what occasion you mean,' Maria said tetchily.

There was a silence. They sauntered on past another cluster of ripe fruit, too small and thorny to detain them. Maria shooed a swarm of midges away. 'I wouldn't say that Mark Bodilly has done so well for himself as might have been expected,' she remarked casually. Then, in a more energetic voice, 'Here, you think that's rain, do 'ee? Over the Lizard there?'

'Very likely.' Roseanne bagged a small handful of blackberries from an overhanging spray, two of which she ate with a guilty sideways glance at her friend. 'Too soft to keep,' she explained.

Maria accepted the assurance with a disbelieving nod. 'Specially when you remember he was always top of the class and that,' she added.

Roseanne remembered the pride she had always felt

when Mark's name was read out, always first. To be the belle of the best had been splendid.

'Auctioneer and cattle dealer!' Maria sighed. 'That's a bit of a come-down.'

'He isn't but twenty-three years old,' Roseanne answered stoutly. 'And what's his father? Only a stonemason, like mine.' She avoided adding, 'And like yours, and all,' for Maria's father, too, was 'only' a stonemason. Maria, no doubt, would be stung into pointing out that her father was an *engineer*-stonemason – merely because he'd helped build ten yards of the sea wall down at Porthleven harbour.

'Mark taking you to Ram-Buck Fair, is he?' Maria asked.

'Very likely,' Roseanne said again.

'He never asked you yet, then?'

'He don't hardly need to. I suppose he can more or less take it for granted.'

Maria sniffed. 'I wouldn't never let no man take me for granted.'

'I never said he do take *me* for granted,' Roseanne countered. 'Only that I'll go with 'n to Ram-Buck same as always.'

'Same as makes no difference.'

They sauntered down the serpentine, switchback lane that led from Breage to the coastal road at Trequean, each trying in her desultory, rather bored way to provoke the other into an outburst of petulant anger – which would have scored a small point or two in the undeclared contest between them. Neither, however, yielded any such satisfaction – which, paradoxically, satisfied them both.

'Here!' Maria declared when they reached the coastal road. 'Look who that is, then!' She had just started to gather blackberries in earnest – by chance, near a gap

6

in the hedge. Now she moved a little to one side to allow Roseanne to peer through it, too. 'On the far side the field there.'

'Young Squire Morvah,' Roseanne murmured.

'What's he doing?'

It was not immediately apparent. He was stooping behind some sort of apparatus, which was supported on a tripod. It was too small for a camera and too complicated for a telescope. He would peer through the back of it, make some adjustments, then stand up and study something on the side of it before jotting down his observations in a little notebook.

'That's like old Coad did out Montpelier when Miss Hervey sold up,' Roseanne commented. 'Surveying, he called it.' She turned wide-eyed to her friend. 'You think that's what 'tis? The squire selling up? Sent his son out to survey the estate before they sell up?'

'Very likely,'' Maria agreed, craning her neck to peer through the gap again. 'Oh my gidge! He's seen us with that thing.'

Stephen Morvah rose behind his apparats and waved at them. His indistinct cry reached them in its dying moments.

'He's coming,' Roseanne said. 'What shall us say to 'n?' She had no notion of the young man's feelings toward her.

'Whatever we please,' Maria replied with more assurance than she felt. 'There's no law against picking blackberries, I hope.'

'Anyway, we're not on his side the hedge. You ever spoken to him before, have you? Since school, I mean?'

'When I was eight and he was about fourteen, paddling in the rocks at Megaliggar.' Maria giggled. 'I never had a stitch on — and no more did he. I don't know which of us was more surprised!'

'Well, don't you dare mention that!' Roseanne rolled her eyes in anguish.

Maria shot her a look of withering pity. 'As if I would.' The young man, now halfway over the pasture, broke into a slow trot.

His sudden move annoyed his sister. It was plainly his intention to hobnob with the two maids through the hedge; but not only would he now have his back to her, he would also obscure one or other of them most of the time. Crouching low she doubled along the headland of the neighbouring field and made a new approach up the road from Trequean.

'He's turned out some proper 'ansum young fellow,' Roseanne murmured appreciatively as he drew near.

Not quite a Greek god, he was nonetheless 'proper 'ansum' with his fair wavy hair and his frank, blue eyes. 'Good afternoon to ye,' he called out when he came within a dozen paces.

'Afternoon, Squire.' The two girls curtsied.

'Oh, I say — none of that, what? Don't I know you both? Miss Maria Curnow and Miss Roseanne Kitto, isn't it?'

The girls giggled, glanced at each other, and giggled again.

'Out blackberrying, eh?'

'There's a burr few down here,' Roseanne told him.

'Indeed. There's quite a harvest this side, too. Why don't you come in? I'll give you a hand — pick for both of you.'

Roseanne gazed up and down the deserted road. 'We shouldn't want to go disturbing you, sir,' she said hesitantly.

'Nonsense! I'm only trying out a surveyor's theodolite I discovered in the attic at home, but I should have brought one of the gardener's boys with me to hold the staff. Now I'm rather glad I didn't.' He took a pace closer to the gap and smiled at them. 'I'm not proposing to *eat* you, you know. Though I might eat a few blackberries. Go back to the gate there. You don't want to tear those lovely dresses trying to get through here.'

Without waiting for an answer he strode back the fifty yards or so to the gate.

The girls looked uncertainly at each other. 'Can't really say no,' Maria offered.

'It would be rude,' Roseanne agreed. So they turned about and made for the gate, too.

'Lovely dresses!' Maria said scornfully, looking at their serviceable blue linen skirts.

'Considerate, though,' Roseanne replied.

He was waiting with the gate already opened and a warm smile of welcome.

Annette found a new vantage that would be side-on to them as they worked their way back along the hedge to the gap where Stephen had first accosted them.

'No bulls or anything?' Roseanne peered cautiously beyond him into the field.

'He's earning his keep in the yard today,' he replied. Then, to Maria, 'I don't suppose you remember the last time we actually met, Miss Curnow? It wasn't a thousand miles from here. I've seen you often since then, of course – out and about – but that was our last actual meeting.'

Maria, too embarrassed to reply, swept past him into the field. He smiled at Roseanne and said, 'Oh dear! Put my foot in it again!'

'It could have been said more tactful,' she chided.

His smile broadened and Roseanne realized he now knew that Maria had just told her of the incident. Perhaps he wasn't so green as he liked to put on.

9

'What's that thing for?' she asked, nodding at his abandoned theodolite.

He was right about the abundance of the harvest on the inside of the hedge; it was twice as prolific as the verge they had just abandoned. Maria was already at work, filling her pannikin as fast as she could.

'I'll pick for you until we've caught up,' Stephen said to Roseanne, reaching for the highest and most luscious fruits. 'And as for the theodolites, well, they enable one to make maps.'

'Ah.'

'Trigonometry and things like that,' he added, dumping his first handful into her jug.

Several were squashed. She looked at them coldly and gave him a tolerant smile.

'I'll do better,' he promised. To the hedge itself he muttered, 'Can't put a foot right, today.'

Both girls laughed and after that the conversation somehow flowed more easily.

Poor Annette now realized that hearing was going to be more important than seeing. Abandoning all attempts at hiding, she wandered up the road, trusting that the hedge would be thick enough to conceal her when she drew within earshot.

Stephen asked the girls what their fathers were doing nowadays. Maria said hers was working on the improvements to the sea wall by Penzance station. Roseanne said nothing. He turned back to her. 'Didn't I hear something about Mr Kitto working for that potty woman over at Helford Passage?' he asked. 'The one who used to live at Montpelier. She's blasting half the cliff away or something, isn't she?'

'Mrs Scawen,' Roseanne said.

'That's the one.'

'He's doing a bit of work for her, yes,' she agreed. 'I don't know about potty. She's making a hanging garden there, so you can walk all the way down to the sea through grottos and tunnels and terraces and that. He says it's proper 'ansum.'

'Proper expensive, too, I'd say,' he commented dourly. 'Not that she's short of it mind. I expect your father could pretty well name his price, eh?'

She looked him square in the eye, laughed, and shook her head.

He wondered how he could look into those eyes, so close, and not die of a heart attack; but he was outwardly all collected as he dropped another handful into her jug. 'Better?' he asked.

She nodded and went on picking. 'I got to get back home and do the milking,' she announced.

'Old Mr Coad, he's got one of them.' Maria nodded at the abandoned theodolite. 'I saw him use it out Montpelier before that Mrs Scawen sold up there. Sold it to your father, didn't he, sir?' She watched closely for any response to the mention of a sale.

'Mr Coad uses it rather more proficiently than me, I hope,' was all he said. After a short silence he added, 'Ram-Buck Fair next week.'

For a while they discussed the prospects for that. The weather had been mixed for some weeks now; they were certainly owed a settled spell. It had rained last year, so perhaps this year would be better. Pity it was held in such an out-of-the-way place. Helston Harvest Fair was much better, really.

'I was at Pallas House last week,' he told them. 'Old Hamill Oliver – you know him, surely – he told me that all Celtic fairs and meetings were held in out-of-the-way places like that. He said we couldn't trust each other enough to invite outsiders into our own villages

11

so we always met on neutral ground.' He sniffed. 'I don't think we've changed much either.'

Listening to him talk, Roseanne decided he was quite a pleasant fellow once he forgot who he was and just spoke about things that interested him. However, she was still a little resentful of the lordly-jocular way he had invited them into his field — when, in fact, he had no right to keep them out. It was well established that anyone could go through the woods and gather all the sticks they could carry. 'Are you going to Ram-Buck Fair yourself?' she asked.

'Roseanne!' Maria shot her a glance of surprise.

'What?' she asked truculently.

'She thinks you're inviting me,' Stephen explained, speaking as if to a foreigner who might not understand the local customs.

His bluntness left her momentarily at a loss. Then, like some spiny creature that cannot back out of a hole it has dug, she pressed onward. 'Well, why not?' she asked.

'Roseanne!' Maria's surprise turned to alarm. 'Pay her no heed, sir. 'Tis her humour, that's all.'

'Oh, is it?' He treated the explanation as a serious diagnosis. 'Is it really?' In fact he was delighted. He had no idea it would be so easy.

Roseanne concentrated on an extra-large bunch of berries. 'As you wish,' she said.

'Oh well, in that case, I accept. I'll be in my gig at the top of Penhale Row with my hair all oiled and frizzed, as they say, at half past one. If that's not too early?'

Now the surprise was all Roseanne's. How had she allowed such a thing to happen? What would she tell Mark, never the world's easiest man to talk to? It was just a joke that got out of hand . . . but all she could think of to say was, 'How did you know I live in Penhale Row?'

With an oddly ritual deference he offered her a handful of perfect berries. 'It may,' he said, 'have something to do with the fact that I am not yet blind.'

She accepted the fruit and then told him she was only joking and he needn't consider himself held to it.

He turned to Maria. 'Did it sound like a joke to you?' he asked.

She grinned and shook her head vigorously.

'Maria!' Roseanne said with an edge of desperation in her tone. 'You know I was! How could I ever have meant that seriously?' Her eyes were wide with pleading. 'And you know, too . . .'

'What? What do I know.'

'You *know*!'

'I know the sky's blue and water's wet.'

He joined in. 'It didn't sound like a joke to her, Miss Kitto. And I'm sorry to have to say that I took you to be in solemn earnest. I accepted your invitation in good faith.'

'Oh, very *well*!' Roseanne stressed the word in her frustration at being unable to stamp her feet — for fear of losing half her blackberries. 'But don't imagine I shall enjoy it.' Her eyes narrowed. 'And don't imagine I'm going to let *you* enjoy it, either!'

On the far side of the hedge Annette hugged herself in a positive ecstasy.

2

Frank Kitto scratched in the stubble of his chin as he surveyed the morning's work. Despite the breeze, the reek of burned blasting powder was heavy on the air — as heavy as the tons of rubble that now awaited his, or someone's, shovel.

'Will it be level, d'you think?' Mrs Scawen asked.

He shook his head gravely. 'No way of telling that, missis, until we've got 'n cleared, see. That's the trouble with the whole of Cornwall — there's no level rock nowhere.' He looked upward, toward the clifftop, gauging the height the debris would now have to be raised. ''Tis starting to be what we do call navvy's work,' he added.

She smiled. 'Hard, you mean.'

'Costly, I do mean. We're down so far now that we'll need to haul the barrows up with a horse and rope. The horse do stay up top, see, and the rope do run over a set of pulleys. So there's all the cost of that — *and* a boy to mind the horse. That's what I do mean.'

The woman scratched thoughtfully at her lower lip. 'What other way is there?' she asked. 'We can't put the rubble to any use down here. I'm beginning to think this was all a big mistake.'

Kitto leaned over the parapet and spat across the wind, watching it eddy and dance all the way to the estuary below. 'That's a good place for it, I'd say.'

She went to the edge and peered over, reaching an arm behind her for his support. 'The Duchy of Cornwall wouldn't like that one bit,' she said.

'I don't suppose they would, missis. But what can they do about it?'

'Sue me?'

''Zackly,' he said.

She turned to him in surprise, giving a little skip to carry her away from that vertiginous edge. 'Well, how would *that* help?'

His grin was all-knowing. 'You ask Mr Scawen, now. What's the law's delays on civil cases at the moment? A year? Two year? I think 'tis even more. So you got two year to tip all the spoilings down there, bring a barge round from Falmouth, and carry 'n off to sea.' His hand pointed vaguely at the wide blue waters of Falmouth Bay. 'And what's left to sue for then? There's no oyster beds just there, is there.'

'I don't know.'

'Well, I'm a-telling of 'ee. There's not. So they couldn't claim no material damage . . .'

As he enumerated the virtues of his idea, it astounded her to realize that his notion of good-neighbourliness and hers should be so much at odds. His unspoken motto seemed to be: *If you can get away with it, do it*.

He let the idea brew a while and then added, ''Tin't liable to be a lot, anyway. We could blast away six month or more and not make much show down there.'

'Oh, really,' she said drily. 'It's a different story when it has to be raised to the top, though!'

'Ah!' He nodded confidently, wishing he had not spoken. 'That's the difference, see, between the *look* of the thing and the *weight* of it.'

She laughed and clapped him on the shoulder. 'You'll do, Kitto,' she said. 'I'll tell you what. Leave it for

15

today. I'll have a word with Mr Scawen. You can go back to rebuilding my front wall — unless you have other fish to fry?'

Kitto did not, at that moment, have other contracts to attend to but he drew out his watch and made a number of apparent mental calculations before he declared he might just as well see out the day, now he was here. He gathered up his shovel and plumbline and together they strolled back across the Trevivian estate. Until a few years ago these had been mere fields. . . . Now one could begin to see Mrs Scawen's gardens beginning to take shape: the terraces, the walks, the borders for what she called *herbaceous* plants and shrubberies, the rockeries and screes, all covered with the peat she had carried by the cartload from Bodmin Moor . . . it was all beginning to emerge from what had been, for three years past, an unpromising wilderness of mud and stone.

He saw her run an appreciative eye over her creation. 'This is the first month,' she told him, 'in which I've been able to take the faintest pleasure in this walk.'

''Es, you,' he agreed. ''Tis a bigger change than I'd ever have believed. Of course, 'tis mostly in the mind, still — but there's something to work on now. He'll look some 'ansum when he's done.'

'Ah, but when will that be, Kitto? Long after we're both in our boxes, I fear. Some of my trees don't grow more than an inch a year.'

'Is that a fact?'

'It is. Still, I don't expect they call me the Madwoman of Trevivian *quite* so often now?'

'I never heard anyone call 'ee that, missis,' he lied.

'Wax in the ears?' she suggested.

She left him when they reached the house. Ten minutes later she was off in her gig to Falmouth to collect yet more shrubs that had been sent down by train. He worked steadily on at rebuilding her front wall, for he was not one of those two-paced men — fast when the boss is about, slow the rest of the time. The work itself was second nature to him now — 'in his hands', as he liked to say — leaving his mind free for higher things.

Today his mind kept returning to the heap of spoil they'd left on that ledge, a few fathoms below the clifftop. Once it was on the surface he felt sure there must be a use for it. *She* didn't want it — the boss-woman, as he called her. It was a mixture of shale and elvanstone, too uneven for a path or driveway. It was good enough for a roadbed, though. But who was laying any roads now? He didn't know of one within paying reach of Helford. The thought of it nagged at him, especially when, in his imagination, he saw himself chucking spoil down the cliff face that might fetch a halfpenny a shovelful in the right place.

Now and then a passer-by would pause to share the time of day. Kitto worked on through their conversation, giving full value both to Mrs Scawen and his companion of the moment. He routinely asked of each if they knew of anyone — farmer, landowner, parish council . . . anyone — who might be looking for a bit of hardcore. Oddly enough, it was Mrs Scawen herself who, on her return, gave him the answer he had been hoping against hope to hear. She told him that the new lunatic asylum above Penryn was adding a separate entrance and driveway to its home farm, so that visitors to the farm would no longer have to run a gauntlet of the inmates. Then she took away all his pleasure by adding, 'So, it all works out for the best.'

'How's that, then, missis?' he asked cautiously.

'I can sell them my rubble, of course.'

17

Kitto hid his disappointment, made a dubious face, sucked at a tooth, and shook his head. 'Still it won't hardly pay 'ee, missis,' he assured her. 'What did they offer? Four bob a load? Something like that? That's the top rate now.'

Of course, he did not for one moment imagine she had actually done anything so unladylike as talk money with Harry Angove, the clerk of the works at the asylum. But she grinned triumphantly and said, 'Well, I got five shillings a load. So I've done rather well.'

He cursed inwardly, being sure he could have risen them to six.

'What's the matter?' she asked, seeing his face fall.

Well, if nothing else, he thought, he could salvage a little moral advantage out of the mess. 'I wish you hadn't done that, missis. You talk to the clerk of works at the asylum, did 'ee?'

'Harry Angove, yes.'

'Well, his daughter Nellie, see, was left at the altar by Harold Knight, whose father is the manager over to Dodman's Quarries. And that's the only other source of good hardcore close to Penryn, see. Old Harry Angove, he'd never have dealt with they, so 'twould have been a nice little market for we.'

'I see.' She pulled a contrite face. 'Fools rush in, eh? How can I make amends?'

He thought rapidly. 'See, 'twill cost 'ee four bob a load just to get 'n to the clifftop.' *Allowing two bob profit for me*, he added mentally.

'But I should still be better off than if we simply shovelled it down the cliff and took it all out by barge later. That won't exactly be cheap.'

He dipped his head shrewdly. 'Don't forget the cost of hauling it from the clifftop and delivering it to the looney bin. You won't do that inside a shilling.'

18

The true figure was more like threepence.

'What d'you suggest then, Mr Kitto?'

'Well, missis, first thing is not to let Harry Angove sleep on that five shillings. If you don't mind, I think I'll go over and see the old feller now.'

She grinned delightedly. 'What d'you think we'll get?'

'We?' he echoed.

'Yes. Let's make it a partnership. I'll pay you your four shillings a load to get the stuff to the clifftop and we'll split all the extra evenly. Doesn't that sound fair?'

He didn't actually care what arrangement they came to — not once he heard that magic word *partnership*. It went very nicely with certain plans he had been fermenting for more than a year now. 'You're a Christian, missis,' he told her.

'She's a real Christian,' he repeated to his wife, Mary, later that evening — after he had beaten Harry Angove up to six and sixpence, spread and rolled. 'This could be what we're waiting for. This is our sprat to catch her mackerel.'

By long habit his wife sought only for drawbacks and disadvantages; the first was also the most glaring. 'That husband of her, Vosper Scawen, he's nobody's fool.'

'That's all the better,' he assured her. 'Seeing as I'm not out to cheat nobody. All I do want is a bit of sound money behind me and I'll not stint on the dividends when it comes to paying back. She won't grumble — and no more will Lawyer Scawen.'

'And how do we know she's as rich as they do say she is? I never see her dressed better than a scarecrow. I've got better dresses than she has.'

'You got better dresses than half the women in Cornwall,' he pointed out.

'Well, they're not the half that concern me,' she replied. 'Anyway, that's no answer.'

19

'Of course she got the money,' he said testily. 'She do put it all into her gardens rather than on her back. Only a woman with money could *afford* to behave like that.'

'And where did she get it from, that's what I'd like to know. People say her mother was that Angwin Vyvyan who left Cornwall in disgrace, belly-out with her and no ring on her finger. How did she lay her hands on so much, eh?'

'People say! People say! That's hardly no concern of ours, is it. *She's* got money, no doubt of it. *She* proposed this here little partnership, not me. *She'll* be pleased as a dog with two tails when she sees what it earned – and I shall give her *all* my profit.'

'Are you mad?'

'I think not. A sprat to catch a mackerel, like I said. And *she'll* listen very attentive-like when I suggest something bigger.'

'Bigger!' his wife exclaimed. ''Twill be like saying, ''Well, Mrs Scawen, we've walked to the bottom of the garden and back without mishap, now shall us walk to London and back?'' That's the top and tail of it.'

He chuckled. 'When you see the size of *her* garden, London-and-back isn't much more. Anyway, 'tis settled now. The worst she can say when the time do come is no. And that'll leave us no worse off than what we are now.'

Mary Kitto shrugged. 'The die is cast then.'

3

Mary Kitto returned from the bakery with a face like a thunderstorm. Roseanne, who was sitting in the window seat sewing a new muslin *balayeuse* into the dress she would wear for the dancing after Wendron Ram-Buck, knew something was wrong even before she saw her mother's face. The way her fearsome silhouette flounced past the gaps in the escallonia hedge was like a ship under flag of war. 'Here's a how d'ye do!' were her first words as she backed into the hall, stamping the mud and gravel from her boots with angry relish.

Roseanne parked her needle and rose to relieve her mother of her messages. 'What now?' she ventured.

The woman lowered her head and fixed her with a button-like eye, as if over the tops of half-moon glasses — though, in fact she wore no such thing. 'Well may you ask miss! Well may you ask!'

Roseanne's heart sank still further. When her mother played these rhetorical cat-and-mouse games, she was in earnest and things were as black as they could be short of corporal chastisement and a regime of bread and water. 'What have I done now?' she prompted.

'What have you *not* done, young lady. That's more to the point. The *shame* of it! I didn't know where to look when Mrs Curnow told me. How could you do it to us? I don't know what your father's going to say.'

'*What*?' Roseanne insisted. 'I'm not aware of having

done anything — nor of leaving anything undone, either. Nothing so serious as all this, anyway.'

Her mother sat down heavily on the hall chair, cracking a wicker hoop in her *tournure* — which only vexed her more. 'Is it not true, then? Oh, but that would be even worse!'

Now poor Roseanne did not know what to think. Whatever she was supposed to have done, or left undone, was bad enough; but now, it seemed, *not* to have done it, or *not* to have left it undone, was even worse. She could not help feeling there was a contradiction in it somewhere. Her mother put her out of her misery at last. 'Is it or is it not true that Squire Morvah's son asked could he put you up Ram-Buck this Saturday?'

'Master Stephen,' she said, drawing in her stomach to prevent it falling away entirely.

'Well, he has no other son so far as I know. Is it true?'

'It was a joke,' she replied airily. 'I never thought no more about it.'

'What do 'ee mean, a joke?' Alarm invaded her mother's face. 'How are you and he on such joking terms all of a sudden?'

'He can't possibly have meant it to be tooken seriously,' Roseanne insisted.

'Well, that Maria Curnow never thought it no joke. *She*'s taken it seriously, sure enough.'

'I'll kill she,' Roseanne muttered.

Her mother rose and began to pace about — as much as any woman with an eighteen-inch *tournure* can pace in a ten-by-ten parlour crammed with china knick-knacks. 'Well, 'tis all over Breage by now. Us'll be in the laughing stocks if 'tis no more than a joke. What did Master Stephen say to 'ee? What were his very words?'

Roseanne sighed, knowing she was going to make a

22

mess of it, as she always did when her mother came at her in such an intimidating manner. 'We was gathering blackberries out Trequean way. And we was coozing on about this and that. And I asked 'n was he going up Wendron Ram-Buck . . .'

'You never!' Mary Kitto put an anxious hand to her mouth.

''Twas only a bit of old cooze, like I said. And Maria started behaving all agape, and I told she not to be so daw-brained, and *he* said Maria must think I was inviting him, Master Stephen, to put me up there. So I said, just for a joke, like, why not?'

'My dear soul! And?'

'And he said why not, indeed.'

Mrs Kitto was bewildered. 'And that's all?'

Roseanne moved her head about awkwardly. 'He did say summat else about collecting me.'

Her mother looked at her sharply. 'And that's what you call a joke? Oh, my gidge! Oh my sainted aunt!'

'What?' Roseanne asked in pained surprise. 'He won't come. He never meant it. I can't see what all the fuss is about.'

Mrs Kitto winced — in fact, because a broken end of wicker had just poked her sharply in the thigh, though Roseanne was not to know that. 'What are you going to wear?'

'He won't come, I tell 'ee!' The assertion sounded increasingly shrill.

Her mother ignored her. 'You can't put up that old thing.' She nodded at the dress her daughter had been patching. 'You'll have to wear my saffron dress. We can get some machine lace in Nicholls's and you can tack on an extra row of flounces. And an artificial rose to cover the stains where Aunt Rose spilled that blackberry wine . . .'

'Mother!' Roseanne chided. ''Tis all needless expense and labour, I tell 'ee. Master Stephen won't come.'

'And you can change in your Aunt Rose's room in Yeol Parc. She do owe us that favour. So you may wear that old thing in the afternoon.' She nodded once more at the dress her daughter had been mending.

'I shall write to him,' Roseanne decided firmly. 'I shall tell him no matter if he thought 'twas serious, *I* never. So there.'

'You'll do no such thing,' her mother responded mildly, as if the girl's assertion were too trivial to be dignified by a stronger denial. 'Three dresses in the one day! That's so much as Lady Morvah do put up most days. Clever Master Stephen can't hardly sneer at that.'

'I don't suppose he'd sneer if I wore but the one dress, either. Say what you mind about him, but sneering isn't his style.'

The shock of it was beginning to wear off for Mrs Kitto. When she had first heard the news from Mrs Curnow in that bantering, teasing manner of hers, she hadn't known how to take it. She considered that her slightly airy but nonetheless knowing denial had, in the circumstances, been rather a good response. But now that it seemed there might be something in it after all, she realized it required some thought, and some rather careful preparation, if it was not to be taken as a joke by both parties and squandered. This first, unthinkable step must be turned into the first of many even more unthinkable steps. Even to herself she did not dare think the words: *leading my daughter to the altar*, but that was the image that dithered in the wings of her mind.

'Sit down, my dear,' she said quietly.

Roseanne, who was by now wishing she had swum out to sea and drowned on that fateful day, instead of 'coozing' with Maria and Master Stephen, obeyed.

'When you say *joke*,' her mother began . . .

'I meant just giddying about.'

'But you never gave Master Stephen no cause to think . . . I mean, you know they do say 'twas *he* got Martha Toy belly-up — which is how she's got ten shilling a week to spend all of a sudden. You never let Master Stephen think . . . you know. Nothing like that, I hope.'

'Mother!' Roseanne blushed deeply.

'Well you might not even know. You could put that thought in his mind without intending it, and be none the wiser. I mean it doesn't take much. One smile . . . one unguarded word — that's all the encouragement many a man will need.'

Roseanne stood up and went out to the kitchen, carrying her mother's messages with her; once her back was safely turned, she raked the heavens with her eyes and let out a silent whistle.

'From your collarbone to your ankle,' the woman called after her, 'that's all trespassers-will-be-prosecuted down there. Just so long as he do understand that.'

Roseanne started putting the groceries away.

Mrs Kitto followed her in and picked up a loaf of sugar. ''Course,' she said in a more ruminative tone, 'I suppose there wouldn't be a bit of harm if he thought you *might*. Not today, nor yet tomorrow, but *sometime*, like. Keep him in his torment till he sees there's only one way you'll ever yield.'

Roseanne listened to her mother in mounting amazement — not least because it was quite clear that the woman was no longer talking directly to her in their own vernacular. She was 'talking posh'. She was stating a case before an unseen audience, somewhere vaguely out there. Her daughter was, by now, a mere eavesdropper.

In the end, though, Mrs Kitto returned sharply to present realities. 'Not a word to your father about this,' she admonished. 'I'll find the way to break it to him.'

That night, as her husband reached across the bed to snuff out their candle, she grasped his arm to restrain him. 'What's all this then?' he asked in amusement.

'Keep your voice down,' she replied, barely above a whisper, as she jabbed her thumb at the wall between their bedroom and Roseanne's. He chuckled and assured her that a good twelve inches of cob and stone separated them and that science had proved . . .

She interrupted to inform him that science was an ass when it came to measuring the hearing of any inquisitive female. And she went on to tell him what had transpired that morning.

'I thought she had a shifty look when she brought me my slippers,' he commented.

'Never mind that now,' Mary grumbled. 'What I'm saying is that if she can fashion it right, she could end up Mrs Stephen Morvah. And Lady Morvah, too, in due course.'

He did his best to suppress a guffaw.

'Only she's so daw-brained she'd just so easy throw it all away.'

He became serious again as the implications of the news began to sink in. 'A gentleman of his class and a young girl of ours . . .' he began dubiously.

''Zackly! I told her plain, and no sparing her blushes, any caper like that and she'll never set foot across this threshold again.'

He made a dubious noise or two. 'I shouldn't think we'd hardly be so scratchy as that.'

'Never mind. Let her think it. But *my* point is, 'twouldn't do no harm if she was to let Master . . . here, just a minute! What d'you mean "a girl of *our* class"? What's wrong with our class?'

'Nothing wrong. I didn't say there's anything wrong.

But if I may put it this way — I don't think fine gentry like the Morvahs do see the same difference between us and Mrs Kitchen next door as *we* do see.'

'Mrs Kitchen! With seven children and seven different fathers to claim them!'

'Shhh!'

'She hasn't even got a parlour! And one good dress between her and her two big daughters! No difference!'

'That's what I'm saying, my dear,' he observed. '*We* can see the difference, higher than Trigonning Hill. But I doubt the Morvahs and their like ever would. And what I'm also saying is, he'd see that Lizzie Kitchen as fair game . . .'

'Which she is!'

'And he might think our Rosie, living next down and all, is much the same.'

Mary, being compelled to accept the logic of that, now wove it into her own argument. 'My point is, our Roseanne should ought to let young Morvah think there's a chance of it — just a chance, mind. Like I said to her — not today, nor yet tomorrow, but a chance all the same.'

'You spoke to her about it?' he asked in surprise.

'Well, of course I did! She'd bring it all down in ruins inside a week, left to herself. I shall push and pull her every inch of this road, till we got that ring on her finger, see?'

He chuckled at her rose-tinted confidence.

'But don't *you* run off with the notion you're left out of it,' she warned him. 'You're a cog in this bit of clockwork, too.'

'How?' he asked.

'That scheme of yours, to ask Mrs Scawen will she throw in a bit of capital, I mean, when's that going to be?'

27

'Lord, woman!' he said dismissively. 'I only now lit the fire. She's made of best Sheffield steel. She won't melt all in one day.'

'Good!' she capped him. 'Because all-in-one-day would be too quick for us, as well. What about next February? March? Sometime before next June, anyway? That'd suit us, proper job.' A cunning thought occurred to her. 'And there's another thing — if it were widely known that our Rosie and young Master Morvah were couranting, all right and proper by then, well, Mrs Scawen would hardly be so inclined to laugh in your face, would she.'

He sniffed. 'That's a thought, now. My dear soul! It *is* like a bit of clockwork and no mistake. Every little wheel must be in its proper place in the train.'

'If Roseanne can spin him out for the next month without saying goodbye entirely, she can hold him off for a year. We shall know one way or the other, this side Christmas.'

There was a brief, thoughtful silence before he picked up the thread: 'Talking of wheels in the train, I know one who's going to squeak mighty loud when news of this gets out — and that's Mark Bodilly.'

'Mark?' Mary laughed at very idea that their daughter's childhood sweetheart would present any problem when the time came. 'He won't say nothing. He'll turn his back, walk away, get drunk, spend a night in the lock-up. And that'll be the last of Master Mark so far as we need worry. Anyway,' she added comfortingly, 'she'll be guided by us in this. Say what you mind, but we have reared an obedient daughter.'

4

Mark Bodilly ran his eye over the four heifers, three in calf and one aborted. It was the aborted one that worried him. Willy Benny, who was hoping to sell them as one lot, claimed not to be worried in the least – but then, of course, he would. 'She just slipped her calf, that's all,' he said. 'Her mother was the same, I recall, when she were first-calf heifer. But she never slipped another, and that's a fact.'

Such a degree of apparent honesty was worrying, too. Why admit to any defect in the line unless you were trying to hide something even more serious? Bodilly allowed his increased worry to show – since it had a certain commercial value in this situation. He ran his palm up and down the heifer's spine, feeling for sweat; he touched his knuckles to her nose; he drew back her lips and studied her tongue and saliva in the gathering dusk; he felt the temperature between her thigh and half-size udders; he pressed her rectum to see how swiftly she reacted; and he parted her vulva to look for residual inflammation in her birth canal. She *seemed* to be a perfectly normal, healthy young heifer – as, indeed, she probably was; but you would never have thought it from the frown that now darkened his face.

'Going to wed the little thing yourself, are 'ee, boy?' Benny asked sarcastically.

Bodilly gave a solemn shake of his head. 'How is she

so healthy, then?' he asked. 'You'd never credit she slipped her calf only yesterday.'

'That's what I'm telling of 'ee,' Benny responded patiently. 'When you get to the bottom of the matter, there isn't nothing wrong with her. She's a proper 'ansum little cooze.' He scratched his unshaven chin thoughtfully: 'Tell 'ee what – I'll knock five bob off of she. You can have her at eighty-five shilling and the other three for ninety apiece. There now!'

Bodilly sniffed dubiously. The farmer had already come down from five pounds apiece. Would he go another half crown? Bodilly had taken the precaution of calling on Roseanne's friend, Maria Curnow, who sometimes helped out at the Queen's Arms, and ascertaining the size of Benny's debt there. He knew it stood at seven pounds and that Michael Edwards, the landlord, had told him he'd chalk up nothing more 'on the slate' until at least half the present owings were paid off. And that was why Bodilly had left this call until the end of the afternoon, when Willy Benny's thirst would be high and the poor fellow would be wondering whence his deliverance might come.

Bodilly half turned on his heel, hinting there was little point in any further discussion at that price. But then he paused and, fishing out a roll of banknotes with elaborate ceremony, he counted out three fivers, a single, and ten shillings, which was a pound short of Willy Benny's price. The man watched as if mesmerized; when he realized that was all he was being offered, he licked his lips and stared unhappily at the huge blue hump of Trigonning Hill, beyond whose flank the sun had set some forty minutes since. The church clock chimed six. The Queen's Arms stood right opposite the tower. The farmer licked his lips again.

Judging his moment to a nicety, Bodilly counted out

30

a further ten shillings and held forth the seventeen pounds. 'I'll take a chance on it,' he said with a magnanimous smile.

Willy Benny seized the wad as if he had won their skirmish. 'Done!' he said and offered his hand.

'You going up Breage, are 'ee?' Bodilly asked.

'Dunno,' Benny replied casually. 'I suppose I might.'

'You give me a hand to turn these four ladies into Frank Kitto's field, will 'ee?'

'Surely,' was the eager reply, for it would give him all the excuse he needed — and Frank Kitto's field was nowhere near the pub.

The four heifers, three heavy with calf and all accustomed to being driven, wandered unconcernedly ahead of them. As they crossed the mowie, Marjorie Benny came out and stood there, barring the farther gate. 'Damn me, woman, what do 'ee want now? Open the gate, can't 'ee!'

Silently she stood her ground.

'Dammit to hell!' Willy Benny strode chest high among the cattle until he stood before his wife. Bodilly wondered if they were about to come to blows — and would he intervene? But, perhaps because he was there to witness it, or perhaps because Willy Benny was more bark than bite, he fished two fivers out of his pocket and passed them over. Still she held out her hand. With a slightly embarrassed laugh Benny turned and explained to Bodilly. 'She's some proper lady, see — she'll only deal in guineas.' He handed her another ten shillings and barked gruffly, 'Go on with 'ee, now!'

She took the money in silence and went back into the house.

'And I must open the gate myself, I suppose!' he called after her.

She did not even pause.

31

The heifers ambled past him out into the half-mile lane that led up a gentle slope to the edge of the village. 'Never marry a woman who gives herself airs,' he remarked disconsolately as he pulled the gate shut behind them. The length of binder twine that served as its hinge frayed and parted; the gate fell flat in the dung and mud.

'The heller!' Benny exclaimed in disgust.

'I'll hold it if you mind,' Bodilly offered. He felt nothing but contempt for the man, letting his wife walk all over him like that; all he should have given her was a good fist between the eyes.

'Oh, leave it go to that,' the other responded. 'There's no stock left to pen back now, anyroad.'

'What, sold all your cows, have 'ee?' Bodilly asked in surprise. He'd heard nothing of it. But Benny told him they were all dried off, so he kept them out in the field all the time now.

Bodilly did a quick calculation. If he'd dried them off now, it would be another six to eight weeks before they calved and were back in milk. So there'd be no income from the creamery all that time. Mrs Benny had her fowls and the eggs. He'd counted a dozen geese in the lower yard. And there was a sow with six weaners in one of the houses. It was touch and go whether the man's thirst would run through that lot before the milk money — and then the spring barley — came to his rescue. He'd get Maria Curnow to keep an eye on the situation for him.

'They won't turn left at the top, will they?' he asked the farmer.

The man appeared unconcerned at the possibility. 'If they do, I can cut across the field to Penbro gate and turn them back. You going Ram-Buck this Saturday, are 'ee?'

There was an edge to the question, which Bodily was swift to catch. However, as no Cornishman will ever anticipate a future pleasure, all he said was, 'I dunno. I suppose I might,' — exactly as Willy Benny had replied earlier.

The farmer brought his stick down lightly on the back of the heifer who had slipped her calf; the animal hastened for two paces and then fell back to its old saunter. 'You belong to go, don't 'ee?' he asked. 'You belong to put that Kitto girl with 'ee, I thought.'

'Very likely I will,' Bodily told him, wondering what all the innuendo was about, and why the tone of secret amusement?

'That's what I thought,' Benny said.

The four heifers, as if they knew they were leaving Sethnoe for ever, behaved impeccably. They turned right at the highway, they ignored the fork in the road before the church and kept straight on through the centre of the village, and when Bodily ran among them to get ahead and open the gate into Kitto's field, they barely moved aside for him. In the last of the twilight the dull red of their coats vanished into the dark of the pasture; a moment later the only sign of their presence was the steady tearing of grass as they settled to graze.

'See again, boy,' Benny called back as he loped off toward the pub. 'See again,' Bodily replied, setting off for Penhale Row to seek his future father-in-law's permission to leave the cattle overnight.

The sour little scene between Willy Benny and his missis repeated itself in his mind. If only men could remember to be men and women, women, there'd be none of those difficulties in marriage.

'Well, you're some stranger,' was Roseanne's greeting as she answered his knock.

He kissed her with his customary awkwardness and

33

hurried inside, rubbing his hands gleefully in anticipation of the warm parlour fire. 'Busy week,' he explained.

'Or fortnight,' she added, like a correction.

'Never!' He raised his eyebrows in shocked query. She nodded accusingly.

'Then I owe you another kiss,' he said hopefully.

'I'm busy too,' she grumbled. But she came to him nonetheless and, after a quick, guilty glance at the door, melted into his embrace. He had to understand that this business with Master Stephen was just a silly mistake she couldn't go back on, but it didn't mean anything and it wouldn't lead to anything — no matter what her mother and father might hope for. It wasn't that she was pessimistic about herself; she simply didn't wish it to lead anywhere. It was just a bit of a lark, that was all — something like a dare, if you want. But she had to tell him before her mother put it in more positive terms.

'Mark,' she murmured, breaking off their kiss and giving him a few compensatory pecks on the cheek. Then, without really meaning to, she said, 'You should ought to have shaved.'

He scratched the harsh stubble. 'That's how I am. Love me or leave me. I bought four heifers off of Willy Benny, down Sethnoe, only now.'

'What about it?'

Despite the thick material of her dress and several layers of petticoats, he could feel her body pressed tight against him, warm and vibrant. 'Nothing,' he replied, abandoning any attempt at an explanation. It was strange that in all the years they had been couranting together, they had never done any of those things that people usually meant by that term. He had never taken the slightest liberty with her. Sometimes he wondered

34

whether she resented his lack of initiative. Did she think him timid? Or worse, did it make him less of a man in her eyes? She never gave hint of it.

He wanted to tell her how deeply he loved her, but he feared it might put him too deeply in her power. Anyway, surely she knew it after all this time? What did she need to *hear* it for as well?

'Maria told me you wanted to know what old Benny had on the slate,' she said.

'It was worth another ten shillings profit to me,' he replied. 'To us, I mean. You want that new dress for Ram-Buck, do 'ee?'

He felt her stiffen. 'Well, now . . .' She smiled anxiously and stroked his stubble with her fingernail, this time without comment. 'That's a thing I wanted for to tell 'ee, see.'

'Mark!' Mrs Kitto stood at the door in her lavender 'evening gown'. She stretched out a hand for him to kiss. 'I thought I heard you. You're some stranger these days.'

He let Roseanne go with guilty haste; she wondered if that awkwardness would ever leave him, even when they were man and wife at last. 'You'll dine with us, of course?' the woman continued.

Mark frowned and glanced at Roseanne, who raised her eyes to the ceiling in an expressive gesture. 'If I'm still welcome here, Mrs Kitto.' He laughed.

'Oh? You've heard our great news then, have you?' she asked disingenuously.

'Mother!' Roseanne exclaimed in alarm.

'*You* still haven't milked the cows, young lady,' the woman said severely. Her daughter sighed and trudged toward the door. 'Mark, come and hold the lantern for me, will you?' she asked.

'I'd like Mark to stay here,' Mrs Kitto insisted. 'If,

that is, he can bear to tear himself away from you after his long and silent absence.'

Roseanne turned pale. 'Then I shall tell him now,' she said.

'And I told you to tend they cows — I mean those cows.' Her mother stamped her foot in her vexation.

Roseanne ignored her and blurted it all out. 'Squire Morvah's son asked I to go to Ram-Buck with 'n. And I thought 'twas just a joke . . .'

'Rose-Anne!' her mother shouted, making two syllables of pure menace out of the name.

'I thought 'twas just a joke,' the girl repeated, gabbling to finish before her mother could physically silence her. 'And I said yes.' She skipped down the passage, just evading her mother's reach, and calling back over her shoulder, 'So now they say I got to go — so that's all the choice I do have.' The door slammed behind her.

Mrs Kitto returned to the parlour to find a thunderstruck Mark staring into the flames. 'Stephen Morvah!' he murmured in a voice she barely recognized as his.

'She's putting it kindly to you, bless her,' Mrs Kitto replied. 'The truth is, dear, dear Mark, that young Master Morvah is very taken with our little girl.'

He held his breath until he thought his lungs would burst.

'And she with him, I fear,' the woman added. 'More than she'll admit. Poor Mark!'

''Tis all wrong. Man like that and a girl like she.'

'Of course, of course,' she responded soothingly. 'Still, I hope you won't stand in her way now?'

'How?' he asked, wrinkling his nose with incomprehension.

''Twould be a selfish love that only wants her for

36

itself. But I dare say you really want what's best for her — and never mind your own interest.'

'There's only one woman knows what's best for her,' he replied desperately — for he was haggler enough to see what was coming. 'Let her tell me what she wants in the matter and I'll . . . well, that'd be different.'

Mrs Kitto bided her time and then added, 'Well, it's not for me say, is it. The days are long gone when parents simply commanded and daughters simply obeyed. And a good thing, too. I'm sure it caused a lot of misery. Far better, I believe, for me to put the whole matter to you and leave you to decide. You're an honourable man, a gentleman. I know that if you truly thought Roseanne might advance herself, you'd never let your own selfishness stand in her way.'

'Well, then, she may do as she pleases!' He flung out of the house, his heart yearning to possess the words and gestures that would forever be beyond him.

5

But what if it *had* been a joke? Roseanne smoothed her dress for the hundredth time, producing — also for the hundredth time — no visible improvement, for perfection cannot be perfected nor the absolutely smooth made even more so. Of course it was a joke. She was going to be the laughing stock of Breage. She shot a venomous glance at her mother, whose back was, fortunately, turned at that moment while she carried her daughter's bonnet to the window so as to straighten a feather and rearrange the gauze and prink up one or two of the silk flowers and anything else that didn't need doing.

Roseanne returned to her looking glass, resisted the temptation to embark on her second century of smoothing, and patted her curls instead.

'If you mess your hair, I'll murder you,' her mother said. She stood aside from the window and let the light fall on her daughter. Her beautiful young daughter. A sharp pang of envy and a great swelling of pride contended for her mood; she was not the first woman her age to realize how scandalously youth was wasted on the young. 'Leave your hair be!' she said crossly as she went to the girl's side; but the moment they were close she gave her an impulsive hug and murmured, 'Oh, Roseanne — just think eh?'

The girl struggled awkwardly out of the embrace,

exclaiming, 'Don't! You'll mess me up.' But then she, too, put an arm around her mother and, in a much softer tone, said, 'I don't hardly dare to think. I'm sure 'twas no more than a joke.'

Mrs Kitto placed the bonnet gingerly on her daughter's head and, startled with the effect, exclaimed, 'Oh!' She clapped hands once, kept them together, raised them to her mouth, and forgot to breathe.

Roseanne stared at herself in the glass and was equally enthralled. She had never thought of herself as a fashion plate. She would look at the girls in the engravings without the slightest envy or wistfulness because she felt no kinship with them at all. She thought of them as creatures in a far-off land whose appearance and way of life had no point of connection with hers. And yet there she was – one of them suddenly! How could a mere bonnet do that? It must be something in the way it made her stand up straight . . . the statuesque line it gave her, around which everything else was suddenly *right*.

'Your gloves,' Mrs Kitto said. 'A lady must always put her gloves on before she leaves her boudoir.'

They both laughed, even though Roseanne knew her mother was not entirely joking; that woman's ambition could easily transform this little box of a room into a boudoir. The white cotton, masking the fingers that scrubbed floors, scoured dishes, and milked the cows, was the final touch of comfort. Mind you, she was careful with her skin. Her father always bought lanolin for the cows' udders, because he said it kept up their yield if their tids were soft, and they also got a better price in the ring; he was forever buying and selling and 'improving his herd', as he grandly described his petty profiteering. She always rubbed plenty of it into her hands and arms, so they were never as coarse and chapped as those of the other village girls. The gloves were a comfort precisely because they did *not* chafe on rough skin and soda cracks.

'Go down and show your father,' her mother said, as if it would be a slightly daring thing to do.

Roseanne lifted her train and picked a careful way down the steep, narrow stairs — which, no doubt, her mother now saw as a grand sweep of a staircase. Mr Kitto, who was puffing his pipe in the parlour, trying to read the *West Briton* despite the day's excitements, looked up casually, ready to prick his daughter's pride with some slightingly humorous comment. He only just caught his pipe as it fell from his gaping jaws. 'Well, maid!' he exclaimed, standing up and reaching out his hand, as if only the touch of her would convince him she was real. 'Well, maid, if that doesn't beat them all!'

Delighted, she did a halfturn to the left and then to the right; it was not the sort of dress you could twirl right round in. 'Well!' he exclaimed again. 'You'd never think that train wasn't sold with it out the shop!'

'That's no shop goods,' his wife said severely. 'That's Mrs Harvey's work, and she's dressmaker to the Morvahs, no less.'

He managed to stop himself from asking what it had cost. Instead, still half lost in admiration, he gave Roseanne a quick kiss on the cheek and said, 'I'm sure 'twill be worth every penny invested.'

'What's the time?' Roseanne asked.

He fished out his watch and tilted it toward the light. 'Half past one,' he announced.

As if it had been waiting for permission, the church clock chimed in with its agreement.

'I must go,' she said in agitation.

'You'll do no such thing,' her mother exclaimed

vehemently. 'You're not putting your nose outside this door till his arm is there to support you.'

Roseanne pulled the gloves an inch or so off her fingers and then pushed them firmly back again, pressing hard in the fork of each finger. Mrs Kitto plucked her sleeve and drew her out into the passage. 'Remember, now,' she whispered. 'No strong drink — nor yet weak drink, neither. None of your shandies and cups.'

'As if I would!' Roseanne answered testily.

'And you're to permit him no liberties.'

'I know.'

'The time he'll try it first is in the middle of a dance. He'll let his hand slip down here.' She demonstrated. 'All sort of accidental-like and "Oh my dear soul! Is that my hand? Tut!" So show me what you'll do.'

'Oh, Mother — really!'

'Come on. Show me.'

The girl implored the heavens to intervene and dealt with her mother's hand.

'No, no!' Mrs Kitto said crossly. 'Give him a little smile — like you know how hard it is for him — and 'tisn't easy for you, neither — but there's a time and place for everything — and the time for that is when there's two rings on your finger.'

Roseanne laughed, despite herself. 'All that in one little smile?'

'And more! When he sees you smile, a voice inside his head will say, "Hold back, boy! The waiting will be worth every minute it takes." You do that, can you?'

'How?' Roseanne asked in exasperation. 'Show me yourself.'

The woman bridled. 'I can't, of course. Not at the drop of a hat.'

Her husband's laugh came from the parlour. 'She's forgotten how — and that's a fact, maid.'

41

'You aren't supposed to be listening to this,' his wife snapped back. 'And if that's all the help you're going to be, you'd best hold your tongue altogether.' She turned back to her daughter. 'There's ways a woman can let a man know she's ardent but she's virtuous. And that's the golden highway to the altar.'

Roseanne half turned away, doubly angry that her train prevented her from turning fully. 'I don't know what all the fuss is about, anyway. 'Twas most likely a joke in the first place. 'Twill be a miracle if he do come at all. And how you can hear wedding bells in one silly little invitation to Ram-Buck Fair I don't know! What about all they times . . .'

'All *them* times,' her mother corrected her.

'All them-*there* times,' her father called from the parlour.

Mrs Kitto turned about and slammed the door.

'What about all those times' — Roseanne smiled sweetly as she found the right word at last — 'Mark put me up Ram-Buck — and nobody never expected my fingers to go sprouting rings next day?' She stared wistfully at the front door. 'I wish I was going along of Mark today, that's all I know.'

'Oh, hark at you!' her mother snapped. 'Did you hear that, Father?' She turned to the parlour door and then remembered she herself had closed it. Now she flung it open once more. 'Did you hear that?' she repeated.

'Hear what?' The newspaper rustled.

'You're some help!' she sneered. 'Leave it all to me as usual!'

'Do 'ee want me to overhear you or not?' he asked in exasperation.

''Course not! Not everything. Just the things you *ought* to overhear — like Miss High-and-Mighty now

42

saying she wished she was going along of . . . going with Bodilly.'

Her tone alerted him to the seriousness of the charge; it was no longer something he could turn aside with a remark about the fickleness of women. He rose portentously, laid down the paper, and processed through the door and down the passage, tapping the bowl of his pipe in the palm of his hand. 'Now listen, maid,' he said quietly — but with a quiet that was charged with significance. 'You should understand what store we do set by this day's work, your mother and me. That Stephen Morvah never yet showed the slightest interest, not decent interest, in any maid in this village. He's got the pick of West Penwith, if he wants to exercise it. But he went and picked you.'

'He never *picked* me,' Roseanne protested. 'Not what you'd call . . .'

'Listen to your father and don't interrupt,' her mother barked.

Roseanne stood, eyes downcast, wishing midnight had already come and gone.

'You quite finished, have 'ee?' he asked with that same quiet authority.

'Yes, Father.'

'Stephen Morvah went and picked you. Now very likely 'twas a bit of daw-brained carry-on. Very likely he never give 'ee a second's thought between then and this. Very likely all he wants is to lift your skirts . . .'

'Father!' His wife was scandalized.

'A spade's a spade, woman. Look where all your mealy-mouthed talk got 'ee!' He turned again to his daughter. 'Very likely all that is true. Well, if 'tis, then you just show him *you've* got an opinion in the matter, too. Let him see you're an upright Christian woman who's the equal of any soul on earth in the sight of God.

43

Respect yourself! Tell yourself that Stephen Morvah's only *just* good enough to put a Kitto up Ram-Buck Fair. Send him home tonight thinking the privilege was all his. I'm telling you no lie if I say all our futures in this house depend on how you fare today.'

Her stomach fell hollow; she had never suspected they'd made so much of the whole sorry business. 'That's like saying we never had no future before Maria Curnow and me went blackberrying last week,' she protested.

'No it isn't,' he replied gravely. 'It's like saying that until now we had only the moon to guide our path. But if you manage today's business well — as I know you can if you put your mind to it — why then in future we shall have the sun. That's the long and short of it, now.'

There was a brisk knock at the door.

'That's him!' Roseanne cried in a sudden panic.

'Oh my gidge!' Mrs Kitto clasped her throat and squeezed, to prevent her heart from escaping altogether.

'Only me!' The door opened and a laughing Maria Curnow let herself in. When she saw the transformation in Roseanne she could only stop and stare. 'Well!' was all the conversation she managed.

Mrs Kitto offered the consolation prize. 'You're looking some pretty, my dear,' she said.

Maria remembered what had brought her here. 'There's a poor, pale, sickly gentleman down on the turnpike, frightened for his life to come up here,' she told them, all her ebullience returning with the memory.

'Who?' Frank Kitto asked.

'Not . . .' his wife began.

'The same,' she assured them. Then, to Roseanne: 'Poor devil! Beside himself with the nerves. I watched him drive three times round the church, inspecting his wheels for an excuse — looking as if he feared the spokes were loose! I told him you wouldn't bite.'

'You never!' Roseanne was horrified.

'I did. I told him you *couldn't* bite. I said you had your teeth all pulled for your twenty-first birthday.'

Roseanne started to laugh, slightly hysterically.

'There was no call to say that,' Mrs Kitto grumbled. 'She never had but two pulled in her life — and they were wisdom teeth.' She looked at her giggling daughter with disdain. 'And maybe we should have left them in!'

Roseanne gathered herself together. 'I'll go down the lane and put him out of his misery,' she said.

Her mother stepped forward and barred her way to the door. 'You'll do no such thing. He'll come to our door or you won't go at all. And he'll give a proper knock. And he'll wait a proper while. Come us on, we'll go sit in the parlour.' Over her shoulder to Maria she asked, 'You going yourself, are 'ee? Up Ram-Buck?'

The girl drew a deep breath and glanced awkwardly at Roseanne. 'Mark Bodilly did ask I,' she murmured.

Roseanne spun round and stared at her in hurt surprise. 'You know I got to have a chaperone if I do go with Stephen Morvah.'

'I never accepted,' Maria replied defensively as Roseanne returned to her side. 'He asked did I know if Lizzie Kitchen next door was going with anyone. So I thought, which would you rather — for Mark Bodilly to put Lizzie Kitchen up Ram-Buck . . . or me? I nearly said yes then, I can tell 'ee.'

Mr Kitto called out softly from the parlour: 'He's now at the front gate!'

Roseanne closed her eyes and offered up a prayer, while Maria stared at her usually-so-confident, devil-may-care friend in amazement.

'He's stopped by the cabbage. He's pulled up a bit

45

of Great King Harry — go on, boy! There's plenty more!'

Roseanne laughed, despite herself.

'No, he's going for the bedstraw now. He won't find much of that but he's welcome to what there is.'

Roseanne, only half believing her father's commentary, prised open the cover of the letter slot and peered out. She found herself staring directly into the eye of Stephen Morvah, a mere three inches away and about to adopt the same spy-stratagem in reverse. But for the wood of the door, she realized, he was close enough to kiss.

6

They both sprang back and stood there, one on each side of the door, looking a trifle sheepish. Then Stephen knocked and Roseanne opened up to him. His jaw dropped and he had to look at her twice to be sure that this elegantly turned-out young lady was the same blackberrying village girl he had so light-heartedly invited to Ram-Buck Fair.

'Why, Miss Kitto,' he exclaimed, 'what a . . . what a . . .' *Vision of loveliness*, were the words that sprang to mind but they sounded much too high-flown for Penhale Row at half past one on a Saturday afternoon. '. . . beautiful dress,' he concluded. Then he recovered sufficiently to round it off: 'But, of course, it is the wearer makes it so.'

'Ooh!' Maria Curnow murmured, turning to Roseanne to see how she took it.

When Roseanne said nothing her mother gave her a nudge. 'There! Did you hear that my pretty?'

'I haven't gone deaf,' she said. 'Are we going today or not?'

'Yes, of course,' he assured her eagerly. 'I have my gig at the gate. And you, Miss Curnow, I take it you will accompany us, too?'

Maria grinned. 'Yes, I'm your pew opener for today.'

Roseanne pinched her surreptitiously on their way down the garden path. 'What's that for?' she inquired, feigning surprise. 'You do know,' was the dark answer.

'Oh, I say!' Stephen called out. 'It's those wretched boys. I *knew* they were up to no good.'

The horse had been unhitched from the cart and led into the field that bordered the lane; then the shafts had been pushed through the bars of the gate until they projected far enough into the field for the animal to be respanned between them. He stood there, grazing contentedly, unable to go forth or back.

Roseanne searched through the neighbouring gardens and spotted them, the Harvey boys from next door, skulking in a gateway about fifteen yards up the lane. They hid as soon as they saw her but she heard their suppressed guffaws. Hitching her skirts halfway up her calves, she ran on tiptoe, using the grassy verge of the hedge to deaden her footfall. Too late the boys, Thomas and Willie, realized her purpose; they stumbled over each other in their haste to escape. She caught them by an ear each, which assisted them to rise quite smartly, and led them protesting back to the gate. 'Now then,' she said sharply when they arrived, 'd'you know who this grand gentleman is?'

'Yes, Miss Kitto,' they grizzled.

'And d'you know which parents of which young idiots are his tenants?'

'Yes, Miss Kitto.'

'So what are you going to do now?'

Rubbing their ears they climbed over the gate and started to unhitch the horse yet again. Stephen and Maria stared admiringly at Roseanne but she was watching the two young rascals like a cat. 'You had the traces all wrong anyway,' she shouted at them. 'You can't do *anything* right, can you.'

Even when they had the horse respanned to the cart — and both on the right side of the gate again — she would still not let them go; she made them stand in front of Stephen and apologize — 'for such daw-brained antics,' she prompted when they faltered.

'For such daw-brained antics.'

'Cut along, then,' he said, tousling their hair.

'They're a waste of good food,' Roseanne said scornfully as she watched them gallop away. 'The whole family.'

'Gertie isn't so bad,' Maria said defensively.

'You don't have to live next down to them.'

Maria gave Stephen a conspiratorial smile of sympathy, much as to say, 'Well, *you* picked her!' Roseanne saw it and realized she would have to rein in her tongue if she wasn't going to spend the entire afternoon snapping at everything anyone said. It was only nerves, anyway.

There was scant room for three upon the driving seat; Stephen assisted Maria into the back, saying, 'Ride in state, eh?'

Roseanne hesitated as to whether or not to join her friend in the passenger seat — until Stephen said, 'I thought you might like to drive a bit, Miss Kitto?'

The temptation was too great. Roseanne had occasionally been allowed to drive her father's horse and cart, and considered herself a fair hand at it; but that was a shire horse and the cart was for carrying stone and timber; she had never taken control of so sprightly an equipage as this. Her good humour returned the moment she had the reins in her hands. Stephen watched nervously for a moment or two until he saw how well she managed to back the gig a short way up the lane to straighten it and then make him go forward — all with only the gentlest movements of her hands and the quietest commands. 'To the manner born,' he said 'It's not the first time you've driven, I can see.'

'Only my father's Clydesdale,' she replied, 'but I suppose they have the same mouths.'

He was a frisky piebald gelding who took some stopping at the main road. 'He's used to the right of way,' Stephen explained ruefully. 'My father reins in for no one.'

Going up through the village, with the wind winnowing her hair, Roseanne felt like the Queen of the May. In her mind's eye she saw herself lashing out with her whip at the passing peasantry, crying, 'Out of my way, damn your hides!' just like Squire Morvah on his way to his club in Helston.

Maria saw her chin go up, and the contemptuous curl of her lips, and, guessing what was passing through her mind, smiled.

'Well, I'm so glad you two young ladies took me seriously,' Stephen told them. 'I've been on tenterhooks all week.'

'You!' Roseanne could not help exclaiming.

'Yes, Miss Roseanne, I thought you might have supposed I was . . . I don't know — pulling your . . . trying to be funny or something. I kept thinking I should call to assure you I had been in earnest, and then I thought no, it would look as if I thought you might think my word wasn't to be relied on, so . . . d'you wonder I say I've been on tenterhooks!'

Roseanne was silent awhile, trying to work through all the implications of what he had said.

'Still,' he added, 'that's all behind us now.' He glanced over his shoulder. 'Are you quite comfortable, Miss Curnow?'

'If I never feel worse, I'll be happy,' she assured him.

After that there seemed to be nothing to say. As the immediate thrill of driving wore off, Roseanne's heart sank once more. Why had she agreed to this ridiculous outing? What had she and Stephen Morvah in common? It was all very well for her parents to stretch their hopes as high as Trigonning — and all over a bit of light-hearted folly — but she was the one who had to try to make the impossible come true. It suddenly struck her as extraordinary that she and this young man at her side had been born within a few years of each other, in the same parish, and had grown up there, hardly ever more than a couple of miles apart — except when he'd gone away to school. Before that, they'd attended the same village school in Breage — and yet what did they know of each other's lives? What had they in common to talk about? Her parents seemed to think she could leave it all to that mysterious attraction between lads and lasses and to a cleverly managed sequence of temptations and denials on her part to manipulate him into . . . well, it was absurd. She wouldn't even *think* the word.

She glanced sidelong at him, feeling increasingly desperate for some conversational gambit to set him talking again. Their eyes met; his, too, were full of perplexity. It occurred to her that he was in the identical quandary. She gave him a wan smile and received a lacklustre one in return.

A few seconds later they both spoke at once.

She said, 'What were you doing when . . .'

He said, 'It's a pity they can't . . .'

They both laughed. He apologized; she said no, go on. He waved a hand vaguely at the passing landscape and said, 'I wish there were some other way of creating wealth and labour. Our grandchildren will surely revile us for what we have done to this beautiful county.'

They were passing through Carleen, which stands at the middle of a crescent of mineworkings, running from Wheal Fortune, back near Breage, up through Grankum and Scott's to Wheal Metal, where the tin lode curves westward through Pallas Consols to Wheal Vor and Greatwork. The mines at each end of this crescent are the richest in Cornwall; indeed, some say that Wheal Fortune makes up the richest five acres in the world; others give that honour to Wheal Vor, where the Great Lode is not only horizontal (a rare luxury in Cornish mining) but is thicker than a church is tall. In a way, both claims are right. Wheal Vor has the richest five acres on earth — but unfortunately they are situated over a thousand feet below grass and well beneath the level of the sea; at Wheal Fortune, though the lode is not so rich, its veins are tight-packed and so near the surface they can be mined open cast.

The result, as far as the landscape is concerned, is identical: vast tracts of neighbouring hillside are buried under great slides of waste tailings. Long ochre fingers lay a slimy, sterile trail down into the valley of the Carleen river, a once-natural stream now kept in permanent and muddy spate by the huge Cornish engines that can lift tons of water to the adits at each stroke; the engine at Wheal Vor was so large that, on the eve of its commissioning, thirteen men sat down to dine within its main cylinder.

'It can't hardly last much longer,' Roseanne assured him. 'My father says they've ripped so much out of Wheal Vor, and done it so fast and in so unsafe a manner, that even if they win the court case, they'll have to abandon the mine.'

The court case to which she referred had, in fact, been going on for the last four decades. Back in the 'thirties two bankers of Godolphin, the Gundry brothers, had overspent themselves in trying to open up Wheal Vor. Their solicitor, a certain Humphry Millet Grylls, had sold up their assets in the mine to a number of venturers — of whom, as it transpired, he himself was the principal. The mine-owning classes detested him for it, saying he was little more than a brigand; but to the miners themselves, and to the local commercial community who had chipped in with the capital, he was the greatest hero. So much so that when he died a permanent memorial was erected to him at the foot of Coinagehall Street in Helston, just above the bowling green — all out of public subscription. The legal wrangle, however, was still going on.

'Do I take it from your tone, Miss Roseanne, that you are not of the Grylls faction?'

'I'm not of any faction, Mr Morvah, having no interest in either the land or the lode. I agree with you in one thing, though — I could wish they had some way of returning the unwanted stone back below ground.' She ran her eye up what looked like a mile or more of 'halvans', the heaps of spoil that cluster around every Cornish mine working. *Lord*, she thought, *are we going to go on talking like this all afternoon?*

His thoughts must have been on something of the same lines for he now said, 'I'm sorry. I interrupted you just now. You were going to ask me what I was doing. . . when?'

'Oh, that day we met last week. No business of mine, to be sure, but I just wondered what you were doing out in the fields.'

'Surveying,' he said in a slightly puzzled tone. 'I'm sorry, didn't I make that clear?'

'Ah,' she said.

Maria cut in. 'She do mean *why*?'

'Oh!' The notion that all activity had to have a *purpose* did not come naturally to him. 'No reason, really. Just. . . something to do, I suppose.'

Roseanne decided to leap in with both conversational feet, otherwise they'd spend all day talking about the mines and the weather and the harvest and Lord knows what else. 'I expect you must have a lot of days like that, sir,' she said. 'When you hardly know what to do with yourself.'

'Quite a few,' he admitted ruefully. 'I don't suppose you have too many?'

'I don't have none — I mean, any.'

There was a further awkward silence before Maria put in again 'And what did your survey tell you, sir?'

'Nothing, really. I didn't actually finish it. Look here, I wish you'd stop calling me sir. It makes a fellow feel . . . well, dashed remote, don't you know.'

'What shall us call 'ee, then?' Maria asked at once.

'When we were at school together we called each other Stephen and Roseanne and Maria. I don't know whether it's for me to suggest it now — or for you.'

'Can't do that!' Roseanne was scandalized. The idea of meeting him about the village next week or next month and shouting out, 'Good morning, Stephen! . . . Good morning, Roseanne!' was unthinkable.

'If we was daughters of some other high-quarter folk . . .' Maria suggested.

He sighed. 'It'd be Miss Kitto, Miss Curnow, and Mr Morvah, of course.'

'Yes!' Roseanne said enthusiastically.

'So be it,' he conceded. 'It seems ridiculous when we practically grew up together. We were in the same class at school, after all.'

'Same class *room*,' Maria corrected.

'Class!' Roseanne echoed.

'Exactly,' he murmured.

It occurred to her that he didn't actually *like* being the squire's son — a possibility that had never even entered her mind. When an idle day like this was a rare luxury in your life, to be treasured for weeks and squandered carefully, you find it hard to imagine that anyone in the world would *not* welcome a life composed of an endless succession of such days. She laughed aloud.

He asked what amused her.

They were approaching the turn to Wendron through Nancegollan. 'This way or up through Pednavounder?' she asked.

'Nancegollan,' he said.

'I was laughing because I've so often seen you out on your horse, carrying your gun, or a fishing rod over your back, and I do always think what a grand life it must be, never being obliged to work at anything.' She smiled nervously to see how he took this piece of mild impertinence.

He nodded in earnest agreement. 'And yet, Miss Kitto, often and often I have returned from that same day's idle "employment", and seen your father washing his trowel and packing up his implements, and I've watched him stand back and run his eye over that day's work − and d'you know, my heart has been hollow with envy. I look at the wall he's built and I think to myself his grandchildren will be able to point that out to their friends and say, "Our grandfather made that!" And it'll still be there. But what of the half dozen tench and dace in my bag, eh? When I get home my mother will ask what sort of day I had and I'll tell her it was capital. I don't suppose your father will talk of his day at all.'

She found it hard to follow his conversation; half his thoughts seemed to lie unexpressed between his sentences. To respond properly − and Roseanne always liked to do everything properly or not at all − she would need a minute's silence to accommodate to his unspoken nuances. Instead, she gave a light laugh and said, 'My father would tell of everyone he met, what they spoke

55

about, what useful little scraps of gossip — sorry, *information*' — she made it sound like an imported word — 'he gleaned from it. And he'd put a price on it, too. I'm amazed he hasn't saved a thousand pounds by now.'

'Roseanne!' Maria chided.

'What?'

'Such disrespect!' She smiled placatingly at Stephen Morvah.

''Tis no such thing,' Roseanne countered stoutly. 'He'd laugh if he heard me say it.'

'My father maintains that Mr Kitto will one day be a substantial master,' Stephen told them.

The two women stared at him in utter astonishment. It was such an outlandish statement yet he had spoken as if he had said no more than that Mr Kitto might be a churchwarden one day, or attain some other minor place well within his grasp. Roseanne had a sudden vision of the conversation in which this opinion might have been voiced: There were Sir Francis and Lady Morvah telling their hapless son and heir that the estate was on its beam ends and that the only way he could save it was to marry an heiress. And out of all the likely and unlikely damsels in West Penwith, the old man had picked her, Roseanne Kitto, adding that, 'Mr Kitto would be a substantial master one day.'

She began to laugh hysterically. The trouble was, you could *almost* imagine it happening. Sir Francis was known to be eccentric to the point of lunacy; the Skyburriowe estate was rumoured to be on its uppers; and her father was, indeed, a cut above the ordinary. He always spoke like a man who was only temporarily engaged at his present level in society, and he and her mother never stopped looking for the next rung on the ladder. But the notion that she and Stephen Morvah

56

might now be sitting side by side because their respective parents suffered complementary delusions about each other's status and prospects was, one had to admit, hysterically funny.

'I say!' Stephen was uncertain whether to join in her mirth or be slightly affronted at it.

'Tell me, Mr Stephen,' she said, 'do your parents know of your arrangements for this afternoon?'

He smiled at the compromise she had unintentionally arrived at in the matter of their names, and he leaped in at once to cement it firm. 'Well, Miss Roseanne, I'm delighted to tell you they do.'

'And do they approve?'

'Again, the answer is in the affirmative.'

'And don't you think that strange?'

He knew what she meant but was not going to admit it. 'In what way?'

'First, that you're going to Ram-Buck at all. It isn't really for the likes of you — be honest. But if you did go, wouldn't you rather take one of the Misses Bolitho or Widow Delamere's youngest?'

'No,' he said.

She waited for more. When nothing came she prompted 'No, what?'

'No thank you?' he tried.

She dug him hard with her elbow. They both stared ahead, smiling and trying not to show it. The questions still echoed in her mind but the urgency to have them answered had evaporated. Or perhaps, in some obscure way, he *had* answered them — enough to be going on with, anyway. She felt a sudden, surprising warmth toward him and for the first time began to entertain the possibility of a romantic attachment between them — something more than an idle dream implanted by her parents' ambitions.

7

There was bowling for a pig, a coconut shy, an Aunt
Sally, a sheaf-pitching contest, a dancing bear, a
cockfight, and − the highlight of the afternoon −
Cornish Wrestling. Normally, as the fair wore on,
sobriety would give way to a general inebriation. But
there had been a huge 'singing funeral' in the parish only
two days earlier, with hundreds following the coffin,
singing hymns loud enough to delight the ghost of their
composer, John Wesley; after which they went on to
drown the sorrow of the occasion at pubs, kiddlywinks
and moonshiners − much to the distress of that same
shade, no doubt. So there was many a delicate head at
Wendron Ram-Buck Fair that day; and though no
Cornishman is ever more than a mile from a good
supply of oblivion, a kind of tactical abstinence was the
order of that particular day.

The moral lessons abounded. The sheaf-pitching
contest was won by Billy Cusack who was so firmly
teetotal he hadn't even needed to sign the pledge nor
join the Band of Hope to shore up his resolve. And the
wrestling was so lacklustre that Stephen Morvah took
it into his head that he might shine at it, on that day
if no other. 'Hold my jacket,' he said, thrusting it into
Roseanne's hands.

'No!' She plucked urgently at his sleeve, unrolling it
even as he rolled it up. She was afraid that if he got

hurt, Sir Francis and Lady Morvah might think she had egged him on.

Actually, she wanted to egg him on. She knew he was doing it for her sake — to prove something to her that neither could have put into words. And what if he *did* get hurt, she asked herself. Well, it wouldn't be much. A broken collarbone, a broken nose . . . that was the worst a man could get in this particular style of wrestling.

Stephen had his boots off by now, for, unlike the Devon wrestlers, Cornishmen engage each other in their stocking feet. The entire aim of the sport is to embrace your opponent and then force him to the ground by means of various leg holds. That is all; there is no wrestling actually on the ground as in Graeco-Roman, catch-as-catch-can, or any of the other styles.

Stephen had just stepped into the ring to challenge the winner of the previous bout, a hulking great miner from Stithians, with an even mightier hangover, when there was a cry of, 'Wait!' from a small group near the back of the throng, somewhere behind Roseanne and Maria.

'Oh my gidge!' Roseanne exclaimed when she saw who it was.

Mark Bodilly was shouldering his way through the crowd. 'No!' she cried out. He ignored her, pointedly. Then she saw he was towing Gertie Harvey and Tamsin Rogers in his wake; if he had scoured the county, he could not have found two female escorts more likely to anger Roseanne. She froze and turned from him, tossing her head in disdain.

When he reached her side, in the front row around the makeshift ring, he halted. She thought he intended speaking to her and prepared at least to be civil; but he had chosen that place to take off his coat and shoes, handing them into the odious Gertie's care with an unctuous charm that even she must surely realize was not intended for her. He even called her 'my love' making that common Cornish endearment into something more particular.

'Come on, Morvah!' Roseanne shouted. 'Up with Breage!'

Stephen smiled gratefully, though he had turned pale the moment he saw his challenger disrobing. Humiliation at the hands — and feet — of a hulking miner from Stithians was one thing; all he had sought from that encounter was Roseanne's admiration for his pluck. But a much more evenly balanced contest with a man his own size and weight was quite another. Stephen began to regret his hastiness, for he had never wrestled in public in his life, whereas Mark Bodilly, he knew, had been something of a champion four or five years ago.

'Up Breage!' and 'Up St Johns!' were the cries from several hundred throats. To Roseanne's dismay she heard ten to one, then thirty to one, and finally a hundred to one being offered against poor Stephen — and there were still few takers, even at that.

Mark smiled sourly at her. 'Five shillings on Morvah,' she snapped at a man offering a hundred to one; it was all the money she had brought with her.

'Roseanne!' Maria cried in a shocked tone. 'She never meant it,' she told the fellow.

Roseanne held forth a half-crown, a florin, and six pennies. 'I do know you,' she told him — just in case he thought of welshing. 'Harry Thomas of Porkellis. That's twenty-five pound you'll pay me.'

'When pigs do fly,' he remarked jovially as he pocketed her stake.

'A fool and her money . . .' Mark commented as he

brushed past her, unnecessarily close, and stepped into the ring.

'Pride before a fall!' she called after him.

The cheers for Breage and St Johns rose louder than ever. The miner from Stithians volunteered himself as referee for the bout, which was set for the best of three falls. The two men squared up and shook hands. Stephen gave a light laugh and said it was all bloody silly. Mark laughed, too, and said they'd soon see about that. Then they stood, legs braced wide apart, and leaned into each other, arms around the other's trunk, hands locked for a firm grip. Stephen felt the knuckle of Mark's thumb dig painfully into the long muscle parallel with his spine. He tried to return the compliment but Mark had some way of arching his back and squirming to one side to avoid it; and while Stephen was trying to discover why the same sort of squirm didn't work in reverse he felt his left leg swept from under him by a shattering blow of his opponent's shin.

A great roar went up from the crowd, who clearly thought the contest as good as over, but by some fluke Stephen got his right leg inside Mark's left. A fraction of a second later and he would have collapsed, but a desperate resolve to remain upright at all costs caused him to wrap that leg around Mark's.

An appreciative buzz from the crowd told him he had somehow done the right thing. He bent his leg, trying to bring Mark's up toward him; and since Mark was half unbalanced, having earlier brought his right leg forward to knock Stephen's from under him, he was suddenly in danger of toppling, himself. But he was experienced enough to throw his weight in the opposite direction and restore the status quo.

Stephen's leg, still coiled around his, was now at a mechanical disadvantage, so he quickly disengaged. A moment later the two men were squared off precisely as they had been at the very start of the bout — except that the contemptuous glint in Mark Bodilly's eye was a trifle dimmed. 'Up Morvah! Up with Breage!' Roseanne's shout rang in his ears, louder than a hundred others combined. The two contenders engaged again, now in deadly earnest.

For five minutes it went on like that, with Mark always taking the initiative and Stephen saving himself by the skin of his teeth. Harry Thomas of Porkellis, who had turned a little pale during the first minutes of the bout, began to breathe more easily again; Roseanne's cries of encouragement grew correspondingly more desperate. But inwardly she exulted at the knowledge that these two men were really fighting over her. The vagaries of fate were truly amazing. Two weeks ago she could have predicted her life in a word or two: She'd marry Mark Bodilly, endure his taciturn ways, accept his inability to express any of the gentler, softer feelings, bear his children, share the ups and downs of his fortune. She'd known him for so long — and thought of herself as *his* girl — that any other arrangement had become almost unthinkable. She knew his every mood, all his thoughts, his ideas about life, his ambitions. Then it struck her that perhaps she didn't, after all, know him so well as she had imagined.

For instance, she'd never have imagined he'd go and challenge poor Stephen to such an unfair contest. It was as if he thought the man a genuine rival! Worse, it was as if he were telling her that all their years of unspoken love and trust in each other suddenly counted for nothing. That was surely a comment upon his own reliability?

What an irony! If Mark had simply laughed it off and been hail-fellow-well-met with Stephen, well, it would have annoyed her, of course, with its suggestion that he took her so much for granted; but that would have been nothing new. In her heart of hearts she would have acknowledged his right to do so, after all the years of proof she had given him. But by challenging Stephen and behaving as if he were a real threat, he made that fear come true. Win or lose, young Morvah had been granted the status of a possible suitor.

'Up Breage!' she yelled fiercely. 'Up with Morvah!'

The two men were still at deadlock. Then, by a lucky stroke, Stephen found himself in exactly the same hold as the one by which he had saved himself at the outset. This time, however, he did not hesitate. Before Mark could lurch back into balance, he drew his leg toward him, wincing at the pain and wondering how close to a fracture it might be – and had the satisfaction of feeling Mark fall away beneath him.

An almighty cheer went up at this unexpected reversal of fortunes. Suddenly nobody was offering a hundred to one against Stephen; the odds shortened to two to one . . . five to four. . . nudging ever closer to evens. Roseanne sought out Harry Thomas with her eyes, found him, and held up a monitory finger. The man pretended not to see her.

The rivals engaged for the second fall. Stephen, who knew by what flukes he had escaped losing the first – never mind the grand fluke by which he had won it – knew he could carry the day only by trapping Bodilly into some idiotic mistake. If he could make the man angry enough, or flustered, he might just stand the faintest chance. In that spirit he muttered to him as they took up their stance, 'I'll let you win this one.'

Mark was too astounded by this effrontery – and then too angry – to respond. And while he fought both emotions, Stephen managed to get that infuriating thumb-knuckle grind going on his spine; and while the man was trying to wriggle out of that, he knocked one of his legs from under him. But, by a superhuman effort that showed what sort of man he was, Mark managed to get up from his knees. Then they settled down to a grim battle of muscle and wit, each man forcing the other to the limits of his tolerance for pain; and even at that extreme, each man swore to himself, neither would yield.

In the end experience told. Stephen having applied a particularly painful lock for some time, and with no apparent effect, relaxed it to try something different. A split second later — for it was all Mark had been waiting for — he found himself flat on his back, staring up at the mocking-helping hand of his triumphant foe.

In the brief respite between that fall and the next Stephen avoided Roseanne's eye; in fact, he did not look at the crowd at all. He stared at the ground, preaching at himself — at his own body — as no evangelist had ever preached at his soul. He told himself that Mark Bodilly may have been a champion five years ago but he'd done precious little in between. Look how the fellow was sweating now — like a horse just off the summer's grass. And he was rattled, too. He'd assumed it would be a walkover — the way he'd strutted into the ring. By now he must be quite shaken. Two or three times in that last fall he'd come close to losing the whole bout — and by an ignominious two falls to nothing. In this way, Stephen convinced himself that the impossible was not even improbable any longer — he *could* actually win. As they closed for the final fall, he murmured, 'This time we'll be serious, eh?'

But when Bodilly merely chuckled he knew that the trick wouldn't work twice. *Very well*, he told himself, *you're not the only one who can learn fast*.

It turned into a battle that people remembered for years to come. The two young men, who had stepped so unevenly matched into the ring, now staggered and grunted and lunged and kicked their way into its every corner, neither yielding, neither gaining the upper leg. Every lock, every twist, every trick known to the game they deployed upon each other — only to be met with the perfect counter. They fought each other to a standstill in which, whoever might technically carry the day, the honours were as even as man might judge.

Finally they stood locked in the centre of the ring, so utterly exhausted that, but for their mutual support, they would both have collapsed. Then Stephen felt Mark stumble a little to the left and, with the last of his own strength, he put out a foot and, with a blow that would not have moved thistledown, sent him reeling to grass.

The cheering split the heavens. Hangovers and queasy stomachs were forgotten as Breage and St Johns factions crowded forward to fête their heroes in the proper Cornish manner. Never mind that half Breage spent most of its time roundly cursing the Morvahs for bad and grasping landlords — one of their number had put the fear of all Cornwall on the other side, and that was enough for this day. A numb, exhausted, and bemused Stephen looked vainly around for Roseanne, without whom none of it would have happened.

But she was half a mile away, haring down the hill to Trenear, chasing Harry Thomas — if not for dear life at least for something that had cost her dear in its toll on her emotions.

8

That curious amity which springs up between men who have fought each other valiantly now brought Stephen and Mark to the same beer tent where, side by side, they toasted each other's health and laughed a good deal.

'I'd dearly wish to know where you learned to wrestle like that,' Mark said ruefully.

'You know damn well already, man.' Stephen gave him a playful punch. 'It was during the first round with you. A dirtier fighter and a better teacher I never met.'

Mark laughed at the insult but shook his head in polite disbelief at the compliment. 'If you learn so fast, then stay clear of Penaluna,' he said, naming the prince of local wrestlers.

They supped their ale and smacked their lips appreciatively. Stephen said it had never tasted better.

'Will I have my chance of revenge at Harvest Fair?' asked Mark.

Stephen shook his head. 'Long before that, I think.'

Mark frowned.

'I mean there was no need even for today's challenge, you know. When I blurted out that invitation to Miss Kitto, it was more than half in jest. Your challenge has given the occasion a solemnity it simply didn't possess.' He smiled as he rubbed it in: 'Until then.'

Mark scratched in the bridge of his nose − a sign of

66

ruminative annoyance. Then, suddenly, he said, 'Your word on it?'

'On what?' Stephen was taken aback.

'That it's all in jest?' He shrugged awkwardly. 'Or whatever you were implying just now.'

Stephen chewed his lip and looked away. 'I can't do that, Bodilly. It *was* true, what I said. But this has rather changed things.'

Mark slammed his tankard down on the counter — a rough plank spanning three barrels. 'Keep her!' he snarled. 'She in't worth nothing, anyway. What she do want is a good fist between the eyes.'

Stephen bridled. 'You have a short fuse, I must say, sir.'

But Mark was already striding away. Roseanne poked her head in at the flap of the tent just as he was leaving; he caught her by the arm and carried her back out with him. 'Women aren't left go in there,' he warned her, 'as well you know.'

'And you can just take your hands off of me,' she replied angrily, plucking her arm from his grasp. 'What d'you mean putting that Gertie Harvey to Ram-Buck with 'ee?'

'Same as you do mean, I suppose, by letting that streak of idleness put *you* here,' he retorted.

She grinned maliciously as she riffled a handful of crisp fivers before his face. ''Tweren't no idle bones as won me this, I'll tell 'ee.'

Mark remembered young Morvah's words, that his challenge had dignified a jest and turned it into a solemn possibility. He knew the man was right. He knew the worst thing he could do was to go on picking away at the same sore point. And yet he could not help it; he was too angry to curb himself and behave sensibly. Above all he was angry at Roseanne; the ferocity of it alarmed him. It was not by any means the first time she had stirred him to such rages.

For the past year or so he had often felt a sort of fleeting anger at her — a sudden wave that rose to a peak and fell away almost before he knew it. He had been able to ignore it because it seemed to have no cause. It could come over him in the middle of a kiss, or when he'd stand at her gate, watching her as she walked back up her garden path and maybe turned to wave yet another loving farewell at him.

Once he had been passing by her house in the small hours after seeing to a heifer that had newly calved, and he had noticed that she still had a candle burning. She told him she'd sometimes wake up in the night and the only way to get off to sleep again was to read awhile. So he'd pictured her up there, reading one of her books — and all of a sudden an enormous anger had overcome him, for no reason at all . . . unless you could say her fondness for reading was a good reason, which would be absurd. And yet the image of her, lying there in all her loveliness, lost to him, unmindful of all the cares of his world, communing with a mere book, had filled him with absolute fury.

And it was the same now. Nothing else could explain why he blurted out, 'You aren't no better than a whore, then.'

His spirit sank as he heard the words come out; he hated himself and the compulsion that had made him utter them. He wanted to shout, 'Stop me! Do something to make me stop! Can't you understand?' But his stubbornness was too strong.

And Roseanne, more deeply wounded than she ever remembered feeling before — and much too angry for tears — said, 'Well there's none better qualified to speak on *that* topic than the man who puts Gertie Harvey to a dance.'

And yet, as she watched him stride away, part of her knew perfectly well what anguish had driven him to such a cruel outburst — and knew, also, just how bitterly he was, even now, regretting it, longing to turn back and apologize, go down on his knees, sweep her up into his arms, beg her to forget this last miserable week and marry him tomorrow.

If he had done so, she would have said yes without a moment's hesitation. She watched him mingle into the crowd; just before he was completely swallowed by it she saw him find Gertie Harvey and link his arm in hers.

She turned to discover Stephen at her side, one arm slightly akimbo — not enough to constitute a definite offer but no accident, either. She slipped her hand through it and said, 'Such a crowd! So many people!'

'Where is Miss Curnow?' he asked, with little apparent interest in the answer.

'I think she's . . .' Roseanne nodded her head vaguely in the direction of the fortune teller's tent.

'Shall we see if we can find her?' he suggested. 'Perhaps she might like to accompany us on a brief walk? Up to the village and back, say?'

The fortune teller's tent was close to the main gate; when they reached it without a sign of Maria, he said, 'Oh dear!'

Roseanne drew a deep breath and came to a decision. 'It's only up to the village and back,' she said.

'Not half a mile,' he agreed.

'And there's people coming and going all the time.'

'That's true.' He pursed his lips as if for whistling and drew a sharp, inward breath — a Cornish gesture of profound assent. 'That's very true.'

'Well, where's the harm?' she asked gaily. Then, as

an idiotic sop to conscience, she added, 'We might even meet Miss Curnow on our way.'

He laughed. 'Stranger things have happened.'

The moment they were on the highway she felt unaccountably shy. People were *not* coming and going; in fact, they had the macadam to themselves — a long, lazy S-bend winding its way up and round the flank of the little hill upon which stand the five houses, the church, and the inn that make up the entirety of Wendron village. It would be a ghost village today, she realized.

'I seem to have upset Mr Bodilly more than somewhat,' he volunteered. 'I'm sorry. I truly had no idea.'

'No idea of what?' she asked.

'You know . . . that you and he . . . you know.'

'Well,' she said vaguely, 'spilt milk and all that.'

'It would be unforgivable of me if . . .' He did not finish the thought. She felt a tension growing in his arm.

'That was a good match,' she told him. 'I'll wager Mark Bodilly never thought . . . Oh! Talking of wagers, look!' She fished out her bundle of fivers and fanned them untidily before his eyes. 'That's what I won on you — for a five-bob stake, too!'

He winced. 'Don't tell me the odds, but I fear they guessed right, Miss Roseanne. I won by the merest fluke.'

'But you did win.'

He folded the money back into her hand. 'That particular contest, anyway.'

'Why were you going to challenge that Stithians man, Bert Whelan?' she asked. 'He'd have thrown you in two seconds.'

'Folly,' he agreed. 'The whole thing was folly.'

What did he mean by 'the whole thing'? That everything — even asking her to accompany him today

– had been folly? He must have become aware of that nuance for he was swift to add, 'Yet I'm glad, really. I'd not take back a single moment. Sometimes, you know . . .' He vanished in a reverie.

'What?' she prompted.

'Oh, sometimes one needs an act of folly just to get out of a rut.'

'Ah.' She suddenly regretted asking.

The sweep of the bend carried them out of sight of the fairground. Their isolation made her aware of their nearness, their physical proximity – and of the conventions of chaperonage and all the reasons for its existence. It was the first time she had been alone with a young man like this.

Except for Mark, of course.

Then it occurred to her to ask herself: Why 'Mark, *of course*'?

But before she could ponder the matter Stephen spoke again. 'Miss Roseanne,' he said, 'may I trespass upon a slender acquaintance and ask you a rather serious question?'

Her heart suddenly leaped into her throat.

'Serious?' she echoed uncertainly.

'Yes. May I ask you what sort of life you imagine I lead?'

'Oh, my gidge!' she exclaimed.

'It's an arrogant question, I know. After all, why should you have an opinion about me or the life I lead? But if you have one, I'd be so grateful to hear it.'

'You lead the life of a gentleman,' she said simply, regaining something of her poise. 'You hunt, you shoot, you take your rod and go fishing, you ride about the lanes, you go to balls and all the big affairs . . .' The list petered out – but surely it was enough, she thought?

'Yes,' he sighed. 'Those are the things I *do*. But what

71

sort of *life* do I lead? I don't mean a mere chronicle of events.'

Now she was completely bewildered. 'Well, what *do* you mean?' she asked.

After a silence he replied, 'I suppose I mean, do you envy me? Do you wish you could lead such a life as mine?'

She hardly knew what to say, or even to think. It sounded as if he were working his way as obliquely as possible toward a proposal. 'What's wrong with it?' she asked cagily.

'I didn't say anything was wrong with it and anyway, that's no answer to my question. Do you wish . . .?'

'You don't hardly need to *say* anything's wrong with it — the way you're going on.'

He shrugged. 'I'm sorry. I shouldn't have asked.'

She felt how keen his disappointment was and answered him then, as best she could. 'I should think a lot of people *do* envy you, Mister Stephen. I remember one time when I was out hoeing a half-acre of turnips . . .' She paused and gave a mildly embarrassed laugh.

'Go on,' he encouraged.

'It doesn't sound much — a half-acre of turnips — but you try hoeing them single-handed in a cold drizzle that no oilskin will keep at bay. And I saw you go riding by inside your mother's coach, off to some Liberal luncheon, I believe.'

'I remember the day!' he cried with all the excitement of a child recalling some forgotten treat. 'In March, was it not? About two years ago? And was that you, standing in the field?'

'If we're talking about the same occasion. I'd like a penny for every time I've hoed turnips in the drizzle — it'd match this twenty-five pounds nearly.'

'And what did you think as you saw us go bowling past?'

She laughed at the absurdity of the question. 'Why, I thought, *Poor people! Poor, poor gentry!* of course. *I must carry them some broth and an improving tract.*'

He bowed his head, accepting her implied rebuke.

'Now tell me 'twas the same for you — you envied me standing out there in the cold and the wet.'

'Perhaps not on that particular occasion. But I have been fishing all day in a blinding drizzle, mind you, so I'm no stranger to that sort of discomfort. However, in general, I believe I *do* envy you your life. I envy anybody whose days are filled with must-do-this, must-do-that.'

'And no time for thought.'

'I'm sure there's always time for thought — if you're a thinking person.'

It struck her that young Morvah was voicing ideas that had flitted through her own mind from time to time — perhaps not in quite the same form, but they were not completely alien and incomprehensible to her; it also struck her that she had never held such conversation with anyone else before. 'Is this what you talk about at balls and dinners with all the grand young ladies?' she asked.

He answered about five further questions in one when he said, 'They don't really understand. They consider me a bit . . . strange, don't you know.'

'So you are,' she replied without even thinking. She bit her lip and waited for his anger to descend.

But all he did was laugh and say, 'Capital!' Then his underlying mood of seriousness came once again to the fore. 'No. One cannot talk of such things at balls, nor at dinners . . . nor anywhere, really. You'll gather I do not much care for my way of life, Miss Roseanne, nor most of the people with whom I am constrained to mingle.'

'What *do* you talk about?' she asked, ignoring the opening he had just offered. 'I've often wondered.'

'The weather. The season, in the social sense. The music. Jokes in *Punch*. Local gossip, provided it is only mildly scandalous. One dance is enough to exhaust most people's stock for the entire season.'

'You'd think they'd welcome the chance to speak of more important topics,' Roseanne commented.

'And do you welcome it?' he asked.

After a pause she said, 'Yes,' as if the answer slightly surprised her.

'So do I.' There was a much longer pause before he added, 'Is this going to be our only chance to converse together, Miss Roseanne? If so, I shall have to squander it all at once.'

'And if not?' she asked, not knowing quite what else to say.

'Why, then we could turn about now and see if the dancing has begun.'

'Oh yes!' she exclaimed. 'Do let's see if they're dancing yet.'

9

Mrs Kitto was up and waiting when Roseanne came home, which was just before midnight. She stood in the darkened parlour, watching the young couple — *the squire's son and her daughter!* — walking up the garden path. As they drew near the door she slipped out into the passage, pressed her ear to the wood, and listened intently for the sound of a kiss or a murmured endearment. But it was too solid to transmit anything so intimate. She was just wondering whether it would be the done thing to invite the young man in when the latch was raised and she had to spring back to avoid being trapped between door and wall.

'A-ha-ha!' She yawned as if she had been startled up from a long doze — reaching behind with her heel to push at a chair, so that its scraping would add to the masquerade. Over Roseanne's shoulder she saw the young man walking away. 'Goodnight, Master Morvah,' she called after him. He, not wishing to raise his voice at such an hour, merely waved an acknowledgement. The casualness of the gesture seemed a good augur.

'Well?' she asked eagerly, fussing her daughter indoors.

'Well, what? You needn't have waited up. I said we'd be home before . . .'

'What happened? What did he tell 'ee?' She peered

75

out into the moonlit dark before pushing the door to. 'Where's that Maria Curnow?'

'Standing with *her* mother and answering the same questions as me, I shouldn't wonder,' Roseanne said wearily.

'She came back with 'ee, then?'

'Same road, same time.' The tone was even wearier − in the hope of preventing her mother from asking if it had been the same carriage. In fact, it had not, for Maria had met Johnny Tregear at the fair and he had put her back home to Breage in his dogcart, keeping close enough behind young Morvah's equipage for her to claim she had just about done her duty as chaperone. 'Fuss fuss!' Roseanne added.

'And you know why, my girl. If you're ever to be the squire's wife, your reputation must be above . . .'

'Squire's wife!' Roseanne echoed scornfully. 'He never even kissed me yet.'

'Ah.' Mrs Kitto's disappointment was plain.

'He held my hand, though,' the girl offered.

'Ah!' The tone brightened.

'And he asked could he see us again.'

'See *I* again,' her mother corrected. 'Well, that's a good start, I must say. Let's have a dish of tay, shall us?' Without awaiting an answer she led the way to the kitchen and drew the kettle on to the centre of the hob. Its desultory whine rose to a singing chorus while three careful spoonfuls of tea leaves were measured into the pot, which needed no heating since it lived at the back of the hob. 'I calculate,' her mother went on, 'that us'll look back on this day as the one that changed our fortunes for us.'

Roseanne's heart sank. 'Mother! I believe you'm putting altogether too much faith in Mister Stephen and me.'

'Mister *Stephen*, is it?' The woman pounced on the familiarity. 'Well!'

''Tis still a long road from there to a wedding breakfast.'

The smile of self-satisfaction grew broader. 'I don't only mean you and Mr Stephen, now,' her mother went on. 'Kitto his self hasn't been idle this day, neither. After you left, he put up his Sunday best and went over Mawnan Smith for a bit chat with Lawyer Scawen and that wife of his. She's the one with the money, mark you, but he's the one to mind it. She's got that spending streak in her blood, see.'

'And?' Roseanne pressed before her mother could ramble off among the branches of Mrs Scawen's family tree.

With teasing deliberation, the woman laid the cups between them on the plain deal table. A light smile tweaked at the corners of her lips. 'They've consented,' she said quietly at last.

The girl's eyebrows shot up in delight. 'You mean, they'll lend us the money?'

Her mother shook her head. 'Not lend, maid. 'Tin't no loan, see? That Lawyer Scawen, he's formed a company, a private company, like — with capital and all. He put up a hundred pound on the spot. They had some old ding-dong by all accounts, but your father, he beat them in the end. Fifty-one percent, they wanted!'

Her talk of so much money reminded Roseanne of her winnings, which she had almost forgotten in the excitement of the dance and the drive home in the moonlight. She had intended simply handing it over and basking in their gratitude, but her mother's tone of cunning self-satisfaction prompted her otherwise. 'This here company,' she said, 'how private would it be?' She

77

sipped her tea and relished its taste. 'Bit of fuggan, now, would go down a treat with that.'

Mrs Kitto rose and took down the cake tin. 'We do deserve it,' she said by way of excuse as she cut a slice for each of them. 'What's it to you *how* private the company is?'

Roseanne took a bite and smiled.

''Tis just the two of them and your father,' her mother added. 'How? Got a bit put by yourself, have 'ee?'

Roseanne laughed to show she knew her mother was joking and the subject was dropped. Then she told her all that had happened at the fair, omitting nothing except the news of her winnings. It was a highly satisfied Mrs Kitto who finally crawled into bed that night to lie between her clever husband and, just the other side of the wall, her equally clever daughter.

10

The day after Ram-Buck Fair, Roseanne found cause to go into Helston without arousing her mother's suspicions. In fact, Mrs Kitto was delighted, since the errand had led to some nagging between them for weeks past: The pail in which they drew water from the pump at the end of the lane had split a seam; Roseanne had been stopping it with cold porridge, which, though it worked well enough, made them look like diddicoys who couldn't afford a new pail.

The trouble was that Mrs Oaksey (this year's owner of the village shop, which seemed to change hands every Lady Day) charged sixpence more for a pail than Gilbert's in Helston, which angered Kitto so much he had told his wife not to buy the replacement in Breage. In fact, there were so many things that were cheaper in Helston that Roseanne went in with a list of messages as long as her arm – not that she minded, for its length would mask the time she devoted to other business. And the new pail would be handy for fetching them all home.

She fairly raced around the shops, not pausing to gossip with any friends she happened to meet and explaining her haste with a quick flash of her list. Then, feeling somewhat guilty at the speed with which she accomplished her errands, for it showed how much time she would normally have wasted on them, she hastened up Wendron Street and presented herself at Lawyer

Scawen's office. She knew him well by sight, of course, but, beyond a passing greeting on a lonely road, had never spoken with him before; she half expected he would put her off and make her arrange an appointment.

She was therefore agreeably surprised when he, having seen her go by his window, came out to greet her in person and usher her into his room at once, steering her past his three clerks, who seemed mildly surprised at this mark of favouritism. But as soon as the door was closed his bland smile gave way to a frown of annoyance. 'You must tell your father not to do such a thing again,' he said sharply.

'Do what, sir?' she asked in bewilderment.

'Why, send you as go-between.'

'But my father knows nothing of this,' she responded stoutly.

That stopped him dead. 'Oh?'

He was a handsome man, she thought, in an unassuming sort of way that befitted his character. She had seen him in court once, pleading for a man who had robbed a neighbour. The more dramatic his point, the quieter his voice had become, so that in the end you could have heard a pin drop. She couldn't remember the verdict but the lawyer's plea had greatly impressed her.

'This is my own affair,' she told him, 'though it concerns the business my father discussed with you yesterday.' And she went on to tell him of her windfall, omitting the names of the parties — for Mark Bodilly was a luncheon crony of Scawen's. 'I don't wish my parents to know of it,' she added.

'But they're bound to,' he pointed out.

'Oh, I'll tell them soon enough. Even this night, maybe — all depending on you, Mr Scawen, sir, and what you do say.'

80

He nodded and made no further interruption.

'I do want it to help my father,' she explained. 'But I'd as soon he never knew nothing about it. So I thought if you was to say you'd found a third party to put up a bit more, but who wished to stay anonymous.'

Vosper Scawen began to laugh. 'It isn't even cunning, Miss Kitto,' he said. 'I can't believe your father put you up to this. Was it your mother? It must have been.'

The vehemence with which she rejected this accusation startled him. If she was acting, she was the most consummate mistress of that art he had ever met in the flesh — and he had met more than his share over the years. 'Is it really as you said, then?' he asked to mollify her. 'But why? What put such a notion into your head?'

Briefly she outlined her conversation with her mother last night.

'So it truly is all off your own bat,' he said at length. 'But your mother plainly omitted all the particulars of our conversation, your father's and mine?'

Roseanne nodded and waited for him to tell her what difference that made. 'She said you had some old ding-dong,' she observed, just to help him begin.

He chuckled. 'That's a mild way of putting it. I desired the ownership of the company to be halved between us, you see. A lot of people are against such an arrangement but I prefer it. Both parties have to be in complete agreement before they can do anything, you see. With any other division, the larger owner can always ride roughshod over the smaller — which is the situation we're faced with now, you see. *If* we decide to proceed.'

'Oh!' Roseanne's face fell. 'You mean, it isn't settled yet.'

He shrugged. 'Your father will get his capital. People

will always get what they want in the end, Miss Kitto, if they work hard enough at it. And no one could possibly work harder than your father, so you need have no fear on that score.' He stared into the distance above her head for a moment and murmured, 'It's a warning we should pass on to you young people more often.' He smiled then. 'Be careful what you wish for now, because in ten or twenty years you'll get it. Where was I?' He became brisk again. 'Ah yes! Your father is determined to have fifty-one per centum of the company. I believe it is against his own best interests but cannot persuade him to do otherwise. We — Mrs Scawen and I, that is — shall probably yield the point partly because the sum involved is relatively small, and partly because even forty-nine per centum of what your father may one day be worth could be a goodly entitlement.' He laughed once more as he saw a neat rounding of his point. 'It's *all* a gamble, as you can see — so you needn't feel especially wicked about your handsome little flutter yesterday afternoon.' He licked his lip and added, 'It was a splendid bout, too, was it not?'

She swallowed. 'You were there?'

He nodded. 'I never miss Ram-Buck. Half my practice was there.'

So now he would know everything. He'd know she had backed Mr Stephen against her presumed young man; he'd wonder why; he'd also be sure to note that she had deliberately withheld their names from her explanation of her windfall . . . he might even have seen her and young Morvah vanish together up the deserted road to the village. She began to wish she'd never placed that wretched bet.

'So you can see,' he went on, picking up a thread from much earlier in their conversation, 'why I immediately assumed your father must have sent you in with this story of twenty-five pounds. That would represent a quarter of the paid-up capital. And though it is true that later calls would dilute that share . . . suppose those calls were never made! Suppose your father made all future growth out of income alone? It's not impossible, given a bit of luck. Why then, between you, you'd own more than three-quarters of the company. Do you wonder at my suspicions, Miss Kitto?'

Ruefully she had to allow that she did not. 'In fact, Mr Scawen, I wonder that you speak as if they're over and done with.'

He grinned, a trifle wickedly. 'To be blunt, young lady, I see your father in you. That's why. You're a Kitto to the very core.'

It sounded like a compliment, but one so flawed she felt reluctant to ask him to explain it.

He saved her the trouble, anyway. 'Straight as a die. You'll work yourself to the bone at anything you set hand to and no man or woman will be able to complain at the quality of the work. Kitto first and Kitto last — that's your watchword, the pair of you, eh?'

The compliment still seemed to have a backhanded edge but she wanted time to work it out. To conclude the interview — as she thought — she said, 'Still, one way or another, you won't accept my twenty-five pounds. And I can't honestly say as I blame you. So, I'll . . .'

'On the contrary, Miss Kitto! Forgive my interrupting you, but I think your altruistic offer has shown us a way out of the impasse. May I suggest to you what I think you should do?'

She nodded warily.

And for the next five minutes or so he told her, step by step.

'It's perfect,' he told Jane, his wife, that night. 'A more independent-minded young woman I . . .' He was on the point of saying 'never met', but hastily changed it to '. . . met only once before in my life'.

She punched his arm playfully and then asked him if he thought he had been entirely wise.

He looked at her askance. 'Are you actually deferring to my judgment for once?' he asked.

'Well, you seem so sure . . . for once!'

'Ah!' He laughed. 'In fact, I am − pretty sure, I mean. Old Man Kitto will suppose he owns his daughter's vote. He'll leap at the chance to let her have a quarter of the scrip and split the remaining three-quarters with us . . .'

'But then they'll have five-eighths between them,' she objected.

'That's how he'll see it, of course. But when the motion is on the table, that girl will vote Roseanne Kitto's interest, one hundred per centum, and the father may fend for himself.' He smiled at the neatness of it and then added, 'The point being that in any conflict among the three parties, her interests and ours will more likely coincide than ours and his. But she will draw his fire away from us.'

His wife shook her head. 'Do lawyers always assume that everything is bound to go wrong?'

He grinned. 'Only the wisest among us.'

'It sounds like nothing but trouble,' she sighed.

'Profitable, though,' he pointed out. 'And if the trouble ever outweighs the profit, we'll sell out to her, the daughter. I saw her at Ram-Buck yesterday, on the arm of young Stephen Morvah. *She* won't be milking cows and hoeing turnips for the rest of her life!'

11

The dark felt warm and moist. The breeze off Mount's Bay was laden with the smell of dying seaweed, uprooted in last month's gales. It gusted over the treeless landscape, soughing in the hedgerows, plucking at the rank, windblasted weeds of winter, and buffeting Roseanne's face and bonnet. 'Cope, cope, cope!' she called into the dark of the field, making two syllables of the word: *coh-oop*! The lantern in her hand cast a fitful light that revealed no more than two or three paces about her — just enough to show the puddles in her immediate path. Here in the gateway, where the cows had poached the land to a mire, they joined to form an almost unbroken sheet of water whose depth could only be guessed at. She stood on a precarious island near the hinge and humped it open, four feet or so — enough to allow Strawberry and Graceful to pass through side by peevish side. They were like two dowagers, neither of whom would yield precedence to the other.

'Cope, cope, cope!'

You called *cope* for a cow, *kip* for a horse, and *chu* for a pig. Who decided such things? The animals seemed to know, for each would come to its own call and to no other.

Raspberry, heavy with milk and eager for the half-weaned calf awaiting her in the yard, was first to the gate. Normally old Greenberry, the doyenne of the little herd, would make life a misery for any young heifer who dared precede her into the lane. But when there was a calf waiting she seemed to understand and would let the *lèse majesté* go unpunished. She was next, anyway, blundering out through the mud with her great milk bag swinging and her rheumy joints grinding like crossed trees in a wind; every step seemed to verge on a stumble. For years past, Mark had advised them to get rid of the cow, but her father couldn't bring himself to it; she was the first cow he'd ever owned — bought in the year Roseanne herself was born. She gave nine hundred gallons in her first lactation. She was the mother, grandmother, and great-grandmother of all the others; twenty-one years, twenty calves — how could you send a creature like that to the knackers? She still milked on all four quarters and yielded over four hundred gallons a year.

Then came a gaggle of cows who had been held back by the old one herself: Strawberry and Graceful, of course, then Youngberry, Dewberry, Jane, and Cloudberry, all trying to squeeze out at the same time.

'Hoo-back!' she cried angrily, thwacking her long blackthorn into the puddle before them. If they broke the gate, her father would blame her for not opening it fully — and he'd send her out with his mason's hammer and a fistful of six-inch nails to mend it. They backed off and stared at her with their big, wary eyes; then they streamed past her in indian file, pretending to be panic-stricken.

Where was Tamsin? Almost dry, of course, so she'd be in no hurry to be milked; and now she'd have the field and all its grass to herself. You couldn't blame her for hanging back, really. 'Tamsin,' she called out. 'Hup now! Cope, cope!'

She strained her ears into a silence that was broken

only by the murmur of the breeze and the clatter of a cow with a loose bowel — one already out in the lane, alas. 'Tamsin,' she cried more tetchily. 'Come us on, now!'

There was a vague noise out there in the dark, a footfall, not too far away. 'I got 'ee, now!' she called in triumph and set off confidently in that direction.

'Miss Roseanne?' asked a voice, and it was a second or so before she recognized it as Stephen Morvah's.

'What do 'ee want?' she asked, pausing a moment. 'Seen a cow, have 'ee?'

He chuckled. 'Can't see anything in this dark.' His voice turned solemn again. 'I have some bad news, I'm afraid.'

'Oh dear! I got to find that cow. I can't leave they others to wander.'

'I heard a cough over there, to your right, a few moments ago. I'm sure it was in this field.' He was already moving in that direction; she turned on a course that would intercept his about halfway to the farther hedge.

'What's this news, then?' she called across the dwindling gap.

'My parents. They were absolutely furious when they learned I took you to the fair.'

'But you said . . .'

'I assumed. I'm afraid I just assumed . . . after the kind things they said about your father.'

'I calculated as much,' she said glumly. 'I never thought you'd have been left borrow that gig if they'd known.'

He was almost at her side now. 'They've forbidden me ever to see you again.'

The news did not sink in all at once. Indeed, she just managed to stop herself from laughing — for it occurred to her to ask whether that was why he'd come out in this dark. Then the seriousness of it struck her. 'How?' she asked.

'They just don't want us to meet. They say it's not fair on you, since nothing can ever come of it . . .'

The words flew around her in the night. She understood their meaning but felt too numb to relate them to herself. 'Ah,' she said. 'I see.'

'You don't sound too . . .' He could not think of a gentle enough word for her coolness.

'That's what *they* say,' she pointed out. 'How about you?' She halted and raised the lantern between them, where each could see the other's face.

The sight of her put new spirit in him. 'I seek the smallest excuse, Miss Roseanne, the most trivial cause to tell them how despicable I think they are.'

'You mean you did — or you mean to?'

'I wished to speak with you first. I suppose it is a measure of how little I truly know you.' Then, with a nod into the dark he added, 'I think that's your missing cow.'

Tamsin, like all of her kind, had waited until they came within ten paces; then, knowing the blackthorn would soon fall upon her haunches, she made a sudden spurt for the gate, as if to say, 'Oh, you meant *me*, did you!'

Roseanne, who had lost all sense of direction by now, trusted the cow and followed the gurgling-sucking noises of her hooves in the mud.

'What I mean,' Stephen went on, as if nothing had interrupted his train of thought, 'is that although my instincts were to give my father a piece of my mind, I did not know whether you would approve of it, or think me altogether too rash.'

It was a novel situation for her. She could not imagine

Mark being deviated one inch from his own chosen path by any thought of her and what her opinion might be. He was his own man. You either liked him as he was or you didn't; but you soon gave up any idea of changing him.

'I would admire you most,' she told Stephen, 'for doing whatever you yourself thought right.'

'Ah,' he replied sadly, 'but it isn't as simple as that. The thing for me must include your feelings, your opinions, surely? Especially in such a matter as this.'

She wondered if all people of his class were equally considerate; then she thought of his father and dismissed the notion. 'I don't hardly know you any better than what you do know me,' she pointed out.

'Ah,' he said as if he had anticipated just such an answer. 'Then if we have so little knowledge to guide us, we have nothing on which to rely but our feelings.'

They arrived at the gate; she held the lantern to show him where to leap across the mire. He held out a hand to catch her when she followed. It would be too easy, she thought, to stumble into his embrace, to slip, to make him hold her tight — and so break the constraints of their all-too-brief acquaintance. And then, having decided against it, she found herself in mid-leap, wondering if it would be so wrong after all. So she let it happen.

He hugged her tight, far longer than was necessary to reestablish her balance. She knew exactly what he was thinking all that while: it would be too easy to allow it to happen this way. When he turned and set her feet on the dry macadam of the lane, the lantern revealed that each was smiling the same smile. After that the atmosphere between them grew easier; the big *if* of their lives had dwindled to a mere *when* — and they both knew it.

They set off in pursuit of the scattered herd. 'Feelings,' he said. 'We spoke of feelings. Perhaps it is easier to say this in the dark. If in losing my father's support I gained yours, it would . . . No — let me start at the beginning.'

He was silent so long she felt constrained to ask, 'When was that?'

'I don't know. Too long ago to remember. I used to see you here and there, going about the parish, in church, in Helston, and so on — more often, I'm sure, than you have seen me, Miss Roseanne. And I've always thought of you as a most particular young . . . I mean, I never considered you as just another Breage maid. I've always looked twice at you — and twice again, if I could. You do not object to my telling you such things?'

She suddenly realized that he had the most beautiful speaking voice she had ever heard; not wishing to break its spell, she took his arm lightly, saying no words.

He went on. 'I don't wish to exaggerate and to say that I have for years been hopelessly in love with you — hopelessly, I mean, across that divide the world would set between us. In fact, I don't think it happened until I met you out blackberrying with Miss Curnow, just a few weeks ago. God, was it only so recently! And even then it didn't strike me until after we'd parted. As I walked away I asked myself what had possessed me to issue such an invitation.'

He laughed self-deprecatingly; she sensed that her silence had dried him up. Was it chivalry or wounded manhood made him say *he* had invited *her*? In Mark it would be wounded pride; but in Stephen . . . who could say? 'And how did you answer yourself, then?' she asked.

He chuckled. 'I decided *I* had no choice in the matter.

When a man begins to feel for a woman the sort of feelings I now entertain for you, why then her very presence on earth is as good as marching orders to him. Before that day I think not a week went by without my remembering your existence — knowing you were somewhere nearby, living, breathing, laughing . . .'

'Hoeing turnips?' she suggested.

He laughed. 'That, too. But now, *since* that day, I believe not an hour has passed without my getting the sharpest reminder of it from . . .' He thumped his breastbone. 'There you have the difference — a week then, an hour now. Soon the very thought of you will expand to fill my life. I shall . . .'

'Master Stephen,' she chided gently, not wishing him to blurt out words he might later regret.

'I walk in places where I know you have walked,' he went on. 'I look into the stones and tufts of wildflowers beside your path — and they are different from all the other stones and flowers in the world because you have touched them. "She has passed this way!" they proclaim. The very air seems still to contain the rare magic of your presence.'

The confession just poured from him now; nothing she might say or do would stem the flow.

'You are all the world to me, and all the world I ever want. I stood an hour or more in that field back there, waiting for you to come and bring in the cows — knowing you would come.'

'That was no clairvoyance.'

He seemed not to hear her. 'And I thought of all the times you must have stood there, or walked across it. I am never alone these days.' His tone changed. 'I know it is too much to expect you to return my feelings — and I can tell by your tone that you are as bemused as . . .'

The moment she leaned her head against his arm he fell to silence.

'No?' he dared to ask.

'No good can come of it,' she murmured.

'Then you do feel something of the sort yourself?' He held his breath, hanging upon her answer.

She stopped and set the lantern on the ground. Then she slipped her arms around him and pressed her lips to his — and trusted him not to let her fall, for her legs were suddenly weak as straws.

The hungry pressure of his mouth on hers was like nothing she had ever felt before. She had often kissed Mark — often in this very lane on their way to or from the fields — and had thought it pleasing enough, and a sure sign of their love, and so forth. But this, with Stephen, had an urgency, a desperation, a grandeur beyond all her past experience. The mere touch of his lips on hers worked some strange alchemy to change her through and through. She felt like a new Roseanne, new and just a little strange. The hands that drew up the folds of his coat and clutched him so urgently to her were not the hands that combed her hair or broke her bread or performed a hundred other mundane tasks; they, and every other particle of her body, seemed charged with a novel significance, with something she must discover anew.

'Oh my darling, darling Roseanne,' he murmured as their lips parted. 'Let us never forget this moment. They are going to place the most terrible obstacles in our way. It won't be easy. But if we can hold on to this moment . . . oh, if we only can!'

'Shush.' She kissed him again, a tender brush with her lips at the corner of his mouth.

'You are so strong,' he whispered. 'Will you stand up to them? I think you will, you know.' After a pause he added, almost to himself, 'I have the disadvantage of knowing them too well.'

She gave a guilty start. 'The cows!'

He tried to hold her a brief while more and then thought better of it. 'No,' he said. 'Necessity is our strength. We shall always act out of necessity — as we love, so shall we live.'

She picked up the lantern and they hastened down the lane, hand in hand. By now she needed no light to guide her, for Raspberry's frantic bellowing was beacon enough; and, fortunately for Roseanne, the heifer's distress had kept the herd together. She found them in the makeshift yard, chewing the cud, all taciturn and still.

'May I help?' Stephen asked.

She felt ashamed of the scene before them, a living illustration of her father's ideas on profitable farming. What sort of advertisement was it that he, the finest stonemason in West Penwith, refused to build a proper cowshouse 'because it cost too damn much'! He could take pencil and paper and show you, six ways to Christmas, that a stone house would never pay unless you owned the land and had a herd of more than twenty in milk at any one time. But it didn't make a casual structure of straw bales, planks, and tarpaulin any the prettier or more acceptable.

'May I?' Stephen repeated, slipping an arm about her waist as they ducked inside the straw-bale milking parlour. Yesterday he would hardly have dared touch her; now the ease of his intimacy was a great comfort to her. She began to understand what he meant when he said he was never alone these days.

'There's a little stone-walled mowie out the back,' she said. 'You take that eevil, if you mind to, and bring in two or three turnips for each cow as I do milk her.'

He hefted the implement in his hands. 'Do I stab them on its prongs or use it more like a shovel?'

'Stab.' She went out with him to fetch a pail of water from the kieve, leaving him the lantern when she went back inside. The first bleary rays of dawn were beginning to finger the eastern skyline. The lone pine on top of Tregathennan was already discernible beside the much nearer tower of the church. The rooks began to chatter and caw; nearby a blackbird joined his more melodious voice to the rising clamour of the day.

'Raspberry!' she called out at the door – or the gap between bales that served as their way in.

Greenberry poked her head inside. 'Ho-back!' Roseanne yelled at her with indifferent ferocity. Moments later a much more nervous Raspberry tore herself away from the door of the little wooden shed where her calf was fattening for veal; the pressure of milk in her bag had overpowered her maternal instincts at last.

Roseanne tied her to the milking stake and then took up a steaming-wet cloth from the pail. She liked the young heifers, with their fine skins and smooth udders; even when they got muddy or dungy, they were so much easier to clean than the warty old cows with their long, lank bags.

Raspberry began letting down her milk the moment she felt the touch of Roseanne's hand. Stephen returned at that moment with the lantern, by whose light she saw the white cloudy liquid swirl into the water. The heifer dried up momentarily as she saw a stranger enter with the turnips . . . but food is food and she let go again with a rush as she bit into the first crisp root. Roseanne just got the milking pail to her in time to catch it.

'This lady almost milks herself,' she told Stephen.

'You mean even I could manage it?'

'Have you ever tried?'

He sniffed. 'When I was about six.' He squatted on his haunches on the opposite side and watched her hands at their work.

She exaggerated the action, opening her fingers wide between pulls to show how she first nipped the teat at its junction with the bag to prevent the milk from flowing back; then the progressive downward squeeze to the outlet at the tip. 'Ever watch a sucking calf, did 'ee?' she asked.

'Not closely. Why?'

'Every now and then they do give their mother a nudge, like, with their muzzle. And that do make her let down more milk. Like that.' She clenched her fist and thrust it upward into Raspberry's bag. 'See? Now she'll let down a bit more. You do that and you'll have no trouble.'

Tentatively he followed suit, expecting the cow to kick or lash out with her tail; to his delight she accepted his amateur fumbling as part of the morning's business. He grasped her teat and tried to copy Roseanne. A firm jet of milk thudded into the wooden pail. He gave a little laugh of triumphant surprise. 'Well, I'll go to blazes!' he exclaimed.

He tried it again, and again succeeded.

'I told 'ee,' she laughed. 'She do milk herself. Use both hands now. And keep the top squeezed off until you've pulled the last drop each time. See? You're letting half of it go back inside.'

For a while they milked the heifer in silence while he exulted in his easy success. Then the feeling of the swollen teats in his hands and the sight of hers, nimbly squeezing and letting go in that steady rhythm, filled him with ideas that he immediately suppressed in shame – trying to expel them from his mind even as he expelled the milk into the pail. But, just as more milk came flooding down to replace what had gone, so those thoughts refilled his mind as fast as he banished them.

To his even deeper shame, he found himself wondering whether similar thoughts were occurring to Roseanne. Suddenly he felt sickened at himself and his own profound unworthiness. How could he even ask such a question? What disease had infested his mind to make him capable of such thoughts? When she laughed and said, 'You'll put the milkmaids to shame at Skyburriowe yet!' he was too disgusted with himself to reply.

Soon the pail was three-fourths filled. She rose from her stool and took it, not to the churn but to a copper pail that stood in the corner. 'That's for the calf, see?' she explained. 'You want to go and feed him while I do finish off here?'

'How would I do that?' he asked, glad of the chance to escape the provocative visions that plagued him.

'Just tilt the pail toward him and hold it about knee high. Then put your finger or thumb in his mouth and he'll start sucking, see. Then lower it into the milk and he'll carry on. You can take your hand away then. Hold the pail firm, mind, or he'll dash it from 'ee.'

Stephen took the pail out into the dawn, whose light was just sufficient by now to show him the dark shapes of the cows. One of them tried to get her muzzle into the milk but he kicked her away. *Just like a real stockman*, he thought with satisfaction, remembering scenes in Helston market.

Perhaps he and Roseanne could go up-country somewhere, to England, and take a small farm? Maybe his aunt in Cheltenham would help. She and his father were always at daggers drawn. Or he could borrow on the entail of Skyburriowe. His father could do nothing to prevent him inheriting the estate one day – and outright, too, since he was third in the line. The old man couldn't bar it without his son's collusion – and there was no chance of *that* now!

He slid back the bolt on the shed door and was almost bowled over by the eager little calf. 'Steady the Buffs!' he cried, then, remembering the market again, changed it to, 'Ho-back, you heller!' That sounded much more like it.

Not that the calf paid the slightest attention to either command.

Stephen did as Roseanne had described and soon the creature was gulping merrily; the way it sucked at his thumb reawakened those earlier, shameful thoughts. But away from Roseanne they were easier to ignore – or, perhaps, to acknowledge. Yes, he thought sadly, they *were* easier to acknowledge as his own.

His reveries drifted back to the coming battle with his parents. He wondered why the prospect of so much strife and bitterness was nonetheless so pleasurable. It was, he decided, the picture of him and Roseanne, living far from here, cut off from all their old ties and allegiances, just the two of them, alone against the world.

As the milk dwindled in the pail, the calf's instinct was to nudge it hard, as he would nudge his mother's bag. He almost knocked it out of Stephen's hand the first time; after that he was ready for the creature, who banged away harder and more often, until Stephen was surprised it didn't put a dent in the copper or spring the seam.

Adroitly he faced the calf toward the corner of the shed, by enticing it with the pail, and thus managed to leap outdoors and shoot the bolt before it could turn and try to follow. As he walked back to the milking parlour he wondered where the knowledge to handle the calf like that had come from. He must have an instinct for it, he decided. He must be a natural stockman.

It suddenly struck him that this was the happiest day of his life. A blackbird sang and he whistled back a joyous, if incompetent, imitation.

Crouched behind the mowie wall, unseen by him, his sister Annette watched and noted his every move. If he truly were a natural stockman, of course, the behaviour of the cattle would have alerted him to her presence at once.

12

Annette had seen enough. She crept back down the lane and then set off for home before the Kitto woman appeared; that one would have noticed the cows' unease immediately, of course. And, though it would not have worried Annette unduly to be discovered there, she preferred to keep her secrets to herself until she could decide how best to use them. Though she was only seventeen, she already had a remarkable faculty in that particular direction.

As she strode out into the brightening day she reviewed what she had learned so far. She was sorry that her parents had learned of this affair from some third party; she would have preferred to tell them herself, though at a more propitious moment. But now she really had something to chew over.

At the heart of her rivalry with Stephen was the fact that he and not she would one day inherit Skyburriowe. He'd manage the place even worse than their father, and that was yet more cause for her anger. Her mother loved repeating the tale of how, when she, Annette, at the age of six had first learned that only boys inherit family estates, she had burst into tears and kicked Stephen and bit him so badly she'd been put on bread and water for a week. Also she'd been whipped every night until she said she was sorry. But her mother always omitted that part, because Annette never had apologized and in the end they'd just given up whipping her, because they couldn't find any unbruised flesh to sting and Dr Moore had said she'd get septicaemia and gangrene if they kept on. So now they all pretended she *had* apologized, and they'd turned the drama into one of those gruesome tales that doting parents love to tell.

Oddly enough, they *were* doting parents. Her father had become quite ill and gone into a decline when he had to keep on with her whipping, night after night. And she knew he was secretly rather proud of her stubbornness and the fortitude of her resistance, especially at so tender an age. Once, in an unguarded moment years later, when she was about twelve, he had told her of old Saxon customs, before the Norman Conquest, and how estates had descended through sons or daughters, depending on the decision of the family elders and who they thought would make the best job of it. She knew why he'd told her that, even though he never said it in so many words. She knew Stephen was a bitter disappointment to him.

Annette herself, despite her chagrin, was actually quite fond of her brother. In fact, everyone was *fond* of him, even their father. It was impossible to dislike someone so amiable and mild. But those very qualities made him the worst possible person to inherit an ancient and run-down estate like Skyburriowe.

For years after her father told her about the Saxons, Annette had dreamed of being at her brother's side, doing all the actual management of the estate while he remained its titular head – rather like the English monarchy and government, which was another of her father's lessons. More recently, though, as she had grown aware of the proper roles of men and women, she had come to realize it would not do. The social positions of the squire's wife and of his spinster sister

100

were like those of queen and beggarmaid. And Stephen would surely take a wife.

From then on Annette had spied shamelessly on her brother whenever he showed an interest in the more nubile females of their circle. In any other young sister in her teens, of course, such an interest could be ascribed to the usual lively curiosity of all females, young and old, in affairs of the heart; in Annette it was no such thing. She assessed them, those potential sisters-in-law, as women who might (or might not) put the missing backbone into her brother. All of them so far had been in the might-not category — darling milksops like himself. Roseanne Kitto, however, was something new.

Their parents were angry because she was socially out of the question. They admired Frank Kitto and acknowledged that he'd do well — in commerce at least. But socially he was beyond the pale. Annette's view of the matter was quite the opposite. As long as Stephen's wife supplied the necessary grit and determination, she did not care whether the woman came from a palace or a hovel. It was Skyburriowe that mattered, the perpetuation of the estate; not the social class of its mistress — or so she had always told herself before this.

It had been an easy thing to say when every candidate was so unsuitable that it would never come to a test. Now she was less certain.

Her thoughts returned again and again to Miss Kitto and she realized how little she knew of the woman. And what little she did know only made her the more uneasy. And that in itself was odd, because it ought to have had the opposite effect.

One often saw her in the fields, weeding this crop or that, lifting potatoes . . . Annette had even noticed her trimming back the hedges on one occasion. And every day she was up and out at five, bringing in the cows to their milking. She wore the same four dresses, each in its season, year after year. Really she should rank no higher in general esteem than any other village maid. And yet she was different; she always had been different.

Annette remembered attending the village school when she was five. Roseanne Kitto had been one of the big maids then, twelve years old and in her last class. Most of the other maids had gone on into service, or the local shops, or to work as bal maidens at the mines. But Roseanne had stayed on until she was fifteen to help Miss Gurney, the school dame, with the infants. She had, in effect, been Annette's first teacher. She had a nimble mind and she certainly knew her figures. Annette had gone in awe of her − and, if she were quite, quite honest, she still did to some degree. They said Miss Kitto could have stayed on and taken over the school when Miss Gurney retired; but when she turned fifteen she said the screech of the slate pencils set her teeth on edge and the chalk dust gave her pimples and so she'd handed in her notice and gone to work on her father's smallholding instead. In fact, she'd more or less taken it over.

The decision had given her something of a scandalous reputation − which was another reason for the squire and his wife to object to her. Why should a respectable girl give up a respectable calling like that and go out and work in the fields in all weathers like some pauper from the workhouse? There was something almost wicked about it. At the very least it was perverse.

To Annette, however, it had a certain magnificence. If she wanted to be like anyone when she grew up, that person was Roseanne Kitto. Not that she wanted to work in the fields or anything like that − God forbid! − but she wanted that same independence of spirit and the determination that went with it.

And yet, she had to admit, those were also qualities that now troubled her. She turned into the driveway at Skyburriowe and gazed around her at the family estate. Her unease deepened. She realized that if Miss Kitto took it into her head to marry Stephen and make a success of this place, she'd succeed. And suddenly that was the last thing in all the world that Annette wished to happen: a stranger coming into the place and doing well what she herself would do even better.

The more she thought about it, the more convinced she became that there was only one fit person to inherit and manage — and rescue — Skyburriowe: herself.

13

After Mark put Gertie Harvey home to Penhale Row he found Roseanne standing at her garden gate, apparently enjoying the evening air. She was staring across the fields to the momentarily calm waters of Mount's Bay and looking as if she had stood there for ages − though, as Mark very well knew, she had not been there only two minutes earlier, when he and Gertie had gone up the lane.

'Evening,' he murmured in a clipped, formal voice as he passed her by.

'When are you going to take they store cattle?' she asked.

He stopped in his tracks but did not immediately turn to look at her. 'How? Looking for rent, are 'ee?'

'A shilling,' she said at once.

Then he turned his great, shocked eyes upon her.

'Or,' she went on evenly, 'you might ask that Gertie Harvey to put them in *her* field.'

He frowned. 'She haven't got no field.'

'Aha!' Roseanne smiled. 'A shilling it is, then.'

He fumbled angrily in his pocket and brought out a handful of loose change, which he flung at her feet without bothering to count it. 'Cheap at the price,' he commented. 'Why not ask thirty pieces of silver − that's more the style for your sort, innit?'

Their eyes met and locked. She fought back an

impulse to be soothing — or at least to talk to him. The trouble was she appeared to love both men equally. That morning, after the milking, when she and Stephen had stood in the mowie and kissed until their mouths ached, her innards had turned over and over with her longing for him. And yet moments later, when, to test herself, she had thought of Mark and all the wonderful times they had known together, she had felt that same hollowing out, that same almost infinite yearning. It made her wonder if she weren't more in love with love itself that with any actual man in her life.

Why couldn't she at least talk to Mark? True, it would mean the sacrifice of at least some of her dignity; but he was so stubborn, he'd never unbend. If she left it to him, they'd go from now to kingdom-come sooner than engage in any real conversation. Was it so great a sacrifice for her to make? She felt her pride beginning to melt and a softness gathering within her; but in that same instant there was a rush of anger, too — anger tinged with fear. If she gave way now, it would set a pattern between them from which he would never deviate. He would always know that if he kept up his coldness long enough, she would be the one to yield in the end.

She bent and counted twelve pence from the coins in the lane. 'A fool and his money . . .' she said, pointing to the remainder, which amounted to fivepence three-farthings.

He took two angry paces toward her and gripped her by the wrist. It hurt but it was also quite thrilling — that and the fury in his eyes. 'Why *should* he come in and just take you from me?' he asked.

She held forth her free hand, her left, stretching her fingers to show that none sported a ring. 'There's no brand there so far as I can see,' she said. It was a particularly unfair comment since both of them knew he had offered to buy her a ring and she had scorned the idea, telling him they'd have better things to do with their money — *their* money. Now, in recalling the occasion, it did just fleetingly occur to her to wonder if simple economy had been all her reason for rejecting the offer.

He raised her imprisoned hand and dashed it against the gatepost — or tried to. But she hadn't been lifting ten-gallon creamery cans full of milk for nothing during the past few years; she resisted him so successfully that her arm barely touched the wood. Yet in struggling to free herself she bent her wrist so sharply that her hand opened and the coins fell out again. It was all he had wanted, anyway.

'A fool and her promises are just as soon parted,' he called over his shoulder as he strode off, adding, 'I'll fetch they stores out the field tomorrow, don't 'ee fret.'

She gathered up all the coins, pocketed a shillings-worth, and carried the remainder up the lane to the field where his stores were grazing. There she left them in a precarious pile on the gatepost.

As she wandered back home she remembered something Miss Gurney had once told her about the Ancient Greeks. They had a different set of gods from the Hebrews and Egyptians and all the other people of those times. The Greeks thought *their* gods had created humans simply for their sport. At times like this, she thought glumly, it would be hard to prove them wrong.

14

May Delamere of Vinery House, a substantial dwelling of cut stone in about half an acre of grounds, was trying to prune a stout hedge of escallonia as Mark stormed by on his way to the Queen's Arms, which was just opposite. He would probably change his mind over two pints, but at that moment his intention was to get paralytic-drunk. And then perhaps go back and heave rocks through that bitch's window. Burn all his boats. It was going to be a fine, moonlit night, perfect for some grand gesture.

'Botheration!' May Delamere exclaimed.

Mark waited to hear whether any cry of pain or distress might follow.

'I say, you out there,' she cried. 'Forgive my rudeness but I can't make out who you are.'

Mark thought that a little odd since, a minute earlier, when he had rounded the corner by the bakery, less than half a furlong away, she had been at her gate and must have seen him quite clearly. Or perhaps not, without her glasses. Did she wear glasses? He couldn't recall. He hardly knew the woman, anyway.

'It's Mark Bodilly, Mrs Delamere,' he replied. 'May I be of any assistance?'

'Oh bless you! If you would, I'd be so . . . If you come in by the gate there, you'll see for yourself.'

He did as she bade. The hinge needed oiling. No man

about the house. Two slates were loose as well, hanging awry. The autumn gales would fetch them down, surely.

She was making futile little leaps at a recalcitrant branch of the shrub, which she abandoned as soon as he drew near. 'I don't want to cut it down this low,' she said, pointing to a spot level with her elbow, 'or it'll leave a gap, d'you see. If you could just bend it down?' She smiled sweetly, a smile both winsome and winning.

For a woman of . . . what? Fortyish? No, her eldest daughter who married that parson must be twenty-eight now — so she must be nearer fifty! Well, for a woman of that age she certainly didn't look it. He smiled back and pulled the branch down. 'Like that?' he asked.

She mashed away at it with her secateurs, making a mess of the wood — which was also odd, because several thicker branches with clean cuts lay scattered at their feet.

'Here.' He took the implement from her and, moving down an inch or so to the undamaged wood, severed it in one neat diagonal slice, just above a bud.

He offered her back the secateurs but she reached beyond them and gave his forearm a light, daring squeeze. 'Oh,' she murmured, fluttering her eyelashes admiringly, 'it just isn't fair. Strong men like you can have no idea of the difficulties . . .' She waved a hand vaguely around the garden — which, in fact, looked immaculate.

'Well,' he offered, slightly at a loss for words, 'is there something else I can do . . . while I'm here, you know?'

'Oh, but I mustn't keep you,' she said, as if remonstrating with herself. He told her he had merely been out for a stroll — with no particular aim in mind.

'Perhaps you'd like to stroll round my garden, then?' she suggested. And before he could demur she added,

'You have an instinctive understanding for nature, I can tell.'

He laughed and, having nothing better to do with the secateurs, slipped them into his pocket before offering her his arm, which he did with jocular gallantry. 'I don't know how you can say that,' he challenged.

'Oh, you may laugh, but it shows. It is always the small things that give us away.' Another winning smile. 'You severed that horrid branch just above a new bud – and you cut it at the slant. See? You understand natural things and how to treat them. You gave yourself away.'

'Ah.' He took up her amicable tone – thinking it nonetheless quite extraordinary, since he and Mrs Delamere had exchanged no more than a dozen words and as many nods of the head in all his life. 'Serve me right, then!' His tone became more serious as he went on, 'I never realized you had so much here in the way of gardens. With those high hedges you get no impression of it from the road.'

'No. I do value my privacy.'

'And all so immaculately kept! Who does it for you?'

'Oh . . . passers-by, you know.' She laughed and gave his arm a squeeze. 'No. Jack Keverne comes over from Ashton three days a week. But I do quite a bit of it myself.' She sighed. 'It's my only true occupation now that the last of my girls is off my hands.'

'Oh, yes. I heard tell as little Bessie married again.'

'She's not so little now – nearly twenty-five, you know.'

'Well, I hope she's happy this time.'

'Happier, anyway.' Her tone was flat, suggesting that Bessie was no longer of much concern to her. 'That's *Acer palmatum dissectum*, you know, the new sport from Japan – *palmatidum*. But it's not thriving here.

109

Some say its roots are too dry, others say no, it's too wet. I think it's the wind, don't you? The scourge of Cornwall.' She seemed to imply that hers was a difficult and hostile world but that he, simply by walking into her garden, had somehow improved it.

She conducted him to every nook and arbour, lingering at none of them, and keeping up a steady stream of botanical information most of which passed far over his head — though he felt absurdly flattered that she should imagine he followed it all. At the innermost wall he looked out over a small field that should have been cut for hay six weeks earlier. 'There's a shame,' he commented.

'What?' Her flow of Latin jawbreakers was stemmed for a moment.

'Whoever let that field go to seed. Is that glebe land?'

She cleared her throat delicately. 'As a matter of fact, Mr Bodilly . . .' She squeezed his arm again to complete the sentence for her.

'My dear soul!' he exclaimed, hitting himself on the forehead. 'I should have thought before I spoke. Of course, you've a perfect right to . . .'

'The only way to reach it is through my garden, you see. I don't want nasty, smelly cows tramping in and out four times a day.'

He eyed her shrewdly, and then the field. 'Well, you wouldn't hardly have to put up with that,' he pointed out.

'Wouldn't I?' She tilted her head engagingly to one side; her eyes were large as saucers.

He scratched his chin, pondering what he might be letting himself in for. Eventually, in a spirit of in for a penny, in for a pound, he said, 'You could put half a dozen store cattle in there for three weeks or a month. They'd leave it looking like a lawn for 'ee.'

110

'Really? I know nothing about such things, of course.'

'If you don't, all they thistles and docks will seed and spread into the garden anyway.'

'Oh don't! We've had an absolute infestation of them this year. Is that the cause, d'you think?'

He nodded sagely and waited for her to ask the obvious question.

A moment later she obliged. 'I don't suppose you happen to know of anyone with . . . what d'you call them? Store cattle?'

'As a matter of fact,' he replied diffidently, 'I've half a dozen of my own up in Kitto's field. I was intending moving them this week, anyroad.'

'Oh well!' she exclaimed, as if that made all the difference in the world. 'I'd trust *you*, of course, Mr Bodilly — not to damage my garden, I mean. You being such a keen gardener yourself.'

'Well, that's kind of you to say so, Mrs Delamere, ma'am. But there's the question of rent.'

'Fie!' She laughed. 'We shan't fall out over that, I'm sure. Whatever you think is reasonable. Now sit you in the summerhouse there, and I'll just slip in and fetch us a glass of ale and a bite of fuggan.'

'Oh . . . well, now . . . I don't hardly . . .'

'Nonsense!' She almost thrust him before her into the arbour. 'I may not know much about the world, Mr Bodilly, but I do know that any arrangement concerning land and livestock has to be cemented over a sup of ale. Am I not right?'

With a perfect blend of reluctance and pleasure he assured her she was, indeed.

While he sat and waited for her to re-emerge, he took stock of this novel and, as far as he was concerned, entirely unexpected situation. As far as *she* was concerned, he thought, it was *not* entirely unexpected. She must have seen him turn the corner by the bakery; and all that wrestling with her hedge, giving out that cry of exasperation just as he was passing — that was no accident, either.

But why? Her reputation in the district, insofar as anyone thought of her at all, was that she was a quiet, respectable, retiring young widow. Well . . . young-*looking*, anyway. She kept herself to herself, performed enough charities to avoid comment either on their excess or their scarcity, and left the rest of the world to its own devices. Not the sort of woman, he thought, to take him by the arm — a relative stranger — and drag him round her garden chatting away like an old friend.

What did she want of him? He thought of the cracked slates, the unoiled hinges, the grass growing in the rain launder at the back, the torn flyscreen of perforated zinc on the pantry window, and several other signs of neglect he had noticed in passing. Well, he thought, becoming easier in his mind, if that was to be his rent, it would be a cheap and easy acquittal.

She returned shortly with a large tankard of ale and a small glass of port; the slices of fuggan were of a similar disproportion — indeed, his was almost half the cake while hers was the merest sliver. He protested his was too much and said she should have some of it; her little portion wouldn't feed a sparrow. She replied that she had to guard her figure, settling herself opposite him in such a way that he became even more aware of it — her figure — than before. 'That's Rosewarne's best export ale,' she warned him. 'I get it directly off Mrs Moore herself.'

He pointed an accusing finger at her roof. 'I see you have two slates working loose up there, Mrs Delamere.' She followed his gaze, tut-tutted sadly, and told him he was right — as if she had never noticed it before. 'Who's the best man to deal with that?' she asked. 'Does Kitto do that sort of thing?'

'I was thinking,' he replied, ignoring her direct question . . . and he went on to list the other odd jobs he had noticed about the place. 'I was thinking, if I took care of those little things for 'ee, would that be acceptable, like, in the way of rent?'

'Oh, Mr Bodilly!' Her startled hands brushed nonexistent fluff from her bodice. 'It hardly seems right, does it. Your cattle will turn that wilderness of a field into a lawn for me, you say — *and* you'll do all those other things into the bargain.'

''Tin't so many other things,' he pointed out hastily. 'It won't take me that long.'

She accepted the assurance. 'Well, what can I say?' She beamed at him. 'If you think it's fair 'change, then I certainly shan't argue. May I put a little head on that ale?'

He withdrew the tankard a token inch. 'Thank 'ee, ma'am. It will be all I require. I'm not a great drinking man.'

She settled herself back into her seat. 'I'm delighted to hear it, Mr Bodilly — not that I'd ever have supposed otherwise. But I wish I could say the same of a dozen others in this village — living opposite the inn, as I do. That's another reason for my good stout hedge, of course.'

He glanced about them and said, yet again, how charming it all was. Their eyes met and she smiled. 'Talking of the Kittos,' she said, 'is it true you didn't take young Roseanne to Wendron Ram-Buck this year? Tell me to mind my own business if you like.'

Mark, who had immediately been racking his brain for some polite way to tell her just that, suddenly felt that of all the people he knew — even among those he knew as slightly as May Delamere — none would lend a more sympathetic ear. He supped his ale, nodded sadly, and took a large bite of fuggan to excuse himself from talking for a moment. He washed it down with more ale and then said, 'I don't know how it happened. She's so stubborn as a donkey and I'm so stubborn as a mule. And that's how it happened.'

She nodded as if she saw it all. 'You and she have been sweethearts a very long time,' she said.

'Since school.'

'Quite so. We hear a great deal, don't we, about lifelong love and devotion, and I'm sure it must occasionally happen. But there's precious little of it' — she waved a hand vaguely about her — 'out there. And I do sometimes wonder . . . I'm sure it's very naughty of me, but I do sometimes wonder if we humans are intended for such monogamy.' She bit her lip. 'Some *men* quite plainly are not. But even we poor females . . . you know?'

He took another bite of that unending cake and nodded warily. Had he been wrong about loose slates and squeaky hinges?

She chuckled and hung her head in chagrin. 'Just hark at me! Talking away like some grand beldame who's seen it all and heard it all. I hardly know anything of life as yet. I married at eighteen and I've just got the last of my daughters off my hands. What do *I* know of life or other people's vexations? Why, I expect you know ten times more than me already, Mr Bodilly.'

'I beg leave to doubt that, ma'am,' he replied. 'I only ever knew one woman well, and she's become a mystery to me — apart from my mother, of course.'

'I thought you had a sister?'

114

'Two. Both married. I couldn't explain them to save my life.'

'Dear me! What is it you find so hard to understand? Perhaps another woman may divine . . .'

She let the offer hang unfinished. He knew she did not refer to his sisters. He tried to think about Roseanne — what it was that so baffled him about her. But it was all too vast, too amorphous for him to pick out one single item of importance. Instead he settled for the most recent. He told her of their altercation in the lane that evening, especially the unfairness of her remarks about her lack of an engagement ring when it was she who had scorned the offer and told him their love was too strong to need such extravagant support.

May Delamere heard him out in sympathetic silence. When he had finished she said, 'I feel there's something you haven't told me. Why did you go to see her tonight? What did you intend saying to her? I mean, did you walk up the lane and suddenly have her springing out at you with all this abuse?'

Sheepishly he admitted that it had all happened *after* he had put Gertie Harvey home. Mrs Delamere hung her head and stared up at him accusingly. 'Well now!' she exclaimed. 'Isn't that all rather different?'

He nodded unhappily.

'And don't tell me you find *that* particular episode hard to explain!'

He shook his head. 'I suppose not.'

'Indeed, if any explanation is needed about anyone's behaviour, surely it's yours.'

Again he shook his head, unwilling to concede so much.

'Perhaps not,' she agreed with a provocative smile. 'After all, if a young man takes another girl past his sweetheart's house in broad daylight and kisses her

115

farewell on the doorstep . . .' She paused. 'I assume you *did* kiss her farewell.'

His nod was barely perceptible.

'Why then,' she concluded, 'he might as well write it in bold capitals and parade the message past her house like a sandwich-board man.'

He stared miserably at the church tower. Half-past eight! The dusk was gathering fast now.

'Of course,' she concluded in the most off-hand tone imaginable, 'one of the difficulties of being a sandwich-board man is that they are often the last, and the least able, to read their own messages.'

15

They were cubbing over Trigonning Hill. Two years ago there had been a great tragedy there when the entire Skyburriowe pack — fifteen couple in full cry — went streaming over the rim of the abandoned quarry above Troon. Not a hound had survived. And, to add insult to the injury, the vixen had been seen loping away on the far side of the quarry, calm as you like. Those who like to embroider such tales even claimed she was grinning, as only a vixen can.

Today was the first occasion Annette had ridden to hounds since that dreadful morning. She had chosen it deliberately because they were drawing the same country and she knew the memory would haunt her forever unless she faced it squarely; also she enjoyed cubbing more than hunting because there were no kills and only the most dedicated huntsmen and women turned out. There were no gaggles of followers whose chief interests were social; such people thought the gallops a bore and longed for nothing more than to mill around at a draw, swigging their hipflasks, and filling the air with their gossip and the smoke of their cigars. Cubbing, she decided, despite its humane nature, was by far the superior sport.

They made good work of it, too, that day. They spread a dozen or more cubs as far afield as Wheal Fortune in the east and Skewjack in the west — stopping just short of the boundaries of the Cury Harriers and the West Penwith. So their own territory was now well stocked with the Red Gentleman and should yield good outings for the rest of the season.

On their way back past Breage she turned aside, up the road that led into the village itself — telling her father she was just going to pop into Mrs Oaksey's to get a hank of black silk twist. The moment they were out of sight, however, she turned back, faced her mount at the hedge on the seaward side of the road and leaped into the field beyond. Two more jumps brought her to the field where she had stood the week before, watching her brother pretending to be a stockman and Miss Kitto abetting the masquerade.

She was there now, lifting creamery cans full of that evening's milk into a great kieve of water to cool off. Annette watched her in awe. They must be almost full, the best part of a hundredweight each, yet she was lifting them with no apparent strain. You could understand it if she was one of those bold, strapping wenches who picked over the rock and ore at the mines, but she had an unremarkable physique in that respect, neither skeletal nor hulking.

'How do you do that, Miss Kitto?' she was moved to ask as she drew up her veil and eased the grip of her hat.

Roseanne, for whom the clatter of the cans had masked the horse's approach, and whose attention had in any case been miles away, turned round in surprise. 'Oh, how d'you do, Miss Morvah,' she replied.

Annette laughed as she slipped from the saddle. 'No, I asked how you manage to lift those heavy cans and make them seem light as a feather.' She peeled off her gloves as she advanced, then held out a hand to shake Roseanne's.

'Oh . . . practice, I suppose.' She slipped off her oilcloth apron and wiped her hands in her smock before she shook Annette's. She felt it rather strange, for the squire's daughter had never offered such familiarity before. She eyed the girl warily and said, 'You were cubbing up Trigonning?'

Annette nodded. 'We had a very good day of it.'

Roseanne smiled, a touch ironically. 'And got spread abroad yourself now, have 'ee? Looking for a new earth?'

'Oh yes! And a new heaven!' Annette laughed, a little immoderately. Roseanne saw the pulse hammering away in a vein in the girl's neck and realized that, despite her control of her voice, she was in quite a nervy state.

'To what do I owe the honour, then?' she prompted.

Annette swallowed heavily. 'Oh dear! And I thought it was going to be so simple!'

Roseanne decided to help her out. 'To do with your brother and me, is it?'

The girl nodded. 'You know what my parents are saying about it? Did Stephen tell you? You know they've forbidden him to see you?'

'He did mention something like that.' Roseanne's eyes gave nothing away.

'Well, I think they're being simply beastly. Also I think they're wrong. Anyway, I was out riding early one morning last week.' She patted her horse's neck as if that somehow proved it. 'And I saw Stephen coming home down the back road by Trequean.' She smiled with mild self-satisfaction as she added, 'And carrying a towel as if he'd been bathing — except he wasn't coming *up* from Trequean Zawn but down the road from Breage.'

'Goodness gracious me!' Roseanne exclaimed in mock alarm.

'No, I want to help,' Annette insisted. 'Honestly.'

'Why?' Roseanne's tone was suddenly sharp.

The girl looked away across the fields and gave an unhappy shrug. 'Because I'm fond of my brother, of course.'

'Oh ah?'

'I *am*! I know we don't always see eye to eye.' She chuckled and bit her lip. 'I can't deny there've been times when I'd happily have murdered him. If you had a brother, that wouldn't surprise you.' She closed her eyes and mumbled, as if she were getting close to tears. 'I know I'm only a silly young giglet of seventeen – and you must think of me still as that infant who couldn't spell *cat* nor add up two and two . . .'

Roseanne leaned forward and touched her arm solicitously. 'By the time I taught you, Miss Kitto, you could do all of those things. And of course I do believe you're fond of your brother.'

'All I wanted to say,' Annette blurted out, 'was that he can't go on meeting you like that. You know what this parish is like. You can't walk a yard without someone noticing it. Word of your meetings is bound to get back to my mother and father. So what I wanted to say was if you need a go-between to carry messages or draw a red herring across the line of the hunt . . .' She sighed with relief now that she had reached her conclusion. 'I mean I'll go leg-bail for you.'

At last Roseanne believed she understood the girl. To one of her tender years these secret assignations in the face of their parents' hostility must seem the very height of romance. To act the go-between in such excitements would be the thrill of her life. Roseanne realized she herself had almost forgotten how one felt at that age; she was suddenly ashamed of her suspicions and her caution of a moment earlier. She took the girl's hand between her own and squeezed it warmly, thanking her profusely and saying how sorry she was ever to have doubted her.

The words released the last of Annette's reserve and she embarked upon an embarrassing paean of admiration, saying Roseanne was exactly the sort of woman Stephen needed and that her parents were blinded by social prejudice when they preferred creatures like Viola Menadue or Wilhelmina Bolitho. Then she paused in midstream and said, 'I'm sorry, I never thought to ask — but what do *your* parents think about it? They must know, of course? Have you finished your chores here? May we walk back down the lane together?'

Roseanne ducked halfway inside the ramshackle parlour and fished a jar of lanolin from its niche between two straw bales. She rubbed a good fingerful into her hands, explaining it was really bought for the cows' teats but it worked wonders on chapped human skin, too. She watched the girl closely while she spoke, thinking that the rather blunt agricultural references might discomfit her; but if so, she gave no hint of it. Indeed, her response was, 'Oh, in that case, I'll try some, too. I hope it's not expensive?'

Roseanne laughed and, taking both Annette's hands between her own, wiped the excess into them.

Annette was amazed. 'I say, they *are* smooth, aren't they!' She raised the other's hands in turn and inspected them closely.

'Time enough for you to worry about that,' Roseanne told her as she transferred the last of the excess.

But the girl would not let her hands go; she continued to massage them between her own, gently and rather languorously. Then she giggled. 'Did you ever read *Moby Dick*? I'm sure you did. D'you remember that passage where the whalers sit on either side of a long trough filled with the spermaceti and scrabble in it for the precious little bits of ambergris? And he describes how the perfume overpowers them so that when their hands accidentally touch they're filled with love and good feeling toward each other. D'you remember?'

Roseanne, slightly embarrassed, nodded. In fact, a vague memory of the same passage had flitted through her mind when she first took Annette's hands in her own, but she did not say so now. Instead she laughed and commented that there was certainly no ambergris in this lanolin – 'only the mildest dose of carbolic'.

Annette was unmoved to hear it. 'I hope we always will love and help each other, Miss Kitto, dear,' she said, breaking contact between them at last. 'There's no one else in all the world I'd rather have as my sister-on-law. And I promise you I'll move heaven itself to make it come true.'

Roseanne, who had meanwhile wiped the last of the cream into her smock grasped the girl's shoulder and gave her a squeeze. 'You are a strange one,' she murmured.

'Can I call you Roseanne?' she blurted out.

'Now how would that appear to others, Miss Morvah?'

'Annette. Please?'

Roseanne sighed. 'Talk about the irresistible force! Only when we're alone, mind – which won't happen too often, I expect.'

'Oh, but we must make it happen, Roseanne.' She linked arms and began propelling her down the lane, leading the horse at her other side. 'I tell you what. My mother's going to stay with her cousin in Bath next month. Well, it's only a fortnight away now and she'll be gone for weeks and weeks. And I'm to do all her parish visits – only she's taking her maid with her, who usually carries the broth and pies and things. Now if *you* were to take her place, we'd see each other every day.'

'Really!' Roseanne laughed.

'Why not? You have time, surely? It only takes an hour or so each morning. Or afternoon, if you prefer. We only visit the *deserving* poor, you know.'

Roseanne laughed again, a touch more desperately. 'But why should I go and do a thing like that, Miss Morvah?'

'Who's she? The cat's mother?'

Roseanne sighed heavily 'All right. Annette! Why should I go and do a thing like that?'

The girl extended a knuckle and dug her in the ribs without weakening her predatory clutch on Roseanne's arm. 'It's what squires' wives are *for*. Didn't you know?'

They came to the cows' present field. Roseanne had left the gate open when she brought them in for milking and they had gone back of their own accord when she'd finished with them. She paused a while and counted the full complement before she dragged the gate to and tied it with twine; well-hung gates with proper bolts were another luxury a smallholding could manage without − according to her father.

They had barely resumed their stroll down the lane before they encountered Mrs Kitto, slightly out of breath. She had seen Annette apparently racing over the fields and had set out to investigate. 'Oh hallo, Miss Morvah. It *is* you. I wondered.' She gasped for breath and patted her breast. 'Nothing amiss, I hope?'

Annette did not proffer her hand. Instead she swung herself lightly on to her saddle, crooked her knee firmly around the post, and said, 'It's only that I'm taking over my mother's parish visits in a week or so, Mrs Kitto,

123

and I wanted your daughter to join me. But she can't make up her mind. Do talk her round, I beg you.' Then, with a bow and a smile, she was off at a measured canter.

'Is that true?' her mother asked excitedly when the clatter had receded.

Roseanne sighed and shook her head.

'It must be true if Miss Morvah said so,' Mrs Kitto insisted. 'Why would she lie, else?'

'I'm not saying it isn't true. Just . . .' She shook her head again. 'Did you ever go outdoors, not realizing how windy a day it was, and almost get knocked down by it?'

Mrs Kitto stared after Annette's receding figure; now only her head and shoulders were visible above the hedge, down near the turnpike. 'She always was a bit headstrong, like.'

Roseanne nodded. 'I'd forgotten.' She took her mother's arm and they started walking back toward the row of houses. 'I suppose I'll have to. Do what she asked, I mean.'

There was a stone in the middle of the lane, tumbled from the top of the hedge by a panicking rabbit. The sight of it reminded Mrs Kitto of something and she exclaimed, 'Botheration!'

'What?' Roseanne stooped to pick it up and replace it.

'I meant to tell 'ee. I should ought to have told 'ee while Miss Morvah was here. Your father got the contract for the new sea wall down Porthleven. That'll be our first big contract.'

'Breage side or Sithney side?' Roseanne asked at once.

Her mother's smile broadened still further. 'Both!'

Roseanne gave a little skip of joy and, throwing her arms about her mother, forced her into an impromptu

124

jig in the lane. After a moment her mother's vexation returned. 'I should have told you it while *she* was here. They could put that in their pipes and smoke it.'

'I should think the old feller's over the moon,' Roseanne commented.

Some of her mother's spirit deserted her as she replied, 'Yes and no. In a way, he said, 'tis too big a success, too soon, see?'

'How?'

'He's going to have to go cap in hand to Lawyer Scawen and his missis and get more capital. He says no one do mind giving away half an acorn, but when 'tis grown to an oak that's when the gift would fret 'ee.'

Roseanne decided there'd never be a better time. 'Would twenty-five quid help?' she asked. 'Or thirty-seven pound, thirteen and fourpence if you count *all* my savings?'

16

In the Kitto household that evening they had to eat standing up; the table was covered with dozens of little cardboard rectangles each bearing some such curious legend as B12: 50″, S27: 47″ . . . and so on. The slightest disturbance to them, Frank told his wife and daughter, could cost them a thousand pounds.

'What are they?' Roseanne asked sceptically, not believing him for one moment.

'I should ought to have done it before I got the contract,' was the rueful reply.

Hesitantly his wife nudged a small shiny object into the centre of the table.

'What's that, woman?' he asked, though he could see well enough it was his gold collar stud, the one he wore at weddings and funerals.

On ordinary days his stud was a patent one of steel, nickel plated. He never wore the starched collar that went with it — just the collarless shirt, neatly fastened at his throat by a shiny stud, gold on grand occasions, nickel the rest of the time.

'I believe you might wear that every day now, Mr Kitto,' she replied. 'And a starched collar to go with it on Sundays.'

'I'll do no such thing,' he asserted stoutly.

''Tin't fitty, like,' she went on. 'You're a contractor now. You can't go about looking like any old stonemason.'

'Master mason,' he corrected her.

'That's still not a contractor. You should have a gold stud for everyday now, not that bit of old iron.'

'Contractor,' he muttered. 'I don't know about that. We shall have to see.'

When they had supped their fill he became more informative as to the purpose of all those bits of card. They represented, at a scale of a quarter-inch to a foot, the blocks of granite that formed the topmost course of the quays where the new sea walls were to be built. Those walls were, in fact, parapets to be added at the edge of the quays in the outer and middle harbours. To give each parapet a good bond into the existing masonry, the contractor would have to remove every other stone and rebed it on a smaller block so as to break the even line of the present top edge of the quay.

'Why not just swap them about?' Roseanne asked. 'Change a big one and a small one about and that'd break the line, surely?'

He shook his head. 'They're all different widths, see. You try it with they ones there. I haven't started on they yet.'

Three minutes of trial and error — mostly error — was enough to show her the complexities of the task. It became a game to her then. 'Can I swap stones on Breage side for stones on Sinny side?'

He chuckled and gave her a congratulatory pat on the shoulder. 'Ah now that's the question, maid. And getting the right answer to it is the difference between rich and poor to us.'

He went on to explain that most of the others who had tendered for the work would have reckoned on wasting a fair proportion of the existing stone, either in shaving it to break the line or in recutting it to fit elsewhere. 'But I was sure, see, that if I could get the

127

contract for both sides, I'd find places enough for every stone, without no shaving nor recutting nor redressing nor nothing. Just moving them round in different places. That's why I put in for both jobs, see. 'Tweren't *just* my greed.'

She pointed at the scattering of cards upon the table. 'And didn't you do this then?'

He shook his head ruefully. 'I drew it out on paper and did it with lines and arrows. And it do work, mind 'ee. There's a place for every stone and I could leave the hammer and chisel home.'

'Well then!'

Another shake of the head. ''Tis twenty-six blocks to move from Breage to Sinny and twenty-two from Sinny to Breage side. 'Tis easy enough with bits of old card, but' — he picked up one of them, measuring about an inch by an inch and a quarter — 'that's more'n twenty ton in that one alone. And there's forty-seven more like him!'

She closed her eyes and gave out a silent whistle; the difficulties were all too clear to her now. It was a good half mile in all, up the cove, along the end of it, and back down the other side — and not too level, either, but with many ups and downs where the original contours of the land had been only partly smoothed out.

'Can't you build a raft and float them over?' Mrs Kitto asked.

He nodded. 'That's one thing to think about. But the best of all would be to cut down the number of swaps from one side to t'other. That's what I'm doing now.'

He was still at it when his wife and daughter went up to bed. Roseanne was at it, too, by then — but all in her mind as she tossed and turned between her sheets. Her father had got it down to eighteen and sixteen swaps respectively. She was sure even that could be bettered.

128

When he came up to bed she waited until he was safely snoring before she tiptoed down to try it out for herself. First, of course, she noted the order in which he now had them, an order that required only thirty-one swaps all told. By five o'clock the following morning, when it was time to go out for the cows, she had it down to twenty-six; she left it for him with a note saying: 'I'm sure this can't be bettered.'

When she came in for her breakfast he was waiting for her by the gate. As they walked back up the path he slipped an arm about her shoulder and paid her the biggest compliment he knew: 'Where's the need for a son,' he said, 'when it's brains that carry the day?'

He repeated it to her mother when they went indoors, which gave her the perfect cue to tell him of Roseanne's offer of her winnings and life savings. At first he thought they were pulling his leg. The betting on Stephen against Mark at the fair had been light, to say the least, and Harry Thomas of Porkellis had certainly done nothing to broadcast his own folly in accepting one at such odds — so the tale had not gone the rounds of the local pubs and kiddleywinks. But when she brought the money from its hiding place under the floorboards in her room, he had no choice but to believe.

The difficulty came when she said she didn't want to give it to him as a straight loan but 'whatever that thing Mrs Scawen give 'ee. Equal-something or whatever she did call it.'

'Equity.' He scratched his ill-shaven chin. 'She'd never accept that. No more would he.'

'You don't know till you try,' she chided; her tone suggested that his lack of resolve was a disappointment to her.

He gave a foxy grin. 'I could frighten them into it.

I could forget how well you solved the puzzle of the stones. Pretend I still have forty, fifty swaps. Put the fear of God into him. Bankrupt on the first contract!'

Roseanne pulled a face; her mother shook her head.

He became downcast again. 'No,' he agreed. ''Twouldn't hardly do.'

'Shall I go and see him?' Roseanne offered then.

He laughed. 'You think you can talk he over?'

'I can try.'

He shrugged, conceding there could be no harm in the idea.

She took the plan of the harbour down off its shelf and unrolled it on the table.

'What now?' he asked, grinning at his wife. 'Here's the new clerk of the works.'

'I was only thinking, while I was pushing bits of card round last night, I remembered what you said about some of them being twenty tons and more. How *are* you going to move them?'

He half turned from her, not welcoming the question. 'Johnny Tayge, I suppose,' he muttered.

Johnny Tyacke, or Tayge, as most people called him, was a diddicoy and a master with the horses. He it was who had carried the great four-hundred-inch Cornish engine almost thirty miles, from East Wheal Rose to Wheal Vor, with a hundred horses spanned. And no men to lead them, no outriders, no traces, no reins, not even a whip − just the power of his command. There was only one Johnny Tayge and he didn't come cheap.

'Could you move the stone *any* distance at all without him?' she asked.

'How?' he countered.

'I was thinking − the stones that are farthest apart are this one and this one.' Her finger stabbed at the chart. 'Two that we've got to move, I mean.'

130

'If you're still thinking of a raft . . .' He shook his head and left the rest unspoken. 'You know what the sea's like once it gets inside that harbour.'

His wife broke in. 'Yes, remember that nurse and babby who got swept off the middle-harbour wall last summer — and they said the swell was hardly running two feet at the time.'

He took up the chant of gloom. 'We'd only need to tip one block in the tideway and then it'd be divers and floating cranes — and we could kiss farewell to all the profit. I don't believe we can risk ferrying stone across that particular bit of water.'

'Not ferrying,' she said tentatively. 'But you know that aerial cable they got down Wheal Fortune — to carry ore from the stamps up to the calciner?'

He nodded, but he also held up a warning finger. 'The foundations for the gantries on that do go down ten, fifteen feet,' he warned. 'We can't do that in they quays.'

'No, but I was thinking,' she repeated, 'last night — if you was to get two big iron carriages like Harveys do use down Hayle for all their big machines and that . . .'

He saw her drift at once and sat down facing her, hands on the chart between them. There was no patronizing jocularity now as he nodded at her to go on.

'If you was to get two of they carriages, one each side, and weight them down with stone, so they'd never tip. And then if you was to stretch the aerial cable between them . . .'

'Yes!' he cried in delight, leaping to her conclusion at once. 'Then 'twould just be up and across! No need to move any stone forth and back along the quay to a jetty or suchlike. Just straight up and across! And we could drop her right where she's destined. My dear

131

soul!' He turned to his wife and laughed. 'What do 'ee say to that, old woman? Never mind "clerk of the works" — I think we reared an assistant manager here!'

'Gusson!' Roseanne cried scornfully, blushing to the roots of her hair.

'Why not!' her mother chided.

'Because how would it look? That's why not. D'you want me for to be the squire's wife or a poor copy of Mrs Moore?'

Mrs Moore, the wife of that Dr Moore who had warned Sir Francis against any further whipping of little Annette, was the local example of the 'woman in a man's world'. Orphaned when young, she had been brought up as a Cinderella in the family of her aunt and uncle. Nonetheless, despite having had her first baby out of wedlock — and hearing her name preached from the pulpit for it — she had started selling her own brew of beer, going door to door in a donkey and cart, and was now the biggest brewer in the West of England. And all in little over twenty years.

'You'd never be a *poor* copy of Mrs Moore,' her father grumbled; but it was a rearguard argument. Their euphoria deserted them as they realized she was right.

'I don't want to be a copy of anyone,' Roseanne replied, 'poor or not.'

'Nor you shan't be, maid,' her father promised fervently. Then, turning to his wife, he added rather grandly, 'Well, Mrs Kitto, I believe you may now fetch me my gold stud.'

17

Part of Frank Kitto's reputation as one of the shrewdest men around was deserved; the rest he gained by pure chance. Just as he had had the good fortune to sire a clever daughter he also had a happy knack of turning up in the right place at the right time − and often just in the nick of the right time, too.

He went down to Porthleven that morning with a gang of masons and labourers whom he knew he could trust. One was Willy Benny Curnow, Maria's father, who had worked on the original sea wall; he was to be the twelve-hour man on the site, Frank's eyes and ears and his deputy during his absence. Frank's first orders − that they were to paint certain cyphers on the top face of every stone along the edge of the quay − mystified them all. One stone, for instance, was to have B4/S29, its neighbour simply B5 . . . and so on. When one man made so bold as to ask him why, he said, "Cos that what I'm a-paying of 'ee for to do, mister. That's why.'

Willy Benny looked at him slightly askance, for this was a Frank Kitto he had not seen before − and they had worked on many a job together. After Frank had gone, Willy Benny, now in charge, told the fellow his own guess as to why they were painting the stones.

'*Move* them?' the man asked incredulously. He stared across the cove, then gauged the length of it. 'Over there? He'll never do that surely? He'll go bust first.'

'You believe he do look like that sort of a fool, do 'ee?'

The man thought it over and shook his head.

'That's how he's where he is and we're where we are,' Willy Benny told him.

Frank's agenda for the morning had been set by Roseanne's overnight musing. He went straight to the mine at Wheal Fortune, which lay a couple of miles up the small river valley that runs almost due north from Porthleven. There was a good metalled road from the village as far as the main Helston–Penzance turnpike. But that was only halfway to the mine; the path from there on was no more than a muddy, rutted track lined on either side by hundreds of rude hovels of earth and stone, the temporary dwellings of those most transitory workers in the most hot-and-cold trade in the land: the Cornish tin miner. Haggard women, their cheeks and spirits alike hollowed out by years of childbearing – and child-burying, too – stared listlessly at him from doors made of sacking. Hungry infants clung to their skirts, which were like as not made of the same material. They watched him with wide yet incurious eyes; he could not even tell what gender most of them might be, for the parish nit-nurse had lately descended like the avenging angel, leaving most of them with their mops shaved to the root. Frank had intended asking if the work at the mines was good, but the answer was there before him, written in rag and bone. Many of the hovels were empty – a sight he had never seen before.

Half a mile from the turnpike the lane turned east and rose steeply up the hillside, bending again and yet again to ease the gradient. Here, too, were further signs of disaster. About ten paces up the slope the road crossed over a culvert. Farther up the valley, out of sight from here, was a sluice, whereby the stream could be diverted to run along the hillside and through this culvert before dashing down to rejoin its natural bed in the valley bottom. On its way it turned a wheel that drove the ore-crushing stamps, and it also washed the lighter rock dust from the heavier ore in the 'buddles' beside the stamps. Normally there would be half a dozen men, freelance tinners, 'vanning' the stream for waste ore from the process. Today, however, the culvert was dry and the river dashed over its stony bed with its full complement of water. There were yet more signs for those who could read them. The wind was northeasterly, straight off the calciner at the top of the hill − or 'callaciner', as miners pronounce it. There should be a strong whiff of sulphur on the air; when the wind was due east, they could even smell it in Breage, a mile and a half away. Yet here, a mere two furlongs from the usually belching chimney, the air smelled as clean as a whistle.

When he reached the hilltop he saw that the furnace was, indeed, cold that day. Gangs of miners stood around the captain's office, hands in pockets, spitting in the dust. Frank went up to one he knew, John Walsh of Trew, and asked him what was ado.

The man raked the heavens with his eyes. 'The venturers do say the price of tin is gone so low, no matter if we do tribute for *nothing*, they still couldn't accept.'

The Cornish miner is unlike any other in the land. He works, not for the mine owner − the venturer − but for himself. The venturer provides all the machinery and buildings at grass level; he sinks the shafts down through the rock and drives the horizontal levels from them into the lode. But at that point the miners take over. Self-employed men, each in competition with the other, they examine the lode, assess how rich or meagre

135

it may be, use their experience to guess whether it will fatten or peter out, and then 'tribute', or bid against each other, for the chance to work the next so-many fathoms of it. The venturers naturally accept the lowest bid and it is then up to each successful tributer to make what profit he can.

So for the venturers to announce that they could not even accept a bid to do the work for nothing was another way of saying, 'This mine is dead.'

'What of the rest?' Frank asked, waving a hand across the downs to the other mines in the district.

A chorus answered him: Pallas Consols was abandoning everything below the adit — the level at which the mine would drain naturally; Grankum and Scotts would continue forking out below the adit but would review the situation before next tribute day; Wheal Vor was having one last, desperate fling before the legal decision was announced, and then would probably close for ever. The venturers at Greatwork were meeting today — 'And I'm bound for Americay,' said the man who told him that.

Frank took aside three among them who had won the drilling championship last summer and told them he'd have a week's work for them, starting tomorrow. The change it wrought in their spirits, from dejection to gladness, showed how fine an edge they lived upon, where a week ahead was as far as they could see.

He had come to the mine intending no more than to learn who had made up the aerial cable and its associated machinery, and what sort of money they had wanted. The closure of Wheal Fortune, however, put a new complexion on it. It was time to see the grass captain himself, William Taylor.

Long before Wheal Fortune had been a mine it had been a thriving farm. The last man to plough its fields

136

had been Barny Hosking, a miller, back in the early years of the century. His fine granite farmhouse was now the mine office and it was there that Frank now made his way. As he crossed the yard he could not help admiring the stonework, not just of the house itself but also of the stables and other outbuildings — every stone cut to fit. It would make a good little farm one day, if the mine really was closed down for ever.

He was just about to knock at Cap'n Taylor's door when there was a stir among the men in the yard behind him. He turned and saw Lawyer Scawen dismounting from his horse. He was the liquidator, Frank guessed as he went to greet him.

'I didn't expect to see you here,' Scawen said.

Frank grinned. 'I do like to be of assistance where I can, see.'

Scawen laughed. 'This'll take more than you've got, or I.'

'Every little helps, as Jack Tar said when he pissed off London Bridge at low tide. If Wheal Fortune's coffers is empty, why, I could put ten guineas in them this very instant.'

The lawyer's laugh was even louder. 'You don't even wait until the iron is hot, man — you strike when the smith first puts it to the flames. What had you in mind, in particular?'

'Oh, something *very* particular, Mr Scawen.' And, with a smile that promised wondrous revelations, he led him to the edge of the crowd and pointed out the aerial cable. 'I do want to hire that for two or three weeks — say a month to be safe.'

'For ten guineas?' the other asked incredulously. 'I should think you could buy it for that — the way things are. But what good is it to you there?'

Frank explained.

Scawen gave a dry whistle. 'You *do* keep your ear to the ground, man! I myself only heard this morning how grave things are.'

'I'll have it for ten, then,' Frank said quickly, 'since you believe that's a fair price.'

The lawyer demurred; he wasn't officially appointed yet; that had merely been his untutored opinion . . . he'd need to take advice. . . blither, blither. Frank said, 'Let's go in and have a bit chat with Cap'n Taylor. If the whole bal is closing, that's the first thing they must dismantle. He'll rust where he is without he's used every day.'

Ten minutes of sparring, coupled with the offer of a further three guineas, got Frank what he wanted — plus the loan of the tools he'd need to dismantle the contraption. Indeed, it was more than he wanted, for he was now the outright owner of the whole thing, pylons and all. He went outside to gather his three champion borers and tell them he could set them on at once if they were willing to become champion dismantlers, too.

When the door had closed behind him, Cap'n Taylor chuckled. 'Well, I take my hat off to that one,' he said. 'You do have to get up early to outsmart him.'

'Who got the best of the bargain?' Scawen asked.

'Hard to say. There's no mine in Cornwall would buy it off of us, as things stand. And who else is there? Newlyn quarries, maybe. But a bird in the hand is worth *ten* in the bush to we. Besides' — he gave a conspiratorial grin — 'if you're to be liquidator, you're entitled to a . . . *perquisite* or two of your own, eh?'

'I?' Scawen was alarmed to think that his association with Kitto might be such common knowledge.

The Captain's grin broadened still further. 'Come now, Mr S, it doesn't take a board of inquiry to realize

138

that Kitto wants that cable to work on a certain cliff in a certain garden not a thousand miles from Helford.'

Scawen laughed, partly at the fact that, until now, the thought had not crossed his mind, but mainly at the realization that Frank Kitto *had* realized it and had played along with the assumption — causing Taylor to believe that the favour was really being done to Mrs Scawen.

And come to think of it, in the fullness of time, who was to say it wasn't?

18

It took a day to mark the stones and three more to bore all the holes. By then there were two huge cast-iron trailers, on hire from Harvey's of Hayle, standing on the quays, one on Breage side, the other on Sinny. There was little enough work for them elsewhere, trade being what it was, so Frank got them cheap. Sunday was an enforced break, twenty-four hours of torture to Frank but a godsend to his hard-worked crew. By the evening of that Monday, the twenty-fourth of October, they had adapted the pylons and erected them on the trailers. Then, by a neat bit of dovetailing, some of the new stones for the parapet were delivered; instead of piling them on the quayside, Frank had them stacked on the landward edges of the two trailers, as counterbalance to the weights they would soon be required to lift.

Tuesday was like a gala day in the little fishing village. Men and women − and children, too − all put up their Sunday best and lined the harbour to watch, at a safe distance, to be sure. Since 'Sunday best' was bible-black they did not make the most festive scene, but their excited chatter and the general buzz of anticipation went some way to compensate. Roseanne stayed at home, saying it would be bad luck to come and watch, but her mother went, nonetheless. Then Roseanne had second thoughts and decided to smuggle herself in along the coastal road, along Bullion Cliffs, and watch unseen from someone's front garden, halfway up the hill.

Unknown to her, Mark had had the same idea. Thinking that the Kittos would all be down beside the harbour, he huddled out of the wind been two granite gateposts belonging to a terrace house that overlooked the middle harbour, the most obvious vantage on the whole of Breage side; he huddled so successfully that Roseanne did not see him until she, too, had taken refuge there.

'Oh my gidge!' she exclaimed at once.

He simply stared at her in extreme discomfiture.

'Cat got your tongue, has it?' she asked, not wishing to lose the initiative.

'A cat may look at a king,' he told her coldly, then, no doubt thinking its connection with their present situation a little tenuous, he added, 'I don't suppose you own this place, high and mighty as you are, these days.'

But for that she would have left and sought another vantage; now the Last Trump itself would not dislodge her. 'A true gentleman would withdraw in like circumstances,' she told the gatepost at her right.

'A true lady,' he murmured to its twin at his left, 'would never put a body to such a trial.'

For a moment they watched the preparations below in silence. In vain she sought for her father though she knew he must be there, directing events, for they'd never start such work without him.

The two trailers were at their appointed stations, one each side of the middle harbour; between them, at about ten degrees to the quaysides, stretched the twin cables of the aerial lift, stretched so taut they made only the shallowest catenary curve; its broken reflection could be seen in a hundred snake-like bands on the face of the almost calm sea. On the far side, Sinny side, an ordinary tripod and tackle had been used to raise one of the blocks from its bed; the gap was immediately beneath the span of the cable. On the near side, in the corresponding position, the champion miners were inserting expanding steel bolts into the block of stone beneath that same cable. They tightened each one by inserting a bar in its eye and walking round the stone like sailors round a windlass. Everything they did had a ritual gravity that inspired the onlookers with the greatest confidence.

As soon as they had the last one tightened, the masons moved in with a mobile block and tackle, which they locked in place and shackled fast to the eyes of the bolts.

'The pulley on the aerial cable looks bigger and stronger,' Roseanne said, forgetting herself and her quarrel. 'Why don't they use that instead?' In her heart of hearts she wanted to ask him where her father was, for she still had not spied him yet.

Mark looked at her askance; it was not the sort of question he expected from a woman. 'Too much bounce, I believe,' he replied.

'I wasn't really asking you,' she snapped, angry at having spoken at all now.

'No more was I telling you, then,' he countered.

'A true gentleman never argues with a lady,' she said.

He leaned forward and spoke to an imaginary person beyond her. 'Get that, did 'ee, boy? She isn't talking to me, so it must be for you.'

He saw her purse her lips tight to avoid smiling. It was a Roseanne he knew so well — as good-humoured as you could wish and as stubborn as a she-devil. His heart was suddenly filled with all his old love for her — though he'd be damned if he'd show it. Nonetheless, he renewed his resolve to get her back, come all Hell against him.

Roseanne, for her part, felt her innards buckle at the

unexpected assault of his old, easy humour; she only just managed to stop herself from smiling — for, of course, she'd rather die than respond as he no doubt hoped she would.

Down on the quayside they hauled on the pulley, just enough to put the stone under strain. Then half a dozen of them set about it with crowbars, easing it from the grip of the three land-facing sides.

'There's two men in a cradle below, with wedges,' Mark said. 'Your father and Willy Benny Curnow.'

She almost blurted out her surprise, and her fear — for surely that was a most dangerous place to be. But all she said was a rather lame, 'Really?'

'They don't want the stone to split, see. All that drilling will leave it weaker.'

'Oh ah?'

There was a cheer from below. The block of stone had obviously shifted, though nothing of it was apparent from that distance. Her father clambered up on the quay and joined his masons as they hauled away on the pulley-chain. Within a couple of minutes they had it poised above ground level, whereupon they slipped the pawl while her father pushed half a dozen thick oak planks to span the gap it had left beneath it. When he had them aligned to his satisfaction he gave the signal and they lowered the stone gently to rest upon them.

'It's amazing,' Mark said.

'Mmm,' she felt constrained to reply.

'No, not that.' He nodded toward the scene below. 'I was thinking 'tis amazing how some people take one ride in a gig and fancy theirselves gentry for ever after.'

She was too angry to make any reply to this sneer — and at the way he had trapped her into responding just before it.

'Mind you,' he went on affably, as if they were discussing the strange customs of a remote people, 'some of they who do call theirselves gentry aren't much better.'

She stood rigid, staring at the scene below, willing herself not to listen to a word.

He laughed. *'Oh, how we fine apples swim, quoth the horsedung!'*

The mobile hoist had been trundled aside by now and they were tightening and checking the large chains from the pulley on the aerial cable.

'Squire!' he sneered. 'There never was such a thing as a squire in Cornwall . . .'

'It's amazing,' she told him, 'how some people can go to one lantern-slide lecture from Hamill Oliver down the polytechnic, and then fancy theirselves the world's authority for ever on all things Cornish!'

'Well, Hamill Oliver do say there never was such a thing as a squire in Cornwall − not with the power to appoint clergy and call theirselves lord of the manor and such like. That's a proper squire, now, and they never had such powers down here. So anyone calling hisself squire is horsedung trading as apples.'

'Amazing,' she repeated.

A gasp went up from the crowd; it was both magnified and confined by the natural amphitheatre of the cove.

'It's on its way,' he exclaimed.

The gasp turned to a cheer and for the next few minutes their grizzling was forgotten as they watched the stone being released gently down the curve and then hauled just as gently up again on the far side. The main concern was the alarming way it bounced up and down any time it moved too fast or was braked too suddenly; once or twice it seemed only a miracle prevented it from

144

bouncing right off the trolley wheels and plummeting to the waters below. On the upward haul it proved a great deal more stable; Roseanne suddenly noticed how sweaty her palms had become. She drew off her gloves to dry her hands and then watched with bated breath while they lowered it into the prepared space on the far side, from which the block of stone had already been removed. Meanwhile, Frank and the miners had rowed across the middle harbour, leaving Willy Benny and the masons to start raising the second stone on Breage side. So Frank was there to direct the lowering of the first stone into its new home.

They had picked the smallest one to begin with, being unsure what weight the two trailers would accommodate, so it sank into its bed and left a gap of about six inches between its top and the quay, even in its new bed of best roman cement. The moment it was settled properly, Frank gave a sign and they slackened off the chain altogether.

Until that moment Roseanne did not realize how long she had been holding her breath. Now she let it out in a rush and gasped for a refill, and again, and yet again. Then, forgetting herself entirely, she turned and grasped Mark by the hands and whirled him round like a dervish. 'They did it!' she cried gaily. 'We did it! It works! My idea works!'

On the far side of the cove, snug in Bert Kitchen's net-making loft, Stephen Morvah lowered his binoculars and turned toward the dark; ever since he had spotted Mark Bodilly hiding between the gateposts on Breage side — to be joined five minutes later by Roseanne — he had watched nothing else.

19

Mark came for his store cattle on the Saturday evening of that same week — not knowing that Roseanne had moved them to a new field some days earlier. He passed her gate twice in his search for them and she, hiding behind her curtains, noted how stubbornly he kept his head averted — and yet how often his gaze let him down by wandering in her direction. After he had passed she threw on her coat and went out to tease him further.

'I was wondering if we'd ever see you again,' she called out when she was still a good way off. 'They're in Mrs Kennedy's field. You remember where that is, do 'ee?'

She meant to imply that if he had forgotten his livestock for so long, he might easily have forgotten the geography of Breage as well but when he turned and leered at her, she recalled that the field in question had other associations for them, too. She was annoyed with herself for forgetting it.

'I never thought to see you on foot again, maid,' he jibed, slowing his pace to let her catch up.

'Ha ha. You won't kill me laughing.'

When she drew level, there was a moment of awkward silence. He made matters worse by trying to fill it with the reminder that he had, after all, paid for the grazing. She just stared at him coldly. Then her mood softened and she said, 'I should think we could at least talk civil to each other, Mark.'

He cleared his throat and said warily, 'I don't see why not, I suppose.' After a further silence he added, 'If you're willing, like.'

'Well then,' she said.

They arrived at the gate. More like farmers than lovers, or former lovers, they leaned upon it and stared out into the field, each turned slightly away from the other. In silence they tallied the cattle. 'The yarling with the white blaze is ours,' she told him quickly in case he'd forgotten what he actually owned.

'Well!' he exclaimed sarcastically. Then he added, 'I never saw you driving round in a gig lately.'

'You shan't bait me,' she promised him. 'That red poll yarling of yours is lame in her left hind quarter.'

'I saw that. Willy Benny's dog — that's what done that.'

'I haven't seen hide nor hair of him for two weeks, if you must know,' she muttered.

'The dog?'

'No! Stephen Morvah. I shan't say a word if you're just going to talk daft.'

'Well, we was talking about the dog. How haven't you seen the gallant squire, then? Got tired of 'ee, has he? Like he did with Gertie Harvey and Millie Beckerleg and . . .'

'Price of hay was down in Helston last Thursday,' she said pointedly. After a pause she added, 'Anyway, 'tin't like with Gertie Harvey and they others at all. His father says he's not to see me. That's where 'tis to.'

'You believe I want to talk about it, do 'ee?' he asked bitterly. 'You think that's all I got time to worry about?'

She eyed him coolly and replied, 'Yes.'

He turned angrily back toward the field.

'And 'tis so daw-brained,' she went on. 'There's no reason we can't be civil with each other.'

'You think he'll marry 'ee, I suppose,' he scoffed.

She closed her eyes and sighed. 'I don't know. And if he was to stand there where you are and ask me now, I don't know what answer I'd give. So there, now! I'm all of a dalver and I couldn't say, one way or another.'

'And if *I* was to ask 'ee now?' he put in quickly.

'I told 'ee — I'm all of a dalver. I don't know.'

'You knew well enough before ever *he* come along. You never had no doubt before that.'

'I never thought I had no *choice* before that, Mark.' Her tone was conciliatory. 'I grew up thinking 'twas only you and me.'

''Tis your mother and father, really,' he said, even more bitterly. 'They believe I shall always be what I am now — which was good enough for them before the *squire* come along. Do they think he'll always be squire? A blind man could see where the Morvahs are going.'

His words awakened strange echoes within her, fleeting thoughts she had suppressed — or not so much suppressed as allowed to flash by; yes, that was it, she had deliberately not followed them up. Now she was aware of them again, mustering at the rim of her mind. She realized that she, too, did not honestly expect Stephen to occupy the position in society that his father presently held. She could not imagine Stephen as a justice of the peace, or deputy sheriff, or even as chairman of the local board of guardians. However, unlike Mark — to judge by his ridicule — she did not feel that such differences represented a come-down in the world.

Another thought flashed by, giving her no time to pursue it to its conclusion. But it left a small impression, nonetheless: her parents were in love with the trappings

148

of the man, while to her they were the one serious impediment.

Mark had meanwhile dramatized his words by picking up a stone, holding it out, and letting it fall. 'That's your Master Morvah,' he said. Somehow it left his argument weaker. Annoyed, he lifted the latch and opened wide the gate.

She, returning from her thoughts, jokingly leaned with it and fell to the ground. He stared down at her and laughed against his will. 'Squire's wife!' he exclaimed. 'I don't know!'

She reached out a hand, which he grasped to haul her upright. The reminder of his strength delighted her. She wanted him to take her in his arms and kiss her once again, as they had kissed so often in the past. He sensed it and curled one arm behind her. But she slipped away, and, thinking to make him chase her, ran toward the cattle, pretending that was her only purpose.

The charade was too well done. He would not risk his dignity on its being a mere tease. 'You going help me drive they up the road, are 'ee?' he asked.

'If you mind,' she replied, turning sharply to cut her own yearling out of the bunch. The rest, being unused to droving, milled awkwardly toward the gate, making short runs, standing and digging in their hooves, looking wild-eyed to right and left.

Mark returned to the lane and went a few yards up it, ready to head them toward the road. For the moment he had nothing to do but stand there, admiring her skill with the nervy little herd. She seemed to know exactly what was going through their primitive brains. Whenever one turned aside in a move that could end in a dash for the open spaces behind her, she already had an arm outstretched to deter it, and in case the arm-waving failed, her body was already poised on the right foot for a leap. And her cry of 'Ho-oe!' and 'Giddaan!' was better than any whiplash.

It almost broke his heart to watch her. What a bloody waste she'd be as a squire's wife — a woman who understood animals like that and who could manage a dairy, too!

His chagrin deepened as they put the cattle before them up the lane. They worked so brilliantly together, she bringing them on, lashing them with her voice when they hesitated, turning instantly calm when they behaved well — and he leaping the hedge and dashing up to head them the right way at the turnpike.

That would be the trickiest moment. They had to come out on to the main road, turn right, then almost immediately left up the side road into the village. It would be hard enough for four drovers to manage with an excitable young herd like this.

'Where are you putting them?' she called out.

'Up Widow . . . in that little field behind Widow Delamere's,' he replied. 'I asked she and she says we can put they through her garden.'

Why didn't he just say, 'Widow Delamere's field'? she wondered. Did she imagine she didn't know the field belonged to the woman?

When they reached the main road he was standing on the Penzance side, to head them off. She gathered her skirts and struggled through a gap in the hedge, raced across the corner of the field, and out by the gate on to the road on the Helston side of the lane into the village — neatly boxing them in.

One yearling — there's always one — tried to turn back the way they had just come. Mark made a heroic bound to the corner of the lane and headed it off. Meanwhile, Roseanne had hidden herself in the gateway, giving them sight of an apparently open road.

150

They took it. She did not emerge again until they were almost at the turn into the village.

From then on it was plain sailing all the way. The most nerve-racking part of it, the short stretch through Mrs Delamere's garden, proved the easiest of all, for the woman herself, mindful of her shrubs and borders, was out there with two carpet beaters and a voice to rival Roseanne's. That, together with the fact that from the main gate they could see the way into the field, sent them arrow-straight for the grass.

'Well!' Mark exclaimed in satisfaction as he tied the gate with twine. 'They were easy-driven from Sethnoe, but a few weeks in the fields and they're like wild beasts.'

By custom so long ingrained they no longer even thought of it, he and Roseanne leaned against the gate once more and watched the cattle settle to their new pasture. The church clock struck four.

May Delamere squeezed herself between them. 'They're like humans,' she said. 'We'd all become wild beasts if we were left out in the fields night and day.'

It was such a wayward sentiment — and so doubly odd, coming from a lady as delicate and refined as Mrs D — that neither knew how to respond. Then Roseanne said, 'The whole of mankind must have lived out in the wild, once upon a time.'

She didn't really mean it as an argument against the other woman's apparent claim that human society inevitably deteriorates, but that is how Mrs Delamere took it. 'Once upon a time,' she echoed. 'Yes, to be sure.' She smiled sweetly at Mark, encouraging him to share her amusement at this untutored girl who lived by fairy tales.

This investment of emotion in what should have been the most casual social encounter took Roseanne aback.

151

She was suddenly aware — and acutely aware, too — that Mark Bodilly was something more than a chance grazing tenant in the eyes of the old widow. Or not-so-old, really, when you looked at her! That flush in her cheeks, that light in her eyes . . . no doubt of it. So the question was, how did Mark see *her*?

Roseanne had to lean forward to glimpse him, past the woman's glowing cheek and over her rather-too-unconsciously expanded bosom — which proved a trap for *his* glance, too, when, becoming aware of Roseanne's movement, he turned to look at her. At last their eyes met and he saw the resentment that burned in hers, perceived Mrs Delamere's happy smile — and understood that here was a situation it would be a shame to waste.

'Near milking time,' he told Roseanne, as if it might have slipped her mind.

For a split second she was equally divided between two quite contrary responses; then some little imp whispered a suggestion in her ear. She turned brightly to Mark and said, 'You're quite right, Mr Bodilly, there's no rest for the wicked, as they say.' Then, turning to the widow, 'But I can't leave without complimenting you, Mrs Delamere, on this beautiful garden. The hedge is so stout I've never seen it from the road, but it really is a picture.'

'Oh . . . why thank you Miss Kitto,' a flustered Mrs Delamere replied. 'It is a labour of love, er, as they say.' Roseanne's genteel sentiments, and the unexpectedly genteel tones in which she had delivered them made it almost de rigueur for her to add, 'May I accompany you back to the gate?' as if she were on a social call. A moment later she could have bitten her tongue out, but that was one moment too late.

Roseanne was quick to build on the advantage. As

one landowner to another she lowered her voice and said confidentially, but still loud enough for Mark to hear, 'I hope he's giving you a fair rent, Mrs Delamere? You know he has a terrible reputation? Er, with money I mean. Most of it well deserved.' She tilted her head toward Mark and smiled — the same cloying smile she had seen Mrs D give him.

He rolled his eyes heavenward and retired from this particular fray, feeling it too complex, and at the same time too petty, for him.

'Why, Miss Kitto!' the widow replied. 'I hardly think that is any of . . .' But some quality in the younger woman, coupled with the unknown nature of her relationship with Bodilly, prevented Mrs Delamere from completing the reprimand.

In any case, Roseanne spotted the broken slates and, in a flash of inspiration, cut in with, 'Or at least make him *work* for it. He's quite the handyman, you know. Mark, my lover, there's a roof up there could do with a patch or two.'

She had trespassed much too far, of course, but quite intentionally. She had also timed it precisely for they were now at the entrance gate once more. Mrs Delamere gathered herself portentously. 'Miss Kitto,' she said coldly, 'such remarks are not well received here, and I wish you to know that, in future you will not be well received here, either. In fact you will not be received at all.'

'Well, I shall have to try and live with that as best I may, Mrs Delamere.' Roseanne smiled and left her standing there open mouthed. She did not even look at Mark, but, rather than sweep past him, which would be too plain a snub, she decided to turn her back on them both and go home by the slightly longer lane past the church and post office.

When she reached the end of the escallonia hedge she risked a backward glance; they had, of course, withdrawn into the garden, and perhaps — who could say? — into the house as well. When she turned toward the church again she was surprised, but not greatly, and not for long, to see Annette Morvah emerging from the gap between the end of the hedge and the beginning of the new graveyard wall.

'That was neatly done, Roseanne,' she said admiringly, taking her by the arm and falling in step with her. 'May we go a little way together?'

'Would it make any difference if I said no?'

'*Do* you say no?'

Roseanne shrugged. 'I suppose not.' She had a fleeting intimation that this, in human terms, was how a yearling felt being driven by a creature with a superior mind, one that could outguess your every move and always be there, one jump ahead of you. 'What was well done, anyway?'

'I've had my eye on them you know.' Annette jerked her head back toward Vinery House. 'After our last conversation I realized how little I knew about your Mr Bodilly, so I . . .'

'He's not *my* Mr Bodilly — as I've just made crystal-clear to him, I trust.'

'*The* Mr Bodilly, then. Young Mr Bodilly. Clever Mr Bodilly. *Sly* Mr Bodilly.' She paused and waited for Roseanne to respond to the last.

When Roseanne forced herself *not* to oblige, the girl continued, unabashed: 'I happened to be passing through Breage a couple of times this week and, just by chance I noticed Mr B going in by the gate of Vinery House. Well, in fact, the second time he was coming out, but the point is, I noticed him.'

'Really?' Roseanne spoke in a slightly childish tone,

a little breathless, hoping to indicate how juvenile she found this turn of conversation.

Annette outwitted her again. 'Reelly and trooly!' she replied, parodying an even younger child, implying that she assumed Roseanne was disguising her avid curiosity with the help of a jest. 'So what I did was I went to the Reverend Martin and told him I wished to make some sketches from the top of the church tower — which, after some toing and froing with my father, he consented to let me. And d'you know what?' She turned and pointed at the tower, which they had strolled past half a minute ago. 'You can see directly down into old Ma Delamere's garden from there. Everything. Every little nook and bower. And d'you know what else? *He* pays her a visit every day!'

'Mark Bodilly?' Roseanne blurted out in her surprise. Then, recovering herself a little, she added, 'Of course, for free grazing he'd walk to London and back.'

'Free?' Annette echoed in a sonorous tone that reminded Roseanne of Sir Francis, her father. 'I don't think it's free.'

Several questions occurred to Roseanne but she was too aware of her own dignity to ask them.

'She is a lonely woman you know,' Annette continued solemnly.

Roseanne swallowed hard; the girl appeared to be hinting at things of which a maid of such tender years should know little or nothing. 'Speak plain,' she snapped.

'I've overheard their conversation, you know. You'd be amazed at the way sound travels upward on a still day. When people walk past you can hear every little scrunch of gravel. You can certainly hear every word they say.'

It might be true, Roseanne thought, but it seemed

more likely to her that the girl had eavesdropped from a much closer vantage. In any case, she was eager to share the fruit of it, notwithstanding her suspicion that Annette was guiding her through each fleeting emotion. 'And what do they talk of?' she asked casually.

Annette giggled and squeezed her arm. 'You know you're dying to hear.'

'I know I might die and never hear it if you don't get on!'

Annette drew a deep breath and said, 'They talk about you!'

'Gusson!' Roseanne was scornful and pleased all in one. 'Me? What do they find to say about me?'

'He says he can't understand you, and she says, "I know, I know." And then he says how much he loves you, and she says, "There there!" And he says why should my brother come crashing in and steal you away? And she says, "I know I know. There there. Poor man!" And so it goes on.'

'You're making it all up,' Roseanne cried out angrily. 'I don't believe a word of it.' But she did, of course, and her anger was really at Mark for letting Mrs D lead him by the snout so brazenly.

Annette, knowing as much, took no offence at the accusation. 'And *he* can't see where it'll all end up!' she added.

'Where?' Roseanne asked scornfully.

Annette squeezed her arm. 'Don't make me say it, Roseanne, dear — but don't imagine I couldn't if put to it. We're not all sugar and spice and all things nice, are we — and certainly not May Delamere!'

Roseanne gave an involuntary shiver. It was as if she and the girl had momentarily joined their entire nervous systems rather than merely linked arms, for she had the most powerful awareness of that daemon which rode poor Annette's back and drove her every minute of her waking day — a daemon of desires, jealousies, and overpowering ambitions.

It took one to recognize one, she thought glumly — meaning not herself and the girl but the girl and Mrs Delamere. For though she, Roseanne, had gained some fleeting intimation of what drove the widow, Annette had divined it at once and in all its malignant strength: a similar daemon of overwhelming force.

Poor man, indeed! she thought, seeing how powerless Mark would be against it. *And poor me, too!* she added, realizing that Annette stood in a precisely similar relationship to her — though her particular needs were, of course, quite different.

20

By the second week of the Porthleven contract you'd
think that forty-ton blocks of stone had been whizzing
forth and back over the middle harbour as long as living
memory ran; the crowds that had cheered and marvelled
at the miraculous passage of the first — and smallest
— stone had long since melted away. The even more
amazing sight of the last, and largest, was watched by
no more than half a dozen urchins and their dogs. As
a reward for their loyalty Frank put them all in a big
bucket, the one normally used for carrying sand and
concrete, and gave them an aerial ride from Breage to
Sinny side and back.

He noticed that two of the brightest lads were taking
a keen interest in the shackles that immobilized the
apparatus overnight, so he told Willy Benny to slacken
off the main cable and dismantle the whole thing. The
trailers would be returned to Hayle in the morning, and
as for the cable and pylons, he had already sold it to
Joel Knight, the manager of Dodman Quarries, for
thirty pounds.

'How can you?' Roseanne asked when she heard of
the sale. Her father, thinking she was scandalized at the
size of his profit, said it was Knight's business what he
paid for it.

'I don't mean that,' she said. 'I mean how can you
just let it go? It saved us a fortune on the Porthleven

job. How can you be so sure we won't need it in future?'

He replied that fifteen pounds clear, in the hand, was fifteen pounds; if they ever needed such a thing again, he'd get it made up — and better, for he'd already devised one or two improvements. Her desire to hold on to it was, he said, sentimental — a charge she could not absolutely deny.

That there was not an ounce of sentiment in him he proved the following day. When he visited the site he found Willy Benny down in a sump they were digging for drainage. Two labourers were standing by, watching him.

'How are you down there and these two gurt lumps of lard leaning on their shovels beside of 'ee?' he asked sharply.

'I'm showing they how I want it done,' the man replied brightly.

'Well, if you're so good at it, you may just so well stop down there,' Frank snapped angrily. 'I'll make someone else my twelve-hour man.'

He did not, however, carry out the threat, though he did force the poor man to work out the rest of the day as a pick-and-shovel labourer. The following morning he greeted him with, 'How are 'ee feeling today, boy? Strong in the arm? Or strong in the head?'

Willy Benny grinned ruefully and supposed he felt stronger in the head.

'That's good,' Frank replied, avoiding a smile. 'I looked all day for a better twelve-hour man than you and never found him.'

He turned on his heel and walked away. Willy Benny followed him with his eyes and, shaking his head ruefully, murmured, 'Well, I'll go to hell!'

'How?' asked one of the labourers he had displaced yesterday.

Another shake of the head. 'I've worked alongside that old boy . . . why, twenty years or more. And never thought him no different from no one else.' Then, turning to the man in an altogether more businesslike tone, he added, 'Now! You see what I dug yesterday? That's in five hours. You've got ten today, and there's 'two of 'ee. So if you haven't opened up four times so much, I shall be looking for two better men this time tomorrow.'

The labourer thanked his stars he hadn't crowed at Willy Benny's demotion yesterday. He now had the strongest suspicion that the whole thing had been rigged between the two master masons.

One of the reasons Frank had been so hard on Willy Benny was that he himself understood so well how strong was the urge in any skilled man to do the job himself rather than stand by and see others bungle it — or even do it slightly less well. How he longed to take hammer and chisel from any of the other masons there and say, 'No, like this!' But he knew he'd still be at it an hour later if he started that sort of caper.

Not that he elevated it into a matter of principle; he was always the most pragmatic of men. Once or twice a week, having resisted the temptation until a mere hour or so of daylight remained, he would unfasten his bag, take out his tools, and work away with all his old gusto and skill — to the despair of the other masons, who considered nine hours of fatigue was already enough to contend with. It set a pattern he was to follow on many later contracts; at least no one would ever be able to say he asked of others what he could not himself perform.

His other, slightly surprising action at that time was to take the three miners, the champion borers of rock, and set them to work on Mrs Scawen's cliff garden overlooking the Helford river. They hadn't been there a day before the top man of the three, Wilfrid Meagor, devised an ingenious rope-and-pulley system whereby a large wheelbarrow was exactly balanced by an iron tub with a sliding bottom. When both were properly filled, a man could wheel the barrow up the steepest slope more easily than on level ground. The end of the run was on a ramp beside which an empty cart was left to stand. When the wheelbarrow was tipped into it, a quick tug on a rope released the sliding bottom of the tub and let its spoil go tumbling down the scree to the river's edge. The empty tub exactly balanced the empty barrow, so the return journey was almost effortless, too. By the end of the day the cart would be full. Then they could harness up the horse, tip the stone where it was needed elsewhere in the garden, and ride home to Carleen.

Frank Kitto marked Wilfrid Meagor down as a man to watch.

There were many throughout West Penwith who felt the same toward Frank himself. Scores of small contractors — carpenters, plumbers, masons, and the like — became employers of anything up to half a dozen men while themselves remaining carpenters, plumbers, masons, and the like. On the site they were indistinguishable. Their workers would look around surreptitiously, muttering to one another, 'Where's the old bugger to now, then?'

But from the very first day Frank Kitto was different. There he stood in his good suit, gold collar stud gleaming, gold watch and chain across his 'corporation' — and no one was ever in the slightest doubt where the old bugger was to.

People who knew he was doing such a sensational job in Porthleven harbour would be slightly surprised to see him in Market Jew Street, Penzance, or striding down Wendron Street in Helston. Quite unconsciously they began to understand that 'Old Man Kitto' was bigger than any particular job he might have on hand; that sort of thing could safely be left to deputies. For Frank's part the gambit was entirely conscious. Years ago his father, having taught him his trade, had gazed with pride at his son's master piece and then had said, with a rueful edge to his voice, 'You've the same failing as your old father, boy: we've a talent will keep us down to the end of our days.'

Frank had never forgotten that fateful utterance. In his mind's eye he could see the first job his father ever carried out, a stone-mullioned window for Carclew Manor, near Perranarworthal. And every time he went to Truro he would visit the new cathedral there and gaze at the last job his father completed, just before the scaffolding gave way and sent him plummeting to his death. It was, by chance, a stone-mullioned window in the chancel, in the purest Normandy Gothic style. Frank never saw it without remembering his father's rueful comment. The two windows, one in his mind's eye, the other before him, neatly bracketed the words, just as they bracketed the old fellow's working life — like two voussoirs that gave it a single point.

If Frank's determination to rise above the level conferred upon him by his trade had any single origin, that was it. So when he strode out down Wendron Street or called cheerily across Market Jew to a friend, he was deliberately and consciously advertising to the world that Frank Kitto, master mason, was no longer detained at that station in life to which Providence had seen fit to call him. He was available for higher things.

Such shrewd advertisement was swiftly repaid.

162

21

Annette stood in the Kitto's doorway, smiling broadly, eager for once to do her charitable round. Her eyes took in Roseanne's dress, which was as plain as the most puritan soul could wish. Just for a moment the smile faded. Then, by deliberate effort, she reasserted it and said, 'Come on, cow's tail!'

The phrase had been Roseanne's in her days as assistant at the school. 'Go and stand in the corner, young miss!' she said severely as she stepped outside, closing the door behind her.

That momentary fading of the girl's smile was not lost on her; but Annette, thinking it had passed unnoticed, said, 'You make me feel rather gaudy.'

'Swap you like,' Roseanne offered.

Annette squared shoulders with her and gave a rueful grin at their difference in height. 'It'll be a few years yet,' she said.

'Yes, I suppose it will.' Roseanne opened the gate and relieved her of one of the baskets as she passed. 'Stephen's not ill, is he?' she asked.

'Why d'you ask?' The smile was arch. 'Hasn't he come a-calling, then?'

'You know full well,' Roseanne told her. 'Does he take your father's commands as much to heart as all that?'

Annette did not reply.

'Well?'

The girl shifted her basket to the other arm and sighed. 'I don't know how much I'm supposed to say.'

Roseanne, who had already decided that the only way to withstand the other's rather persuasive personality was to mount a jocular attack against her, said quietly, 'You'll tell me just so much as it suits you to tell — and you very well know it.'

Annette darted a wounded glance at her. 'Is that what you think of me?'

Roseanne laughed and looked away.

'I shan't tell you a thing, then,' she said huffily. 'Anyway, here's Mrs Roseveare's. D'you know her? She won't know you, of course — she doesn't know anyone any more.'

'We do pass the time of day if we do meet in the village. Last time she thought I was Jane Eyre — asked me did I want to come in and wash my feet after my long walk.'

Annette gave the brass knocker a peremptory rap. 'It was the same with us. She thought my mother was Mrs Anstruther, who must be dead these forty years.'

'Oh thank you, thank you,' Mrs Roseveare began saying even before she opened the door. 'So kind!' She peered at them through the cataracts that clouded her eyes. 'Don't tell me now. I never forget a face. Miss Anstruther, isn't it. Yes. So kind. How is your mother today? I was so sorry to hear she was ailing.' The bleary focus shifted to Roseanne. 'And . . . why, bless me! Miss Vyvyan, isn't it! Well-well-well!'

To the astonishment of her two visitors she blushed scarlet and patted her bosom as if to still a racing heart. 'Of course, I would *never* cast the first stone,' she added, staring nervously up and down the deserted village street. 'Do come in.' Her tone made it clear that this was an enormous social concession.

Intrigued, Roseanne did as she was bid. At the back of her mind was a vague memory that Mrs Scawen's mother had been a Miss Vyvyan before her marriage to . . . the name escaped her though she could see the man himself clearly enough — tall, cadaverous, solemn of mien. Bought Montpelier and died within the year. About ten years ago, when she herself was still a child. It would come back to her.

The cottage was chill and damp. A meagre fire struggled to survive in a grate choked with ashes. While Annette doled out a few slices of cold tongue and a jar of damson jam, Roseanne stooped and began to rake out the grate.

'Oh, please don't do that, my dear!' Mrs Roseveare called out anxiously, between her cooing at 'Miss Anstruther's' largesse. 'I can make it last all day, you know.'

'But Mrs Roseveare,' Annette chided, 'you have tons of coal out the back. You know you have. Your brother brought it last time he came down.' She nodded at Roseanne. 'Go on, give her a good blaze.'

'Poor Arthur,' Mrs Roseveare sighed.

'Not Arthur,' Annette reminded her. 'Arthur died last year. It was Harry who brought it. He'll be very angry with you if he finds you haven't been burning his coal. And you'll only take a chill, and your rheumatics will get worse.'

Roseanne found a sheet of wrapping paper, which she stretched over the mouth of the fireplace to draw up the smouldering ashes to a cheery blaze.

'Don't set the chimney on fire,' the old woman warned.

It amazed Roseanne that such practical wisdom could

165

exist in a mind clouded by such utter nonsense. Then she wondered if there were any real difference between the two. In point of fact, they were all memories. When she said not to set the chimney on fire, she was repeating a memory, something a grown-up had once told her, or perhaps even a memory of an actual chimney blaze. And when she peered out through her almost ruined eyes and saw a young woman of a certain height with russet hair, her memory said, 'Miss Vyvyan'. It wasn't so very different, after all.

She stood back and peeled away the paper. Bright, dancing flames cheered the room at once. 'There now, isn't that better?' Annette exclaimed as if she were the true author of the improvement.

Mrs Roseveare gestured for them to sit; she kept catching Roseanne's eye and smiling at her with an awkward kind of bonhomie.

'Did you get your money this week?' Annette asked.

'Yes,' the woman said genially. 'At least, I think I did.'

'May I see your purse?' It was not a question but a command.

'Certainly not!' Mrs Roseveare exclaimed.

Annette rose, crossed the room, and took up the purse for herself. 'You didn't,' she said mildly. 'Never mind. I'll write to him again. You have enough here to be going on with.' She wagged a finger at the woman. 'Which is very naughty! You know you have to spend it. You have to eat. That's why he sends it to you.' She winked at Roseanne. 'I'll just go out and have a peep in the larder.'

Mrs Roseveare had obviously decided that her best strategy was to ignore the obstreperous young woman who had chosen to gatecrash her life. The moment Annette had gone she smoothed her dress, smiled at

Roseanne, and said, 'It is a very brave thing you have done, my dear. I shouldn't like to be in your shoes, I know that much.'

Roseanne shrugged awkwardly. 'One does what one has to, you know.'

'I'm sure. Mind you — people in general are much more understanding about such matters than when I was a gel. Look at Mrs Moore! Such a *good* woman — you can't deny it. Despite the Dreadful Thing she did, she is a good woman.'

It was impossible to know what decade the old lady's mind was rambling through. Mrs Moore and Miss Vyvyan would be much the same age, Roseanne reflected; yet here she was, talking about the one in the past and the other in the present — to the extent that she actually confused her with Roseanne. Still, it was fascinating to discover that Mrs Scawen's mother might have done something scandalous, comparable to Mrs Moore's having a baby out of wedlock and being denounced from the pulpit in Breage church. Could it have been the same Dreadful Thing? She pondered ways to induce the old woman into letting slip some further nugget of scandal.

'How is Vienna?' Mrs Roseveare asked suddenly.

'Oh.' Roseanne was taken aback. 'Gay, you know.'

'Mr Roseveare and I spent our honeymoon there.'

'I expect it was even more beautiful in those days.'

'Yes, so I was.' She patted her hair modestly. 'Henry had to keep his eye on all those officers, I can tell you. I'm sure they plague the life out of you — a woman on her own . . .?' Her voice trailed uncertainly up toward the interrogatory.

'They're no match for the sons of the Cornish gentry, Mrs Roseveare. Now *they* are baptism by fire, if you will!'

The old woman glanced nervously toward the open door and then leaned forward to say in a conspiratorial tone, 'Not to mention Kinghorn Jago, eh! A baptism of fire and brimstone, wouldn't you say?' She cackled merrily and then, appearing to recollect herself, put her knuckles to her lips and exclaimed, 'Oh my dear, do forgive me! I don't know what possessed me to say such a thing. What must you think of me?'

Roseanne leaned forward and patted her arm. 'Please,' she begged. 'Don't take on so. I'm not in the least offended. Truly.'

She became aware that Annette was, as usual, eavesdropping just beyond the door. For a moment she was angry − until she realized that she, by pretending to be Miss Vyvyan, was, in effect, doing precisely the same thing: eavesdropping on history, or on the old woman's time-warped memories of it, anyway.

Annette came breezing in then, as if she had walked in one unbroken sweep from the kitchen. 'If you don't eat the last of that game pie today, you'll have to throw it away,' she said sharply. 'D'you promise me, now?'

Mrs Roseveare nodded primly and gathered her shaky dignity about her.

Annette sat down, saying conversationally, 'Miss Vyvyan has decided to face her critics and come home.'

The old woman stared at her in bewilderment. 'Miss Vyvyan?' she murmured. 'Didn't she marry old Pellew in Falmouth? Yes. They had several children who died tragically and two daughters who made the most lamentable marriages in Scotland. Or was it Ireland? My memory's going, you know.' She smiled at them wanly. 'More tea?'

Annette rose. 'No, thank you, dear Mrs Roseveare. We really must be going.'

Roseanne put more coal on the fire before they left.

When they reached the daylight again the woman jabbed a finger at her and exclaimed triumphantly, 'Miss Kitto! I never forget a face.'

'I sometimes wonder if it isn't all deliberate,' Annette said as they walked away. Her tone implied she wouldn't in the least mind if it were. 'It would be her way of alleviating the boredom. She's young enough still to be visiting the poor and needy herself. It allows her to escape all that, you see.'

Roseanne said, 'She's not really poor and needy at all. Only she's so daw-brained, she might just so well be.'

'I wonder who Miss Vyvyan was. Vienna, eh? Bolted to Vienna.'

Roseanne laughed. 'I knew you were listening.'

'Why not? I've heard of Kinghorn Jago, of course.'

'I've heard him in person,' Roseanne boasted. 'He do sing bass in the Falmouth Operatic Society.'

Annette darted her an accusing look.

'What?' Roseanne asked.

'You didn't talk all common like that when you were with her.' She jerked her head back toward the widow's cottage. 'You can talk properly when you want to.'

'When I'm not me, you mean. I was pretending to be Miss Vyvyan.'

'Me!' Annette responded scornfully. 'What's *me*? Me is what me makes me.' She paused at the gate to old man Austin's cottage and murmured, 'Now, if you really want to see "poor and needy", here you are!'

At first the old fellow would not let them in, but Annette was merciless with him. 'I know why,' she shouted through the crack of the door. 'It's because you haven't mended that window yet, isn't it? But it's so silly not to let us in because I can see it even better from the outside. What did you do with the money my mother

169

gave you? Spent it all on drink, I suppose.' She winked at Roseanne and whispered, 'He loves to be scolded by women.'

Austin opened the door then and Roseanne noticed that there was, indeed, a sort of aura of pleasure about him, though he spoke plaintively enough. 'I got no will, Miss Morvah. That's where he's to. No will, see. I heard tell as John Tregembo were up the Queen's Arms so I went up there to give he the money you give I for to fix that glass. But he weren't there after all.'

'Nor ever was,' Annette accused him. 'Well, now you can jolly well stew in your own juice. If you wake up dead one morning, frozen between your sheets, you'll know who to blame.'

They left him some tongue and another pot of damson jam and went on their way.

'Will you really?' Roseanne asked. 'Leave him to stew in his own juice.'

'Of course not. He just wants to be talked to like that. My mother says his wife never stopped, morning till night. No, this time I'll give the money directly to John Tregembo.'

'That was a nasty cut on the back of his hand. It looked like it had gone bad.'

Annette nodded. 'I saw it, too. I'll send word to Dr Moore. He'll call by and see to it. My mother should have given John Tregembo the money in the first place. The reason she doesn't is she says if we do everything for them . . .' She bit her lip and half covered her face, glancing uncertainly at Roseanne.

'What?'

'It's a bit rude.'

'Dear, dear!' Roseanne laughed.

'She says we'll end up wiping their bottoms for them!'

Another laugh. 'There's a lot of truth in that.'

170

Annette cleared her throat and added, 'The word she uses, though, isn't *bottoms*.'

'Well now,' Roseanne replied with jocular severity, 'I do believe I've heard other words for it.' Then, closing the subject, she added in a more serious tone, 'You do interfere in their privacy quite a bit, don't you.'

'Interfere?' Annette bridled at the accusation. 'What d'you mean?'

'Going through her purse. Looking in their larders. Sending down the doctor . . .'

'But it's all for their own good,' the girl protested.

At the centre of the village they took the Carleen road. Mark's store cattle stared morosely at them from Mrs Delamere's field, which was well grazed by now. 'They'll have to be moved again before this week is out,' Roseanne commented smugly. 'He'll make no profit on them.'

Annette caught her tone and responded at once. 'Oh? Do you still care?'

'About what?'

She grinned. 'About *who*? I mean, whom?'

Roseanne tossed her head. 'If he wants to make a great pillack of his self with some old widow-woman, that's his affair.' She turned to see the girl staring at her calmly. 'It *is*,' she insisted.

'Hmmm.' Annette pursed her lips. 'You still have a hankering for him, though.'

'Is that what Stephen asked you to find out?'

The girl shrugged. 'It's what worries him, I know. He doesn't need to *ask* me. We're like that!' She hooked her two index fingers into each other and pulled firmly.

'Scroff and attle!' Roseanne exclaimed scornfully. 'You wouldn't give him the time of day.'

Annette made no reply to that. After a silence Roseanne went on, 'Anyway, I don't see why a woman should have to marry *at all* – just because everyone says so. Do you?'

'What else is there?' Annette asked.

Roseanne stared at Mark's cattle. She regretted starting this particular hare now. 'I don't know,' she replied.

'There you are, then,' Annette concluded bleakly.

A toddler wandered uncertainly out of a nearby field – whose gate had long since been chopped up for firewood. The land had been set aside for cottages but the depression in tin had put paid to that scheme; now it was just a bit of waste ground where diddicoys and the workless could squat until the law took its ponderous course. Roseanne caught the child by the hand – one of the grubbiest she had ever seen – and said, 'Now, now, little cooze. You'll get run over out here. Where's your mammy to, eh?'

The infant, a little boy, blue with the cold, said, 'Ma-ma-ma-ma . . .' His eyes wandered all over the place.

'Smell the gin!' Roseanne commented. She saw a man leaning against the hedge and asked him who owned the child. He nodded toward a patched scrap of tarpaulin stretched over withies bent in low hoops, both ends stuck in the mired ground; then he returned to his contemplation of the skies.

Beneath the tarpaulin a young woman, almost naked, lay in an indecent embrace with an older man, a rough fellow with long, wild hair. Both were drunk. She was laughing at him and he was muttering threats at her. Neither paid their callers the slightest attention.

With a sudden shock Roseanne realized that she knew the young woman: Mary Williams. They had been at school together.

Annette drew breath to berate the couple for their neglect of the child but Roseanne put out a hand and stopped her. She nudged the boy forward, making him stoop and then fall at his mother's side. She at once started yelling at the child — incoherent oaths that only made him cry.

Roseanne plucked Annette by the sleeve and they walked away. The man stuck his head out from under the tarpaulin and called after them. They turned. But nature caught up with him at that moment and all he did was vomit in the grass. Then, suddenly sober, he raised his eyes and stared directly at her. She thought she had never seen such malevolence in a supposedly human countenance. Matted black hair framed a swarthy hatchet face that was divided from a simian forehead by a single, continuous, bushy eyebrow. But it was the coal-black eyes beneath them that held her; they seemed to smoulder with a hatred for the whole world — but chiefly, at that moment, for her. She shivered and looked away. It was not a face she would easily forget, though she attempted to do so from the moment she left that baleful scene.

The sky-gazer by the gate did not move as they passed back on to the road. There they stamped the mud from their boots and set off for the next of the *deserving* poor.

22

When Mark sold off his stores at the next market —
and at a handsome profit, too, considering that most
of their grazing had been free — there was a new
emptiness in his life. It was, to be sure, nothing like that
far greater emptiness caused by the loss of Roseanne;
but it was there, nagging away inside him nonetheless.
He had always considered himself a most equable man,
hail-fellow-well-met, quietly confident, destined without
too much struggle for a better life than he was born to
. . . all that sort of thing. But the loss of Roseanne
seemed to have made him moody and introspective.

Some days he would be up at four, long before the
lark, working like a demon, muttering 'to hell with her!'
— and generally consigning the whole female tribe to
outer darkness. Who needed them? What a paradise
this wide and beautiful earth would be without their
constantly petulant, prettifying, pettifogging presence!
At such times he was, indeed, a monster of raw energy,
dispatching two days' work in a morning. But then the
black dog would leap on his back and he'd linger in
bed till noon, hiding his eyes in the pillow and
murmuring *her* name until he had ladled the well of
self-pity dry.

The new emptiness came on top of all that, driving
him to the edge of despair and making its cause seem
more important than it was. And the cause itself? It was

the fact that he could no longer meet Mrs Delamere and tell her all about it.

She was the kindliest, most sympathetic soul imaginable. From his first shy hints at the torment he was undergoing to his later baring of his utter despair, she was never at a loss for a sympathetic word or phrase to show how profoundly she understood what he was going through. 'I, too, have known the deepest loss,' she would murmur as she patted his arm in her gently soothing way. Sometimes it was hard for him to believe she was almost twice his age.

Having endured their separation as long as he could, he called on her the following week, just before Christmas; he was actually on his way to the Queen's Arms, so it wasn't as if he went out of his way to engineer the encounter. Also it had rained heavily the night before, and what could be more natural than that he should want to know how well his handiwork had withstood the wintry onslaught?

But the moment she heard him announce his name to the maid, the widow herself came hotfoot into the passage with, 'Why, Mr Bodilly, you're quite the stranger! Thank you, Bridget, you may return to the kitchen. Come in, come in! What a raw night to be sure. You'll need some fortification. Don't argue – I know! In there by the fire with you!'

Before he could squeeze one word among her thousand, he found himself standing with his back to a cheery blaze, watching her measure out as large a tot of rum as a sober man could wish for. How delicate she was in all her movements, he thought. Of course, she was a *real* lady. Her late husband had been the Honourable Owen Delamere, heir-presumptive to an earldom until the childless heir-apparent had, in his dotage, sired a son at last. Then the Hon. Owen had

175

to go out to work for the first time in his life — not least to pay off the debts he had run up on the foot of an estate he would not now inherit. Oh yes, May Delamere had known tragedy long before the Grim Reaper passed by her door. Not for the first time he found himself wishing she had been born just twenty-five years later. She would have made the perfect wife — so understanding of all his needs, so attentive to them, so appreciative of anything he did for her.

'I was wondering if those slates did their job last night, ma'am,' he said as she approached with his glass.

'Oh dear man, you have no idea how I blessed you last night! The leak is — or was — directly over my bedroom ceiling, as you know. And last night was the first rainy night this year when I did not have to endure the lullaby of raindrops in that old pail in the corner. I just lay there, feeling *so* grateful to you and . . .' Her smile begged his forgiveness at her poor way with words. 'Well, just thinking about you.'

As she put the tumbler into his hand, her own lingered long enough to give him a comforting pinch. 'And worrying about you.'

He laughed awkwardly, though her words filled him with pleasure. 'You shouldn't ought to do that.'

'But I do. You know I do.' As she returned to the decanter she added over her shoulder, 'I've missed our little chats, my dear. Always when people we . . . we've grown to . . . to like — when they're absent from us, we worry about them and imagine things are far worse than they probably are.'

She poured herself a good snorter, he noticed. Then she sat on the sofa, at the end nearest the fire, where she had to look up at him — and in a way he found most appealing. At the same time he, in looking down on her, could not help but notice how soulful were her eyes in that situation, how finely modelled were the curves of her cheekbones and chin, how neat and rounded her bosom . . . He swallowed heavily and began an intense study of the plasterwork which was, indeed, rather fine, as his auctioneer's eyes informed him.

She sighed. 'But men are men. The world and its work is ever ready to claim them. I don't suppose you missed . . . having to come and tend to your cattle here at all!'

He cleared his throat and took a grateful gulp of the rum. By harry, it was good stuff! 'I was thinking, ma'am — if you got no immediate need for that little field out the back there, why, I got a dry cow due to calve down, end of February. That bit of grass would just about suit she.'

He glanced her way for a bit of help.

'Yes?' she murmured, absently smoothing her dress over her limbs, the gesture fleetingly revealing their form. Did she do such things deliberately, he wondered, or was it all quite unconscious? Did she know what disturbance it must cause in a man — to be made so aware of how good-looking she was still, and how desirable her person? She gave no sign of it. She certainly did not look up at him to see what effect her action might have had; she just stared into the flames with an enigmatic smile. The firelight dancing on her cheeks and glowing in those faraway eyes was especially entrancing.

'Come the new year,' he went on, 'I should have to start steaming she up, of course.'

'Steaming her up!' She laughed at the odd phrase.

'Mangles and hay, like,' he explained. 'But I could throw they over the hedge from the road, see. I wouldn't have to carry they in through your garden, like.'

'Any excuse not to call,' she murmured with pretend

sadness; but the twinkle in her eye assured him it was a joke.

' 'Course I'd come visiting,' he assured her. 'I missed our bit chat, too, if you must know.'

'I almost began to wonder if you and Miss Kitto hadn't made it up again.'

He shook his head morosely and stared deep into the rum before knocking back another draught.

'She hasn't been seeing the Morvah boy, so I hear.'

'He haven't been seeing she.'

'A-haa! Is that the way of it.'

'Seemingly.'

As the rum began to take effect, he found it increasingly hard to think of Roseanne, much less to feel his loss of her and keep alive his pain and bewilderment at her rejection of him after so many steady years together. 'Six years,' he muttered.

'I beg your pardon?' she asked.

'Near on seven.'

'Ah!' She caught his drift then. 'Yes, that's the worst thing in life, I think − the way it allows you to grow used to a situation, so that you utterly depend upon it. And then . . . pffft! All gone!'

''Zackly!' he said, putting up a hand to steady himself against the mantlepiece.

'Poor man, you must be roasted by now. Come and sit by me here.' She patted the sofa and moved herself diagonally into the corner between its back and armrest, leaving him little choice but to comply − or appear churlish. 'There, isn't that better?' she cooed as he settled himself.

He agreed it was, half turning to face her and the fire. Their knees touched. She did not move hers, so he withdrew his a careful inch. They were still touching her dress, but no one could make anything out of that; it

178

was so voluminous. He shook his head as if to clear it of confusion. *Make anything out of it?* What could he be thinking about!

'Yes,' she sighed, picking up the echo of her earlier words. 'Pffft! All gone! The mind can accept such losses, of course. At least it can discern the *fact* of loss. It can ask why. It can struggle to adjust. But our poor, dumb, sightless bodies have no such relief.'

He stared into the flames and nodded. It was so true, so very true.

'Even now, after all these years, you yourself can see how I miss dear Owen's hand about the place – the thousand and one things a man would notice, and know how to put right again.'

He gave another ruminative nod and glanced briefly at her before returning his gaze to the merry flames. The image of her lingered on in his mind: her eyes, unreadably dark with the firelight so bright on the flesh around them – her delicate cheek, her clear brow, her fine, patrician nose. In such a setting her eyes became two pools of enticement and mystery. And then there was the image of her lips – full, soft, and restless as they gathered more words for him. . . .

'I miss him in so many ways,' she confessed.

When he did not at once respond, she added, 'In every possible way.'

He took the merest sip of rum this time and savoured it to the full.

'You understand me, I'm sure.' It was not a question. There was a discernible tremor in her voice.

He stared at his tumbler and nodded. How on earth had they leaped from a leaking roof to *this* – and in just a few minutes? He trembled to think what another few minutes might achieve – but it was not the trembling of fear.

'Is it like that with you?' she asked hesitantly. 'I have no right to put such a shocking question, I know — and you may strike me to the floor if you wish. But I feel so . . . I don't know what . . . toward you, dear Mark. Believe me, I feel your pain as if it were my own. What am I saying! It *is* my own. When we first became friends, you know, I looked upon you as the son I never was able to give dear Owen while he lived. But that's no longer how I see you at all. I don't know how I see you now. I only know I want to help in any way I can. Say something, dear man! Stop me talking my head off in this foolish way!' She leaned forward and took the tumbler from him, placing it on the whatnot beside her own; he noted that the two levels were precisely coincident. 'You needn't clutch it like grim death.' She laughed. 'I promise not to steal it.'

It gave him the chance to smile. He drew a deep breath, shrugged his shoulders, and let it out in a sigh.

'You're quite right to ignore my question,' she told him. 'It was most impertinent of me. I can't imagine what you must . . .'

'No, no!' he hastened to reassure her. 'I want to tell 'ee. I want for 'ee to understand. There isn't no one else who *could* understand, I believe.' He leaned forward, elbows on knees, hands clasped as if in prayer. ''Tweren't never like that with Roseanne and me. Never . . . we never went . . .' He smiled awkwardly at her.

'Never went all the way,' she said mildly. 'Never jumped the starter's flag. Common expressions, I know. But no more so than the situation itself!'

He gave her a grateful smile and reached for his glass; again he took only the merest sip, which he savoured with relish.

'It was the same with Owen and me,' she went on, to his surprise. 'Afterwards, I regretted it, of course.'

180

'How?' he asked, bowled over at this confession. 'I mean how "of course"?'

'When I discovered what intense pleasures we had postponed. All those lost opportunities. Who said, "Gather ye rosebuds while ye may, Old Time is fast a-flying"? Something like that, isn't it? Anyway, it's true. 'Ever at my back I hear Time's winged chariot hurrying near." Don't you? Or are you still at that age when you imagine yourself immortal, and even an infinite postponement is of no consequence?'

'No,' he admitted reluctantly. ''Tis of consequence, right enough.' He eyed her shrewdly. 'How did 'ee rear they four daughters, then? Gather ye rosebuds, or what?'

She hung her head ruefully. 'No, I brought them up just as my parents brought up me, I must confess. We are such slaves to convention, aren't we.'

He replaced his tumbler beside hers; the levels were now half an inch apart.

'Aren't we?' she repeated, making it a question this time.

'I suppose so.'

'And it's so silly of us!' She grew quite vehement. 'Convention! What is it? I was sitting among the other dry old women at the church social the other night. Of course, these village maids have no idea how to manage a dance programme, so their swains just congregate together between dances, chatting about wrestling and hurling or whatever it is they chat about . . .'

'Village maids,' he told her with a wry chuckle.

'Well, you certainly wouldn't think it from the reluctant way they shuffle toward those same fair damsels when the music starts! You'd imagine there was a heavy fine for getting there first. I watched them, glancing sidelong at one another, racked with

181

the fear of getting too far in front, and I thought to myself — what makes them behave so? There they are, longing to get those maids in their arms, to get a hand round their waists, to hold them tight in a swirl, to brush limbs with them.' The tremor was back in her voice. 'What on earth is preventing them? And the answer is: *convention!* And I'll tell you another thing. Why was it, when my daughters were little girls and had their friends round for birthday parties — why did I insist on their eating plain brown bread with their jellies? Because if I hadn't done so, the other mothers would have remarked upon it and I should have gained a reputation for laxity. Convention again!'

'Reputation's important though,' he remarked — not knowing quite what else to say.

She pounced on the statement: 'No one gives a farthing for the reputation of a widow in her forties, my dear. Set your mind at rest on that score at least.'

Mark, who had intended nothing so direct, could only stare at her.

Her lips parted in a slow smile. 'And what is convention preventing you from doing now?' she asked.

He looked away, then back at her, then away again. 'You aren't drinking no more.'

'I've had all I *need*. She emphasized the word heavily, but her touch upon his arm was light as she added, 'Mark?'

'You know what,' he mumbled.

'If it's only convention . . . I've told you my opinion of that,' she went on remorselessly.

He nodded.

'Or are you afraid I might bite?'

A morose little laugh.

'Perhaps you find me repellent.'

'Dear God, no!' he exclaimed fervently, daring to meet her eye at last.

It was all she had been waiting for. 'Oh Mark!' She moved her face closer to his, offering her lips in an unambiguous invitation.

For a brief moment more he hesitated; then he lowered his head to hers and began to graze at the warmth and softness of her mouth. She, who had steeled her body to withstand a clumsier passion, was agreeably surprised at this finesse; she relaxed and yielded herself to his tenderness.

But he remained tense beneath his fervour. She moved her lips to his cheek; she nuzzled his ear, kissed his eyelids, gently ran the tip of her tongue down his nose, pressed her lips to his again, opened them, darted her tongue at his teeth, chased his into the warm cavern of his mouth, invited it to follow hers back — and still he would not relax. At last she asked what troubled him still.

'The maid,' he explained.

'Oh, that!' Laughing, she rose and went out to the kitchen, blowing him a kiss as she left by the door. He raised his glass to his lips and then returned it to the whatnot, its contents untouched. She had left him in no possible doubt as to what was about to happen between them. He wondered at his lack of feeling about it, either way. To test himself he began thinking in the most cynical terms: She wasn't a bad bit of stuff . . . desperate for a loving stroke or two . . . get his feet under the table . . . and so forth.

None of it raised the faintest echo of agreement within; no part of him resonated to such ideas. And yet there were no positive feelings about her, either. His heart was not racing as it had on those few occasions when he and Roseanne had come equally close to this same irreversible moment.

'There now,' she said as she returned.

'What?'

'What d'you suppose? I've given her the rest of the evening off — that's what.'

'But she'll know the reason,' he objected.

'Naturally — just as I know why she is so avid to get out. And she knows I know — and what's more, *he* is a married man. We may be mistress and servant but we are also a pair of women who understand each other. Our secrets are safe.' She raised her massive skirts behind her and settled herself on his lap. 'And now — no more words, eh?'

23

'Murder most Foul!' proclaimed the *Helston Vindicator* when it reported the tragedy. Almost any other description would have been more accurate — 'Murder most pathetic . . . most sordid . . . most pointless . . .' — but of course they would have sold fewer copies. It did not become foul until the dog . . . but let us start at the beginning.

As it happened, Roseanne and Annette were the first on the scene. The day until then had been a close copy of the same morning of the previous week: a visit to Mrs Roseveare (who appeared to have forgotten the very name of Vyvyan during the intervening seven days); a call on old Austin (who had healed without even a scar); a pause at the junction while they stared into Mrs Delamere's field. And that was where the differences began.

'He's sold they stores — those stores, then,' Roseanne said. 'I wonder what price he got?'

'I wonder whose cow that is?' Annette countered. 'But not much.'

'Why d'you say it like that?'

'It would give him an excuse to go on calling, of course.' A new note of intrigue crept into her voice as she nodded toward Vinery House and said, 'Now there's a funny thing! Two funny things, in fact.'

Roseanne followed her gaze and saw a couple of

shapes moving around in one of the rooms — not in the main house but in the wing on its western side. One of the shapes approached the window, threw it up, and shook a large dust sheet out over its sill.

'That's Bridget Walsh,' Roseanne said. 'Old Widow Delamere's maid-of-all-work.' She turned to her companion. 'What's funny about that?'

'That wing has stood locked and empty ever since she bought the place. So why are they giving it a spring clean two days before Christmas, eh?'

'Perhaps one of her daughters is coming to stay?'

Annette dismissed that with a shake of the head. 'There's more than enough room for them in the main house. Even when Rosa came with all those ridiculous servants in wigs and livery, they didn't open the annexe.'

Roseanne laughed. 'You know a lot about it.'

'Breage is *our* village. It's my duty to know a lot about everything.'

Last week, Roseanne realized, she would have added a taunt to the effect that she, Roseanne, would have to become that same sort of know-all when she was the squire's wife. The girl's failure to do so must, she felt, be significant. 'Perhaps they're *all* coming for Christmas,' she replied.

Reluctantly Annette had to concede that possibility.

'What's the other funny thing?' Roseanne continued. 'You said two.'

'Oh, the fact that Mrs D is helping in person rather than leaving it to Bridget and one of the dailies.'

'Then it must be the whole family coming home.'

'Yes.' Annette sighed. 'I suppose it must.'

Roseanne patted her comfortingly, mockingly, on the back. 'Why — what did you hope it was?'

'I thought she might be hard up and preparing to take in lodgers, that's all.'

186

Roseanne felt a small pang of disappointment. It would have been a most pleasurable outcome to contemplate. 'Actually,' she said slowly, 'now you say it, it does sound more likely than all four daughters and their husbands coming home. Surely she'd have said if it was that? She'd never have kept that to herself.' She giggled happily at the thought of old Widow Delamere coming down in the world.

They turned, as they had last week, on to the Carleen road.

'Oh no, not you again!' Roseanne exclaimed.

Mary Williams's little toddler was once more stumbling down the road, this time howling his eyes out.

'Let's see if we have any better luck this week,' she sighed as she bent to lift him up.

He stopped crying at once. He was, without doubt, the filthiest bundle of rags and swaddling Roseanne had ever seen, and certainly the worst she had ever held. The ammonia-reek off him made her eyes water; other smells, even more pungent, almost caused her to retch. She turned at the gate and stepped out smartly over the field, her eyes seeking the spot where the tent had been last week.

A patch of yellowed grass, a rotting rabbit skin or two, some well-gnawed bones and a sheep's head, and a wad of rag with blood on it were all that marked the site. Roseanne, thinking she knew what the bloodstained rag might be, curled her nose in disgust.

'Gonk,' the lad said, stretching a crooked finger toward the patch of litter. Whether it was an actual word or just a coincidence, Roseanne couldn't tell. He didn't repeat it.

'Have they?' she asked him. 'Have they gone?'

He just stared at her and then broke into a broad grin. A dishevelled woman poked her head out of a nearby tent − a piece of sailcloth tied down over two rusting bed ends and stopped off at the back by a broken tailgate from a farm wagon. The rest of her followed, shivering, into the raw December day. As near naked as made no difference, she squatted to one side of the entrance and pissed like a mare. The steaming water ran back toward the tent. 'Damn!' she said.

'Have they gone?' Roseanne asked her, nodding at the abandoned site.

'I dunno, my lover. There was some bailin' and bawlin' last night, I can tell 'ee.'

'Did you see them? Did anyone try to separate them?'

The woman shook her head and muttered something about 'slippin' a babby'.

At first she thought the woman must be referring to Mary Williams; that, too, would explain the blood-stained rag. But as she turned and went to rejoin Annette at the gate, she glanced at the side of her informant's tent and saw a small bundle of rags with a tiny human foot poking out of it at an odd angle; then she realized the woman had spoken of herself.

'Well,' Roseanne said to the pathetic little lad in her arms, 'and what's to be done with you now, eh? Give 'ee a good wash first, then take 'ee down the work-house, I suppose. What do they call 'ee? Got a name, have ee?'

'Gonk!' He stared over her shoulder and reached that same crooked, dirty finger toward the site of his erstwhile home. Roseanne wondered if it were a deformity or just a habit, that crook of his finger.

'One more that fell upon stony ground,' Annette said as they drew near.

Roseanne's hackles rose at once. Though she herself might easily have made such a comment, somehow on

Annette's lips it seemed so unutterably smug she was stung into replying, 'Speak for yourself!'

'Hoity-toity!' the other exclaimed. Then, laughing 'Why — going to keep him, are you?'

'No!' The very idea horrified Roseanne — and then she wondered why. The notion was so unthinkable, so plainly intended as a joke, she ought merely to have laughed. "Course not.' She gave a belated laugh at last.

Her eyes met the little boy's and dwelled there a moment. They were a beautiful bright blue, almost violet. His curly hair was probably flaxen-fair under all that filth . . . He smiled at her again. Little pearly teeth, beautifully regular. 'Bet you're hungry,' she said. 'I wish I knew your name.'

'Jik,' he said, bouncing aromatically up and down in her arms. 'Jik-jik-jik . . .'

'Jake?' she suggested.

Something like recognition flared briefly behind his eyes, so she decided that was it: Jake was his name from then on.

'If his parents really have done a flit,' she said, 'he'll have to go on the parish, poor little bugger. Where can we wash him?'

'Mrs Tregew's?' Annette suggested.

Mrs Tregew lived in the first house in the terrace known as Troon Row, which ran at right angles to the Carleen road and whose back gardens fringed on the field where the diddicoys and squatters had their temporary camp. They were now mere yards from the point where the field hedge became the hedge to her garden. Annette stood on hillocks of grass at the roadside verge to make one last survey of the field. 'We might just have overlooked it,' she said — then, a moment later, 'Ha! Told you so! They've moved. Isn't that their tarpaulin just here against Mrs Tregew's hedge?'

Roseanne craned her neck and peered over. Her heart fell as she saw it was, indeed, the same wretched bit of material. It was even bobbing up and down in the same lewd manner. 'At least we can wash the poor little mite,' she said, turning angrily back into the road. 'Plainly that slut never bothers.'

Mrs Tregew eyed the filthy infant with distaste, but she lent them the little zinc bath that hung on a nail by her back door, together with some soap and a pail to draw water. The pump stood beside the main road, just beyond her front gate.

Jake seemed impervious to the cold, as well he might, considering the season and the miserable rags that he wore. He didn't like being washed at all, especially when they ducked his head and started to soap his hair. But he discovered he liked the bubbles, playing patacake with them between his hands. That kept him amused until they had removed the worst of the dirt – which took no fewer than three changes of water.

By then he was such a different little boy that Mrs Tregew herself, all unprompted, told them to bring the poor mite indoors and dry him by the fire. She even looked out some drawers and a petticoat and a blouse that her little niece had outgrown. 'Poor little cooze,' she said as she carried his old rags away between two bits of kindling wood. 'I speck he's some hungry, this weather.' She returned and tousled his hair, which proved as flaxen and curly as Roseanne had imagined it might be. 'Like a bit of fuggan, would 'ee, boy?'

'Fuggan, fuggan,' Jake replied.

'He's got a tongue then,' she said as she reached for the tin where the precious cake was hoarded.

Privately Roseanne doubted it; the lad was a good mimic, no more. But she kept the opinion to herself.

He ate the cake ravenously, washing it down with

buttermilk. Roseanne could feel he was desperate for more but, from the way he avoided looking at the tin or giving any sign of his longing, she guessed that the only second helpings he'd ever had were from the back of the hand.

'More?' Mrs Tregew asked, reluctantly holding the tin near him. He turned on Roseanne's lap and buried his face in her bosom. 'Thank 'ee kindly, Mrs Tregew,' she said with a smile. 'I'll take he back home and feed 'n up a bit afore I put 'n back to his mother.'

Relieved, the old woman tousled his hair and chuckled. 'Pretty little cooze, isn't he? Proper 'ansum.'

Annette seemed rather subdued as they left and returned to the road; she had been staring down Mrs Tregew's garden while the other two had been vying to spoil Jake. 'I most earnestly hope I'm wrong,' she said when the woman had closed her door, 'but I don't think what's going on under that tarpaulin is . . . well, what we thought it might be.'

The squatters had broken a gap in the hedge, through which the two women now hastened; Roseanne still held Jake in her arms. Instinctively, as they drew near, she put a hand over the boy's head to shield him. Almost at once he fell asleep. She rested her chin on his curls and, for no reason she could think of felt tears sprouting behind her eyes.

A moment later, though, her mood changed abruptly. The wriggling mass under the tarpaulin *growled*. The two women halted at once. The sound was unmistakably that of a dog at his meal, warning off some approaching marauder.

Annette took one further step and the growling doubled in ferocity. She picked up a bit of an old furze branch and stuck it under one edge of the material. The dog went into a frenzy, which so frightened the girl that she jerked the stick back at once. But some bare threads got caught in a snag of a side-shoot and so, in pulling the furze away, she drew the tarpaulin with it.

The horror that now lay revealed before them was something that neither woman ever forgot. The dog, a starved little black mongrel, stood at bay beyond his grisly meal, snarling like a demon.

Roseanne covered Jake's head even more firmly and ran for the main gate; Annette followed hard behind. When they reached the roadway they paused for breath. 'What now?' the girl asked. 'We must fetch Sergeant Evans, I suppose.'

Roseanne admired her more than ever then. She could just imagine how she herself might have felt at the age of seventeen on seeing such an appalling sight. You couldn't say Annette was completely unaffected by it, but it certainly hadn't robbed her of any wit or sense.

A movement in the field caught their eye. A Romany — a superior diddicoy with a caravan of his own and two horses — was running up the field from his rather exclusive little encampment near the far hedge. Half-way, he noticed the dog, saw what it was doing, and turned and ran back home.

'Why did he do that?' Annette asked.

'I have a feeling I know what's going to happen,' Roseanne replied.

'I suppose she *was* dead. She must have been. She couldn't possibly have survived.'

'No, not possibly,' Roseanne reassured her. 'Going by what that other wretched woman told me, I think it all happened last night. And the man will be ten parishes away by now. Probably in Falmouth, looking to work his passage to Australia or somewhere. God, I can't even remember what he looked like.'

Annette gave a little laugh, almost against her will.

'The only bit of him I'd know again was his' — she glanced furtively about them — 'his b-t-m.'

A loud report spared Roseanne the necessity to laugh at such an immature comment. They both spun round and saw the Romany stirring the dog's carcase with the smoking muzzle of his shotgun.

'Oh, thank God!' Annette exclaimed.

A barefoot labourer ran across the field and began berating the man for shooting his dog; but when he was shown what the creature had been doing, he decided it wasn't his after all. He ran back to his tent and began at once to pack up his few belongings.

'Sergeant Evans?' Annette repeated.

Roseanne nodded unwillingly. 'I suppose we must. Here! Where are our baskets?'

Annette smiled. 'I wondered when you'd notice. While you were looking for Jake's mother, I slipped them behind the Johnsons' garden wall.'

'And I never gave it a second thought!' Roseanne jerked the infant higher up her chest. 'Ooh, you are getting heavy, little mite!' She raised an eyebrow at the girl. 'Want to take a turn?'

Annette raised her hands in mock horror. 'Nothing to do with me, my dear! The Evanses are only round the corner, anyway. You'll leave the lad with them, I suppose?'

'Mmm, I suppose,' Roseanne agreed.

Sergeant Evans was feeding sugar to his bees. He did not appear greatly perturbed at their tale but he did reluctantly agree to take off his nets and smock and put up his official 'hemlet', as he called it, and accompany them to the scene of the brawl. He gave the impression that one dreg of humanity more or less was of little moment, no matter how appalling its end.

But the sight of Mary Williams, or what remained

193

of her, clearly shook him; the brawl was promoted on the spot to a proper murder.

Annette had accompanied him to the spot — not that he needed a guide; it was now quite thronged with curious and idle villagers. Roseanne, still clutching the now somnolent Jake to her, remained at the gate. She stared at the rest of the field in amazement — for, apart from the Romany who had shot the dog, not a single squatter remained. They were no doubt, she reflected, already well settled in similar camps in similar nearby fields or patches of waste ground, where their new neighbours were ready to swear they had all been living for weeks.

Sergeant Evans began making notes as to the lie of the body and the nature of its wounds. He was an impressive man and everybody's eye was fixed upon him — which was as well for the woman who sidled through the gate and walked, with that shy reserve of the very poor, to where Roseanne had last seen her, pissing in the mud. There, quite casually, she stooped and picked up the incriminating bundle, strolling back to the road with that same unhurried humility. 'Shocking!' she exclaimed to Roseanne as she passed back out again.

'Cover up that babby's leg, for heaven's sake,' Roseanne told her.

Guiltily the woman obeyed as she hobbled away down the road.

The Sergeant sent a lad into Helston with a telegraph message for the Falmouth constabulary. Then he took depositions from Annette and Roseanne. It was all very perfunctory and he clearly expected no arrests. Finally, as the merest afterthought, he asked about the lad.

'She asked I to look after he for a few days,' Roseanne said calmly. Behind her she heard Annette clear her throat.

'She said she was tramping to Redruth, looking for work, and she'd send for 'n. She said her mother was living over there, over to Bissoe.'

The Sergeant made a note of that, saying the last *he'd* heard of Mary Williams's mother, after the father was killed down Wheal Vor, she was in Exeter bridewell.

'Well, after Christmas I'll just see if she isn't down Bissoe,' Roseanne replied. 'And if not, I'll put he to Helston workhouse. If that's all right by the powers-that-be?'

He laughed. 'I don't expect they'd come after 'ee with writs, maid, not if you was to keep he for good!'

'No fear of that,' Roseanne said firmly.

Annette accompanied her back home; it was assumed between them that the girl would finish their round on her own now.

'Roseanne?' she asked warily when they were out of hearing of the stragglers around the Evans house.

'What, dear?' Roseanne asked lightly.

'You know.'

'What do I know? I know lots of things.'

'You know it's impossible. It's out of the question.'

'What is?'

'Keeping Jake for good.'

'Oh my gidge!' Roseanne turned great innocent eyes upon her. 'Is *that* what you think? My dear soul!'

'Roseanne.' Annette's gaze did not waver.

'What now?'

The girl just shook her head; but the gesture was so ambiguous Roseanne could not say whether it was in sadness or prohibition.

Not that she cared much, either way.

24

'Only over Christmas,' Roseanne explained. 'You couldn't put a babby like that up Helston workhouse, not Christmas Eve.' Her eyes pleaded with her mother, avoided her father. 'Specially not after what happened to poor Mary,' she added.

'Poor Mary!' her father scoffed. 'First time ever I heard you talk about she like that.'

'I taught she in school,' Roseanne added, with no particular relevance.

'And come home every blessed day ramping on about she — what she wouldn't do and what deviltry she got up to. You never had a good word for she then. How is it "poor Mary" all of a sudden?'

'Fuss, fuss, fuss!' Roseanne exclaimed. 'And just over two days. Christmas, that's all.'

Jake sat on her hip, grinning indifferently at each speaker, pointing his crook finger at anything that took his eye.

'Where'll he sleep?' Mrs Kitto asked nervously. She reached forward and ran her fingers through the boy's curls. 'Eyeable little edjack, isn't he.'

'He's no edjack,' Roseanne assured her. 'He's quick as cress.' She thrust her hip forward. 'Go on, Jake. Go to Aunty Mary.'

'None of that now,' her mother warned. 'Aunt Mary, indeed!' But she took the child nonetheless and dandled him warily on her arm.

He showed his beautiful teeth and tried to see if her nose screwed off.

'Here!' Mrs Kitto's wounded annoyance mingled with her laughter. 'He's got some strength in that hand — haven't you, my lover. Yes you have! Yes you have! My, he'll be some bowerly young man when he grows up.'

'Not on workhouse gruel, he won't.' Frank leaned forward and, jabbing a finger at the boy, said, 'Gruel and skilly, my lad. That's what's in store for you.'

Jake gurgled with delight and made a grab for the accusatory finger. A brief tussle ensued, ending only when Frank remembered he wasn't supposed to be smiling at all. ''Es,' he grumbled as he extricated himself from Jake's powerful grip. 'Some strength in that, all right. Don't feed he no meat while he's under *this* roof, or there's no telling what he'll do.'

'So he can stay under this roof?' Roseanne asked swiftly.

He stared at the boy, realizing he had unwittingly conceded the point yet still reluctant to admit it. 'Mary Williams!' he repeated scornfully. 'A coxy maid she was! On and off the boats with all they sailors afore she was sixteen. Who's the father, I'd like to know?'

'So would the police, I expect.' Mrs Kitto put Jake down. 'Or where he is, anyroad.'

The boy went directly to Roseanne and clutched at her skirts. She grinned at her father and risked asking, 'What you going to give he for Christmas, then?'

'A clip round the lughole if he don't comport hisself,' was the growled reply. At the door he paused and turned to her again. 'And 'tis four days, not two. But the day after Boxing Day — hear me now maid — the day after Boxing Day, I'll put he to Helston Union meself, if I have to.'

197

Roseanne bent and lifted Jake back on to her hip. 'Come us on, then, boy. Time you earned your keep. Let's make a cowman out of you.'

Her mother followed her out to the gate; by then her husband was a dwindling figure, stumping down the lane — and anger in every step. She put a hand to her daughter's arm. 'He do mean it, my lover,' she warned. 'Don't 'ee build no fairy castles now. That poor little bugger's going in Helston Union next Tuesday, no matter what you do say.'

'I know that, Mother.' She smiled reassuringly. 'I never thought to keep 'n at all. 'Tis everyone else put that in my mouth, not me.' Jake struggled to be put down again. He wanted to run after the man with the strong finger, but Roseanne soon seduced him out of that with the promise of 'cows'. He had no idea what cows were. He had seen them, of course, but no one had ever bothered to tell him their name; so he was eager to make what sounded like a new discovery. However, when he realized that 'cows' were just *those* things, he ran to her and begged to be taken up again. She wiped the mud off his feet in the grass before she obliged. 'Must get you some little boots,' she told him. 'And don't you pay no heed to what *they* did say. You aren't going in no workhouse while I live and breathe.'

'Cows!' he said.

25

'Happy Christmas, my lover!' May Delamere archly dropped into dialect as she whispered the words into Mark's left ear. She followed them with the tip of her tongue — warm, sensuous, and writhing in a way which, as he had already discovered, would drive him wild with desire. At least, it had done so at eleven last night; now, at four-thirty in the morning, it did not seem quite so efficacious. She redoubled her efforts, lying half on top of him, parting her right thigh over his left, hoping for a renewal of that most ancient miracle of all. 'Mark?'

He groaned and turned to her, caressing her clumsily with a sleepsodden arm.

'One more,' she whispered. 'Quick as you like. Then you must go. Bridget'll be up and about in less than an hour.'

It was wonderful having a man in her bed again after all these years. No child in the kingdom, waking up this morning to find a new toy at the foot of his bed, would be half so ecstatic as she, waking up to find *him* — big, beefy, powerful Mark Bodilly — lying at her side, conquered and docile. A real *bowerly* man, as the locals would say. To confront him in that torpor and provoke him to one more encounter before banishing him to the outer cold and darkness of his unslept-in bed would now be the supreme feather in her cap.

Ten minutes later, with the sweat on him turning chill,

he drew on his nightshirt, for the first time that night, and groaned and shivered his way to the door — followed by a barrage of shushes and blown kisses from her.

After he had gone she stretched herself across the bed, luxuriating in the manwarmth he had left behind, and wondering if this was not actually the happiest day in her life. She thought back to her wedding with Owen, to the arrival of her daughters and the peculiar pleasures of bringing them up, and decided she could not, in all fairness, say that those wonderful occasions had been any less happy than this. Nonetheless, it felt like the happiest *something* so, in the end, she settled for the happiest Christmas.

Yes, she thought, that could be said without the slightest fear of contradiction; her past Christmases had generally been disastrous, one way or another. Remember the time when the dog had run off with the goose! And then when Bessie had come weeping and wailing home, just when she thought she'd got at least one daughter safely off her hands; that hadn't happened at Christmas but it had cast a pall over the whole season. And then there was Rosa's and Dicky's first bankruptcy — that had actually happened at Christmas, or just days before. Yes, this very day (or yesterday, now) five years ago. And again . . . no, she didn't want to think about all that now. The point was, this one certainly looked like being the best Christmas of her life.

You didn't have to be in love with a man to enjoy the congress of his body. Well . . . in a way she *was* in love with Mark, of course. But not romantically. That was the point: You didn't need to be *romantically* in love with a man to enjoy him like that. In fact, it was much better when you weren't. No yearning, no pining away, no sighing, none of the pains of love, just the pleasures.

The brute pleasures?

Reverend Martin would say so, to be sure; but they weren't brutish at all. In fact, Mark showed surprising finesse at it. He said he'd never gone that far with Roseanne Kitto, even though they'd been 'betokened' so long. And she believed him. Yet someone had taught him his bedside manners . . .

What about jealousy? That was certainly one of love's pains. Why had she left that off the list just now? Did she suffer its pangs at all?

She tested herself, trying to picture Mark and Roseanne entwined in each other's arms, kissing, touching. She imagined him pouring out his love in words and caresses − words he had not whispered to her last night, not even at the height of his passion. But her feelings remained quite calm and neutral. That settled it. She did not want his love, so she did not resent his giving it to another. She heaved a great sigh of relief and, turning on her side, settled to sleep, glad to have the bed to herself, glad to be alone again, glad to have the best of both worlds.

Love would be a nightmare if it insinuated its way back into her life now, she thought, feeling her mind begin to turn a slow, familiar eddy as the drowsiness stole over her. If she loved Mark, she'd spend all day wondering where he was, who he was seeing, what they were talking about, what they were doing, when he'd come back . . .

She'd lived through all that.

Once was enough.

Once a week?

Twice a week. *I wasn't talking about that.*

Never mind. Two or three times . . . that was all she required now . . . and the rest . . . even tenor of her ways . . .

At that same moment, not a hundred paces away (not even twenty, if you removed a few walls), Mark lay shivering in his bed, wondering if it would ever get warm and trying to remember where he'd seen that advertisement for a slow charcoal burner you could safely leave in your bed, for hours if necessary. He was going to need something like that if *this* was now to be his way of life.

Also the ability to catnap for twenty minutes after lunch — and breakfast, tea, and dinner, too, if she was going to go on being so demanding as last night. He'd never encountered anything like it — not that his experience was all that wide — but May Delamere took the gold diploma. She'd warned him she'd wake him up and send him off before five, but she'd never said she'd send him off like that!

Funny thing — in the dark you could imagine she was twenty again. Even in daylight she could stir your bowels to discomfort.

Was it love?

His thoughts turned to Roseanne; and the anger and bitterness that rose up within him told him at once that, whatever his feelings for May Delamere might be called, they certainly had nothing to do with love. He couldn't survive one hour of the day without thinking of Roseanne and cursing her hold upon him; he could happily go from dawn to dusk without once thinking of May, except, perhaps, the occasional warm memory of her lithe, comfortable little body and her genial smile.

So it wasn't love.

Suppose she got a taste for it now? After all, as she herself said, that was why she'd gone to such pains to keep all knowledge of such things from her four daughters — because women can get a taste for it and

202

then become insatiable. What if that happened to May, now, after all her years of abstinence?

He shivered again, though his bed was no longer cold enough to cause it. He'd have to find other men to help share the burden. No two ways about it. He smiled to himself. At least that proved it wasn't love.

The thought then occurred to him that it might be something even better than love – which, until this week, would have sounded like a perverse kind of cynicism. He had noticed an odd change in his nature since Roseanne had taken up with Stephen Morvah. He had never wanted to go all the way with her . . . no, that wasn't true. He had never courted her for that purpose; he had wanted to postpone the consummation until after their marriage. And it had never been a burden to him because she was such a wonderful girl in every other way as well. They could walk the lanes of Breage and Germoe, talking for hours about everything under the sun – never even touching or holding hands. And yet he could come away feeling richer inside and happier than . . . well, than he felt now after going all the way with May Delamere, for example. Even four times all the way.

But since losing Roseanne he had found his eye roving toward other girls – that serving maid at the Angel Hotel, Beth Davey, for instance, and Kitty Pascoe in the bakery, and Jean Berry, who looked after old Miss Grylls. His eye would stray toward them and *that* was the main thing on his mind. Fornication. Love was nowhere in it. He wanted to possess them as a kind of revenge on Roseanne; and on them, too – on every girl he desired. A revenge on them just for being women and provoking him to so much misery.

So perhaps May Delamere had made her offer just in time to save him from something awful. Perhaps, in the end, he'd have turned into one of those sour old mysogynists people were always writing about. Or perhaps the very opposite – one of those rakes who needed a new woman every week.

As the bed warmed up he allowed himself to uncurl, to heat its still-frozen corners. The glow of health. The power of his flesh, casually deployed. Good feelings coursed through his limbs. Beyond all doubt he had made the right choice in coming to live here. He and May could cater to each other's needs without stirring those profound emotions that make such a misery of most people's lives. Who knows? Perhaps he'd look back one day and see these coming times as the golden years of his life – the years when May Delamere set him free to manage his business and turn the corner to real prosperity.

Yes . . . the golden years.

He yawned.

Golden years . . . He went on repeating the phrase in his mind until it lost all meaning and only the glow and comfort of it lingered on. And it was at that precise moment that Roseanne felt a sharp stab of pain at the tip of her nose, accompanied by a maniacal little giggle.

'Jake, oh Jake,' she groaned. 'Not again. It doesn't come off. It's not made that way.' She tweaked his nose and the giggling stopped.

'Wee-wee,' he said. 'Wee-wee-wee . . .'

'Yes! All right. I heard 'ee. Good boy!' She struggled from the bed and guided him through the dark of the room to the night commode, where, a moment later, she was rewarded with the delicate tinkle of his performance. 'Where's it all come from, eh?' she asked. ''Tis a miracle to me.'

She lifted a corner of the curtain and saw the first blear finger of dawn upon the eastern horizon. 'Happy

Christmas,' she half said, half yawned as she reached in to shake the last drops off him. Then, lifting him to her hips — a now familiar riding seat to the pair of them — she whispered, 'Well now, the question is, do I rock 'ee off to sleep again or take 'ee out milking along of me?'

He flung his arms around her neck.

'Silly question,' she muttered as she felt for the matches to light the candle.

She dressed him quickly, then herself, before carrying him downstairs for a slice of heavy cake and a sip of the thick, black tea that had stewed on the hob all night. She took two blankets to wrap him in, shrewdly suspecting he'd drop off to sleep once they reached the milking parlour. She wouldn't allow him down on the ground, where a cow might easily crush his feet; and he'd soon grow bored just sitting there, watching her by the dim light of their only lantern.

And so it proved. Before she was halfway through milking old Greenberry of her measly half-gallon, he was fast asleep again; he didn't even wait for a sip of the udder-warm milk, which had sent him into such ecstasies yesterday. As she turned the old cow out, she settled the lad into a safer little nest among the straw. 'If you aren't the best Christmas present ever!' she murmured, stroking his soft cheek with the back of her fingers. Then she went out the back for Raspberry's fodder.

The young heifer's calf had gone to market last week; her tiny udders were strained to the limit with over four gallons of milk. Not that size had anything to do with yield, mind you. Look at Greenberry — with a great bag that made her sway as she walked, and yet she never gave more than three gallons even in her flush. And Mark had once told her that a mare could give her foal

205

five gallons a day — and you couldn't even *see* her udders, just the teats.

Where was Mark this Christmas? she wondered. Gone over Nancledra to his people like last year, she supposed. What would he say when he heard about her keeping Jake?

She bridled at the question. What did it matter *what* he thought. Or Stephen Morvah, either. They could both go and jump in the sea for all she cared.

What a fool she'd been! At the back of her mind there'd always been this thought that she had to belong to a man. She had to be betokened, even if there was no actual ring on her finger. If there wasn't that man there, more or less propping up her life, then it would all fall to pieces!

Of course, she wasn't alone in that. Nine tenths of the chatter she'd enjoyed with other girls — and with her mother and aunts and all the female tribe — had been about men, getting men, keeping them in their place, keeping them happy, and above all keeping them. And until now it had seemed as natural as eating when you were hungry or putting on more clothes when the weather turned cold.

Yet all it had taken to open her eyes was for two men to fight over her — and then shun her as if she had the plague. She didn't care now if she never saw Stephen again. Nor yet Mark, neither. One day the right man for her might come along. If so, she hoped she'd recognize him and make the most of it. But until that blessed or cursed day she wasn't going to fret her life to a ravelling in the belief it had all turned wrong.

Besides, there was Jake to think of now.

She finished washing Raspberry's swollen udders, which seemed stretched to the point where they must surely tear; then she sat at the stool with the milk pail clenched between her knees. She prodded gently at the heifer's udders and felt her let down her milk; but it was so ticklish that she raised her hind foot to kick the very hand that relieved her. The first of her kicks wrote a long, painful diagonal of dung and mud across Roseanne's forearm; the second found Roseanne ready with the point of a hairpin just where it would prick the animal's knee. Three times more she tried it before the pain convinced her that a mild tickle, however irritating, was the better option.

Roseanne began to sing: *Oh, I shan't forget the day that I was born* . . . It proved better at calming the heifer's spirit than a sting from her hairpin; and when the last chorus was over, the heifer's bag was half empty and the ticklishness had stopped.

'Am I mad, Raspberry?' Roseanne asked with a sigh. 'They're all going to say I am. And I know what you're going to say: "How can I take your calf from 'ee one week and go and ask 'ee a question like that the next!" Well, my lover, I haven't got no answer to that, so I'll say no more.'

After a moment she added, 'Excepting this: I got today and tomorrow to change the old man's mind. So if you've any thoughts on how I'm to do that, I should like to hear 'em.'

Later, to Dewberry, she said, "Course, he always wanted a son. He never said as much but Aunt Doris told I he did. You believe that's the way to his heart, do 'ee? Might be a bit late now, though.'

Graceful had this more practical nugget to chew over with her cud: 'I could go back and teach in school anytime. They're crying out for infant teachers over to Rosudgeon, Goldsithney, Leedstown . . . lots of places. And I could put Jake in class with I, and they couldn't say nothing to that.'

Youngberry had a repeat of the same argument, plus its corollary. 'And the old man do know it, too. So he can't just hand out the orders.'

When she went to the door to call in Cloudberry, she got the shock of her life. The figure of a man loomed out of the dark, one hand raised, and for a moment she thought he was going to strike her. She reeled back and, as he came into the light, she saw he had both hands raised, not in menace but in surrender.

'Stephen!' she exclaimed. 'My gidge, you did give I a fright — give me a fright!'

'Sorry.' He smiled warily. 'Thoughtless as ever!' He saw she had taken in his gesture and so lowered his hands. 'The other thing you could do,' he said, 'is marry the squire's son.'

26

Stephen was so enthusiastic that her doubts began to yield; against every cautious instinct within her, she actually tested his plan for drawbacks. It was an instinct of a different kind that made her hand Jake over to him, saying, 'Here, see how you like the burden of that.'

But Jake burst into howls and reached desperately for her warm embrace once again. Stephen, nervous of the child, handed him back at once.

''Tis nothing to do with you,' she said, 'that great scroggan Mary Williams took up with must have abused the boy. That's all. He's just taken against men.'

Stephen, more discomfited by this 'consolation' than he had been by Jake's rejection, said stiffly, 'I trust I resemble that blackguard in no particular manner.'

'He was dark. Spanish-looking. He had pock marks on his forehead and a scar on his cheek . . .' Her voice tailed off . . .

'What?' he asked.

'I forgot all that when I told Sergeant Evans. But why? How does it come back so clear now? Should I go back and tell he, I wonder?'

'If they haven't caught him by now, he'll be on the high seas and well away.' His scan of the horizon brought him eye to eye with Jake, who now showed the impenetrable logic of the near-two-year-old and beamed at him. 'We'll be on terms soon enough,' Stephen assured him, holding out a finger of friendship.

Jake shrank from him, buried his face in Roseanne's neck, and then peeped to see what response this brought.

Stephen chuckled. '*His* terms, I'm sure.'

Roseanne reverted to their earlier conversation. 'What would we live on?' she asked. 'There'd soon enough be more mouths than this to feed.'

He did not know how to respond to such bluntness. 'My parents wouldn't stop my allowance,' he assured her.

'You have that in writing, have 'ee?'

He made no reply.

'Anyway,' she went on, 'what makes you suppose you can stop away a month or more and then just come back and say "marry me"?'

There was an awkward pause before he said, 'I was wrong.' They had reached the gate of her house. 'Look, we can't start talking about all that now. The child will get cold out here — and so will you.'

'Come on in and have a bit breakfast,' she invited; when he hesitated, she added, ''Tis Christmas, so you'll fare so well as you would home, I dare say.'

'But your parents . . . how may we talk in front of them?'

'I'll take up a dish o' tay and a morsel of bread and ham. They won't stir.' She knew, however, that her mother would be out of bed and lifting the loose floor board before she, Roseanne, was back in the kitchen.

However, her words were reassuring enough to allow him to accept her invitation. As he got his legs under the table, the scraping of his chair masked Mrs Kitto's eager footfall — and kneefall — on the floor above; only Roseanne, ears straining for them, heard the telltale sounds. She set a plate before him and ladled out a good helping of steaming porridge, hot from its overnight haybox. He smacked his lips and made other appreciative noises as he sprinkled it with salt and drowned it in scalded milk — the milk from which the clotted cream had been scraped.

Now that he wanted to eat in peace, Jake desired nothing more than to climb up on his lap. 'Missed your chance, son,' he told the child, fending him off with a jovial thrust of his knee.

'You may carve the ham while you're eating.' Roseanne thrust the knife into his hand and placed the joint before him. The moment Jake saw him holding the utensil he ran and hid behind her skirt. 'Oh dear,' she said, hoisting him up on to her hip again. 'I know what you're thinking. Well you just sit there and watch the nice man cut you a bit breakfast. You'll soon see there's no harm in it.'

The boy became utterly absorbed in the carving, watching the knife glide back and forth in lethal silence as the pale pink and white meat curled over and fell to the plate. She stared into his eyes, in near-profile to her, and wondered what hellish re-enactment going on behind them. She didn't know whether infants' hearts beat faster than grown-ups' but his was certainly doing so, much faster. 'Give he a bit,' she said.

Stephen speared a scrap, half fat, half lean, and proffered it on the point of the carver. Her reassuring grip on Jake tightened. 'Go on, little cooze, 'twon't hurt ee. 'Tis food.' She smacked her lips and helped his hand make the decision.

It was a battle royal between whatever foul memory was making his heart flutter so, on the one hand, and his trust in her, fortified by his hunger, on the other. Trust and hunger won and he mashed the morsel into his open mouth and chewed voraciously.

'Why does he do that with his finger?' Stephen asked. 'Make it like a talon? Is he deformed?'

'No. He do just do that when he's a bit mazed or spronsey or something of that sort. Give he another bit.'

Stephen obliged. This time Jake took it unaided. Soon he had no fear of the knife at all — not *that* knife, anyway.

'If you truly want to do something for the lad,' she told Stephen, 'you could get he a little old pair of boots.'

Stephen hit his forehead with the side of his clenched fist and went to the door, where his greatcoat was hanging; he returned with the very items in his hand, of soft leather and fine workmanship. 'A grand stepfather *I'll* make!' he commented. 'Annette told me you wanted some. These were my excuse for coming to see you.'

'Excuse?' she echoed in surprise.

'You know what I mean. You'd best set him on my lap while I put them on.'

She watched in fascination. Jake seemed to have forgotten all his terror of Stephen — or was it that his curiosity over the strange objects in his hand left no room for fear? 'Where did 'ee get they to?' she asked.

'They were mine once. I think I must have been a little older. They're not a very good fit. Side-to-side, anyway. Lord! But his soles are so thick they fit up-and-down pretty well. There you are, young fellow my lad!' He tied the second lace and then cried out in pain as Jake tested the possibilities of these strange new toys. 'The champion hurler of 'eighty-six!' he commented as he set him down again and fended him off.

Roseanne smiled to think what her mother might be making of that bellow of pain. Moments later she herself was adding to the confusion with cries of 'Stop it, you varmint!' as Jake hacked at the table legs and cupboard

doors. 'Look what you've been and gone and done!'
She stooped and gathered him into her crouching
embrace as she pointed out the marks in the paintwork.

He giggled delightedly.

'Bad boots!' She gave them what would have been
a hard slap had they been flesh. 'Bad, bad boots!'

He joined the game, hitting them, too, and crying
'Bab-bab-bab!'

Stephen sighed. 'They make all rational discourse
impossible, don't they? The nursery, the nanny, and the
green baize door are the grandest institutions, I'm
thinking.'

'And will your allowance run to that?' she asked as
she came to sit at the table. She lifted Jake on to her
lap to share her porridge.

Stephen gave a noncommittal shrug.

'And you never answered my other question, neither:
how did you stop away all those weeks? Never a word
from 'ee?'

He finished carving the ham and returned to his
porridge, unwilling to look her in the eye. 'Does it
matter?' he asked. 'I'm not proud of it. Even if my fears
had been . . . anyway, it's over now. I was wrong. I'm
sorry. Won't that do?'

'If you don't want to say the reason . . .' She
floundered a moment and then, on sudden inspiration,
concluded, '. . . at least you could tell me *why* you don't
want to.'

He grinned and shook his head. 'I'm sure *you* can
see a difference between the two! Oh, very well! I
thought you were deceiving me. There!'

She could only stare at him in blank amazement.

'I know. I was wrong. But you must admit it *looked*
awful.'

'What did? I've no idea what you're on about.'

'Didn't Annette say anything?'

She shook her head. 'Not about all this. Anyway, I'd never discuss it with a maid her age – your baby sister and all.'

'*Baby* sister is not what she is. Sometimes she's so . . . self-controlled . . . self-assured – what's the word? You know what I mean. She makes me shiver.'

Roseanne nodded, 'Anyway, what might she have told me?'

'About my seeing you dancing in Porthleven with Mark Bodilly.'

'I never did!' The vehemence of her protest startled Jake, who coughed on his porridge.

While she patted him on the back (which he thought an amusing new game) and wiped his drool (which he resented), he explained: 'I don't mean at a dance or anything. Just in the street. On that terrace-road up on Breage side, the day your father moved the first block . . .'

'Oh that!' She laughed with relief. 'My dear soul! Is that all!'

He cleared his throat delicately. 'You did tell me you weren't going down to watch, if you recall? You did say you and Bodilly weren't seeing each other. Yet the very next day I see the pair of you in Porthleven, at a place where you could hardly meet by accident, dancing hand-in-hand.'

'And at the sight of that, I suppose, your tongue tied itself in a knot and your legs took an instantaneous ague so you could neither walk to me nor ask me to explain!'

He stared at her as if she had slapped his face. 'You have no idea what jealousy is like, do you,' he said bitterly.

'If it's like that sort of folly,' she began – and then thought better of it.

214

Jake crooked a finger at the ham.

'Just wait!' she snapped.

The lad began to grizzle.

Stephen reached his fork across, speared a sliver of fat, and offered it to him. Roseanne said nothing.

'It's either we talk or he wines,' Stephen explained. 'When I saw you and Bodilly there on the hillside, I thought the whole world had come to an end.'

'Then you're a fool,' she said curtly.

'I don't care about that,' he went on doggedly. 'That's not the point. I'm trying to make you understand what jealousy's like. My heart started going so fast I thought I was going to die. Sometimes I couldn't see anything. I looked across the harbour to see if you were still there and I'd see nothing but great black . . . it was like flying clouds of needles in front of my eyes. My innards kept falling away inside me, endlessly falling. I couldn't say a word because my mouth was so dry. And it didn't stop. I couldn't sleep for two nights. I kept thinking of you being back with him again . . .'

'Stephen!' She felt she'd heard enough. 'It's all very flattering, my lover, and I'm sure any of the young ladies in your circle, with nothing better to do than embroidery and flower pressing, would have the feet knocked out from under them by now. But don't you see? 'Tweren't called for, none of it. All you needed to do was walk half a mile and say, "What's all this to, then?" In five minutes you could have been at ease again. That's not jealousy, my lover. That's asking for sympathy 'cos you got a stone in your boot.'

He stared morosely at his empty bowl, shrugged, and gave a little laugh. 'There's no answer to that — except to repeat that you obviously don't know what jealousy is. Of *course* it leads to stupid, idiotic, self-destructive

215

behaviour. So does love.' He nodded at Jake and added in a quieter, more reasoned tone, 'So does parenthood – even adoptive parenthood – as you may yet discover.'

He saw the sudden dart of fear in her eyes and knew he had at last penetrated that ultra-reasonable exterior she held up to the world as the real Roseanne. 'Does the agony of it rouse nothing in you? Is there no other response within you – apart from this sneer that it leads to folly?'

She bit her lip but said nothing.

He scraped a good helping of ham on to his plate and soused it with pickles, making it seem that the questions had been merely rhetorical.

'Anyway,' she said guardedly, 'how did you come around to the truth in the end?'

He chuckled and, speaking round his mouthful with obvious relish, said, 'That was only last night – when Annette came bursting into my room with the news that Bodilly has moved into Vinery House with the merry widow Delamere.'

Roseanne's spoon went clattering to the floor. She paid it no heed. Jake began struggling to be let down – until he realized there was no resistance, anyway. 'Never!' Roseanne whispered, remembering how she and Annette had watched part of the preparations for the event.

She could see nothing but great black . . . it was like flying clouds of needles in front of her eyes. Her innards kept falling away inside her, endlessly falling. And she couldn't say a word because her mouth was just so dry.

27

The powers that be in Breage parish were, nominally, the parish councillors; in practice, it was their wives who determined what was what – the all-important Ladies Committee under its chairwoman, Lady Morvah. They also determined who was who. Among the poor, for instance, they separated the deserving, who qualified for private charitable relief in their own cottages, from the rest – who were therefore cast upon the cold mercy of the workhouse. And among themselves they separated those who were in from those who were out, or – an even more delicate discrimination – those who, having once been in, were no longer in that sublime state of grace.

May Delamere escaped the latter fate by an eyelash. Christmas Day that year fell upon a Sunday. When Mrs Haynes noted that she was missing from early communion and Miss Martin threw in the fact that the widow had taken a lodger – the handsome young Mark Bodilly, no less – storm cones were hoisted. Between then and matins the streets were swept bare by the hems of the scurrying great and virtuous as they passed to and from one another's houses.

Mrs Willoughby said, well, she herself had been thinking of doing just such a thing because what with all the miners made idle there was bound to be disaffection and no one would be safe in their beds and it was all very well for those with big manly husbands to make innuendoes but a defenceless woman on her own was quite another matter . . .

Mrs Trent said surely it all depended on how May Delamere comported herself in future. After all, she *was* a widow; and she *had* been left without a penny *and* with four daughters under the age of eighteen to get off her hands; and she had managed the task supremely well — thanks to which she now enjoyed independent means once again. If anyone was entitled to a little understanding . . .

Miss Marchmain said indeed, indeed, times *were* changing.

Miss Fryer said it was an out-and-out scandal. One could not touch pitch without being defiled. The ladies of Breage should immediately cease all intercourse with the scarlet woman. She certainly intended doing so. The others said nothing as to this, though many privately wondered how she intended to make Mrs D. aware of her ostracism, since she had not communicated with the woman in years — not since Susan Delamere, the scarlet woman's eldest, had married Argus Nicholl of Antron, who, everybody said, would be a bishop one day and at whom Miss Fryer had once set her cap.

Mrs Deakin, a widow herself, said it would be rather strange to cut May Delamere and yet go on accepting hospitality from Fenella Morgan when they all knew that while she'd been 'housekeeper' to the late Mr Liggat of Liston Court she'd kept all her costumes in his bedroom wardrobe and everyone knew what had been going on between them.

Mrs Trent said that was just her point. The maid at Liston Court had taken a pot of tea to Mrs Morgan's bedroom early every morning and always found her there, even if the bed did look rather pristine and feel quite cold. Mrs Morgan knew how to manage the whole business with decorum; she never made an open gesture of intimacy and was the soul of propriety on all public occasions. May Delamere should now be given a chance to show the same genteel discretion.

The last word on the matter lay, naturally, with Lady Morvah, who had returned home only the previous night, since when, of course, the excitements of the murder and the hunt for the villain had occupied most of her attention; but when dear Mrs Lanyon of Parc-an-Ython sent her a hastily scribbled note, telling her what machinations were afoot in the village, she turned her mind to the new dilemma. In the normal run of things she could have given the answer out of hand. A widow who has done her duty by society and who has reached the age of discretion should be given every chance to show that she knows how to use its unspoken privileges. However, the beneficiary of the said privileges on this particular occasion was the beau of the belle who had cast such a dire shadow upon the life of her ladyship's own son. It was an intractable problem. She discussed it with her daughter, in a manner of speaking, in the carriage on their way to church that same morning. Her manner of speaking was to address all her remarks to her husband, who said yes and no and made what he supposed were helpful comments, as appropriate; Annette merely sat beside him and listened, knowing her turn would come.

'You see, my dear,' she said, 'if we put it to Mrs Delamere that she must choose between her continued acceptance among us and this Bodilly person, I'm sure she'll show him the door,' she said.

Grunt.

'Which would suit us admirably. It might then encourage the man to take up with the Kitto gel again

219

— which, in turn, might bring the boy to his senses. Where *is* he, by the way?'

'He went out for a walk earlier,' Annette told her. 'He said he'd meet us at church.'

'A walk!' her mother said heavily.

The girl nodded.

'Oh dear, oh dear! What have we done to deserve such vexations?'

'Fishin',' Sir Francis said firmly.

'I beg your pardon, dear?' his wife replied.

'Too much fishin'. Solitary pursuit. No harm in the occasional spot of it, don't you know, but needs a judicious mixture of companionable sport as well — shootin' and huntin', what? The boy never struck the right balance. That's where he went off the rails.'

By long habit Lady Morvah contained her impatience. 'There's a great deal of truth in that, dear. However, I don't think we should write him off as already having passed beyond the pale — especially as he is the third in the entail and will inherit the whole estate outright one day.'

'He's insane,' Sir Francis said morosely.

She sighed. '*I* know that, and so do you. But for every doctor we found who'd agree with us, there'd be three who wouldn't. We've been through all that. There's not the slightest hope of getting him certified so we must somehow persuade him to drop all this madness quite voluntarily.'

'Send him away. Buy him a commission in the Duke of Cornwall's.'

Another sigh, even deeper. 'One can no longer buy commissions, dear. We asked, you remember? And he won't go away of his own accord. And we have no way of forcing him.' She tapped her forehead crossly. 'Besides, none of this helps *me* decide what

220

to do about May Delamere. That's our immediate concern.'

'Buy off the Kitto girl,' was his final shot as they laboured up the hill to the south of the church. 'You can't cut a widow for taking in a lodger — as long as she doesn't frighten the horses. I doubt she's ever seen a hundred guineas all at once.'

'Mrs Delamere?'

'No! The Kitto. Buy her off.'

They arrived at the church gate. 'You go on in, dear,' she told him. 'I need Annette to help me adjust this dress.'

'Well?' she asked her daughter when he had gone. The incongruity of it, that she, the queen bee of the district, should consult her young daughter on a matter of such delicacy, did not strike her; she had long ago realized that Annette was no ordinary young miss.

'Stephen would only run off with Roseanne,' was the calm reply.

Her mother nodded glumly. 'And there's no point in asking what they'd live on — he could borrow all they wanted on the strength of his expectations. Yes, I can just see it happening.'

'I can't.'

Lady Morvah glanced at her sharply. 'Why ever not?'

'She wouldn't let him. Earning is all she thinks of. She could never tolerate a debt.'

'Earning?' Her mother spoke the word as if it were slightly indelicate — certainly alien and suspect. 'But what could the boy possibly earn *at*?'

Annette made a gesture of ignorance. 'She'd think of something. He could join old man Kitto's new business and go round drumming up trade for them. His name would open doors that Kitto wouldn't get a toecap through.'

221

Annette did not actually believe what she was saying, but some instinct informed her she would do well to turn her mother's disquiet to something nearer panic – in which, she certainly succeeded. Then, as if it were not nightmare enough already, she added, 'And if the worst came to the worst, he could always become a teacher.'

It was the most miserable Christmas service Lady Morvah could ever remember. To crown it all, Stephen came late, during the first hymn, and, rather than disturb the congregation, slipped into one of the pews at the back, where – Lord, what a surprise – the Kitto creature just happened to be sitting with the murdered woman's brat on her lap. Annette had told her the complete tale of it last night. No doubt Miss Kitto was very noble to give the child a home over Christmas but, in her ladyship's opinion, it was a little *de trop* to flaunt her charity so publicly. Humble people should hide their light under a bushel as the Bible commanded. Instead here was the woman letting it shine out over the parish as if . . . well, as if she were already the squire's wife, frankly. And now there was Stephen adding colour to the masquerade!

It so vexed her that when May Delamere approached her after the service, looking so radiant and with such a friendly smile, she quite forgot that any question mark hung over the woman and responded in like vein.

Mrs Haynes, Miss Martin, Mrs Willoughby, Mrs Trent, Miss Marchmain, and Mrs Deakin, to name but half a dozen, saw that judgement had been cast and pressed forward to signal their delighted acceptance of the new situation at Vinery House.

Miss Fryer alone withheld her accolade but she was not so incautious as to mention anything remotely connected with the colour scarlet. All through the service she had cast about as inconspicuously as possible to see

222

where Bodilly might be seated, if, indeed, he was in church at all. To her chagrin she found him at last, two seats behind his former sweetheart, Roseanne Kitto, and twenty pews distant from his new paramour. And after the service, all during the ten minutes it required for the chattering little groups to break up and go their ways, there was not so much as a glance between them. Quite clearly they were going to behave impeccably in public. The uphill labours Miss Fryer had espied ahead of her were turning into an ascent of Everest. The wretched man even had the impudence to approach his old belle, the Kitto girl, smiling as if all that were still . . . Ha! There was some small consolation at least — for whatever his opening pleasantry, she quite clearly put a flea in his ear!

'How could 'ee?' Roseanne asked vehemently, glancing about to see how much she dared raise her voice.

'What now?' Mark asked in wounded bewilderment.

Stephen cleared his throat and said, 'I'll just go and explain matters to my parents.'

The moment he had gone, Roseanne made for the north gate, saying to Mark as she passed, 'You may walk along of I a bit.'

'I shan't,' he muttered.

She turned and stared back at him until he followed; he caught up with her opposite the inn, where they were just taking down the shutters.

'You want a glass of ale, do 'ee?' he asked awkwardly.

'I've never taken liquor in this parish, as well you know,' she replied. 'How could you, Mark? How *could* you?'

He stared at the sky, avoiding the high escallonia hedge around Vinery House. 'I suppose you do know what you're gassing on about, for I'm blessed if I do.'

As they passed the gate, portions of the façade slipped across their view. 'Which is *her* bedroom?' she asked.

Jake crooked his finger at the annexe. 'Yes,' she told him, 'you were a very good boy in church. I was proud of you.'

'That one up there.' Mark pointed at the main house.

'You don't even try to deny it!'

'What? That I know Widow Delamere's bedroom? Seeing as I patched the slates over it, I should hope I wasn't losing my memory that badly!'

'She's old enough to be your mother!' Roseanne almost withered the words with her scorn.

But he, knowing she'd find no chink in his armour no matter how many darts she let fly, responded mildly, 'A landlady is a kind of mother to her lodgers, so there's no harm in that.'

Sergeant Evans came round the corner at that moment. 'Ah, Miss Kitto,' he called out. 'The very person! The Falmouth constabulary have sent to say they've an eye on three possible villains but they can't make no arrest without a better description. I don't suppose you remembered nothing else, did 'ee? Only what you said was burr and vague.'

'No!' Roseanne replied, crossly at first; then she repeated the word in a more conciliatory tone. 'No, I'm sorry, Sergeant Evans. I'll have another talk with Miss Morvah. She saw the man, too, I think — perhaps if we can jog each other's memories . . .'

The sergeant said he'd be grateful, only time was short.

After a few paces in silence, Mark said, 'Anyway, what's it to you if I choose to lodge along of Widow Delamere?'

She shifted Jake on to her other hip and speaking to

the road directly before them, said in a flat tone, 'Because I do love 'ee, that's what.'

'Oh,' he replied.

'That all you got to say?'

He sniffed, taken aback. 'Well, 'tin't the first time, like, you told I, that is it!'

''Tis the first time *after* I thought I loved another.'

He tugged at the point of his beard, twirling and untwirling it.

'It do make a difference,' she added.

'I suppose so.'

'Don't it!' she insisted.

'I already said yes.' He cleared his throat hesitantly. 'What do 'ee want, then?'

'Get married,' she said at once. 'If there's nothing between you and old Widow Delamere and she's only doing it for the rent, she won't mind the extra income.'

He walked on in silence.

'Unless there *is* something,' she added.

'No!' he assured her.

'That's all right then,' she said happily. 'We may put up the banns next Sunday.'

'And what about Stephen Morvah?'

'He's a nice enough fellow, but' — she slipped her one free arm through his — 'he's no Mark Bodilly.'

He drew a deep breath; she risked a glance and saw him smiling broadly. An enormous wave of relief passed over her. She *did* love him after all. Her brief flirtation with Stephen had only confirmed it for her. He had been her sweetheart since she was fourteen. They had so much love and companionship invested in each other — too much to squander in silly bickering. From now on, whenever her love for him was challenged, she'd remember Stephen, what a good man he was — what a worthy rival to Mark indeed – and yet how, in the end, he had not been worthy enough.

She was just about to tell Mark all this when he said, 'You've got the wrong idea about she, about Widow Delamere, maid.'

'How?'' she asked warily.

'I'd have gone mad if I hadn't been able to talk to she – like a mother, just like you said.'

'What about?'

'Feelings and that.' He made several more attempts to speak and then gave up.

'You can talk to she but not me,' Roseanne observed.

He nodded. ''Cos she's more like a stranger. I don't mean she haven't got no sympathy, mind, but . . .' More silence.

'So . . .' Roseanne spoke hesitantly '. . . she's, er, soft-hearted, really?'

'Very. She surprised me, 'cos she don't look it, I admit.'

'And fond of 'ee, like a mother?'

'Exactly!' He was delighted she understood at last. 'She never had but daughters, you remember. That's where it's to – her being so fond of me. She never had no son of her own.'

'Nor grandson, neither,' she said gaily, hefting Jake higher on to her hip. 'What's she going to say to my little fellow, here? *Our* little fellow, now!'

He came to a sudden halt. 'What?' he asked incredulously, looking first at her then at Jake.

She walked on for several paces. 'Our little fellow,' she repeated over her shoulder. But her smile was beginning to fade.

He shook his head. 'I aren't having that,' he told her. 'You never said nothing about that.'

She turned and stood her ground, hugging the boy

tightly to her, cheek-to-cheek, two pale green eyes and two of dazzling blue, beseeching him.

'You never said that,' he repeated.

'I never thought I needed to.'

He gave out a bitter laugh. 'Oh, I see your game now! The wonderful Mr Stephen Morvah took one look at the babby and said no thanks very much! So now you think you'll come back to I and twist I into accepting . . . the brat! You must think my brains have addled since we parted ways.'

'Hah!' she exploded in triumph. 'You couldn't never be more wrong. *Mister* Stephen Morvah kept away from I for weeks, ever since he saw you and me dancing on Breage side that day. 'Twas Jake here brought him back to me. When he heard about the boy he come and offered his hand in marriage and a home for the babby.' She stamped angrily back up the road, the way they had just come. Passing him she said, without turning her head, 'That's the measure of a real man, Mark. He do make you look no taller than a worm.'

Ten yards past him she turned and called back, 'You've found your level all right − an old woman who's got no choice but to thank God for small mercies, no matter how small!'

After ten more paces she cast one final pearl. 'I was only testing of 'ee, anyroad − which shows me up for the fool I am!'

His complete lack of response, either by word or gesture, unnerved her. She spun angrily on her heel and resumed her walk back to the church. All the way she tried desperately to shut out a nagging little voice within her, telling her it wished what she had said was true − about only testing him.

How easy it would then be for her to make the urgent choices that now faced her!

28

Roseanne lifted Jake into the gig. Her father grumbled that they'd have to go the long way round because of the extra weight. She made no reply. He couldn't even bring himself to hold the child, she thought bitterly, just to steady him while she climbed aboard. Her mother, divided equally between a desire for her daughter's happiness and her husband's (and, to be honest, her own) desire *not* to have the house turned upside down by Jake for the next God-knows-how-many years, watched miserably from the upstairs window.

A moment later, still with no word spoken, they were off.

At least if they went the long way round, they wouldn't be passing Vinery House. Merely to go into the village had become a test of her nerves. The sight of that place, so smug behind its high, all-concealing hedge, would rouse her anger. The lace curtains were enough to suggest that what went on behind them was not for the eyes of curious outsiders; the heavy velvet ones the Old Widow drew at dusk hinted at greater iniquities yet; and that extra bulwark against the prying eyes of the world seemed to confirm that it went beyond all imagining. And the smugness of it all taunted her with the fact that there was nothing she could do about it. Not a thing.

How curious that she had never seen the place in that

light before. Until now Vinery House had seemed no more than a rather sad, shy, withdrawn sort of dwelling – the sort where, if someone whispered to you that they kept a mad old granny locked up in the attic, you'd easily credit it.

'I got better things to do with my time,' her father mumbled as, at the last minute, he hauled the pony round on to the shorter road, even though it would mean negotiating the steep valley between Breage and Sithney. 'I'll walk up Trelissick hill,' he added. ''Twill still be quicker.'

As they passed Vinery House, Roseanne saw Mark up on the roof of the annexe, standing over a chimney pot and making a long arm into it to fish out an old rook's nest. When he saw them, he stopped and stared – rather bashfully, she thought. 'You putting the boy to Helston Union, are 'ee?' he called out.

''Es,' her father replied. 'Good riddance to 'n.'

'Happy now?' Roseanne added.

'There's a thing I wanted to tell 'ee about that,' he replied.

Two lunchtime revellers, straight from the pub, walked an uncertain line between them and the gate. When they saw Mark up on the roof, one of them called out, 'How are 'ee standing all alone up there, then, boy? I heard tell as there's work for chimney sweeps next door!' The remark struck them as the height of wit and they collapsed alternately on each other's shoulders all the way to the corner.

'What?' Roseanne called out.

Jake caught the infection of laughter and pointed a bent finger at Mark.

'What did 'ee want to say?' she prompted.

But he was too angry to speak; he turned his back on them and plunged his arm deep into the chimney

229

flue. A moment later the all-obscuring hedge came between them.

Work for chimney sweeps! she thought. She had occasionally heard the phrase, never dreaming it had such a connotation.

'That's what people are saying,' her father commented drily.

'Chimney sweep!' she replied bitterly. 'If 'tis true, 'tis black work right enough.'

'The man's a fool. I never thought him other.'

'Father! You told me he was the smartest man you . . .'

'Smart, yes, that I'll grant. He's smart as new snow. Clever. But he's one of they smart, clever *fools*. That's what he is. Taking up with a lawdydaw widow-woman like she! Where's that going to lead?' He glanced at her sidelong. 'You still feel a bit . . . *hurrisome*, like, for he, do 'ee?'

'Bit,' she confessed reluctantly. 'I felt for sure he'd give Jake and I a home, but he never even thought about it. He just took fire. He's so quick to get maggoty.'

He reached over and patted her hand. 'You're best off out of all that. A maggoty man – or woman – is a heller.' When she said nothing to that he risked adding, 'And you're best off without this encumbrance, too, maid. The lad'll do well enough in the Union. Look at Tom Hampden, who do work for I over to Mrs Scawen's cliff garden. Proper 'ansum fellow, he is, and he was ten year in that place.'

Roseanne thought of asking what age the man had been when they took him in; but she knew it would do no good. They had ruined Boxing Day with that sort of argument. She glanced at Jake and smiled, rather wanly, though it was the best she could manage. He knew, of course – not what was going to happen to him but that some misery was on its way and that he was caught up in it. How desperately she had hugged him to her all through last night. How she had wept, and tried to keep him from realizing it. How she had racked her brains for some way of keeping the boy, and not ruining Stephen's life – and her own. But nothing had occurred to her. Her dreams of being a public teacher and being allowed to keep a child not her own were – as in her heart of hearts she had always known – quite idle. All she could do now was sit back in some fatalistic way and hope for a miracle.

Instead, what she got was Annette Morvah. As they drove out past Sethnoe gate, she came cantering up behind them and reined back to a walk as she drew level. 'Phew!' she cried out, 'I thought it was you when I saw you go past the church.'

Roseanne knew at once that she had been waiting to waylay them down on the main road.

'Good afternoon, Mr Kitto,' she went on cheerfully. 'D'you mind if I walk with you a bit? What a lovely day after the storms last night.'

He tipped the brim of his hat, lazily rather than respectfully. 'Afternoon, Miss Morvah. Always pleased for a bit of bright company.'

'It will help the road rise to meet you, as my old Irish nanny used to say.'

'What's that mean?' Roseanne asked.

Annette laughed. 'I haven't the faintest idea. Something to do with their drinking habits, I suppose.'

Frank laughed loudly. Jake, always drawn to laughter, squeezed between him and Roseanne and clutched his arm. Brusquely Frank jerked his arm away. Roseanne saw Annette's sharp eyes taking the whole thing in. 'Come to Rosie.' She put her arm round the boy. 'Don't bother that old bear.'

For some reason Annette shook her head disapprovingly at this quite natural response. But she said nothing. Indeed, she chatted on about this and that, nothing of consequence, all the way down into the valley bottom. There Frank passed the reins to his daughter and said gruffly, 'I'd best get out and walk, I suppose.'

In the corner of her eye she saw Annette shaking her head vehemently. On impulse she threw the reins back into her father's hands and jumped down before he could protest, saying, 'I'm as able to walk as you.'

When the trap started up the steep incline Jake clutched again at Frank's sleeve, and again was fended off. 'If any harm befalls that mite,' Roseanne shouted after them, 'I'll never forgive 'ee.'

Reluctantly he pulled Jake back to his side and let him hold his sleeve.

Meanwhile Annette had slipped down from her saddle and was standing, waiting at the bottom of the rise. When Roseanne drew level she linked arms with her and fell in step, leading the horse on a long rein to let him walk on the soft verge at their side. 'You really want to keep the little fellow?' she asked. 'It's a different tune from last Saturday.'

'He's a different boy from last Saturday, too.'

'But can't you also see your parents' point of view?'

They both began to pant as the slope took its toll of their stamina.

'I asked Mark would he marry I and give the lad a home.'

She felt the girl give a start. 'But what about Stephen?'

'He would, of course. But I don't want to ruin his life, too.'

'Because you love him? Or why?'

232

'I love both of them. Or I don't know who I love. I don't know what love is no more.'

They had just rounded the first corner of the hill. Annette nudged her and pointed at the trap ahead. Only the stark silhouette of her father's back was visible.

'Where's Jake?' Roseanne asked in a sudden panic.

The girl laughed. 'Can't you guess? He's on your father's lap, holding the reins.'

Roseanne gave a chuckle of disbelief but said nothing.

'Why d'you think your father's so short with the boy?' Annette went on. 'Why does he shake him off so quickly?'

'He says he can't abide him.'

Annette merely sighed and said, 'Well, well.'

Roseanne wondered if the girl really was as superior and all-knowing as she liked people to think. It was so easy to gain that reputation if you never actually said anything but just confined yourself to knowing smiles and vague comments like, 'well, well!'

'We're putting he to Helston Union,' she explained.

'So I supposed. If your father said you could keep the boy, what would . . .'

'He won't do no such thing, so there's no point even asking.'

'Bear with me. Just suppose. What would you do about him? How would you live?'

Once again Roseanne felt herself being overwhelmed by the girl. It didn't matter whether her all-knowing air were truly deserved or just cleverly contrived, it gave her a power that was hard to resist. 'What's it to you, anyway?' she asked gruffly.

The hill was no less steep but they were beginning to get second wind – which was more than could be said for the horse, who now began to drag. Annette clucked him some encouragement and then said to Roseanne,

'D'you know, that's the first sign of sense in you since last Saturday.'

'What?'

'Asking what it is to me. It's the first sign that you're trying to see this affair from some other point of view than your own.'

'Go on,' Roseanne said cautiously — thinking how often that emotion cropped up in her conversations with this young lady.

'D'you want me to tell you everything? There's just time between here and the hilltop. I think I'm going to have to, anyway.'

'I've nothing better to do at the moment.' Roseanne felt herself warming to the girl against her will; it was almost as if she had said, 'Come sit here by me and I'll tell you a tale full of wonders.'

'What does life hold in store for me?' Annette said. 'Precious little! Anything connected with agriculture looks like a high road to ruin — which means that nine-tenths of Cornwall's eligible bachelors will be wanting a goodly dowry before they'll even look at a girl. But there's no question of a settlement for me. And my father will leave nothing but debts, so no settlement, either. I've a good enough income for one, but it's all tied up. And tightly, too.' As with so many of Annette's explanations, this was indeed almost half true.

'Mr Right will surely come along,' Roseanne offered.

Annette looked at her pityingly. 'That's the way you go about managing your whole life, isn't it! Something will turn up!' She shook her head and went on in a milder tone: 'I've read too many romances to believe that. No, there *must* be a dowry.'

'But how?'

Now Annette's eyes brimmed with amusement. 'Can't you guess? Isn't it obvious?'

234

'Sell Montpelier? No one's living there.'

'That would only pay the debt. We shall have to do it one day, of course, but it won't be enough. No, the only answer is — Stephen must sell Skyburriowe. Father can't. Stevie's the only one who can, legally.'

'Just to help you!'

The sarcasm drew nothing but Annette's scornful: 'No! Do you still not understand? How do I get my own way — and I always do get my own way? I see to it that other people get theirs as well. If I can, of course. Usually I can't, because I'm only me. So I have to bide my time and wait for the right moment. But I think it's come at last. I never knew so many . . . I mean, it's all bubbling to the top at once. Too soon, perhaps. For me, anyway. But that's better than too late.'

'I wish I knew what you're on about,' Roseanne complained.

'Opportunity. Tell me — d'you believe Stephen will make a good squire of Skyburriowe? If we don't agree on that, there's no point in . . .'

'I said that before, didn't I? Didn't you ask me that already? Anyway, I don't. He's too soft and too decent.'

'Good. So, if you were married to him, you wouldn't want to . . .'

'I told 'ee,' Roseanne interrupted again. 'I aren't going to spoil his life.'

'And that's what I want to talk to you about. If you and he were married, you'd be much happier to have him doing something else, rather than be squire?'

Roseanne agreed reluctantly, just for argument's sake.

'What?' Annette snapped, taking her by surprise.

When Roseanne merely stammered and said she'd never thought about it much, the girl's scorn redoubled.

'Well, think about it now,' she suggested. 'Wouldn't he make a good working partner for your father? Father and son-in-law. Stephen's a superb angler, you know. He has all the right instincts for it . . . patience, cunning . . . he can keep a secret . . . knows just how to play all the different fish. I think he might find an excellent outlet for his talents in a business like your father's.'

Roseanne stopped in her tracks and stared at the girl. How could a chit of a thing like that, just short of eighteen − how could she see things so clearly? And be so *right*! The moment she heard the suggestion every particle in her rose and cried out 'Yes!' She had never encountered anything before that hit the nail so absolutely on the head. How could the girl do that?

Because she took the trouble to *think*, Roseanne told herself caustically. You couldn't say she had no feelings about it. In fact, she was consumed with feelings. But she also knew how to put them on one side, so as to let herself think.

Roseanne shook her head as if to clear it. 'Just suppose,' she said, 'grant all that . . . I mean, that wouldn't mean he'd have to sell Skyburriowe.'

Annette took her arm again and they resumed their slow, uphill plod. 'You'd be amazed what you hear out foxhunting,' she replied. 'People pay no attention to a little girl milling around on her horse while they're drawing a covert. They talk away as if she's just not there. You know that Mr Vyvyan, Abraham Vyvyan, who's manager of Bolitho's Bank in Helston? You'll hear people say what's a man like that doing, hunting two full days a week? How can Colonel Bolitho permit such laxity? Well, I promise you, he gets in more trade for Bolitho's in those two days than he gets in a month when the season ends. And it cuts both ways. I sometimes think the hunt would collapse if he weren't there. Half the field only turns out so as to get the chance to sidle up to him at a draw and ask for a renewal on their bills, or for credit for some new business idea. The things I could tell you about the mercantile "gentry" in West Penwith! Anyway, one thing that's no secret is that *every* business is *always* short of the old spundulicks. Your father's will be no exception. If Stephen becomes a partner, he'll look at the glittering ventures you could be undertaking if only you had the money, and he'll look at the millstone of Skyburriowe, and he won't be able to sell it fast enough.' She laughed and hugged Roseanne's arm tight to her. 'Now you're going to think me truly dreadful, but if you could manage to stave off that point for, say, two or three years? That would suit me best.'

Roseanne's laugh was mildly embarrassed. 'But your father,' she objected. 'I mean . . . surely Stephen won't be able to sell it while Sir Francis survives.'

Annette was still laughing. 'Don't go jumping to conclusions now! When I say dreadful I don't mean *that* dreadful. But it will take my father a little time to see the wisdom of passing the estate on to Stephen pre- rather than post-humously. Can one say *pre*humously? You know what I mean, anyway.'

Roseanne was intrigued. 'Could he do that? I never thought such a thing possible.'

'According to Mr Coad, who has handled more inheritances than any other lawyer in Helston, I should think.'

'You asked him?' Roseanne asked in amazement.

Annette smiled. 'If he ever asks you how my romance is coming along, by the way, tell him . . .'

'What romance?'

'The one he imagines I'm writing. It's amazing what people will tell you if they think it's for a book, which

237

they wouldn't dream of saying if they thought it was just out of childish curiosity.'

Her use of the word childish made Roseanne think back to the time when she taught Annette at the village school. She had surely been a child then, hadn't she? There was no hint that she'd turn into this scheming, precocious young hoyden? All she could remember was a rather solemn, self-contained little girl with large, staring eyes. You never had to tell her off, nor correct her for the same mistake twice, in spelling or arithmetic, for instance. Yes, she certainly had been a solemn one. At the time Roseanne had ascribed that to the girl's rather solitary life, mingling with no children of her own age, only grown-ups, at the big house; now she considered the same cause might better explain her present personality.

'Have you talked any of this over with Stephen?' she asked at length.

For a while Annette just stared at her, as if sizing her up; then, breaking into a slow grin, she said, 'I shall if you don't, of course.'

They were approaching the top of the hill by now, almost within earshot of her father, who had reined in at Trelissick gate and put Jake firmly back on the seat at his side. 'What's my next step, I wonder?' Roseanne mused aloud.

'I think,' Annette replied in a low, measured tone, 'that when we get to Helston you should let your father know you can't bear to go another yard and that if he's determined to see it through, he must hand Jake over by himself.'

'And he'll surely do it,' Roseanne objected. 'He wouldn't think twice.'

Annette stopped and asked to be helped back up into the saddle. Roseanne plucked a handful of grass to keep the mud off her gloves and then cupped her hands for Annette's boot — all of which gave them time to complete the plan.

'He'll surely do it if you *are* there,' Annette pointed out. 'You've made it a matter of his pride. You left him no choice.'

'Will you go with him?'

'Of course.'

A strange sense of relief overcame Roseanne. If Annette took charge, somehow it would work out all right. But in its wake came the contrary emotion: If she resigned her control of affairs like that, it would happen again and again, each time more easily and more completely, until the girl was running her entire life. 'How will you talk he out of it?' she asked.

'I shan't even try.' Annette seemed surprised at the question. 'Jake will. I mean perhaps he will. I can't promise. But haven't you watched them together?'

It was no good. Even though she knew that the girl was manipulating her every move, and all in the interests of Miss Annette Morvah not of Roseanne Kitto, she felt control ebbing from her. 'And what do I do for half an hour, kicking my heels in Helston?' she asked. 'I'd go mad.'

Annette gave the matter some thought. Then, as if the notion had only just crossed her mind, she said, 'I know! You could call on Lawyer Scawen and find out how best to go about adopting an orphan.'

29

When Roseanne made all that fuss about not being able
to go another yard, Annette volunteered to take her
place. She left her horse stabled at the Angel Hotel and
— literally — took Roseanne's place beside Mr Kitto.
Jake, as treacherous as any of that age, never gave a
backward glance, happy as a sandboy with his new
minder.

Roseanne watched them all the way up Meneage
Street, wondering if she'd ever see the lad again, biting
her lip to hold back the tears. Then, rather than watch
them until they vanished altogether from sight, she
turned resolutely into Wendron Street and set off for
Lawyer Scawen's office, praying only that he was there
and would have time to see her.

'I can't understand anyone wanting *boys*, can you,
Mr Kitto?' Annette spoke the word as if it were
inherently nauseous. 'Such hard, knobbly, awkward
things. And so full of violence and aggression. When
I marry I want nothing but girls.'

He grunted.

'Still,' she babbled on happily, 'they knock the
stuffing out of them in *that* place right enough!' She
gave Jake a friendly tickle under the chin. He had a most
appealing laugh. 'Ho ho,' she teased. 'Laugh while you
may, little chap! If you knew what's in store for *you*,
just minutes away, too — why, I think you'd sooner

throw yourself under this trap than go another pace.'
She concluded with a tinkling laugh that induced
another burst of merriment from the lad.

Mr Kitto shook the reins angrily. 'Two days in the
stall and this fellow's forgotten how to pull,' he
grumbled.

She let the observation sink in a brief silence and then
continued: 'I told Roseanne she must be out of her mind
to want to take on this burden. Granted he's an amiable
little thing but he's obviously feeble minded.'

Mr Kitto darted a surprised and venomous glance her
way. 'Feeble minded?' he echoed.

'Oh, I think so. Look at his eyes.'

Rashly he obeyed, only to be discomfited by their
limpid friendliness and trust. 'Don't see nothing feeble
minded there,' he muttered as he returned his gaze to
the way ahead.

The horse had slowed once again but, Annette
noticed, he did nothing to make it hasten.

'At least he's not deformed,' she said, adding, after
a brief silence, 'but he's bad seed. Or so I gather. Mary
Williams — she wasn't much to be proud of, was she.'

He made a dubious noise in his throat.

'Of course, I hardly knew her. She was a class or two
ahead of me.'

'She weren't such a bad little maid, as I recall. And
her father, now, he was a burr fine fellow. Albert
Williams. One of the best tributers in the whole district.
When he died, now, that's when little Mary went to the
bad. Her mother married again, see. Some rough old
fellow from up Crowntown. After that she turned into
some wild cat. He used to beat she black and blue, but
it never made no difference. You couldn't hold she after
that.'

Annette drew a deep breath and risked saying, 'So

241

would Jake have any cousins or anything like that? Where did Mary's father come from — her real father?'

'Why, his family had a farm over Goldsithney, I believe.'

'*Had* a farm?'

'They sold up years ago and went to America. I believe there's a brother there still, a brother to old Albert.'

'Jake's uncle, in other words.'

''Es, that's what he'd be.'

'A farmer?'

'Not really. He's got a few acres like me but he do earn his bread in Leedstown mill.'

'Perhaps he'd be willing to take little Jake into his own household. Is he married?'

''Es, I believe he is. Married a girl from up Nancegollan. Martha Chigwidden.'

'And have they any children?' It was like squeezing wine out of granite — but she hoped she knew the cause of his reluctance to speak without prompting.

'They got a boy, about ten, but they never had no more.'

'At least we can let him know about Jake.' She looked at the lowering sun. 'Too late today but I can ride over there tomorrow morning. Leedstown mill, eh?' She turned to the lad. 'You hear that, Jake? You may not have to cast yourself under a cartwheel after all! Oh dear! If you could only understand what I'm saying, you'd be ever so much happier tonight than I fear you will be.' She looked about them and chided, in the same maddeningly bright tone, 'Well, here we are then, safely delivered to the gates of hell!'

The pony sauntered to a stop. Mr Kitto stared at his knuckles, saw a thorn in his skin, and tried unsuccessfully to draw it with a battered thumbnail.

242

'Well, well, well, Mr Kitto!'

They looked up to see Mr Hourican, the workhouse master, striding jovially down the sloping front drive to meet them. 'I had a feeling I'd be seeing you before too long.'

Mr Kitto glanced at Jake and nodded unhappily.

'But you're here even sooner than that!' Hourican added.

The sentiment did not entirely accord with his earlier comment − or, at least, with what Frank had inferred from it. 'How's that, then?' he asked in puzzlement.

But Hourican had turned his back on them to berate a young workhouse boy for idling − a hatchet-faced lad, all soap-shiny skin and bone, shivering in thin flannel clothes three sizes too big for him while he struggled to pull weeds from among the severely regimented rose shrubs that garlanded the entrance in summer. It did not help that he seemed to have a large, septic gash in his left hand, between thumb and forefinger.

'Go on, you great bag of idle bones!' the master yelled. 'There's no meat for you till you've cleared it all, right up to the gate.'

He turned back to them with an apologetic smile. 'There's no point pulling weeds this weather, I know,' he explained, 'but the stupid oaf put a hatchet through his hand before Christmas, chopping kindling. There's no other employment for him.' He rubbed his hands and became brisk again. 'Well, Mr Kitto, that's where our new walls are to go − from the road up to that corner, and from the other corner down to the road again. What d'you think? The board is most sensitive to recent criticisms in our ill-informed Liberal press. They desire to give the place an altogether grander appearance, without' − he laid a gentle stress upon the

243

word and touched the side of his nose – 'bankrupting themselves, if you take my meaning?'

Frank descended from his trap and passed the reins to Annette. Then he went off with the master to walk the line of the wall and discuss at their leisure how to please the guardians – without depriving themselves of their own just rewards.

Annette took Jake on her lap and, holding his little hands in hers, showed him how to cross his fingers. 'This is all we can do at such a time, little thing,' she told him.

The conference went for quite a while. Annette grew bored of the crossed-fingers game though Jake could have played it happily for hours. She tightened the brake a further notch and got down to give the pony his nosebag. Then, lifting the lad down on to the footpath, she wandered hand-in-hand with him, with no apparent aim in mind. She reached the boy with the cut in his hand just as the two men approached. She peered intently at the poor young fellow; he tried to look at her but seemed unable to focus his eyes on anything. A cold sweat beaded his brow.

She stared the master straight in the eye as she said, 'Hourican! This boy is ill. He has a fever.'

''Tis only the appearance of it, Miss Morvah. They're past masters at all such kinds of dissimulation.'

'No, Hourican,' she replied evenly, still not taking her eyes off him, 'he is ill.' She held her breath, not knowing whether he would let her carry it off. Sir Francis, who was Chairman of the Board of Guardians, would skin her alive to see her behaving so – but Hourican wasn't to know it.

She watched the calculations going on behind his eyes before he lowered them and, with his mouth pursed to a mere slit, said, 'As you say, Miss Morvah. I'll send

244

for Doctor Wilson directly. You, boy, go indoors now.'

The lad knew he was being addressed but the words had no meaning. He just stared at the master and gave out little placatory laughs, in case the man took it into his mind to deal out a few cuffs.

'The infirmary. I'll take him,' Annette volunteered. And before he could stop her she had seized the boy by the sleeve — the cleanest, or least dirty, bit of him on offer — and hurried him up the path to the gaunt granite building beyond the gate. 'Mr Kitto? If you'd be so kind?' She gave him a radiant smile — and Jake — as she passed.

The 'infirmary' was a single, cheerless room just to the right of the gate, so she was not away for long. The nurse was slightly sympathetic and slightly kind to her new patient. At least, Annette thought as she went outside again, it was better than outright coldness. She lingered just inside the gate, apparently reading the inscription in the foundation stone there. The two men had wandered a few paces up the path and were just within earshot; they seemed to be concluding a conversation on the terrors of bossy, interfering females. Then Hourican said. 'Well, and who's this little fellow, eh? That's a grand pair of boots on him. Not one for us, I'll wager!' He laughed immoderately.

Annette held her breath.

'Noooo,' Mr Kitto replied — the word seemed to be dragged from the tormented depths of him. ''Tis just some little cooze we're minding a day or two.'

30

Vosper Scawen saw at once that Kitto's daughter was in something of a state, and, though he was in the middle of drafting a complicated settlement for an impatient client in the village of Gweek, he had her shown into his office at once. She said it was very kind of him to give her his time so readily. He replied that she could have no idea of the tedium of a lawyer's average day and that it was always a pleasure to see her because she brought him *real* issues for his advice. And how many thousand pounds did she have to invest this time?

Roseanne began to cry.

He shed his jocularity at once, gave her a clean silk handkerchief, pressed her arm reassuringly, and placed a small glass of madeira within convenient reach. She took a hold of herself and, haltingly, told him the entire story. By the time she finished she was calm once again, and would have felt ashamed of her outburst if he were not so kind and sympathetic. She expected him to answer her question about adoption at once but instead he said, 'The only person who can decide what's best for Stephen Morvah is Stephen Morvah, you know. And the same is true for you: Only you can decide what's best for Roseanne Kitto. It sounds very selfish, I know, but it's the way we all work.'

He clasped his hands together and leaned forward

over the desk, smiling at her while he let his words sink in. Then he prompted her: 'So let's ask what is best for Roseanne Kitto? If you can live independently, you could foster the infant on your own. I'm sure you don't need me to tell you how fraught with difficulty such a course would be. If you can't live independently and yet feel unable to yield up the lad, you have three choices. You can seek to change your father's mind. You can make your peace with Mr Bodilly — and change his mind, too. Or you can go for the downhill run.'

She gave him her first smile since entering his office. 'Stephen,' she said. 'But I'm not sure I love him.'

'Ah!' He waited for more.

She stared out of the window in mild embarrassment. 'I'm sorry, Mr Scawen. This isn't really legal business. I shouldn't ought to take up your time.'

He nodded sadly and replied, 'Yes, in a way, it's putting me *out* of business. I'll sell you an ounce of prevention and cheat myself out of a ton of cure! Is there anyone else you could talk this over with? Your mother, perhaps?'

She shook her head. 'I don't want she to take sides. I keep thinking about that poor little mite in the workhouse tonight.' Tears began to well again.

'You're very considerate. Perhaps a comparative stranger, then? Who can I suggest?' He closed his eyes and scratched his head. 'Do you know Mrs Moore of Lanfear? I'm sure you know *of* her. She's a most approachable woman, and a wise one, too. You won't get a pat answer from her, straight out of *The Ladies' Drawing Room Companion* — I'm sure you know what that august publication would advise!'

Roseanne smiled again and the danger of fresh tears receded.

247

Scawen continued 'She was most helpful to my wife around the time her father died.' A new thought struck him. 'Indeed, my wife might suit you better — being somewhat closer to you in age? If you'd rather take it out of the parish altogether and yet keep it within the family, so to speak? Think it over, anyway. Don't decide now.'

Roseanne said it was more than kind of him, but it was Jake that occupied her mind at the moment — Jake and how best to care for him.

He became rather grave, warning her to expect little comfort. The law, he said, had nothing to offer her or Jake in their present situation.

'But what about adoption?' she asked.

He shook his head. 'There's no such thing, I'm afraid. It's one of the glaring gaps — one of the many glaring gaps — in English law. And Scottish. And American, incidentally. There is no legal institution of adoption.'

'But . . .' Roseanne thought of the dozens of children she knew who had been brought up by relatives and in-laws, and even mere neighbours, after the death of their own parents. Indeed, the best-known case of all had just been mentioned between them. 'What about Mrs Moore?' she asked. 'I heard tell as her uncle and aunt adopted she.'

'Not formally. There simply is no formal mechanism to permit it to be done. The legal term, anyway, is fostering. Mrs Moore was fostered by her uncle and aunt. In France and Germany — in most of the Continent — things are different. Most of them permit legal adoption with inheritance of property and so on. In France a child must live with you for six years before you may adopt it, and you must be at least fourteen years older than it. But they also have this strange rule that you can adopt *anyone*, younger or older, immediately, if he or she has saved your life! I sometimes think that French law is designed entirely to serve the needs of stage melodrama!' He went on talking in this inconsequential vein to give her time to absorb the bad news.

'So Jake couldn't come and live with us anyway,' she said glumly.

He put his elbows on his desk, made a spire of his two index fingers, and rested his chin upon them. 'Legally, as an orphan, he is now in the care of the Board of Guardians.'

She closed her eyes and shivered.

'They, *in loco parentis*, could appoint you, formally, as Jake's foster mother. I need hardly tell you there is little hope of that while you remain a spinster of uncertain means and under the age of, say, forty. On the other hand, if you were married to the son and heir of the Chairman of the said Board . . .' He smiled. 'I'm not necessarily advising it, mind. I simply point out the fact.'

Roseanne ran a dry tongue around her lips, drew a deep breath, and asked, 'And what if, when we were schoolgirls — I mean, we were good friends, Mary Williams and me — what if we made a pact, like, that if one of us died and left orphan children, the other would, like, adopt them?'

'And did you?' he asked, staring at her coolly.

She swallowed heavily. 'Yes.'

'It seems an extraordinary thing for two young . . . what age were you, after all? Fourteen, if you were still at school. An extraordinary thing for fourteen-year-old girls to promise.'

She stared out of the window. Half of her wished she had not started this particular lie; the other half thought of Annette and how she would not hesitate for a moment if it helped her get what she wanted. 'It was after a big fall down Wheal Vor,' she said. That was safe enough. There was a big fall down Wheal Vor more than once a year — or had been in those days. 'And there was dozens of babbies and infants left fatherless, and with mothers who couldn't earn enough to keep them. Two girls in our class — Cissie Mollard and June Davey — they had to leave and go directly into service. That's how we were talking about it, see.'

She saw him jot down the two names and was glad she had picked true examples.

'It might carry weight,' he allowed. 'What would carry most weight of all, of course, would be if she had repeated the request just before her death. If she knew she was dying, that would have legal force. I don't suppose she did?'

Looking into his eyes Roseanne realized this was a test not of her truthfulness — that had already been tested — but of her recklessness. 'No,' she said reluctantly. 'She was dead when I found her.'

The answer appeared to please him. 'Another way out of your dilemma — if you feel that marriage to Stephen Morvah is a little drastic — would be for your parents to agree to foster Jake. I'm sure the Guardians would leap at it. They're not exactly overburdened with offers of that kind.'

He smiled again at her while his left hand fidgeted with the papers on his desk.

She took the hint and rose, thanking him profusely and apologizing for taking up his valuable time. And yes, she would consider his kind suggestion that she should talk matters over with Mrs Scawen.

'You could come over with your father, to see the progress we're making with the cliff garden. That would justify your visit well enough, I think?' As he saw her to the door, he added, 'The greatest threat to your *title* to the child – if I can so express it – would be the father. But against that we must weigh the fact that he could only claim his right to the child by appealing to the very system that would hang him by the neck until dead.'

As she went out a clerk took the opportunity to slip into his master's room and rebuild the fire.

When he was alone again Vosper Scawen tipped the untouched madeira back into the decanter. Abstractedly he carried the glass to the fireplace and shook the last few drops into the reviving flames. Then he stood awhile, one foot on the brass fender, staring into the heart of it.

'Extraordinary!' he murmured at last. 'Quite extraordinary!'

31

'A most extraordinary thing happened today, my dear,' Vosper Scawen told his wife Jane as they came downstairs from the nursery that evening. But she was only half listening, being rather worried over little Courtenay's cough. The other three had recovered quickly enough from their winter snivels but the baby of the family, now almost two, couldn't seem to shake his. 'If it's not improved by tomorrow,' she said, 'we'll get a second opinion.'

'Ah,' he said, 'yes, of course.' He cleared his throat. 'Talking of second opinions . . . well, that's what I was coming to. I'm afraid I rather volunteered your assistance to a client of ours today.'

That certainly caught her attention! She could not remember the last occasion on which he had discussed a client's affairs with her. He was so scrupulous about that sort of thing. 'Me?' she replied, in a mixture of alarm and pleasure. 'What do I know of the law?'

'The laws of human nature?' he offered.

'Oh dear!' She sat beside the fire and took up her embroidery. 'It sounds worse by the minute.'

He told her all that had happened during Roseanne's visit. 'And then later,' he concluded, 'I was coming up Meneage Street when I ran into old Doc. Wilson, just leaving the workhouse. We talked about this and that, and then I mentioned Jake — because he has to examine all new admissions there. But he said he hadn't seen the lad.'

'Really? How strange.'

'In fact, not. He also told me that *Frank* Kitto and young Miss Morvah had called by with a message about some urchin who'd cut his hand up at the workhouse. And he said the little lad — Jake, obviously — was with them! In short, they'd been up to the workhouse and come away again without leaving him.'

His wife chuckled. 'Poor old Kitto! He likes to think he's hard as granite you know, and really he's as soft as a duck. So! What is your difficulty and what is left for me to accomplish? Miss Kitto's dilemma would seem to be resolved.'

'Is it?' he asked.

She thought about it and shook her head. 'I suppose not.'

He prompted her for some more positive response. 'I still can't quite believe what I saw. The ferocity in that young woman!'

'Hmmm,' she said. 'And how old is little Jake — two, did you say?'

'Rising two, she thinks. He was probably never registered or baptized. "Jake" is just the name she's given him. He can walk and is just starting to talk.'

'He's younger than Courtenay, then. Courtenay can talk quite well.'

'Yes, but he's got a brother and sisters, not to mention Nanny and the maids — none of whom ever *stops* talking. I doubt if anyone ever spoke to Jake much before last . . . whenever it was. Friday. Anyway, what has his age to do with it?'

'I was just thinking. What would *we* do if someone kidnapped Courtenay?'

'I'd offer a swap for Trevanion, like a shot.'

'No, be serious. What would you do?'

'I'd go to the very limit of the law, of course. But her case and ours are hardly . . .' He faltered as he saw her shaking her head. 'What?' he asked.

'Go to the limit of the law?' She put scorn into her echo of his words. 'Is that all? *I* would cheerfully commit murder to get him back.'

He poked the end of a half-consumed log into the fire with the toe of his boot. 'Cheerfully?' he asked.

'Yes. And so would you when it came to it.'

He sat in the chair facing her and reached his hands toward the reviving blaze. 'I hope I would always remember I am a civilized man, my dear. If not, then my whole living, not to say livelihood, is a sham. However, that's another discussion. What I mean is . . .'

'No it's not. You seemed astonished that Miss Kitto, who is obviously an upright, godfearing young woman, should be prepared to perjure herself with this lie in order to . . .'

'It was the look in her eye more than anything. Frightening. So implacable. So determined.'

'Would *she* commit murder to keep him, d'you think?'

He shrugged awkwardly.

'You see! You can't be sure she wouldn't. That's what I'm talking about.'

'Yes,' he conceded. 'And yet there is one huge difference: Courtenay is ours, but Miss Kitto didn't even know of Jake's existence a month ago. Before last Friday she'd done no more for him than any passing stranger would do for a toddler that had strayed on to the highway.'

Now it was Jane's turn to concede the point — and yet she could still understand Miss Kitto's actions. 'How do you explain it then?' she asked. 'You have the advantage of knowing the young lady.'

It was the opening he had been waiting for. 'Well.' He leaned back in his chair and crossed his legs. 'I have the advantage of watching her expression while she unfolded her tale. I know you think I always look for the most devious and far-fetched explanations of people's behaviour, while you believe there's a much simpler reason for it, but hear me out.' He uncrossed his legs and stretched his toes toward the hearth. 'Ever since she was a young girl, fourteen or fifteen, Miss Kitto has been "promised", in her own mind, anyway, to Mark Bodilly. They are, or were, a pair of real childhood sweethearts.'

'And did it cut both ways?'

He smiled at her alertness. 'I suspect — she didn't say as much, but reading between the lines I get the impression that Bodilly had become a mite casual about the whole affair.'

'Otherwise why did she respond so readily to young Morvah?'

'Precisely. So then there's a few heady weeks while she's the centre of attraction. Two splendid young men vying for her affection! They even wrestled over her — everything short of coming to blows. But then, as the novelty of being courted by the squire's son wears off, the old feelings begin to reassert themselves until, last week, the strain became intolerable.'

His wife frowned. 'But in that case why add to it, with all the complications of taking little Jake under her wing?'

He stared into the flames awhile before replying. 'While she was telling me all this I couldn't help thinking of a case we have coming up next month. I was working on it, in fact, when she called. And I was thinking how

255

much I pity the judge. We have two sterling characters, plaintiff and defendant, salt of the earth, both acting out of the highest of motives — yet they find themselves in head-on contention without the remotest chance of a compromise. It's an almost impossible case to decide. As I say, I was working on it when Miss Kitto called and yet, busy as I was, I had her shown in with a speed and delight which, I know, amazed her. But the fact is, I would have welcomed anything, almost any distraction, rather than face the issues in that impossible case. And I couldn't avoid wondering if her sudden obsession to care for Jake isn't something of the same? On a much more profound scale, of course.'

Jane, too, stared at the fire — rather a long time. 'You're a terrible man,' she said at last.

He smiled.

'Noble deeds, romantic actions, fine sentiments . . . they never cut the thinnest ice with you, do they!'

'You think I'm wrong, then.'

'No.' She sighed. 'When you put it like that, it sounds all too likely. I can't tell you how grateful I am for volunteering me as her advisor.'

He hung his head. 'That was wrong. I plead guilty, offer no defence, and throw myself upon the mercy of the court.'

She reached across and dug her needle gently into his kneecap, until he winced. 'Actually,' he said, 'I volunteered Mrs Moore first, but then I thought no, she's getting a bit long in the tooth for such giddy and girlish conundrums.'

She raised her hand and held the needle poised menacingly over the same knee. 'Take that back,' she commanded.

He pretended to cower and then became serious again. 'In fact, as soon as I'd said it I saw it was a mistake.'

'Why? She'd be the perfect one to advise Miss Kitto. Remember how helpful she was to me once upon a time?'

'She'd be too perfect. I'm sure she'd offer to take the boy into the home she and Dr Moore founded in Redruth, for the orphans of their own servants and employees.'

Jane clapped her free hand on the arm of her chair. 'But you're right. It is perfect — the perfect answer to the whole thing!'

'Too perfect,' he repeated calmly.

She frowned. 'I simply don't understand you, Vosper. One minute you seem to be saying that Jake is just a device to allow her to avoid any decision about Morvah and Bodilly. And next minute you're implying it would be wrong to remove that device.'

He pursed his lips and nodded. 'Like a good lawyer, I can see all sides of the issue with equal clarity. Now I need someone to come along and persuade me to act for one side or the other.'

With an amused smile she glanced right and left, as if there might be other volunteers for the task — which she then accepted with an ironic shrug.

'There are one or two other things you ought to know,' he added at once. 'She omitted to mention one of the most salient points of all. It may have been her maidenly modesty, but I don't think so.'

Jane's eyes gleamed. 'Go on, go on! It's starting to sound most interesting.'

'You know May Delamere, of course.'

'I'm hardly likely to forget *her*!'

Jane had, in fact, been the incidental matchmaker for two of the widow's daughters — and had helped a third through the crisis that had resulted in the annulment of hers. May Delamere was certainly no stranger!

'Well,' he went on, 'it seems she has suddenly found Vinery House rather too large and lonely for her. So she has taken a lodger.'

'No! Who?'

'None other than Mark Bodilly!'

Jane closed her eyes and fanned her face. 'My, my!' She glanced at him. 'And what does the private dining room at the Angel make of that? As if I need ask!'

'It believes that a kind, experienced dame and a young bachelor with too much ambition to allow him to marry just yet have found a mutually agreeable solution to their difficulties.'

'A conclusion hard to resist,' she commented.

'The whole of West Penwith is buzzing with it. By no stretch of the imagination can Miss Kitto *not* have heard of the arrangement. Yet she said absolutely nothing about it.'

'If I were her, it would make up my mind for me at once.' Yet even as she spoke the words Jane found her mind straying back ten years or so, to a time when she, a young heiress, had imagined herself in love with a penniless young man in Falmouth. She had been quite ready to elope with him – even after certain vipers had whispered in their ears (falsely, as it later transpired) that they were half-brother and -sister. Such knowledge surely ought to have 'made her mind up at once', yet it had not.

She sighed. To advise Miss Kitto in her present dilemma had never seemed an easy prospect. The more she thought about it, the more it stirred old memories within her – memories of feelings that a decade of happy marriage had comfortably buried.

And the more daunting the task became.

32

Throughout the first weeks of his new domestic situation Mark Bodilly braced himself for the odd matrimonial hint or two. That such hints would come he had no doubt; women didn't bestow their jewel for nothing. He wondered how 'Mrs Delamere' would first broach the topic with 'Mr Bodilly', as she insisted they call each other, even in their most incandescent moments; when she spoke his surname in such bizarre circumstances, he had the uncomfortable feeling that a third party shared the bed with them. So how, when they could never be May and Mark would she drop the first hints of what must surely be uppermost in her mind?

Would she sigh and recall happy moments with the Hon. Owen? Or draw attention to other supposedly happy couples of their acquaintance? Leave copies of the *Companion* open at the bridal pages? Or come straight out with it?

It would be none of these, he suspected. 'Coming straight out with it' would be most like her — yet even there she would find her own way of managing the business. She was a revelation to him. By no stretch of the imagination could it be said he was in love with her, and yet he thought about her almost all the time. The enigma of her personality, the contradictions between its public and private faces, had come to obsess him.

He had known Mrs Delamere, by sight at least, almost

all his life. She was a feature of the landscape. He could dimly recall a time when, as a little boy, he had seen her and her husband with two or three little daughters in tow at various public occasions. She was a pretty woman who caught the eye and turned the head — but impeccably modest, for all that, and always so attentive to her family. Then there was a long gap in his recall; during that time she had undoubtedly been there, somewhere, but not part of his day-to-day life. Perhaps that was when the Delameres had lived up in North Cornwall, when he was land agent to the Lanyons of Parc-an-Ython.

His next conscious memory of her was when he'd been about fourteen. She had just been widowed and was living with her four unmarried (and, everyone feared, now unmarriageable) daughters in one of the Lanyons' grace-and-favour cottages in Sithney. In the normal way he'd never have passed near that village, but at that particular time he had to avoid passing Tom Hampton's house because of what Tom's father threatened to do after a fight in which his son had come off worst. Mark had caught up with Widow Delamere struggling with a pail of potatoes that Billy Meagor had let her dig out of his headlands. He had offered to take the burden from her but she insisted on their carrying it between them. 'It will avoid chafing our limbs,' she said with a most engaging smile.

He had formed an immediate picture of her limbs swinging under her dress — but then, at that age, he tried to picture the limbs of most females old enough to wear skirts that were long enough to make the daydream necessary. He remembered wondering what it would be like to drag May Delamere into one of the fields and have his way with her; but that, too, was an almost hourly speculation with him, as it was with every other lad of his acquaintance. What was different about the day with the potatoes was that he had somehow gained the impression that *she* might be entertaining similar idle speculations concerning *him*. Nothing was said. Nothing was even hinted at. Yet she had by some witchcraft managed to fill his mind with the notion.

Of course, the moment he formed the thought he was seized by a terror that she might act on the impulse. The mighty hunter, whose imagination had only moments earlier been filled with glowing pictures of his conquest, was now all a-tremble with the thought that his victim might at any moment make the first infinitesimal sign of her surrender. He brought her to her gate but would not step over its threshold. He stood in the roadway and bolted the milk and bun she offered him before haring off as fast as his legs could carry him.

Now, eleven years later, he could not help thinking of that as a significant moment — even though, at the time, he had seen its absurdity before he was halfway home. He had mocked the very idea of it then. Dammit to hell, the woman was more than twenty years his senior! Did his fevered imaginings know no bounds? Was no woman safe in those wild and unswept corners of his mind? Sadly, with a kind of shamefaced pride, he had to admit they weren't. And yet when Widow Delamere refused to let him carry the pail alone, all she had wanted, probably, was to avoid having to give him a tip.

Three or four years later, during most of which time he'd been Roseanne's steady beau, he prided himself he had learned the self-control and respect for a lady that is the natural armour of the true gentleman. Then he began to win at local wrestling contests and to be seen about the village, bruised and bleeding after parish hurling matches. Then he had swiftly become aware that

261

ladies 'of a certain age' were no longer untouchable grown-ups in a remote world of their own. Certainly not in their own estimation! They would eye him with a candour that was unmistakable. And one or two went even further.

Mrs Furnival, for instance. The month before she and her family moved up to Devon, she cornered him in the linen press. He'd only gone into her house because he had happened to be passing by at the time Willy Rodda was carrying in some furniture she'd bought. One moment she was remote and commanding – 'Put it there, if you'd be so kind . . . careful now!' – and the next she was all over him like a tornado: 'Oh, Mr Bodilly, you've no idea how lonely I am and how vilely Furnival neglects me!' And trying to smother him with kisses and tear his clothes off. For weeks after that he had cringed with shame when he recalled how he had simply turned and fled from her advances. But once she was safely in Devon, oh what a man he had then become! Night after night he replayed the event in his mind, replacing his cowardly retreat with scenes of conquest and passion.

Funnily enough, he'd been placed beside her at a tribute supper the very next evening, and she'd talked to him in the calmest, sweetest, remotest manner – as if nothing so stirring had happened between them less than thirty hours earlier.

So Mark Bodilly had every reason to know that women were just as hypocritical as men in such affairs; only it was somehow different in their case. Society, in all its arrangements, seemed to acknowledge without ever actually saying so that, while men were supposed to be 'like that', women weren't. Nobody chaperoned men; nobody forbade them to go out of doors without the company of a servant or a responsible adult of mature years. True, a gentleman was taught it was as much his duty to protect the honour of a *lady* as it was hers — but that was tantamount to assuring him that nine out of ten of the female tribe was fair game. In short, he had long ago ceased to be surprised by the vast discrepancy between, on the one hand, the Nature of Woman, as universally described (in public) — a view to which most women avidly assent (in public) — and, on the other, the individual natures that many of the 'gentle' sex had revealed to him in private. Yet he also knew how strong was their desire to conform to that universal ideal. Look at how Mrs Furnival had behaved the very next day! She swallowed all her wounded pride and self-esteem and bent every effort to patch over the rift — until there was no sign it had ever existed.

With such experiences behind him, leading to such views concerning the hypocrisies of men and women in their most intimate dealings with one another, it is hardly surprising that Mark prepared himself for a matrimonial onslaught from Mrs Delamere. When nothing of the kind materialized, far from relaxing him, it merely deepened his suspicions. At last he grew so wary of her that May herself, snug though she was in her newly discovered bower of happiness, asked if anything ailed him.

'I can't get over that Roseanne Kitto,' he replied, instantly misdirecting her.

They were lying side by side in her bed at the time. It was the first occasion on which they had done so without any passionate engagement and May was still trying to decide whether it was a novelty to be encouraged or something she should stamp upon firmly. Part of her wanted Bodily *only* for those moments of ungovernable rapture; for the remaining hours of the day she would prefer to be free of the encumbrance of a man — indeed, not just of a man but of any other person. She had enjoyed the management of her own life and the pleasing of herself within the limits of her purse, for the best part of ten years; and now that her purse had lately been so generously augmented by her daughter Rosa's good fortune, she was loath to yield one inch of her precious freedom.

But another part of her — perhaps a remnant of that little girl who had once played so fervently with her dolls — desired Bodilly as a kind of animated pet. She wanted to cosset him and do nice things for him and bask in his gratitude, entirely without reference to that *other* part of their association.

Mark, feeling that his choice of words had been a trifle unwise, qualified them by adding: 'Taking in that babby!' — as if *that* were what he could not get over.

'Ah!' May thought she understood. 'Did it frighten you, poor man?'

'Frighten me?' he echoed, half scornful at the idea, half puzzled at it.

'It's one thing for a man to contemplate connubial bliss with the object of his adoration — fully realizing, of course, that sooner or later there will be the pitapat of tiny feet. It's quite another to find the feet ready-made, and, indeed — if my eyes did not deceive me last Sunday — wearing a substantial pair of well-cobbled boots!' She leaned her head on his shoulder. 'Am I not right?'

He combed her hair gently with his fingers, caressing her scalp with their tips. 'I can't make you out at all,' he murmured fondly.

'In what way?' She imitated the purring of a cat.

'Well — when I go and blurt out something like that — about not being able to get over Roseanne, which

264

you might think I meant in a different way . . . I mean, don't you mind? Don't you think it's, like, insulting to you?'

'Goodness, what an odd idea!' She gave a little giggle and then, kissing his neck, added, 'Oh! Did you want me to be jealous, then?'

More than a little miffed he told her it would be only natural.

The word amused her even more. 'And what about our usual nightly activity, my dear — is that not natural, too?' But before he could answer, other words began to pour from her, words that came welling up from somewhere deep inside, taking her as much by surprise as they did him. 'Listen! To be jealous one must first be in love. Surely you realize by now that love is the last thing I seek to add to my life? Or, rather, to allow to complicate my daily existence. I have learned to live alone — God knows I had chance enough to practise the art! I have learned to manage my feelings and keep myself in harmony and balance. Look at all the miserable people in the world around us! I don't mean the starving and wretched and poor. I mean people in comfortable circumstances who enjoy four square meals a day and servants to wait on them — people like that who are nonetheless consumed with misery. And why? Nine times out of ten it's because *love* has misled them, trapped them, confused them — and finally, having led them into an indissoluble union, has abandoned them to their fate.'

She drew breath at last and then laughed. 'Hark at me!' Then, in a less boisterous tone, she concluded, 'No, Mr Bodilly, the day I feel myself falling in love with you is the day I give you your notice. And the same goes for you, I hope you realize? If I ever suspect you of feeling for me more than the simple warmth of honest

265

friendship . . .' She gave him a token push away from her. 'I trust that's plain enough for you?'

He began to laugh, not harshly, in fact, rather self-deprecatingly.

She asked him what was so amusing.

'Me,' he admitted. 'My dawbrained fears. I don't suppose I shall ever understand women, or not a woman like you.'

'I hope that's a compliment. You're very good, tonight, at saying things that may be taken two ways at once.'

'What I mean is, all the world knows that a woman's life has but a single aim. The wife basks in it while the maid and widow can only dream of joining her. I mean, that's the wisdom of the world, isn't it! And yet, just "hark at you!" as you yourself put it. You speak like it was a nightmare instead.'

She was silent a while before she replied, 'I certainly didn't mean to do that — imply it is a universal nightmare. My years with Owen were as happy as the most artless maid could dream of. But he has gone before me and I am not so naïve as to imagine I might repeat the experience with another. And even if I were, I should know better than to choose a partner of your tender years!'

'Why *did* you choose me?' he asked — and instantly regretted it.

Her answer was an unambiguous gesture that needed no verbal accompaniment.

'Couldn't we just lie here and talk tonight?' he asked. 'I want to get these matters straight between us.'

Reluctantly she conceded its necessity. 'That's another particular upon which the wisdom of the world concerning Womankind is not the best guide to a long and happy life.'

'I'm beginning to agree,' he replied heavily. 'Are you speaking for yourself or all women?'

'It would be rash indeed to claim to speak for all women. Yet I think I may safely speak for all those whom I know. Who, would you say, is the most respectable woman in the entire neighbourhood? Who is the one to whom the rest of us . . .'

'Dorothy Lanyon,' he said at once.

'Hah!' Her single laugh told him it was the name she had expected him to pick. 'Would it surprise you to learn that her eldest daughter was fathered by some unknown gentleman in Paris? Known to her, of course, but not to us!'

'Did she tell you so?' he asked in shocked tones.

'Of course not, or I shouldn't be telling you now. No, but it's quite plain she had an *affaire* when she accompanied Mrs Scawen to Paris about ten years ago. Mrs Scawen was then Miss Hervey of Montpelier House, of course, and Mrs Lanyon was her guardian. For years and years the Lanyons had been trying for a child, without success. Then off she goes to Paris and, on her return, she gives birth to a bonny little girl whose term was either ten and a half or seven and a half months − depending on whether you date La Lanyon's *enceinture* from the night of her departure or that of her return! Little Angwyn Lanyon was the biggest, bonniest seven-and-a-half-month baby *I* ever saw, I may tell you.'

He gave a long, dry whistle in the dark. 'Dorothy Lanyon!' he murmured. 'Who would have thought it! But the other two are surely his? They have his nose − and ears.'

'Why else would he have tolerated it? He can count up to nine as well as the next man. No, that act of infidelity unlocked something between them that made the next two children possible. So there you are! Nothing that takes place between men and women will ever surprise me.'

There seemed to be nothing to say to that.

After enduring his silence awhile she chuckled, close to his ear. 'Poor man! And were you afraid I had designs on you?'

He sniffed.

'And have I now set your mind at rest? I hope so, for I'll tell you this – a less designing woman than I never drew breath.'

33

By February, 1871, Jane Scawen's cliff garden at Trevivian was beginning to take its final shape: a series of terraces, amphitheatres, grottoes, and steps, all hewn from the living rock. Her original plan had been to continue all the way down to the river edge, but she soon realized that most of the lower half would be wasted, for no casual visitor would undertake such an exhausting vertical stroll. However, since she had planned the rest of her enormous garden to accommodate the spoil — as the basis of paths and hardcore for ponds and paved areas — she had decided to complete the walk by creating a series of sloping tunnels with hewn staircases that linked the terraces. These were close enough to the exposed rock face to be lighted naturally through windows cut at convenient intervals, while still leaving enough gloom to arouse a sense of mystery and excitement.

'The idea, you see,' she explained to any visitor curious enough to inquire, 'is that people will descend by way of the tunnels, which will give them enticing glimpses of the terraces and the river mouth and so on — and then they'll emerge into the sunlight on the lowest terrace of all and be able to enjoy a much more leisurely, meandering walk back to the top again.'

It required all the skill of Wilfrid Meagor and his two assistants to place charges that would excavate the tunnel without bursting out the yard or so of rock between it and the face of the cliff. And no one was more aware of their skill than Jane herself. She had not only taken a course in explosives at the School of Mines – the only woman ever to do such a thing – but she had also attended Professor Nobel's first demonstration of 'Dynamite' in England, which had been some three years before Frank Kitto took on the contract. She had sent to Sweden for a supply of the stuff and had even made a few experiments with it before Vosper put his foot down – baby Courtenay being by then well on the way. There was still a good supply left, all of it stable, when Wilfrid Meagor came on the scene.

Until then he had experienced nothing but blasting powder. He had tried gun cotton but did not trust it. He trusted the 'new fangled Swedish muck' even less. But Jane persisted and, after his third go with it, he reluctantly admitted it 'wasn't bad'. Half a dozen charges later and he swore he'd never willingly go back to any of the older explosives.

Toward the end of that February, the moment approached when the last yard of the upward tunnel was to meet the last yard of the one they had earlier drifted down from the surface. It was only fitting, Meagor thought, to yield his place to her and allow her to plan, set, and detonate the final charge.

The Scawens made a gala day of it, with all their friends in attendance – or as many as cared to come for such a bizarre spectacle. Dorothy Lanyon summed it up for them all when she said, 'You know, Jane dear, my only reason for accepting your invitation is that I've been longing for months to tell your maid, "Yes, I know she's blasting, but *today* I have an invitation to attend!" '

Jane stared about her in surprise at the laughter raised by this remark.

270

'But it's true!' Angelica McDougall assured her. 'The number of times I've paid you a call, only to be told, "Sorry, you caaan't see she today, she's blaaastin'!" It was so chagrin-making.'

Frank Kitto was there, too, of course, and he had brought his wife and daughter — and, after much grumbling, Jake, as well. For the other ladies present this was something of a bonus. They had heard so much about Kitto that, though most of them knew him well enough by sight, his recent rise in the world had somehow given him a new aura, which they were anxious to see at close quarters. And the same was even more true of his daughter after the strange goings on with the murdered girl and her abandoned child — not to mention the rather serious attention young Morvah was said to be paying her nowadays. All in all, they could hardly wait for the dynamiting to be over and done with. The weather did not help. It was a blustery February morning with a southeasterly half-gale blowing across the estuary to give those without sticks something else to lean against. The one good thing that could be said about it was that the rain had eased and did not look like returning all day. Bright, fleecy clouds filled the sky and even allowed an occasional finger of sunlight to wander across the face of the sea and make an intermittent stab at the land about them.

'Now, all you'll hear,' Jane shouted above the gale, 'I *hope*, is a muffled explosion. And there may also be a small cloud of dust. That's all. If you want something more spectacular, you'll have to wait for the summer tattoo.' She looked around the circle of eager faces. 'Ready?'

'Yes! Yes!' came the impatient replies. People stamped their feet in the spoil of previous 'blaaastings' and triced themselves up tighter against the wind.

'Right, then. Count slowly up to thirty.' Meagor handed her a brand of smouldering tow. With a flourish she touched off the safety fuse, which burned an inch before igniting a wad of cordite, which, in turn, ignited half a dozen safety fuses at the identical moment. She did not relax until she saw they were all burning.

Dorothy Lanyon, standing at her side, noticed the change in her and asked why she was so relieved.

'That's the trick you see,' Jane replied. 'The charges are placed in three concentric rings.'

'Ah!' Dorothy began to regret her question.

'The innermost ring must fire half a second ahead of the next one, which must fire half a second ahead of the outer ring. The first blast makes a small hole in the middle, which the next two can fill with their debris, you see.'

'But how fascinating!' Her eyes glazed and she went on ticking off the seconds with her fingers in her pockets . . . eighteen, nineteen, twenty . . .

Jane could see she hadn't grasped the point and so continued: 'If they all blasted together, we'd simply blow the face off the cliff.'

'I see, I see,' Bessie Tanner, at her other elbow, said brightly. Anything to fill the suspenseful seconds.

'People think blasting is just a matter of putting in the dynamite and lighting the fuse,' Jane complained.

. . . twenty-four, twenty-five . . .

Roseanne clutched Jake tight to her and murmured in his ear, 'Thunder coming, my lover. Just harken to the thunder.'

There was a muffled booming, with three barely discernible peaks − and that was it! If they had not known what it was, most of those present would have guessed at a brief roll on a big bass drum about a hundred yards away. A cloud of dust was carried swiftly downwind — their only visible assurance that there had, indeed, been an explosion.

'Is that all?' asked a score of disappointed voices.

Frank Kitto stepped forward at once. 'Ladies and gentlemen,' he cried, 'I say this knowing full well that Wilfrid Meagor, master shotfirer of Wheal Fortune mines, is standing right here beside of me, but I say I never saw shot placed so pretty nor fired so sweet. Three cheers for Mrs Scawen — hip-hip-hip!'

When the cheering was done Jane led them forward to the edge of the tunnel; and now there were quite genuine gasps of amazement. They had all seen it five minutes earlier, or dimly glimpsed it, anyway — a face of rock at the blind end of a twenty-yard hole, sloping down at about thirty degrees. Now the tunnel was half-filled with debris and they could see clear through it to daylight at the far end.

'And just look how she fired it nearly all *up*hill,' Frank pointed out to those nearest him. 'Why, she's some master-woman, she is!'

His hearers were aware of the incongruity in his description but could think of no alternative.

'And now' — Jane clapped her hands for attention — 'if that brief ceremony has given anyone an appetite, I think we may find one or two things to nibble back at the house.'

Laughing, and more than a little grateful, they turned their backs to the wind and let it nudge them up the sloping headlands to what they knew would be a banquet of a buffet. Jane singled out Roseanne, though she made it seem as if it were Kitto himself she wished to consult.

After a brief conversation with him she leaned forward and asked Roseanne whether the child had minded the explosion.

'I had my fingers stopping his ears,' she replied. 'I don't believe he heard nothing, poor mite. I felt it under my feet, though. I can tell you that.'

Jane turned back to her father. 'You'll stay behind after the others have gone, I hope, Mr Kitto? I want to go over my plans for the next month with you.'

He agreed readily enough.

And then, as if it were no more than an afterthought, she turned again to Roseanne and said: 'And you, Miss Kitto — perhaps you'd be good enough to accompany me around this wilderness?' She swept a hand across the landscape. 'I'd welcome your opinion. Your father tells me you're quite the gardener at home.'

It was true that Roseanne had for some years now done all the gardening at home; but since the entire 'demesne' consisted of some twenty small shrubs, all of them very commonplace, and three beds where she sprinkled packets of mixed annuals every spring — oh, and an unruly hedge of escallonia — she considered her father was being somewhat boastful. However, since she knew Mrs Scawen had quite a different purpose in making the suggestion, she accepted with outward pleasure, though with a sinking heart.

34

The weather improved steadily throughout the afternoon. By the time the last of the 'blasting-day' guests had taken his leave, the wind was the merest zephyr and the sun and clouds divided an equal sky. Jake and Courtenay had discovered a common fascination for Maria Scawen's dolls house — which she tolerated because it gave her unfettered access to her brother's toy fort; so they were all left to their devices while Jane Scawen took Roseanne on the promised tour of the garden-to-be.

In fact, as Roseanne saw once they were in the thick of it, much had already been achieved. All the slow-growing subjects, which needed to get a start before the faster ones could overtake and smother them, were already established — the oaks and beeches, the maidenhair ferns, the baytrees, the yews, the Portugal laurels, and some of the more elegant viburnums — these were already well settled, while the ground at their feet was kept ruthlessly bare of competition.

'It looks quite dreadful,' Mrs Scawen admitted, 'but the final result will show it was worth it — as I tell Mr Scawen when he complains of my curling papers.'

Roseanne laughed and said her father was the same about the lanolin and carbolic she put on her hands after milking. 'But see the result!' She peeled off a glove and held out a hand that was almost as smooth as a real lady's.

Mrs Scawen did the same with hers, revealing at once that she could be nothing but a gardener who went in for the occasional bout of dynamiting. 'That puts *me* in my place!'

'Oh, but I didn't mean . . . oh dear!' Roseanne began to stammer her apologies.

The other laughed and patted her arm. 'Don't take it amiss,' she said stoutly. 'I'm proud of them – just as I'm proud of all that.' Her eyes swept the skyline.

Watching her, Roseanne was filled with a sudden envy. Here was a woman who knew precisely what she wanted to do with the world, or her small corner of it – and who had the means to achieve it, too. That was the sort of woman *she* would like to be one day. But what did she want to do with the world, or her small corner of it? No easy answer suggested itself. 'Did you always want to do this, ma'am?' she asked. 'Make a big garden and that?'

'Heavens no,' came the immediate reply. 'The idea didn't strike me until . . .' She broke off and stared quizzically at Roseanne. 'D'you mind my asking how old you are, Miss Kitto?'

'I was twenty-two last Wednesday, ma'am.'

Considerately Mrs Scawen added a year or two to her memories. 'I think I was twenty-three before the idea for all this came to me. And very suddenly, too. I was journeying down by train from Paddington, I remember. Have you ever done that?'

'I never went beyond Truro, ma'am.'

'Well, that's a treat you have in store. It was May, I think, or early June, with the whole countryside looking its very best after a rather wet spring. And the line from Paddington takes you through Buckingham-shire, which is chalk, with huge forests of beech and lush pasture in between. Then Wiltshire, which is still chalk but much higher, with great rolling hills and dry plains. Then down into Somerset, which is all rich farmland and yellow sandstone hills. And on to Devon, where the valleys are deeply carved into red sandstone. The greens you get there are simply beyond description. And finally, when you cross that amazing bridge of Brunel's, over the Tamar into Cornwall, where it's elvanstone and granite and china clay and more granite, and poky little fields with stony hedges, and the terrible beauty of the mine tailings, and . . .'

'Beauty?' Roseanne echoed in surprise.

'Oh yes! The colours in the stone when it's wet — every colour of the rainbow. And the dark fingers of ling clutching at all that barrenness and struggling to colonize it. The ling and the gorse. But it wasn't just the rock and the plants that struck me on that journey. It was the buildings, too. Walls of local stone with plants seen against them. And glimpses of little streams dashing over rock. And ruins. And the marshes near Exeter. And follies on rich men's estates. Quaint *things* on hilltops and carvings into the chalk. When I closed my eyes that night and tried to sleep, I couldn't. My mind was crammed to bursting with scenes like that. And then I knew that what I wished to do with the rest of my life — make a big, big garden with surprises and delights like that around every corner.' She laughed at her own intensity as, darting her eyes about the landscape, she concluded, 'And, as you can see, we've made a start. We've got the rock, if nothing else! And the weeds, to be sure.'

And the money, Roseanne thought.

Henry Blight, one of the miners, came past with a

cartload of rubble from that morning's work. 'Is this for the fishpond or the folly, missis?' he asked.

'Put it where the windmill's going to be,' she told him.

He tipped his cap and went on by.

'Windmill?' Roseanne asked.

'Yes, the one thing these grounds lack is a natural stream. So I'm building a windmill at the top to pump water from a new pond down there at the cliff edge to a watercourse at the top of the garden. Keep it circulating, you see. Won't it be nice?'

Roseanne shook her head in amazement. 'How d'you think of it all, ma'am? How d'you keep it all in your head?'

'But isn't that something we all do? Don't you? It's daydreaming, really. I'm sure you must daydream about things in your life?' When Roseanne did not immediately respond, she added, 'Jake, for instance?'

'Ye-es,' Roseanne admitted reluctantly.

After another brief silence Mrs Scawen went on, 'Of course, it's no business of mine . . .'

'No,' Roseanne said at once — then, realizing her reply could be taken the wrong way, qualified it with, 'I mean no, it's not that. I do want to talk about it, but I don't hardly know how to begin.'

Mrs Scawen, who still held her arm, gave it another comforting squeeze. 'My husband told me of your visit, of course, and he mentioned your perplexities. I thought that, as I hadn't seen you since then, the whole business had blown over and everyone now accepted the new status quo.' There was merriment in her voice as she added, 'I must say, Jake would win *my* heart any day of the week. How could such an adorable little boy have come out of such a situation?'

She could not have chosen better words to win Roseanne's confidence — nor a better opening to get her talking. 'She wasn't such a bad mother as they made out in the papers,' she said. 'And even though they lived in old henhouses and barns and that, she always fed Jake proper, and clothed him proper, too, until her last few weeks. I don't know what changed her then. But the papers made out as she'd neglected the babby from the start.'

'They spoke very warmly of you.'

Roseanne made a rueful face. 'That never helped me with the old man, either. Getting in the papers like that. It made us look like we were kin to Mary Williams and slummocks like her.'

'All the more credit to him, then, that he's come to accept the lad, eh?'

'I suppose so.'

The rubble path gave out at that point. They stood awhile and admired the play of colour on the waters of Falmouth Bay. Then they turned and retraced their steps. 'You don't sound too certain,' Mrs Scawen said, as if there had been no interruption at all.

Roseanne sighed. 'In the beginning, see, I thought that would be my difficulty — talking the old man round. But when Miss Morvah went with him up the workhouse, well, I don't know what she said, but he went up there resolved to put Jake in the orphanage and he came away holding him by the hand. And when I saw them, after I'd talked with Mr Scawen, I thought, *There now! All my perplexities are over*. But it wasn't so.'

'And what are your perplexities, then?'

Roseanne's eyes implored her not to take the next words as a joke: 'I don't know why I done it. That's my perplexity. I mean, there's little boys like him, and girls, too, go into that orphanage every month. They don't *die*, do they. They don't live on pilchards and

279

cream, I know, but they don't die. They come out and lead good, useful lives. Look at Tom Hampden, who works for my dad. And that Beth Davey in the Angel – she's from that orphanage. They both are. I can see it now, so why couldn't I see it then? Why did I lose all reason? Honestly, I'd have cast myself down a shaft if they'd left Jake there that day.'

Mrs Scawen shivered. 'Don't say such things,' she said – with such anguish that Roseanne apologized profusely, suspecting she had touched on some tragedy from the woman's past.

'No, you weren't to know.' Mrs Scawen drew a deep breath and gathered herself. 'Let's go up this path and I'll show you where the grotto is to be. The folly, I mean. Well, it's a bit of both.'

Roseanne said nothing.

'You weren't to know,' Mrs Scawen repeated, 'but only last week quite a dear friend of mine tried to take her own life. She's in the infirmary in Truro now. I don't think it was a very serious attempt on her actual life – but I certainly took it as a *very* serious attempt to tell me I had failed her.'

'Oh, I don't believe you should ought to take it like that,' Roseanne said to assure her.

'I know I shouldn't, my dear. But it's hard not to. Knowing's one thing, feeling's another – as you've just pointed out in a different way. The poor woman had led a very *unfortunate* life.' She put a certain stress upon the word, which Roseanne could interpret or not, depending on her degree of worldly wisdom. 'And then she met and married a wonderful man, a truly wonderful man. But despite that, and despite all the comfort and support I *thought* I had given her – I believe I am her closest friend – despite all that, she has never been able to reconcile those two facts in her life.' She gave a wan smile and stepped out more briskly, for her sad tale had brought them to a snail's pace. 'I'm telling you all this just to warn you that I may not be such a wonderful counsellor and friend as I may once have imagined − and you may have hoped.'

Her self-control was admirable, Roseanne thought. From the brink of tears only moments earlier she had brought herself back to this robust self-mockery. 'I don't know what I hoped, ma'am,' she said. 'But I didn't see why I should plague you with my troubles.'

'Then don't, pray,' the other replied. 'Simply tell me about them, instead. For instance, tell me why you now think you did it? Since you can see so clearly that the workhouse, though not a bed of violets, is certainly no murder factory, either − why do you now think you were so stubborn and insistent?'

Roseanne shrugged awkwardly. 'Dunno.'

'*Really?*' The answer seemed to surprise her. 'Surely you've had some thoughts about it?'

Roseanne hung her head and dragged her feet again. 'I suppose . . . in a way . . . I mean, I *do* love little Jake and I shan't go back on my promises nor nothing like that . . . but I suppose, in a way, I was also testing Mark Bodilly and Stephen Morvah. Mr Scawen tell you about they, did he?'

'Yes,' she replied hastily, as if it went without saying. 'Testing them?' she repeated. 'To prove what?'

'Well, 'twas a dawbrained test, wasn't it! It never tested nothing at all.'

'But if Mark Bodilly had said yes, he'd accept the little lad along with you . . .?'

Roseanne nodded glumly.

'Then it wouldn't have been a silly test at all,' Mrs Scawen insisted.

'I suppose not.'

'So he's the one you want, when it comes down to it.'

She shook her head. 'I dunno. Maybe I want him the way I wanted to keep a hold of Jake − against all reason and my calmer judgment. Maybe if I got my way and got Mark's ring on my finger . . . maybe after a month or so I'd come to my senses and see it was no more than me being rash and headstrong again, like over Jake. Maybe I should do what my head tells me is the sensible thing, even now.'

Something shimmered beneath a shrub to one side of the path. Mrs Scawen stooped and picked it up. 'Snakeskin,' she commented. 'Grass snake by the look of him. Isn't it beautiful.'

Roseanne stretched forth her hand and touched it, almost reverently. 'Just think if we could do that!' she replied.

The older woman was about to laugh when she caught sight of the other's eye and realized she was not joking. A perplexity filled her suddenly − and a sense of despair that she would never be able to help in this case.

They came to a large, round area of flattened stone rubble. 'This is where *my* folly is going to be,' Mrs Scawen told her with an amused smile. 'I saw an illustration once of a folly in a large country house in Bedfordshire. Picture it − I'm going to build my own version of it here. A small circular temple with a domed roof of cut stone blocks. Massive blocks − only a bolt of lightning or some fiery retribution from the gods has broken the roof, just moments ago. And here are the stone blocks, actually frozen in the act of tumbling down!' Her hands vigorously defined the tumbling stones. 'Like in these latest photographs, where the camera can actually freeze things that are in motion. Imagine it! Four-hundredweight blocks of stone just held in mid-air!'

Roseanne frowned. 'How are 'ee going to do that, then?'

'Ah!' Mrs Scawen grinned and held up a magician's finger. 'Just look a little closer and you'll see that each block in that cascade of masonry is actually touching its neighbour! Your father has worked it all out. That's what being a master-mason means, you know. And there will be a bar of steel running right down through them, sealed in lead so it will never rust — holding them all in impossible suspension!'

'But why?' Roseanne asked, fascinated at the intensity of her pleasure in this vision.

'Because! Just because!' She laughed. 'Can't you see it? Don't you think there's something awesome about it — the impossible, happening before your very eyes! And you can walk round it and study it from every angle, and *still* say it's impossible! It'll be the crowning glory of the whole garden, you just wait and see.'

Again her gestures sculpted the folly in the empty air — so vividly that Roseanne had a fleeting intimation of the wonder that so plainly gripped her companion. There *was* something grand about it — and almost dangerous, too, in a spiritual sense, as if Mrs Scawen were setting out to mock the laws that kept the whole material world in its proper place.

'Come on! I'll show you the watercourse and then we'll go back home.' The woman was all brisk again. 'We've had quite enough idiotic dreams for one day.' Almost in the same breath — and certainly in the same jocular tone — she added, 'By *the sensible thing* I suppose you mean accept young Morvah's offer of marriage?'

'Yes. I don't see no other way.'

'Ah!' Mrs Scawen's tone suggested that Roseanne had at last said something of great significance.

283

'Don't *you*?' she asked, hoping against hope.

'Well . . . what about going out into the world, finding a position somewhere — just for a year or two . . . or three . . . however long it may take — and supporting yourself and Jake that way?'

'Well, I'd surely like nothing better,' Roseanne answered, with a sarcastic edge to her voice. 'I can't stop home much longer, I know. But, I mean, finding a place like that! On the moon, is it?'

'No,' Mrs Scawen said simply. 'Here.'

PART TWO

ONE'S COMPANY

35

It was the first summer that the Trevivian gardens looked anything like presentable, in their earthly creator's view, at least. The paths were properly paved in the more formal areas, smoothly gravelled where the intention was more natural, and, in the wild fringe, they had all the appearance of ancient packhorse trails, but so well grazed they would not bedew a lady's skirts as she promenaded there. And though there was still nothing you could call a tree, the intention was plain enough. Here you might see a specimen false acacia with fifty feet of growing yet ahead of it; there a grove of walnut and birch over which a good athlete might still make a leap; while the cork oak, an acclimatized usurper of many south Cornish estuaries, was already darkening the fringes of the demesne though no taller than a flowering currant.

The terrace gardens, too, were beginning to show their potential. The summer of '73 having been so desperately hot, Jane Scawen and Roseanne had spent whole days on the beach with their children — as many beaches as they could manage, for they wanted as many different shells as possible. Over the weeks they had gathered several hundredweight, with the help of the children and servants. And thanks to those labours the first two grottoes of the downward walk were now completely encased in what Vosper called 'molluscery'. Cuttlefish framed the entrances; smooth carpet shells alternated in bands with rough hoofs, divided by razors, each from the other; tellins the colour of marigolds shone among banded cockles, flaxen and brown; and at the heart of it all Smooth Artemis winked a luteous eye from beds of Oval Venus, as well he might. The radiance that picked out their mother-of-pearl iridescence filtered in through what now had all the appearance of unglazed cottage windows — squared-off holes in the rock, filled with cast-iron window frames in and around and through which the tendrils of species roses were beginning to trail.

The upward walk, from one open-air terrace to the next, was flanked by cut-stone columns with massive oak lintels to form a pergola that framed a series of views down over the river and its estuary. Already wisteria, jasmine, and clematis were softening the harsh lines imposed by chisel and saw. One of the unexpected advantages of such a vertical garden, they had discovered, was that on the hottest days, when not the faintest soothing breeze could be found among the more conventional walks above, there was always either an upward or a downward draught to be enjoyed down there above the river — and often enough, both: upward off the sunstruck cliff; downward through the cool tunnels behind its face.

Today, however, the third Saturday in June, there was just enough breeze to support the Helford regatta, which is where Vosper and Roseanne had taken the children. There had been an altercation about that. The day had dawned overcast and drizzly, so the two women had decided not to go. The opportunity to water and mulch some of the borders was too perfect to miss. But then, around eleven o'clock, Vosper, who had taken the day off especially, called them out of doors to witness

288

the most amazing sight. It was as if some mighty hand had drawn a ruler-straight line across the sky, from due west to east. North of that line the vault of the sky was unrelieved grey; to the south stretched a blue and cloudless heaven.

No one could remember having seen such a thing before, though Harvey Moyle, the oldest of the gardeners, said he'd seen it happen the other way, from clear blue to heavy rain, back along a good while.

'It's going to be a scorcher,' Roseanne said — and then, without so much as a what-d'you-think, she'd decided to take Jake to 'see the brave boats' after all.

Following that, how could Sarah, Trevanion, Maria, and Courtenay be denied their treat, too? In pique Jane had developed an unspecified malady, a minor, moving feast of an affliction, which sadly prevented her from accompanying them. How Roseanne's face had fallen at that! Now aged twelve, Sarah was handful enough for any grown-up to manage — never mind the other three, whose ages spanned that unbridgeable gulf between ten and five — as well as Jake, now assumed to be almost six. Yes, that'd teach her to go making decisions off the top of her head!

So Jane took her telescope down to its tripod on the first terrace, where she now sat in blissful solitude, enjoying every moment of the regatta without having to endure one bit of it — the press of the sweaty mob and the constant demands of the children for ice cream and sugar niceys, and gallons of pop to wash it down. They were the dearest, sweetest things, and she wouldn't hear a word against them, nor did she regret a moment of their rearing, but one had to admit that one day with them around had all the wear-and-tear of a week without. Their ability to walk into a room and destroy its order was beyond belief — not through romping and horseplay but by such simple acts as taking books from shelves (why was *one* book never enough?), playing the musical box (why did one of them always want the selection the others had wanted on some previous occasion?), and making cuttings for the scrap book (why did one shape produce twenty offcuts — and how did those offcuts migrate to the farthest and most unvisited corners of the room? And how, with a paste brush you could use for painting miniatures, could they accidentally cover a greater area than your average paperhanger could manage deliberately with his twelve-inch monster?).

She closed her eyes, leaned back in her chair, and stretched luxuriously in the shade of her parasol. Poor Vosper! He'd have his fill of being paterfamilias by this evening. Still, he only had himself to blame. He shouldn't have taken up Roseanne's decision quite so eagerly, before consulting his wife. She leaned back still further, the bamboo chair sliding with her, and listened to the sounds of summer. A cuckoo on the far river bank was singing her late-season 'oo-cuck!' She'd taken ages to find a mate this year. Roseanne had made a joke about it, comparing herself to that poor bird in a self-deprecating fashion; Jane had stoically held back from pointing out that Roseanne was, if anything, the *victim* of another cuckoo.

There was a starting gun from the regatta, followed by distant but frenzied shouts of encouragement and insult from the estuary shore. Without opening her eyes Jane pictured the scene — the slack sails, every yard set to catch the slightest puff of wind, the prows miraculously cutting the water at half a walking pace when there seemed no breeze to produce it, all on a sea like badly made glass.

Then there was a sound from much nearer at hand

– feet upon gravel, voices . . . visitors! She groaned inwardly, assumed her hostess smile, and sat up to receive whoever it might be.

June Moyle, the gardener's granddaughter and one of the maids in the house, handed her the card: *Sir Francis Morvah* was the printed legend but underneath was the handwritten addition: *Miss Morvah*. Jane's spirit, which had dipped at the first name, now rose at the second. The famous Annette – Roseanne's tireless correspondent from Paris, Venice, and Rome – home at last. 'Ask her to come down here,' Jane told the girl. 'And you may bring out tea, with the new saffron cake.'

She had a fleeting memory of Dorothy Lanyon, years ago, passing the most scathing remark on the habit of serving cake with afternoon tea – and her father, God rest him, taking it all so solemnly. Lord, how people put themselves on the rack over the most trivial matters!

As she heard Miss Morvah's foot on the terrace steps, she rose to greet her.

'Oh please!' Annette called out from halfway down. 'The last thing I wanted was to disturb you on such a tranquil day, Mrs Scawen.'

'But you don't, Miss Morvah,' Jane assured her. 'And you surely won't deprive me of the pleasure of showing off my handiwork to you? It's so long since you saw it last.'

'It's very good of you.' Annette approached and shook her hand. 'I'd *love* to see it again. I can already see how much you've done.'

'We'll go back through the shell grottoes,' Jane decided aloud. 'It's a cooler way up. Well, I expect you hoped to find Roseanne here?' They sauntered along the terrace to the second downward flight of steps.

'Oh, I can see her some other time,' Annette replied lightly. 'In fact, I'm rather glad of the opportunity to talk to you, Mrs Scawen. I say, those columns are rather fine. Italian?'

Jane allowed herself to be taken in by the implied flattery. 'Kitto,' she said. 'The great man carved them himself. He still has two more to finish.'

'Really? I shouldn't have thought he had the time these days.'

'He doesn't, of course. But he says he wants to keep his hand in at it. So I just . . . live in hope he'll deliver them one day. He is good, isn't he.'

'And how is Roseanne these days?'

You would have thought it mere gentility that prompted the inquiry.

After a pause Jane replied, 'It all depends. Her health is as robust as ever.'

'I worried about her every minute I was away.'

Jane glanced at her in surprise. A young woman less consumed by worry would be hard to picture.

Annette, knowing what was going through her mind, smiled and added, 'Thought about her, anyway.'

'You were certainly a most faithful correspondent, Miss Morvah. If the packets were delayed by storms, Roseanne was quite out of sorts for days.'

Annette narrowed her eyes and stared out at the scene; it was as if she had not heard the last remark.

'Why d'you do that, if I may ask?' Jane said.

The younger woman started guiltily, as if she had been caught scratching herself indelicately. 'Habit,' she said. 'A painter's habit.'

'Yes, I've often seen Roger Moynihan do the same.'

'It reduces a scene to a few simple tones.'

'D'you do a lot of painting now?'

Annette shook her head. 'I dabble. It's an *accomplishment*.' She put sarcastic emphasis on the word.

It struck Jane that they were very alike, give or take the thirteen years between them. She, too, when she came of age, had hated the confinements society placed upon genteel young spinsters, trapping them in a zoo of 'accomplishments' and denying them any chance to make their mark upon the real world. The gardens at Trevivian were her answer to that challenge; Miss Morvah, she suspected, had yet to find hers.

'How *is* Mr Moynihan these days?' Annette asked.

'Do you know him?'

'No, Roseanne wrote and told me. It was tragic. His wife was a very close friend of yours, I understand?'

Jane gave a tight-lipped nod. 'For her the tragedy was that she could see no other way out. She threatened to end it all, many times, but her attempts were always half-hearted. I don't think the last one was any different. It just went that little bit too far.'

They had descended by now to the lower terrace. Jane halted and leaned against the parapet. A light onshore breeze had developed and the racing boats were making better headway now. 'She was a proud woman,' she said. 'She was left an orphan, you know. Quite penniless. Her parents gave her a good education. They managed an inn, one of Mrs Moore's inns, in Redruth. And they were both overcome by fumes in their own cellar. Together. A dreadful shock for the poor girl. She went as a governess to a family in North Cornwall, not a very nice family, as it turned out. But if she'd just sat tight, some young man would have married her.'

'Why didn't she?'

'Because she had too much spirit, I think. It's the ruin of many a maid. She simply couldn't accept that it was her lot to sit tight and wait. She had to cut her cable and go out into the big ocean and . . . make things happen.' Jane smiled dreamily. 'That's one reason she and I grew so close. There's a bit of that in me, too. Hence all this.' She laughed as she waved a hand vaguely about her.

And then she returned her elbow to the parapet and waited.

'Me, too, I suppose,' Annette confessed awkwardly.

Once again Jane turned a surprised gaze upon her.

'All women, perhaps?' Annette offered.

'Oh no. Not Roseanne, for instance.' Jane chuckled. 'In fact, just to show the perversity of the whole thing, *she'd* be quite content to embrace that world which poor Esther Moynihan found it so hard to accept.'

'But before her father became so prosperous she used to work out in their fields all the hours God sent.'

'Don't I know it! This garden wouldn't be half so presentable were it not for her. But that's my point, you see. There's Roseanne, brought up thinking she'd have to make her way in life by the toil of her hands – and yet now she has the choice, she'd happily settle for a world that ended at her garden fence. And here are we, brought up thinking that tiny kingdom would be our world – the hearth and home – and *we* want the rest of it, too!'

'I don't.' Annette joined her at the parapet and stared out over the estuary. 'All I want is Skyburriowe.'

'Ah,' Jane said. 'Not a *tiny* kingdom, anyway.'

There was a long, ruminative silence.

Annette broke it at last. 'I begin to understand,' she murmured, 'why nothing has changed.' She repeated it more emphatically: 'In four years, nothing has changed!'

'Nothing?' Jane frowned.

'I mean, Roseanne is still here. Jake is still . . . Jake. And . . .'

'Oh! If you think *he* hasn't changed!'

'No, but you know what I mean. He's still . . . just Jake. My brother is still besotted by Roseanne. I didn't know he'd moved out into the gate lodge at Montpelier, by the way. Roseanne never mentioned it, and nor did he. I wonder why? Anyway, you know what I mean. Nothing's changed since I left. In fact, since Roseanne came to live here. And Mark Bodilly still living at Vinery House, too — I never thought *that* would last. It's all so . . . so . . . thwarting! What's the word?'

'Frustrating?'

'Yes. Don't you think she ought to *do* something? Make a decision?'

Jane smiled. 'So you think you've come back not a moment too soon? Time to stop her mouldering here, eh!'

'Well, it's hardly fair on Stephen.'

'Is he complaining?'

Annette, unable to say that he was, simply shrugged and said, 'He's just as bad. And what about Mark Bodilly? What does she say about him?'

'I rather think that's her business, don't you,' Jane replied — sounding a little more prim than she intended.

Miss Morvah stared at her so pityingly that, for a moment, their ages seemed reversed and Jane became the *ingénue* who didn't understand the ways of the world. She remembered Roseanne describing how, even at the age of seventeen, the girl had had that effect on her; now she saw what it meant. Half against her will she responded 'If you want my own opinion, I think *that's* where most of the trouble lies: Mr Bodilly.'

'She's still in love with him?'

'Oh, if only it were that simple! She just doesn't know.'

'And she's too proud to find out?'

Jane softened her words with a kindly squeeze of Miss Morvah's arm. 'If you'll just stop putting in questions?'

'Sorry!' Annette bit her lip and went on staring out at the horizon. No smile. Jane felt her arm, stiff as bone.

From above came the silver tinkle of a small bell. The tea had arrived. As if the sound were some order for release, Annette peeled herself away and said, 'Can we go up through the shell grotto?'

As soon as her eyes grew accustomed to the gloom she cried out in amazement. 'Oh, but it's even more beautiful than Roseanne described it.' She touched a dog whelk delicately, as if it might fall off — as it would have done in a rock pool. 'It was worth all those *hours* of sweated labour.'

'Is that how she described it? There's lots more still needed, if you wish to join our beach parties this summer?'

Annette made vague murmurs of an even vaguer commitment. When they came out into the sunlight again she gave another cry of delight: 'A telescope! Oh, I adore those things — did the maid bring it?'

'No, it was there when you came.' Jane went directly to the table and took up her duties as hostess.

'I didn't even notice.' Annette put her eye to the instrument. 'Let's see if I can find her. Such a feeling of power, isn't it. You can see *everything* they're doing and they don't even know you're there. Papa gave me one for my fourteenth birthday. I was never without it at one time.' She scanned the regatta crowds methodically, working in small, overlapping circles. 'This is the best I've ever looked through. I could almost reach out and touch them! There's Jake!' She stopped and peered intently before resuming her search. 'No, it isn't.'

'They're there somewhere,' Jane assured her. 'D'you take sugar?'

Annette, reminded of her duties as a guest, removed

her eye from the telescope and came to the table.

But Jane handed her the cup and said, 'Take it back there with you. I shan't think it in the least bit rude. I know the fascination of that instrument. I could draw the face of every fisherman on the Helford — and tell you which of them to approach for a good brandy!'

'I know!' Annette laughed. 'I could do the same for the Porthleven lot.' She stared reluctantly at the telescope. 'Are you sure you wouldn't mind?'

'As long as you keep up a good commentary. I'd be quite interested to find out where they are . . . and if any of them have drowned yet. That sort of thing.'

Annette needed no second bidding, but returned to the balustrade at once. Jane pointed out that she could adjust the tripod; she didn't need to stoop like that.

In leaving the telescope she had given it a slight knock, leaving it pointing out to sea — which was how she found them so quickly now. 'That *is* Jake!' she exclaimed. 'They're on one of the boats. Yes, there's the girl herself!'

'Dark green?' Jane asked. 'With two masts?'

'That's the boat.'

'Bother!'

Annette glanced briefly at her. 'Why so?' She took the chance of a sip at her teacup.

'Oh, we had a little tiff before they left, which is why I stayed behind.'

'Ah. I did just slightly wonder.'

'Oh, it was nothing. Quite petty. But I was relishing the thought of her trying to manage my four as well as Jake. But if they're on the *Arethusa*, John Walker's boat, that's their seventh heaven, so she'll have no difficulty.'

Annette, staring through the eyepiece again, bit her lip and giggled.

'What?' Jane prompted.

'There we were, talking about Stephen and Mark Bodily . . . perhaps they'd both better look to their laurels!'

Intrigued, Jane almost sprang from her seat and dashed to see for herself. But when she had focused the eyepiece to suit her own sight her smile changed from conspiratorial to long-sufferance. 'Oh,' she exclaimed in disappointment, 'that's only Scawen. Their laurels are safe — more's the pity, perhaps.'

'Oh, I say, I'm sorry . . .' Annette stammered as her hostess resumed her seat. 'I thought he'd be in Helston. I mean, I thought you said she'd be looking after all five youngsters on her own.'

'So she is, my dear! When it comes to keeping petty discipline, I'm afraid, Scawen's about as useful as a stepladder in a rowing boat.'

Annette laughed and went on peering through the telescope.

After a pause Jane asked, 'What made you say our two young gallants should look to their laurels just now?'

'Oh . . . nothing.' With an almost guilty abruptness, Annette left the instrument and brought her cup back to the table, sipping at it to give herself cause not to speak. 'Just jumping to wild conclusions at the sight of her standing within three feet of a handsome gentleman. That's one of the dangers of those things.' She jerked her head back toward the telescope as she sat down.

'Yes,' Jane replied, and busied herself with pouring a second cup for them both. 'Do cut us some cake.'

Annette complied and then flopped gratefully beneath the parasol into the all-embracing clutch of the other wicker chair. 'You never finished telling me about

298

Roseanne — how she couldn't decide about Mark Bodilly and so on. Do they see each other at all? She never so much as breathed his name in her letters.'

Jane paused and then rose to her feet. 'It's a strange situation altogether,' she said as she went back to the telescope. She put her eyes to it, readjusted the focus but did not change its alignment, and continued, 'When you say nothing has changed — in that sense — you're quite right. She never sees Mark now. Since her parents moved to Helston, she has no . . .'

'I know!' Annette interrupted in tones of amazement. 'Liston Court, no less! Who would have thought it! My mother thinks it an utter scandal, of course. And my father's quite sure old Kitto bribed his way to where he is.' She put a hand to her mouth. 'Sorry! I interrupted?'

'Yes, I was saying, since they left Breage, she has no call to return there herself. So they don't even have the chance to glower at each other over hedges and across the aisle in church. But for all that — she just can't forget him.'

'Has she told you so?'

Jane still staring intently through the telescope, replied, 'She doesn't need to. If one of them doesn't get a hand to Jake's collar soon, he'll be in the drink.'

'Can he swim?'

Jane was interested at the lack of alarm, or even concern, in the question. 'Like a pilchard,' she replied. 'The thing is, Roseanne seems utterly contented with this . . . limbo. Your brother seems afraid to force the issue . . .' She allowed her voice to rise slightly on the thought, making it as nearly a question as possible.

'Not in that way,' Annette informed her, taking the cue. 'He doesn't want to live off her money. She must be quite rich by now, I imagine?'

Jane ignored *her* cue. 'Then you can tell him from me he's a fool. He could keep her quite well now in the style she'd prefer, which is simplicity itself. She thinks even we live too grandly here! Mrs Moore is her pattern. Only last week she said to me, "Mrs Moore could buy and sell the lot of us ten times over — and look how simply she lives!" So you tell your brother . . .'

'It wouldn't help,' Annette cut in. 'I think he knows that already. But he's developed this prejudice against having an income. He wants to *earn* his keep by the sweat of his brow — or the sweat of his pen, anyway. So, as long as they keep returning his effusions to him with those polite little letters of rejection, he's very happy for Roseanne *not* to come to any conclusion about anything. He could never have contrived this situation, mind you. *He's* utterly lacking in that sort of guile.'

Her stress on the word was interesting enough for Jane to leave off her perusal at last and return to the tea table. 'Well,' she said, with a disarming smile, as she seated herself once more, 'I have to confess that when she came here first, I never imagined she'd be staying so long. *Not*, I hasten to add, that I now wish to see the back of her. Perish the thought! She's a wonderful companion, devoted to the children. . . . Jake's so adorable — and I've already said what a stalwart helper she is in the garden. All the same, I feel guilty' — her eyes flickered briefly toward the telescope — 'that we have possibly made *too* comfortable a home for her here, and are thus only contributing to the difficulty she obviously has in making the next important decision in her life.'

Annette sighed. 'What an awful dilemma! Any suggestion from you . . . I mean, there's no way you could . . . however tactfully . . .' She relapsed into silence.

Watching her pretending to think, Jane suppressed a smile; for she had not the slightest doubt but that Annette had decided what to do next, long before she left home that afternoon. The next words only served to confirm it.

'I think,' Annette said slowly, 'that something must happen, something to shake all three of them out of their complacency.'

36

Montpelier House had once belonged to Jane Hervey
— before she married Vosper Scawen and decided that
the grand life was not for her. Even before old man
Hervey had bought the place, its farms and estate had
been sold off to the Pellews of Skewjack Hall, but
Squire Pellew had cannily decided against buying the
house itself. After her father's death and her own
marriage, Jane had sold the place to the Morvahs of
Skyburriowe. Tin had been strong at the time.

Now, although tin was strong once again, it had failed
to take the Morvahs up with it; their principal venture,
the Wheal Fortune lode, was finally exhausted. So
something had to go, and the lot fell to Montpelier
House. In the normal way Sir Francis would have called
upon Coad and Snell, Helston's leading auctioneers and
valuers, to handle the business for them, as they had
for generations; but Annette managed to persuade them
to give young Bodilly a chance, instead. He had made
quite a name for himself these past few years, having
shifted a number of properties that had been considered
almost unsaleable.

All of which goes to explain why she was standing
before Montpelier, in the middle of the carriage sweep,
on that hot July morning, waiting for the man himself
to arrive. She had gone to extraordinary lengths over
her appearance — considering his station in life and

the humdrum nature of their business there. She wore a white dress of a fine, silky-textured gauze, spotted with hand-embroidered flowers in purple, yellow, and green and tied in with a broad waistband of white sateen. Bustles, having almost vanished five years ago, were now back with a vengeance; hers had no fewer than three hoops. Their tapes bore hard on the back of her thighs, so great was the weight of material they supported. Part of her rebelled at the discomfort of it all, and the awkwardness involved in such simple acts as walking and sitting; but the rest of her had to admit it did make one rather grand and stately, especially now that shoes with proper heels were 'in' again. They made one so tall and gave one's walk such statuesque grace.

'Something has obviously delayed him,' she told her maid, Margaret Chigwidden.

'Mrs Moore,' the girl replied laconically.

Annette turned to her with interest. 'Oh?'

'She's putting up a new brewery over to Redruth. She can't enlarge no more in Penzance, and they're working double-tides now and can't keep up.'

'No matter what the price of tin, there's always money for beer, 'eh!'

'You know her first brewery is still there in the coach house at Lanfear? Ever see it, did 'ee?'

'No.' Annette moved back into the shade of the portico and folded her parasol. 'Tell me more about Bodilly. Why is she dealing with him in Redruth? Surely they've plenty of estate agents there?'

'Bodilly's a man of greed, Miss Morvah. And that Mrs Moore, she's got a nose for it.'

'He's certainly done well for himself lately. When I went away he was trading mostly in cattle and selling the odd cottage. And now . . .' A wave of the hand at

Montpelier completed the thought. 'He'll have his work cut out for him here, though, I think.'

Margaret looked hesitantly at her, drew breath to speak and then thought better of it.

'Go on,' Annette urged.

'Well, I was only going to say, like, that his *connection*' – she gave a slight sniff – 'with old Widow Delamere done him no harm.'

Annette felt that the description 'old widow' hardly fitted the vivacious lady she had spoken to only an hour or so earlier in Breage. 'Well,' she said, 'Mrs D may have opened a few doors, but he was the one who had to go through them and give a satisfactory account of himself. When you're buying and selling properties, you can't make too many mistakes.'

'Oh, he's a clever fellow, right enough,' Margaret agreed, though in such ambiguous tones that Annette could not be sure it was a compliment. 'Here he comes now,' she added.

'You've better hearing than me,' Annette commented.

''Tweren't hearing, Miss. I saw the rooks go up in the spinney by the gate lodge.'

A moment later they both heard the sound of a carriage on the gravel drive.

'Talking of the gate lodge,' Annette remarked, 'my brother will have to move out again now.'

Her maid chuckled. 'I should think Bodilly would take the job for nothing – just to be able to do that!'

Was she fishing, or voicing the local gossip and opinion? There was no time to probe, for Mark's gig was now in sight emerging from the woodland that fringed the drive.

Though he was now going at a smart enough pace, and pulled up with something of a skid, his horse was

304

in no lather; indeed, the creature was hardly out of breath.

'I'm so sorry to be late, Miss Morvah,' he exclaimed as he leaped down. 'I was only in Germoe, too.'

'Think nothing of it, Mr Bodilly. We have barely arrived ourselves.' She held out a hand to shake his — which startled him somewhat.

'When I lived just down the road from Breage school,' he said ruefully, 'I was the last to get there each morning!'

She absent-mindedly kept a hold of his hand, enjoying his slight discomfiture — and, to be honest, the touch of him, too. 'And are you always late for *church* now?' she asked with a coy smile.

'Ah!' He was at a loss for any more meaningful reply. One-handed, he slung a binoculars case around his neck.

'That would be telling, eh?' she suggested, letting go of him at last.

'Indeed.' He clapped his hands and soaped them vigorously. 'Would you mind if I took a quick look at the exterior of the house first? No need to trouble you. I'll ring the bell when it's time to . . .'

'It would be no trouble at all, Mr Bodilly.' She took his arm and propelled him down the steps again. 'I want to know exactly what you think about the place. What you discover. All the faults. Everything.' Again she released him. 'Chigwidden can take your horse round to the yard, where Martin can unhitch him and put him in a stable.'

'Well . . .' he fingered his chain but did not actually pull out his watch.

'Or are we such small beer that you can't spare us the rest of your valuable morning?'

'Of course, of course!' He clapped his hands and soaped them again. 'You can manage the horse?' he

305

asked the maid — who gave him a sarcastic smile and led the beast away.

He was, Annette realized, a very different Mark Bodilly from the tetchy, tongue-tied fellow she remembered. She wondered whether Roseanne knew it, too. How often did they meet these days?

She set off for the garden; he followed, saying, 'The place is in much better repair than I expected, Miss Morvah.'

'Well, the Martins have nothing else to do but keep it shipshape. And two of the gardeners from Skyburriowe come up here every week and trim the shrubs and things.'

'So I see. It'll make it much easier to sell.'

She stopped and turned to him with a grin. 'You're an odd one, I must say!'

Once again her friendliness took him aback, though not so much as last time. 'How?' he asked.

'Everyone else we deal with from the plumber to the vet shakes his head and sighs and generally suggests that our particular difficulty is something quite out of the ordinary and will call for an almost superhuman effort — which, to be sure, is reflected in the final bill!'

He took out his binoculars while she was speaking and trained them on the house. 'I've no patience with all that,' he told her. 'There's a tuft of grass up in that launder. That's where it's been overflowing — see the discoloration down the wall?'

She drew forth a note book and pencil and made a jotting. 'Tell me every little thing,' she said. 'No matter how small. Everything a buyer might use so as to abate the price. I'll make sure it's remedied before the first of them comes.'

'Well, well!' he said admiringly. 'I believe you.'

After that he held back nothing — the moss gathering at the corners of sills and panes, the efflorescence by the basement lights, the cobwebs choking the ventilator grilles — he pointed out each one.

'And those cracks in the wall?' she asked, thinking he had missed them.

But he shook his head. 'Hair cracks. It's only in the stucco. People expect them in a house this age. If they don't see them, they grow suspicious and start wondering how big they were before the plasterer came along.'

She made a note of that, too, in case an enthusiastic builder exceeded his instructions.

On their way back to the front portico he said, 'I wish everyone I had to deal with was like you, Miss Morvah.'

'Oh!' she replied archly. 'Now I, on the other hand, am rather glad there's only *one* of me!'

He laughed apologetically; why did she make him feel so much on the defensive? 'I mean as thorough and as businesslike, of course.'

'Of course,' she echoed as she led him indoors. 'Shall we start at the top and work down?'

She beat him to the foot of the stairs and went ahead of him. With each step she managed to get the end of the lowest hoop of her bustle behind the bend of her knee — so that when she straightened it, the most alluring wriggle was produced, which, coupled with the swish of the gauze and the suggestion of perfume, made him catch his breath.

She had had a lot of practice at this manoeuvre, especially in the art galleries in Italy, where gentlemen made no secret of their admiration for a lady — and yet never forgot they were gentlemen. Their flattering attention had been most pleasing to her; nonetheless, Mark Bodilly's breathless and tongue-tied response was, somehow, more pleasing still — and in a way she could not easily explain.

He found every excuse to remain ungallantly behind her at least until the first landing; he shook the banister rail to test its soundness and pressed every other tread for squeaks.

'If we . . . whoo!' He paused for breath and mopped his brow. 'I *am* out of condition!'

'A great Cornish wrestler like you?' she asked in surprise. 'Or have you given that up, too?'

He tilted his head ruefully. 'I've done little enough of it lately. It's a young man's game.'

'Pff!' she exploded scornfully. 'What are *you* then? Come on, there's lots to see yet.' And she started up the next flight.

Manfully — or gentlemanfully — he raced ahead of her this time. 'If we could lay a bit of carpet,' he suggested. 'I always think that helps. And arrange for flowers in the principal rooms when I show people over . . .'

It all went down in her notebook, everything he said during the hour or so that followed. He, for his part, made a rough plan of each floor and took precise measurements. She held one end of the tape for him, always against a door or the glass of a window or the back of an alcove.

'You've done this before,' he accused jovially. 'That's one of *our* tricks — to make a room seem as large as possible.'

But she denied it. 'It wouldn't cross my mind to measure from anywhere else,' she replied.

He felt quite at ease with her by the time they had worked their way back to the front door. There she told him she had brought sandwiches, not knowing how long their inspection might last. Would he not share them?

She had far more than she needed. And there was surely some bottled ale in the house. 'And anyway, you ought to see the gardens. They were always the glory of Montpelier, and could be again.'

He needed little persuasion, of course.

Notwithstanding all Miss Morvah's friendliness that morning, it still surprised him to see Margaret Chigwidden keeping a discreet distance behind them. No ordinary valuer, or doctor, solicitor, or other professional servant, come to that, would require such chaperoning. The suggestion that he was in a somewhat different class intrigued him.

They ambled among the shrubs and flowers, chatting amiably enough, and came at length to a small courtyard garden of stone troughs and alpines. To one side of it was a little arbour where they could sit in the shade and unwrap their sandwiches at last. Margaret took hers and strolled slowly away, passing eventually out of sight.

'These gardens are just right,' Mark said. 'They are not so neglected as to break the heart, nor so perfect they leave nothing to stimulate the imagination.'

'Yes, yes.' Her brusqueness informed him she'd had enough house-sale talk for one day.

He took the hint immediately. 'You'll be sorry to see the place go, Miss Morvah,' he said.

'Not at all,' she assured him. 'All I want is Skyburriowe.'

He darted an astonished glance at her, forgetting to chew for a moment. 'But . . . your brother?'

She shrugged. 'He's the residuary legatee. Or is it reversioner? I never understand all those terms.'

He suspected she knew precisely what 'all those terms' meant. She was just giving him the chance to say, 'You mean he'll own it, lock, stock and barrel.'

She smiled.

'I see,' he said slowly. 'Yes. And he's the sort of man who'd be far happier in the gate lodge than the big house.'

It was wonderful, she thought, to sit beside a person and to know exactly what was passing through their mind. At this moment, for instance, she had not the slightest doubt but that he was thinking: *How well endowed is she? Could she afford to buy her brother out?* And, in a quick thinking mind like his, that would lead directly to the further question: *Why has she been so very friendly with me this morning?*

'Just before you came,' she told him, 'Chigwidden suggested to me that you'd waive your commission on this sale.'

'Oh?' He shifted nervously. Her tone suggested it was a joke, but there were some things one hardly joked about.

'Can't you guess why?' she asked. 'Your mention of "gate lodge" put me in mind of it.'

'Oh!' He groaned and collapsed his shoulders, as people do on hearing a feeble witticism.

'That was my response, too,' she assured him. 'Still, I'm glad to know it's yours.' After the briefest pause she went on, 'I wonder . . . Jane Scawen used to live here, didn't she. I remember seeing her father when I was a child.'

His eyes narrowed. He looked at her sharply. But his tone was mild enough as he replied, 'Yes, that's right. Tall fellow with an old-fashioned stovepipe hat. Thin as a rasher of wind. Yes.' He laughed as if there were other details he might supply but chose not to.

Annette said nothing. She waited to see if this new seed would germinate and sprout.

Soon enough he said, 'That's some garden she's built over to Helford by all accounts.'

'Have you not seen it, then?' Her smile was arch enough to show she was teasing.

He stared at her uncertainly and, not for the first time, she became aware of an uncomfortable feeling inside her. In a certain mood and a certain light, his gaze could be . . . disconcerting. 'Sorry,' she said — without quite knowing why.

Again his eyes narrowed, but this time his tone was hard as he asked, 'What does all this mean?'

'Mean?' She swallowed.

'You know full well what I'm talking about, Miss Morvah,' he said evenly.

'What d'you think it means!' she snapped as if he were being deliberately obtuse — though really she was playing for time.

'I'll tell you exactly what I think it means,' he went on in that same deadly calm. 'I think it means you've been a-visiting Mrs Scawen.' He raised his voice an octave and parodied her grossly: 'Oh, she used to live here at Montpelier, didn't she!' Then back to his quiet voice again: 'And you had a good little giggle with a certain person who lives over there. And she said — or one of you said — "I wonder how Mark Bodilly feels about it all now?" And *you* volunteered to find out.'

'How *dare* you!' Annette tried.

He laughed in her face, but quite amicably. 'I can think of no other reason for you to be so pleasant to a person like me.'

She rose and walked a pace or two away, keeping her back to him. What had happened? Why had she so completely lost control of the situation? Normally she would have relished a contretemps like this. These were precisely the circumstances in which she *never* grew heated, *never* lost her calm. Yet here was her heart, thundering away like a butter churn; her knees felt so weak the tapes of her bustle threatened to cave her legs in; and her hands were so feeble she couldn't have clenched them to save her life. 'Oh, can't you!' she heard her voice saying.

What was he doing? Why did he remain so silent? She told herself to turn and face him but the paralysis still gripped her.

Suddenly she felt his hand delicately touch her arm, on the inside, just above her elbow. 'Forgive me,' he said simply.

She turned and looked at him. Her chin lifted itself an inch or two, tilting her face toward his. None of these things she willed, yet she did nothing to prevent them, either.

And he, looking down at her, suddenly thought she was the most beautiful and desirable woman he had ever seen. It was also the first time he had thought of her as that − a woman − rather than the little cooze who had given Roseanne so much trouble at school, or as the young giglet who had spied on him, and everyone else, backalong, or, indeed, as the kitey female who had pitched up to him on the stairs just now. For a moment he stared down at her, seeing her as she really was − confused, vulnerable, and ready. He lowered his lips to hers.

But she turned and ran.

37

For weeks after that encounter Annette avoided any situation in which she and Mark might run across each other. Her few unavoidable visits to Helston were nightmares of vigilance and terror. Terror! She couldn't understand it. She who prided herself on being so cool and controlled, who thrilled at any sign of strong emotion in others because it made them so vulnerable – *she* now walked in mortal terror of meeting a man whose only connection with her was that he was handling the sale of one of her father's properties!

She had known Mark Bodilly all her life – in the sense that she could recognize him from a distance, knew the sound of his voice . . . had heard all the tales about him, scurrilous or otherwise. At anytime before that meeting she could have passed him with a friendly nod and would have forgotten him moments later. There were plenty of men in the district she'd follow with her eyes – or school her eyes not to follow; most of them she couldn't even name. But Mark had never been among them.

In a way she had known him too well for that. True, she couldn't have repeated his opinion on any particular topic, social or political; she couldn't have said how deep was his faith, how great his charity. But, for all that, she felt she knew him. The men she followed with her eyes (or forced herself not to) were men she'd deliberately never know. For such knowledge would destroy the images she made of them in the incandescent darkness of her imagination; they were phantasms who kept all true feelings of that kind safely at bay. They left her free of entanglements and able to take on the world. Between them and real men, men of her actual acquaintance, there stretched a vast, unbridgeable chasm.

And now Mark Bodilly had somehow leaped that divide. He had become the only man *unknown* to her who could stir those dangerous passions. Time and again her mind replayed their meeting at Montpelier, their walk around the house, their wandering through its rooms . . . and yet she could remember no moment of warning. She stared at the notes she had jotted; her firm, bold hand gave no clue as to what had lain in store. Even their stroll through the garden to that fateful spot was as carefree as she could have wished. Where had it gone wrong?

The skin and flesh of her arm remembered his touch. The nape of her neck tingled again at the murmur of his voice: 'I'm sorry.' Her lips remembered reaching for his. But every time she felt the luxury of those moments begin to steal through her, she pinched herself hard, so hard that a lesser creature would have cried out loud – all in a vain attempt to expunge those moments of weakness from her memory.

How could such a thing have happened to her? The anger in the question begged another: How could she have permitted it to happen? At what moment did she drop her guard? What clue had she given him that the fortress of her self-sufficiency was, just for that moment, wide open to him? She had to know the answers if she was ever to lead a normal life again.

Any parent whose carelessness has led to the death

of a child will tell you that they replay the moment of tragedy over and over in their minds, giving it a happier outcome – 'If only . . . if only!' In that same spirit, Annette rewrote the garden scene a dozen different ways to salve a wound that seemed no less pernicious to her. It was only a flirtatious moment – she kissed him lightly and tripped laughingly away, calling 'Catch me if you can!' Or she had simply asked, 'Is there a midge or something in my eye?' and the danger had blown over. Or – and this was the one she liked best – she kissed him tenderly, once and once only; and then, in a sincere and well-modulated voice, she had explained to him how such things could never be between them; and he had sighingly agreed and enlisted in the colours.

None of it had the slightest effect. At best it would help her sleep; but come the dawn and the dreadful knowledge of what she had done, and so nearly done, was there again to mock her. And yet, over those weeks, there was at least some change – a change in the emphasis if not in the actual cause of her anger. In the beginning it had been *her* fault. She had allowed . . . she had risked. But gradually the burden of guilt was shifted on to him. He had planned it. He had watched her all morning, dropping little bombs with long fuses, all timed to detonate within her at the moment when he knew she'd be most off her guard. He was the devil.

A small, sarcastic voice whispered to her: 'That, to be sure, is why *he* brought those sandwiches and suggested you eat them in the garden, dear!' But it did not prevail. She simply could not face the thought that it was her weakness rather than his superhuman cunning that had led to this catastrophe. The one thought that never occurred to her was that Mark himself might be undergoing precisely the same sort of torture, and for very similar reasons.

315

38

May Delameré leaned across the bed and blew gently in Mark's ear. 'Time my darling boy was gone,' she whispered. He stirred, made a few noises that were not quite groans, and settled again. 'We don't want a repeat of last week, do we,' she insisted. 'Or what so nearly happened last week.' He linked his fingers behind his head and stared at the ceiling — just to show her he was not dropping off again. He seemed to be haunted by things that *nearly* happened. Midnight struck. The church tower and the grandfather in the hall were in rare unison. He looked at the curtains. The nights were definitely drawing in.

'Remember to duck as you pass the candle,' she added.

Still lying flat on his back, he bent his left knee a few degrees — the first of what might be a thousand signs he was preparing to go. 'If we were married . . .' he said.

She no longer bothered to reply to the suggestion, though she longed to ask why it had become such an obsession with him lately.

'You can't say it's because of the difference in our wealth any longer,' he pointed out.

Stifling a sigh, and a yawn, she laid her head on the pillow beside him. There was one way to make him leave.

'I've probably got enough put by to keep you *above* the style to which you are accustomed,' he pointed out.

She put the tip of her tongue against his ear lobe.

He shivered. 'And I owe it all to you,' he went on.

Her tongue began to explore.

'Rent-free . . .' He swallowed. 'Never having to pay out on . . . whoo!' A tremble passed right down him. 'I can't!' he complained. 'You know I've given . . . my all.'

'Mmm!' Her delicate fingers reached for his nipples.

'Anyway!' he cried more briskly, raising himself on one elbow and fending her off with a long, iron hand. 'I know exactly what you're trying to do. You don't want any more, really. You're just trying to shame me into going.'

'. . . which you'll have to do sooner or later. And this poor, tired, raddled old frame of mine just wishes it were sooner.'

'Why won't you marry me?' he asked.

'The reasons haven't changed since last time. Nor the time before. Nor the time . . .'

'But life changes. I change. Don't you like me any more?'

'Far too much to marry you, my dear.' She kissed his hand.

But his words struck a chord within her. He *had* changed lately and she knew that the usual trick would not make him leave her bed tonight.

She sat up and shrugged herself back into her nightdress. 'Put that on,' she commanded, throwing his nightshirt over his face. While he complied she poured a glass of water, returned to the bed, pulled the sheet, which was their only covering, off him, and then sat cross-legged in her half of the bed, facing him. 'Now,' she said, 'what's really behind this *idée fixé* for us to marry? You know it would be disastrous.'

'I think it's my only possible salvation,' he murmured lugubriously.

'Sit up!' she snapped. 'Anyone can lie down and maunder on and on. Sit up and talk properly. What's all this nonsense about salvation?'

She handed him the tumbler, which he sipped for politeness' sake. Then, finding himself thirsty indeed, he finished it off.

'Better?' She rose and replaced it by the carafe.

He nodded.

'Well?' she prompted, sitting and facing him once again.

'You might as well know. There's a . . . a female . . . girl . . .'

She wanted to tell him they usually were, but held her tongue.

'I mean . . . it's not even as if I *like* her! I've never thought of her as anything but a spoiled little . . . I mean an interfering nosey-parker . . . hoity-toity . . .'

'Annette Morvah!' May Delamere was at a loss to explain the sudden little squirt of fear in her belly.

He was staring at her in amazement. 'Has she communicated with you?' he asked.

'No.' Her tone was acid-sweet. 'Your description was enough.'

'I have the sale of Montpelier for Sir Francis.'

She frowned. 'Today? Was it arranged today?' If so, it would hardly explain his behaviour these weeks gone by.

'No.' He licked his lips nervously. 'Back in July. Tuesday the twenty-first of July.'

'And what happened . . . to make you say it in that tone?'

He shook his head at the impossibility of explaining it. 'At first I blamed myself. I mean, she is burr good

318

company – and she was so friendly. She didn't behave like the squire's daughter or anything. And I thought I just got a bit carried away.'

'For heaven's sake!' May's heart was going like a hammer. 'What are you trying to say?'

He ploughed doggedly on, keeping to his chosen furrow. 'But now I see it was her all along. She planned it. She tricked me into it. I don't know what her game is.'

May stared at him aghast. 'Why *her*?' she asked. 'That creature, of all people! Oh . . . men!' Her eyes impeached the ceiling.

'Men?' The word stung him. 'We're no match for a scheming woman, I'll tell 'ee.'

'What an excuse!' she sneered. 'If you knew how feeble you sounded!' She gave out a single, heavy sigh. 'Well, what's to be done about it? That's the question to ask ourselves now.' A thought struck her and she turned to him, asking bitterly, 'And did you suppose that marrying me would relieve you of your responsibilities?'

'No, you stupid . . . old . . .' He stopped in horror. It was the one word he had sworn to himself never to use of her, not even in his innermost thoughts – and he had just blurted it out like that! 'See what she's gone and done!' he said.

'What did you call me?' she asked icily.

'The one thing you're not,' he said with more spirit. 'Nor ever will be to me. And that's the power of that witch, so you take heed of it, woman.'

'Old,' she repeated. 'You said old.'

'Oh *hell*!' he cried. 'I'm going!'

He forgot to duck as he passed between the candle flame and the drawn curtains.

319

39

Roseanne and Jane Scawen spent the morning with the children on Breage Rocks, collecting limpets and cockles. Jane could remember a time when she had swum here almost every day, when the two Pellew girls had come over from Falmouth to stay with their aunt and uncle at Skewjack. 'They were the two who made such unfortunate marriages,' she said, describing those times to Roseanne. 'Angelica and Jemima – I must have mentioned them to you.'

At least once a month! Roseanne thought.

'I feel so sorry for them. They were such a bright, happy pair. Oh, the first time we swam here! It was a day like this, except it was at the beginning of summer, not the end, and the sea was *freezing*! But it was oily calm like this. And we swam right out there.' She pointed beyond the headland. 'Just three gossiping heads on the water.' A new thought struck her. 'I say, would you care for a swim now? There's nobody about to see us – and what if they do, anyway? And Bridget can keep an eye on the children.'

Roseanne agreed that it would be most refreshing.

They got down among high rocks and changed into their bathing costumes; then they negotiated the awkward bit between there and the point where the sea covered the exposed portions of their limbs. But once they were safe from prying eyes (which were, in any case, nonexistent), they halted and smiled encouraging after-you smiles at each other, and shivered and stared without enthusiasm at the vast expanse of uninvitingly cold sea ahead of them.

'This is quite the wrong way to go about it,' Jane said. 'We should run down the sand and hurl ourselves full tilt into the water. Get it over and done with quickly.'

Sarah, the only child old enough to need a bathing costume, came from nowhere and ran vigorously between them, putting up great sheets of water and making them scream. Jake saw the fun and ran to join in, and soon all five of them held the women hostage in walls and curtains and stinging jets of cruelly cold water.

However, once the shock wore off, the victims began to retaliate. The battle was so even that eventually they all collapsed in the shallows, laughing, coughing, spluttering, and fighting for breath.

'Who wants to swim out to the headland and back?' Jane asked.

The youngsters, who had done it twice already that morning and who considered their parents' idea of swimming much too sedate and uneventful, groaned and returned to the Great Congo Dam they were building across the freshwater stream that ran into the cove. Roseanne and Jane began a stately breaststroke through the slick, calm water, out to the edge of the open sea. Halfway Jane turned on her back and, treading water gently, just enough to keep more or less horizontal, closed her eyes and gave out a great sigh. 'I wish moments like this could go on and on forever, don't you?' she asked.

'Mmm.' Roseanne trod water and wondered what was really going on inside her companion's mind. She was trying to work around to something, no doubt of it. For weeks now she'd been dropping remarks that sounded like the start of a conversation but proved not to be, and giving little searching looks, and smiling at things that weren't really worth a smile. Ever since that day Annette had come back from Italy and paid them a visit. Something was afoot, and Jane knew of it and couldn't think how to tell her.

'Oh, I forgot,' Roseanne said. 'You belonged to live up Montpelier then, didn't you. This beach was yours.'

'Only to the high-tide line. The Queen owns the rest.'

'It must be funny to own land you'd never, ever visit.'

'Oh, I don't know.' Jane made a few vigorous trudgeon strokes to bring herself horizontal again. 'We owned a hundred and fifty acres at Montpelier. I'm sure I never walked in half the fields, only stared at them over the gate. And there were some rooms in the house I never set foot in until the sale. Talking of which' – she opened her eyes and started swimming vigorously once more, but this time on her back – 'I suppose you've heard it's on the market again?'

'No.' Roseanne struck out to catch up.

'Oh, I'm sorry. I meant to tell you. It must have slipped my mind. But I thought *you'd* know, anyway.' An archness in her smile alerted Roseanne to what came next: 'Mr Bodilly has the agency for the sale. I think it was Annette's doing, really, because the Morvahs have always dealt with Coad and Snell for all their previous land transactions.' There was a fractional pause before she added, 'Wasn't it kind of her?'

To Roseanne, the thought that Annette might do something out of *pure* kindness was so unlikely that she immediately began to wonder what other motive the woman might have – even as she knew that Jane had intended her mind to start working that way.

'Indeed,' Jane went on, 'I thought that, as we're in the neighbourhood, we'd send the coach back to wait for us in Ashton while we walk up through the fields and through the gardens at Montpelier. We could see if there aren't one or two subjects that could do with dividing at this time of year.' She laughed as people do when they propose something a little cheeky. 'But if you'd rather not, you can go with the coach.'

'What ever for?' Roseanne asked.

'If you'd rather not meet Stephen.'

'I meet him quite often,' Roseanne said defensively.

Jane laughed. 'When was the last time?' She began to tread water. 'That's far enough, I think. I wonder how deep it is here?' And she plunged below the surface, leaving a diminishing trail of bubbles to mark her course.

'Mummy!' Jake shouted from the shore, followed by an unintelligible complaint.

She waved back and shouted, 'Good boy!' A moment later she felt a tweak at her toes and dived below to fight her attacker. They grappled and wrestled at arm's length for a few moments before Jane, who had been below for longer, kicked her way back to the surface.

'He writes to me quite often,' Roseanne spluttered as she broke the surface.

They laughed and said no more until they had recovered their breath.

'Ah, writes to you, eh?' Jane's tone implied that was quite a different matter. 'Still, if you don't mind meeting him, we'll go up through the gardens. Have you ever seen them?'

'Not since I knew a thing or two about gardening,' Roseanne admitted.

An hour or so later, having consumed a salty-sandy picnic, they toiled up the overgrown path to the accompanying whine of disgruntled and argumentative children.

'Mummy, mummy! Maria took my bucket and said it was hers,' Jake complained to Roseanne.

'Dear-oh-dear,' she intoned.

'Yours is red. Mine is pink. You must be going blind,' Maria told him, using the same, woman-weary tone she heard from her mother when her father came home with unnecessary mud on his unmentionables.

Jane chuckled and took Roseanne's arm. 'One no longer actually hears it, does one.'

They came to the stile at the bottom of Montpelier's gardens. 'Look, there's a clump of pampas grass, ripe for splitting if ever I saw one.'

Once they were inside the ground, they made their zigzag way among the many paths, noting more than a dozen subjects, all ripe for division. Jane always called them 'subjects', as if she were their monarch. They were just starting on the borders surrounding the lawns when there was a 'Coo-ee' from one of the attic windows. They turned and saw Annette, leaning out and waving. 'Stay there, I'll come down,' she called.

'That's a bit of luck,' Jane commented. 'We can get permission at once. Then old Martin can give them a good watering tonight, and we'll come back and divide them tomorrow.'

Roseanne had an intuition that luck had little to do with this encounter. 'Yes,' she said.

'Children, dear!' Jane clapped her hands for attention. 'Why don't you go indoors and ask Mr Martin to show you the cellars. They're very gloomy and absolutely crawling with ghosts.' The children rewarded her with excited gasps and groans at this news. 'And then you could ask him ever so kindly to put up the badminton set on the side lawn, and have a nice quarrelsome game there.'

Five pairs of flying heels left them in relative peace — peace of an adult kind, full of undercurrents but calm on the surface.

As the children vanished in the direction of the kitchens, Annette appeared from round the front of the house. 'What a pleasant surprise!' she called as they converged in the middle of the lawn.

Jane did her begging act, perfected in many another friend's garden long before this day; Annette played milady, waving a hand airily about her and saying they could take whatever they wanted.

'I'll go and mark them,' Jane said at once. 'I see a bunch of canes by the hot house there.' When Roseanne made to accompany her she added, 'No, dear, you stay here. It won't take a mo. You haven't seen Annette for ages.'

'Yes, have you been avoiding me?' Annette asked as soon as they were alone.

'Me avoiding you?' Roseanne asked in surprise; the very same question had been on the tip of her tongue.

'Well, you're not a prisoner of the Scawens, are you? There is a gig at your disposal — which is more than *I* can claim, most days . . .'

'All right! All right!' Roseanne patted her arm. 'Anyway, I haven't been avoiding you. We've just been rather busy, as always. What a thing to suggest!'

Annette brightened. 'Have you ever seen the house? This could be your last chance, you know. Bodilly says he has two or three very strong nibbles.' She linked arms with Roseanne and started walking her up the lawns.

'That was kindly of you,' Roseanne told her.

'What?'

'You know what — getting Mark the agency for this house. It'd mean a lot to him.'

Annette gave a baffled laugh. 'I just don't know about you, Miss Kitto,' she said. 'You talk as if there'd never been anything between you and him.'

'Sometimes it feels like that,' Roseanne replied guardedly.

'Really?' Annette stopped and stared into her eyes. 'Is that really how you feel now?'

She shrugged awkwardly. 'I dunno. I'd like to be friends but, somehow, whenever we meet we go for each other like Johnny Scatho's ganders. Anyway, what's it to you?'

Annette became all breezy again as they resumed their stroll toward the house. 'You know me — can't keep my nose out of other people's affairs.'

'Stephen never put you up to it, then?'

'Heavens, no!' She laughed. 'He'd throttle me if he knew. A long engagement suits him very well.'

'Engagement!' Roseanne said scornfully. 'We aren't engaged.' She held out her hand to prove it.

'Long courtship, then. He wants to be able to keep you by the sweat of his pen. He thinks work is noble, whereas people like you and me, who just live off our incomes, are contemptible. Well, not you, perhaps, but me, definitely.'

Roseanne laughed, slightly against her will. 'Me, living off an income!' she said as they mounted the steps and went in through the wide-open door.

'You do, don't you? Or d'you mean your father doesn't pay dividends? I thought you owned a large bit of Kitto & Co.'

'Annette!' Roseanne laughed in protest.

'That's what Stephen told me, anyway. Between you and me, I think *he* thinks *your* income is all right because your initial investment came out of your winnings on his wrestling bout with Bodilly. So it's not tainted like all the other money in the world. And they accuse women of being creatures of emotion!'

Roseanne looked about her; they were standing in the large classical entrance hall immediately below the dome. 'It's big!' she said. 'You'd never think it from outside.'

'Ah!' Annette assumed a jocular, preachy voice. 'Like so many of life's little troubles, my dear – they loom so large when we're in the thick of them, yet how small they seem to those who view them from the outside!'

Laughing, they went up the stairs, intending to start at the top and work their way down to the grandest room on the ground floor.

'Why have you started calling him plain Bodilly, all of a sudden?' Roseanne asked.

To her surprise she saw that the question brought a slight flush – something short of a blush, but a touch of colour nonetheless – to the other's ears. 'Have I?' she asked with elaborate carelessness. 'I suppose it's because he's now a kind of servant. I really don't know.'

Roseanne, not wishing to press the point, looked about them again – they were up on the first-floor landing by now – and said, 'Well, this is certainly a step-up for him.'

Annette, regaining her composure swiftly, asked in a slightly teasing tone, 'Would *you* like to live here?'

Roseanne glanced at her and puckered her lips in a soundless whistle.

'You would!' Annette punched her playfully. 'Well, there's a turn-up! We're only asking three and a half thou', you know.' She put her lips conspiratorially close to Roseanne's ear. 'But between you and me, anything the right side of three would get it.' She laughed as a new thought struck her. 'Then you could throw pennies out of your carriage window — to Stephen, you know — when he opens and closes the gate to you.'

Roseanne decided to make a game of it after that. 'Come on,' she said, now leading the way up to the attics, 'I'll look it over as if I were a real buyer.'

But, as they wandered from one empty maidservant's room to another, the game soon palled.

'Could you?' Annette asked as they went back down to the main bedrooms. 'I'll bet you could. Live in a grand house like this.'

Roseanne sidestepped the answer. 'It isn't the outlay, my lover. It's the upkeep.'

'It's a very solid, substantial house, you know. Not the sort of place where things are constantly going . . .'

'I don't mean that. Not up-keep but keeping-up. The servants, the carriages, the entertainments — dinners, At Homes, garden parties . . .'

'Your parents seem to manage well enough at Liston House,' Annette pointed out.

'They make it pay, though,' Roseanne told her. 'My father says if they give a garden party and he doesn't see at least a thousand pounds in new business out of it, then it was a failure. I can't abide all that. I'd sooner live like Jane Scawen.' She nodded out through the window, which gave a view over the gardens. Jane was stalking the paths with a quiverful of canes, marking each trophy with a triumphal stab at the soil around its roots. 'She was twenty-three when she decided to create the gardens at Trevivian. And now she's got something that'll keep her happy for the rest of her life.'

'Vosper Scawen.'

'Well . . . yes. Him, too, of course.'

'You know the first thing Vosper Scawen did when he married her?'

'What?' Roseanne giggled.

Annette sighed wearily. 'All right! The second thing, then. He gave all her money back to her! She was a considerable heiress, you know, both from her mother's side and her father's. And none of it was in trust or anything like that. It was all hers, absolutely. And so when she married it automatically became his. But he made a trust to exclude himself from any ownership or control of it. He gave it all back to her.'

It was news to Roseanne, for she and Jane had never discussed such matters. 'I wonder why,' she said.

'Because he's a lawyer, my dear. And he's seen how squabbles over money have torn so many families apart. Look at us Morvahs! Stephen and my father won't talk to each other, and the only reason I can live at home in some kind of peace is because I'm well enough endowed to keep my independence of them.' She sniffed. 'Don't you think the Scawens are the happiest couple you know?'

Roseanne, alert, though slightly buffeted by these mercurial changes of topic, said, 'I don't know many other couples, but they certainly seem very happy.'

'Even lately?' Annette asked.

Roseanne frowned at her.

'It's just that I ran across her in Helston last week and she dropped one or two remarks about him — well, about men in general, but wives always mean their husbands in particular when they talk men in general, don't they! It just set me wondering.'

'I'm a guest in their house,' Roseanne pointed out awkwardly.

Annette smiled. 'Well, naturally, I wouldn't *dream* of prying. But I think of her as a friend. She was certainly a good friend to me when I was at loggerheads with my parents. If it hadn't been for her, I'd never have got away to France and Italy. So I think it's only natural concern on my part if she's troubled in some way.'

Roseanne sighed and admitted that Jane hadn't been her old self lately, and, yes, she had been a trifle cooler toward Vosper. 'But I think it has something to do with that friend of hers in Falmouth, Mrs Moynihan — the artist's wife, you remember?'

'The one who took poison,' Annette said bluntly. 'Yes, she told me about her. You think that's behind it, do you?'

'What else?'

Annette smiled a little sadly and shrugged — thereby conveying that, while she herself could well imagine other reasons, if Roseanne couldn't, then it was not for her, Annette, to enlighten her. But before Roseanne could follow it up, the young woman was off again on the opposite tack. 'Of course — going back to the question of money — all this applies to you, too, now, doesn't it! You're moderately wealthy in your own right. And whoever you marry would get it all.'

Roseanne shrugged.

'You mean, it never crossed your mind?' Annette pressed her.

She shook her head. 'The only thing I ever used it for — my income, I mean — is so that no one could ever take Jake off me again. I'll never forget that day at the workhouse nor what I owe you, Annette. But, thanks to my income, they can't say I'll never afford to give him a proper home and good rearing.'

They went to the side window and stared down at the children, who were now arguing over the right way to put up a badminton net.

At that moment they heard the sound of carriage wheels on the sweep before the house. They dashed to the opposite window and saw Mark stepping out of an

330

open landau and handing down an elegantly dressed young lady. Behind her stood an equally elegant middle-aged gentleman who was conducting a slow, careful survey of the house. At last he saw the two women, standing at the last window up on the first floor. Slightly nonplussed, he raised his hat to them.

'Christ!' Annette murmured, barely audibly.

Roseanne stared at her sharply, never having heard her profane before. To her surprise, the woman had turned pale as chalk.

40

'Do you know that man?' Roseanne was still getting over her surprise at Annette's astonishing outburst.

The other nodded unhappily. 'I just hope to God he doesn't recognize me, that's all.' She stared at the party down below. 'D'you think he saw us clearly? Or would we just be two shapes at the window?' She brightened. 'Actually, there's still a chance to slip down the servants' stair, isn't there.' Without further ado she tripped to the door, Roseanne following close on her heels.

'Where d'you know him from?' she asked as they reached the first-floor landing.

'Shh!'

They tiptoed across to the stairhead and listened intently. From the entrance portico came the sound of voices — Mark's mostly, extolling the virtues of Montpelier.

Annette whispered, 'You stay here and if they ask, say I was just Mrs Miller or something.'

'What about me and Mark?' Roseanne complained. 'He's the last man I wanted to meet.'

They went down by the back stairs and then a good way along the passage toward the kitchens before they paused to listen again. Hearing nothing they relaxed and spoke normally once more. 'Go on with you!' Annette chided 'You know you're longing to meet Bodilly again.

I mean Mark. And he can't bite your head off now, not in front of Mr and Mrs whatsit.'

'Yes, what is his name?'

Annette shrugged. 'I've forgotten, even if I ever knew it. I only saw him. We never spoke or anything. He's not the sort of man you forget. But if he recognizes me . . .!'

'Why? I don't understand this at all. Where did you see him? Or he see you?'

'In Vienna.' She dashed toward the back door.

A thousand questions buzzed in Roseanne's mind as they went out into the yard — especially as she had no idea Annette had ever been to Vienna. But the first thing she asked was, 'What now? Are you going to hide till they've gone? Isn't Mark expecting to meet you here?' She was thinking even while she spoke, so her conclusion made the questions unnecessary: 'If they are serious buyers, you're going to have to hide, or be ill, or have some prior engagement every time they call. Every single time! And what if they do buy Montpelier and move into the district? You'll be in purdah for ever.'

Despite her desperation, Annette looked askance at this; she knew that Roseanne had lost the broadest elements of her dialect since living with the Scawens, but she had no idea it had gone so far. Roseanne smiled and added, 'Doan 'ee fret, my lover — I can still talk fitty-like if I mind to. But seriously . . . you have to face it now. Get it over with.' Her voice acquired an encouraging lilt: 'Perhaps he won't recognize you. Perhaps it wasn't him after all.'

Annette leaned her forehead against the jamb of a stable door, forlornly seeking some other way out. At last she sighed and said, 'You're right.'

Roseanne felt inordinately pleased to be the sensible

one, the one who knew what to do, for a change. 'Come on,' she said, taking Annette by the arm and leading her back into the house. Her borrowed fear quite masked her own trepidation at coming face-to-face with Mark again after . . . she couldn't recall how long. More than a year, anyway.

The relief was relative, however; it just meant that instead of almost fainting and losing her voice and not being able to think of a word to say, her stomach fell away endlessly inside her and a cold sweat passed over her in waves − and she was sure she'd lose her voice and not be able to think of a word to say.

'Dear God,' Annette murmured at her side, 'if I come through this unscathed, I'll never . . . never . . .' She swallowed heavily as they went from the servants' quarters into the main hall. They made a statuesque group, Mark and the two visitors, standing at the foot of the great staircase, looking up at the domed light almost directly above them. Mark was pointing out some of its features and his upraised arm gave a vigorous focus to the scene. It would have been quite classical had it not been for the fashionable young lady; the broad, diagonal stripes of her silk dress, dark plum alternating with warm caramel, struck an incontestably contemporary note − as, indeed, did the gentleman's dove-grey morning coat, which set off her colours to perfection.

Roseanne had to hand it to Annette − especially after having seen her in such a funk only moments earlier. 'Tissot!' she cried, marching gaily toward them, arms upheld in delighted welcome. 'You look just like a painting by Tissot!'

The woman, especially, was delighted at the comparison, which made all three of them smile.

'Allow me to introduce myself,' she continued

without a tremor in her voice — you would never have thought her the same person who had fled in terror at the sight of these strangers.

Mark then introduced them as Mr and Mrs Edward Dawson. His voice faltered on the final syllable as he caught sight of Roseanne, who was still in the shadow of the staircase.

'And here's my friend Miss Kitto,' Annette said, stepping into the breach.

Edward Dawson, close-to, was rather older than he had seemed from the upstairs window. Roseanne guessed him to be in his early fifties — a vigorous, athletic man, clean-shaven with mutton-chop side-whiskers and a full head of steely grey hair, cut fashionably long to show its natural waves. His nose was sharp and the set of his mouth and jaw was firm, even a little hard. His blue-grey eyes were calm and watchful. Not a man to trifle with, Roseanne decided; she admired Annette all the more for daring to face him like this.

But if Dawson recognized her, he gave not the slightest sign of it. He shook her hand, made a flattering remark or two about Montpelier, and then turned to Roseanne and accorded her precisely the same degree of polite attention.

All this while his wife's eyes were travelling between Mark and Roseanne. She had noted that catch in his voice and was avid for some further clue. She was, without doubt, one of the prettiest, daintiest young ladies Roseanne had ever seen, with flaxen curls and huge, powder-blue eyes above a delicately retroussé nose and the most perfect pair of cupid's-bow lips. And as for her figure . . .!

Most females of her age aspired to the proverbial eighteen-inch waist, regardless of medical opinion.

Many, reckless of that same opinion, managed with the help of whalebone, rawhide, steel eyelets, two maids, and a stout bedpost, to get somewhere close to their ideal — and then they groaned and creaked and panted for their release all evening. In their opinion, the Mrs Dawsons of this world were the special creations of some malign and mysogynistical spirit, liberated to flaunt their natural eighteen inches in silk so fine, so tucked, so darted, so exquisitely seamed, that not even the thinnest steel nor the most meagre shaving of whalebone could it conceal. Annette and Roseanne quite detested her at sight.

They were, therefore, especially cordial and attentive to her as the whole party went upstairs to inspect the main bedrooms.

No, she had not had a long journey; in fact, they were staying at an hotel in Penzance. Yes, this was her first visit to Cornwall. Yes, it was quite different from any other English county known to her. She was from London, herself — or *near* London, anyway: Hampstead. Did they know it? A beautiful and leafy village on an eminence overlooking the city. She would miss it, of course, but, what with the improvements in the railways, London was really on *everybody's* doorstep these days, wasn't it.

Mark was talking about manly things like dimensions and joists to a Dawson who was plainly not at home with such items — but equally plainly thought he ought to be, or appear so. At each halting site he stood, legs slightly apart, right elbow in left hand, chin cupped between thumb and index finger, nodding sagely — Pharaoh with his master builder, enduring one technicality after another when all he wanted to hear was that *his* pyramid would be the grandest ever.

'The best thing about Montpelier,' Annette put in when she thought the poor man had taken enough, 'is that it's unencumbered with farms and tenants and all those things that used to be so profitable.'

In the astonished silence that followed this announcement, Dawson said, '*Used* to be?'

'Yes,' she went on briskly. 'There's only one farm, of about a hundred and thirty acres, let to Hubert Tiddy, one of the most progressive farmers in West Penwith.' She gave a disarming smile. 'If you doubt me, Mr Dawson, as to the burdens of being a substantial landowner, come to Skyburriowe any Tuesday morning at ten. That's when we receive tenants and their complaints – though demands would be a better word for it these days.'

Man and wife exchanged glances; it was a point they had not appreciated before, though they clearly did so now.

Annette slipped in the *coup de grâce*: 'And yet it *looks* like the sort of country seat that surely has at least a thousand acres to support it.'

'Mmm!' A thoughtful Mrs Dawson went to the window, stared out over the well-tended gardens, ran an approving finger up and down the fumed-oak panelling. Her husband joined her and murmured something in her ear.

Annette risked a small, triumphant nod in Mark's direction. He came and stood beside her, giving Roseanne a curt nod. 'Going on,' he said.

'Proper 'ansum,' she told him, not taking her eyes off Mrs Dawson, who, though still apparently interested in the garden, had gone rigid with curiosity and was no doubt wishing that the eyes in the back of her head were just a tiny bit larger.

Annette chose that moment to drop a little bomb. 'Is

it true you and old widow Delamere have fallen out?'
she asked Mark.

He stared at her in consternation, being quite
unprepared for anything so direct. 'I . . . we . . . that
is . . .' he floundered.

Roseanne thought furiously. It had been clear to her
from the outset that some of today's 'coincidences' had
been arranged between Annette and Jane; though to
what purpose she could not even guess. But neither of
them could have foreseen that Mark Bodilly would turn
up in the middle of it all — much less that he would
bring with him a gentleman who either was or who
resembled to a remarkable degree another gentleman
Annette had met in Vienna — a city she was supposed
never to have visited. Their appearance on the scene at
least was a genuine surprise.

Therefore, whatever the two women's purpose might
have been, it was now frustrated. Annette knew it; but
Jane did not.

Roseanne crossed to the side window, overlooking the
lawn where the children had by now settled to a serious
game; for once they were laughing rather than
quarrelling. The fact that Jane was umpiring at the net
may have had something to do with it; she saw Roseanne
at the window and gave a cheery wave.

Mrs Dawson joined her at that moment, saying, 'I
thought I heard children somewhere. How jolly! Is that
their nanny?'

It was a natural error; any woman who dressed for
a shell-picking expedition with five children could easily
be taken for their nanny. But Roseanne could not help
laughing out loud. 'That,' she said, 'is Mrs Scawen.
Fourteen years ago she was the owner of Montpelier.
Now she has a large estate about five miles the other
side of Helston. I am her companion.'

The woman took a pair of lorgnettes from her pocket-book and peered briefly at Jane through them. Any other person with the slightest leaning toward the social graces would have said, 'Ah yes. How stupid of me! I see my error at once now.'

Mrs Dawson said, 'Hmm!' and replaced her glasses. A moment later she proved she had not the slightest need of them by adding, 'And the children are hers, I presume. Are the two youngest boys twins?'

'No,' Roseanne told her evenly. 'The boy playing back in the right-hand court is mine.'

The woman swallowed audibly and was unable to stop herself turning round to compare Jake with Mr Bodilly. But Mark and her husband had wandered off into the next bedroom.

Annette, who had started to accompany them, changed her mind and was now crossing the room to join the two ladies at the window. 'The children are very quiet,' she said. 'I hope that doesn't mean they're up to no good.'

In fact, she barely glanced at the children, but trained her broadest smile on their visitor and continued, 'I do so hope you take Montpelier, Mrs Dawson. It's far and away the most *stylish* house in the whole of West Cornwall, you know. And it does so need people who *understand* style.'

Roseanne held her breath to see how the other would respond to this crudest of flatteries; not entirely to her surprise, Mrs Dawson basked in it.

Annette's smile became a shade conspiratorial: 'Between you and me,' she went on, 'and please don't breathe a word of this to Mr Bodilly – who is so well-meaning – but some of the people he has brought here . . .' Her eyes raked the ceiling for words to describe them. 'They would be desperately trying to live *up* to the place all the time. D'you know the sort? One's every call here would be a torture.' Her panoramic glance of approval included the lady herself. 'What Montpelier cries out for is people who can live here effortlessly. To the manner born, you might say.'

'You are almost too kind, Miss Morvah,' she replied, showing she was no stranger to compliments, no matter how far-fetched. 'Tell me — who is that gaunt young rustic who opened the gate to us?'

Roseanne tried to stifle her laughter and failed.

Annette, thoroughly annoyed at the question and her friend's unseemly response, blurted out, 'Why, he is Miss Kitto's fiancé.'

Roseanne stopped laughing at once. 'He's no such thing, Mrs Dawson,' she said. 'In fact, he's Miss Morvah's brother — and heir to the Skyburriowe estate.' She added the latter because she knew how Annette hated to be reminded of it.

'Goodness gracious!' Mrs Dawson showed the first genuine remorse Roseanne had seen in her. 'But how dreadful! I made Dawson throw him a penny.'

'Oh, he'll thank you for it.' Annette smiled thinly at Roseanne. 'Come the winter it will buy him a candle to light his labours a further hour or two. He is struggling to live by his pen, you see.'

'Yes, I see,' the woman echoed, though her grip on local reality was beginning to feel distinctly tenuous.

Mark returned at the moment, wondering what was keeping them. 'There's lots more to see,' he told Mrs Dawson.

Roseanne, feeling she had to do something dramatic to show what nonsense Annette had been talking about Stephen, tripped gaily to him and took his arm. 'Leave it to Miss Morvah, my lover,' she said. 'She's ten

340

times so good as you. And I want a word in your ear.'

In fact, she had no idea what she was going to say, but the look on Annette's face at that moment was worth every ounce of the effort she was going to have to make in order to extricate herself.

41

It was the strangest feeling to be arm in arm with Mark again — even to be touching him. It was somehow novel and exciting while also being ancient and familiar. Best of all to her, though, was the effect such a simple gesture had on Annette. If taking Mark aside for a private word had startled her, the sight of them with arms linked, as if such casual familiarity were commonplace between them, produced a veritable consternation.

Mrs Dawson saw it, too; she turned to her husband to see whether he had noticed. Indeed, he was watching Annette, but the expression in his eyes soon took the smile off his wife's lips. 'Do come on,' she said sharply, 'we have several other houses to see today.'

'Does she take us for fools?' Mark asked Roseanne as soon as they were out of earshot. They went down by the servants' stair. 'Several other houses! There's only Chyandour — and that needs a thousand or two to make it even habitable.'

Reluctantly she let go of his arm; now that there was no one to tease, she thought . . . and then paused. Why would it be teasing Annette to behave with such familiarity? Mark meant nothing to her. It didn't make sense. But then, very few of this day's events did. 'That woman has no idea of what life in the country is like,' she replied. 'How we all know each other's business.' She laughed. 'She thought Mrs Scawen was a nanny and she called Stephen Morvah an honest rustic or something. Talk about fools rushing in! Yet she *looks* like an angel, don't you agree?'

'She wants a good fist between the eyes,' he muttered. They had reached the back door by now. 'What do you want, anyway?' he asked.

It was the last thing she had intended asking, but his aggressiveness put her to it. 'D'you hate me?' she said.

He darted her a swift, uncomfortable glance. 'What do 'ee want to ask a thing like that for?'

'Do you?'

He strode away from her, out into the stable yard. 'Come us on, if you're coming,' he snapped.

She smiled to herself. If he was truly as annoyed as he was trying to appear, he'd just turn about and rejoin the others. She caught up with him and diverted their steps toward the back lawn, where the shouts of the children indicated that the game was reaching its climax. 'Do you?' she insisted.

He shrugged. 'S'pose not.'

'So there's no reason why we can't be civil to each other when we happen to meet.'

A second shrug conceded her point. She wanted to take him by those shoulders and shake some actual words out of him. Why could he never say what was on his mind? 'Is it true about you and old Widow Delamere?' she asked.

'She's not old.'

'She's got a daughter your age.'

They ducked beneath an arch in the wall that divided the yard from the back lane. Jake came running to her, bubbling with excitement. 'Mummy, mummy, we beat them. Courtenay and me beat Maria and Sarah.'

'Gusson, boy! They let 'ee win,' Mark teased.

'They didn't, they didn't!' Jake showed how close to tears his excitement was.

''Course they didn't, my bird,' Roseanne assured him, giving Mark a venomous stare. 'He's only teasing.'

'I've found a fuzzy-pig!' Trevanion shouted from one of the flower beds. Jake ran off to share the new excitement, his bruised pride all forgotten.

'Hedgehog!' Jane called out a weary correction over her shoulder as she approached Mark and Roseanne. 'I saw you had visitors. Prospective buyers?'

''Es,' Mark said. 'A Mr and Mrs Edward Dawson of Lunnon.'

'Nice people?' She raised her eyebrows at Roseanne.

'Very à la mode,' Roseanne replied – and *her* eyebrows promised a whole budget more, but later. 'And no longer prospective, I believe,' she added. 'Annette could sell water in Wales.'

Jane glanced at Mark to see how he took this gentle insult but his taciturn face gave nothing away. She cocked an ear toward the children, who were starting to quarrel again. 'I think we should be off quite soon,' she warned, and went to join them – or, rather, to separate them.

Mark chuckled. 'She *do* look like a nanny.'

'What d'you want to say a thing like that for?' Roseanne asked, sharp again.

He turned to her in surprise.

'To Jake,' she added. 'You could see how pleased he was to beat those girls. You can't abide it to see anyone happy, can you. You've got to spoil it for people. Especially me – and *especially* Jake.'

He gave a derisive snort. 'Seeing as I haven't spoken a word to either of 'ee for years . . .'

'And the first words you do say are those!' But her

anger suddenly evaporated. You could be annoyed at Mark Bodilly for ever, but not angry. It was a puzzle. She seized his arm and shook it vigorously, turning him toward the front of the house – where they now saw Annette bidding farewell to the Dawsons. 'Oh, you're such an unforgiving . . . prickly . . . *bear*!' she exclaimed, laughing against her will.

But he was staring at the group in front of the house. 'There's a man to watch,' he said darkly. 'I can't take to him, somehow.'

'Dawson?' she asked in surprise, letting him go again.

'The way he do look at her. 'Tisn't right.'

'I don't know.' She gave a slightly embarrassed laugh. 'I should think any man with a wife like that . . .'

'Not *she*,' he said contemptuously. 'He can look at she any way he do want. I'm talking about the way he do look at Miss Morvah.'

Dawson raised his hat to them as he took up the reins; his wife dipped her head with a gravity that, in her, was slightly comical. As the carriage turned, almost in its own length, they saw Stephen approaching. Being hatless he merely touched his forelock to the departing visitors. Roseanne laughed and hastened to greet him, leaving Mark to stew in his own anger. Nothing had changed, she thought with resignation. It was still the case that she was never happier to see Stephen than after a set-to with Mark – and never more keen to see Mark than after a placid hour with Stephen.

'What an ornament to the district *they'll* be,' he commented, nodding his head backward at the now departed carriage. He took her by both hands and gave her a quick buss on the cheek.

She glanced hastily over her shoulder to see how Mark

responded; but he was walking directly toward Annette, who had a guarded smile of welcome for him. But he walked straight past her, saying, 'I suppose you think that was clever.'

She stood quite rigid for a moment, fists clenched, eyes tight closed. Then, suddenly, she relaxed and smiled. 'Mr Bodilly,' she called after him.

He walked several paces more before he deigned to turn.

'You're impossible!' she told him.

He stood irresolute a moment or two and then continued his long exit up the drive.

Annette turned her smile on the other two. 'Why didn't May Delamere just simply murder him?' she asked.

'Because murder's too good for him,' Roseanne replied. Then, feeling she ought to say something to Stephen, asked how his writing was going, though the question had become almost embarrassing, for he had enough letters of rejection to paper a ballroom.

'That's what I came to tell you. Or tell someone. The *Western Morning News* has taken a little thing I wrote.'

'Your essay on modern French novelists?' his sister asked excitedly.

'No.' He cleared his throat and gave a rueful smile. 'A little piece about the thrush. They said it was very good and they wonder if I'd be interested in doing a regular . . . sort of nature piece for them. Weekly, you know.'

'What do they pay?' Roseanne asked.

'A thousand words for nineteen shillings. I could live on it, just about. And it would only take a morning. Still . . .' He smiled wanly. 'Me a nature-notes man!'

'Mummy, mummy!' Jake came running up, all

excitement again. 'Aunt Jane says I can take that fuzzy-pig home if Aunty Netty says she doesn't want it.'

Roseanne turned him to face Annette, of whom he was unaccountably shy. 'Then you'll have to ask her nicely, won't you — because people just don't give away their fuzzy-pigs every day of the week, you know.'

But Stephen dropped on his haunches beside the lad and said, 'I'm the one to ask, young fellow. I'm the caretaker here, you know.'

Annette gave a hollow laugh at this gloss on his rights.

He continued, 'And I'll say yes at once. You can take him home with you provided . . .'

Jake's eyes sparkled with delight — until he noticed Uncle Stephen's upraised finger and heard the condition:

'. . . provided you say goodbye to your Mummy, this instant, and goodbye to Aunt Jane, and Courtenay and the other three and come and live here with me for ever and ever. Now, d'you agree to that?'

Jake shook his head slowly.

'Wouldn't you *like* it?' Stephen persisted, as if the answer would not surprise him hugely.

Again that shake of the head — but now, behind those large, solemn eyes there was an inkling of what was coming.

'But why ever not?' Stephen asked. 'It's what you're asking the fuzzy pig to do. He's got all his brothers and sisters and friends and aunts and uncles here. And you're going to take him away from them all. Why d'you think he would like it when you wouldn't?'

Jake drew a deep breath and stared at his bare feet; he tried to pick up a piece of gravel with his toe.

'Come on.' Stephen rose and took his hand. 'Let's go and tell the others what you've decided.' As they walked off he added, 'And I'll tell you how to get a fuzzy-pig of your very own — one that already belongs in Aunt Jane's garden.'

Roseanne, watching them go, murmured more to herself than Annette, 'I'm a bloody fool, aren't I!'

Annette stared at her in astonishment — never having heard her swear before.

42

The badminton had tired them out. Jake fell asleep on his Aunt Jane's lap; Courtenay gave the scene a certain symmetry by doing the same on his Aunt Zan's. The two women smiled faint apologies at each other and resigned themselves to the discomforts of their petty martyrdom. 'They're such bony things, boys,' Jane complained.

Trevanion and Maria were sitting one each side of Harold Bennett, the groom, taking it in turns to drive the straight bits of the road — which were few and jealously measured. Only Sarah remained in the body of the vehicle, sandwiched been Aunt Zan and two sacks of seashells. 'Who were those people?' she asked, staking her claim to a part in any subsequent conversation.

'A Mr Edward Dawson and his wife,' Roseanne told her. 'I don't know her name. Araminta, probably — something like that.'

Jane chuckled. 'Yes, she looked just like an Araminta. Like a Dresden figurine, I thought, though I didn't see her close to. Was she well spoken?'

'Oh yes. She told us she's from Ham . . . something. A village on a hill outside London.' She gave a brief laugh and said, 'Lunnon!'

'Is that how she said it?' Jane asked. 'Rather old-fashioned. My father always said Lunnon. And laylock instead of lilac.' She smiled at Sarah to show her she still had a toe in the conversation. 'And what will you find amusing in our speech when we're the oldest generation?'

'Are they going to buy Montpelier?' the girl asked, getting a whole foot in the door.

'If they don't,' Roseanne told her, 'it won't be Aunt Netty's fault.' She turned to Jane. 'Honestly, she ran circles round Mark when it came to selling the place. All he could talk about was the joists and the plumbing up in the roofvalleys.' And she went on to describe how Annette had charmed the Dawsons into thinking they and the house were each other's destinies.

'She and Bodilly would make a good pair then, eh?' Jane asked with a roguish smile.

'Maybe they would,' Roseanne agreed glumly. 'Maybe they do.'

Jane raised an interested eyebrow.

'Why *did* she talk her parents into using him instead of Coad and Snell?' Roseanne asked. 'And how did *she* know about him falling out with old Widow Delamere?'

'Oh, has he!' Despite her interest Jane gave a warning lift to her eyebrows.

Roseanne put an arm around Sarah and gave her a brief hug. 'You can keep a secret, can't 'ee, my lover.'

''Course I can!' The girl stared resentfully at her mother.

'Besides,' Roseanne continued, 'she'll be out of the nursery soon enough.'

It was a winning argument and Roseanne knew it, for Jane had so often bemoaned her own parents' desire to keep her 'in the nursery' as long as they possibly could. 'Did he confirm it to you?' she asked.

'In his own sweet way. He said old Widow Delamere

350

wasn't all that old and then he changed the subject and got angry. He was very *scadgy* with Jake, too.'

'He's that sort of man, though, isn't he,' Jane said. She gathered Jake up and resettled him in a more comfortable position; he slumbered on.

The ability of young children to abandon their bodies just anywhere, to leave them totally in the trust of the grown-up world about them, never ceased to rouse Roseanne's sense of wonder. 'What sort of man?' she asked, staring at Jake and feeling her whole being stir with love for him and wondering how she'd face the day when he'd grow up and leave her.

'They can't meet the challenge of beauty. It frightens them. They look at a sunset and sneer. They want to tell you how deeply it moves them but they can't. They're afraid you'll just laugh. Look at him!' She stared down at Jake. 'Like a beautiful little faun! He'd melt the heart of Herod. No wonder Mark Bodilly had to say something wounding.'

'Oh, it was hardly as bad as that.' Roseanne now felt she had blackened the poor man more than he deserved. But then she remembered. 'He said Mrs Dawson wanted a good fist between the eyes.'

'There you are, then.'

'And he was scratchy with poor Annette, too.'

Jane made no response to that — which, in its way, was just as significant.

'You think there's anything . . . hurrisome between them, do you?' Roseanne pressed.

Jane shrugged, as if unwilling to say the actual word yes.

Roseanne smiled down at Sarah, who was goggle-eyed at being permitted to overhear this conversation. 'Enjoy your peace of mind while you yet can, maid,' she advised lugubriously.

Sarah almost boasted back about how Arthur Bennett, the groom's elder son, had disturbed her peace of mind of late, but then decided that discretion had points in its favour, too.

'How do *you* feel about that?' Jane asked casually.

They were now approaching Breage. In fact, they were passing the end of Penhale Row, where Roseanne was born and reared. Her eyes sought out the one that had been 'Kitto's' and could not immediately find it; someone had painted all the woodwork black. Only four years, she thought. It was like looking into someone else's life. But she missed the cows. She remembered all the times she'd cursed them up and down that lane . . . the sheer awfulness of early-morning milking in a 'shed' made of straw bales and tarpaulin . . . and her sense of loss was suddenly acute.

'Eh?' Jane said.

Roseanne sighed. 'I suppose it's time I made up my mind.'

The other nodded sadly. 'You'll never wake up twenty-four hours younger than the last time.'

'Do you know what I'd really like to do?' Roseanne flung herself back in her seat and ruffled Sarah's hair. Her jovial tone informed them she was joking as she said, 'I'd love to just buy a farm somewhere and . . . work it. Yes, if I'm to marry anything, I'd like it to be a farm!'

43

Mary Kitto had 'taken well' in Helston society. To be sure, there were plenty who were amused at the thought of a journeyman mason and his wife, the daughter of the Duke of Leeds's old stockman, taking a grand house like Liston Court. Some were even outraged and resisted all her efforts at forming an acquaintance; but they were a dwindling band. Season by season her circle grew wider. It was not simply that a social occasion at Liston Court was always good fun. Indeed, that was nothing new, for the place had enjoyed a slightly rash reputation for as long as anyone could remember — first with Lady Nina Brookes, a very merry widow, and then with John Liggatt, a retired publisher from London who had been able to singe the ears with his scabrous tales of goings-on in that great metropolis. Now, with Frank and Mary Kitto installed, the fun was supplemented by something even more desirable: information. Liston Court had become a high 'change of commercial intelligence, too.

In an earlier age, that would have been a point against them. Gentlemen and their ladies had once been able to rely on a good quarterly dividend from their ventures in copper and tin — topped up with steady if unspectacular rents from their farms. They had, therefore, found it easy to despise commerce and trade and to exclude all who dabbled in either. But as those ancient reservoirs of wealth ran low, attitudes began to shift. And when a labouring man and his wife were able to rent a place like Liston Court and go about in a carriage and four, while ancient families were turning their sheets sides-to-middle and giving the London season a miss this year, clearly it was time to ask if the Grand Old Merry-go-round could not be moved to a more salubrious site in the great Showground of Life. A little closer to the trade winds, perhaps?

Almost overnight it became wonderfully clear to the rulers of society — what had been clear to the rest of the nation for more than a century past — that the kingdom's wealth no longer depended on large lands and great families. Commerce now was king. It was almost one's patriotic duty to encourage it. And, by a happy chance, the exercise of that duty led to an almost miraculous refilling of the coffers — *if* one only went about it the right way. The secret, it seemed, was to acquire good information and acquire it early. And Liston Court had become one of the very best places to carry out such a design. No one could quite explain why. It wasn't as if Frank Kitto himself was the source of all one heard; in fact, he was as guarded and discreet as any man in Cornwall.

There are people whose parties are always a feast of jollity. They don't serve the best wines; their table is nothing very remarkable; they hire the same bands as the rest of the district and play more or less the same programme. Yet, by some strange alchemy, their occasions 'go' when those of others just languish. The Kittos seemed to have the identical knack when it came to matters of trade and commerce — and without sacrificing the sheer fun for which Liston Court had always been renowned.

So, people might laugh at some of Mary Kitto's gaffes and blunders — indeed, she'd laugh at them herself, louder and more jovially than any — but they assured each other that her heart was in the right place, and they never missed an invitation to cross the Kitto threshold.

One blustery October morning, shortly after the Dawsons completed the purchase of Montpelier, Roseanne paid one of her regular visits to Liston Court. She found her mother head over heels with arrangements for 'a select little ball for about a hundred', on the coming Friday evening, which was in three days' time.

''Tis to welcome they new people up Montpelier,' she explained. 'Your friend Annette has tooken the invitation only now. Pity. She could have put you with her. You want to come, do 'ee? I'll ask Stephen, too, if you mind.'

'Mother!' Roseanne gave her a hug of loving exasperation. 'You'll never give up, will you.'

Her mother drew breath to speak, thought better of it, and simply smiled.

'Actually,' Roseanne went on, 'I think I would like to come, if the Dawsons accept. You met them, have you?'

'Met her.' She ran a fingernail down a pile of napkins, counting them with practised speed. 'Mary Ann! I told 'ee before — when you do put these napkins in a pile, all the folds are to be the same way. I can't count them like this.'

Mary Ann came to reorder the pile; her angry glance at one of the other maids revealed the true culprit without any actual preaching.

''Es,' Mary Kitto resumed the conversation with her daughter. 'Met she to Mrs Lanyon's. Pretty little mite, but she never had much to say for herself.'

Roseanne smiled. She could hardly imagine what the modish Tamara Dawson would make of a woman like

355

her mother, who, having tried for a heart-breaking six months to 'talk proper', had reverted to talking 'fitty-like' and challenged the whole world to sneer.

'Still,' she concluded, 'your father says mister is a proper fellow, and that's good enough for me.' She started counting the cutlery out into piles.

Roseanne joined in. 'Does anyone know how they made their money yet?' she asked. 'They're obviously not short of it. Jane thinks he inherited it but Vosper's equally sure he made it somehow, but no one can guess what. Jane said no one ever suspected her father had been a wholesale tea merchant until he told them.'

'Well,' her mother answered with a grimly satisfied smile, 'there's one man can find out soon enough.'

Annette appeared at that moment, walking in unannounced. 'Oh, what fun!' she cried, picking up a knife and peering at its markings. 'Is that what real silver looks like? Perhaps we'll get ours back now.'

Mrs Kitto laughed. 'You were some quick, my lover,' she commented. It struck Roseanne that the two of them, Annette and her mother, were alike in many ways. They both knew how to disarm the world's mockery by making a parade of the very shame that others would rather emigrate than reveal. Then it occurred to her that she had done much the same over Jake — not that there was shame in it, but people had thought it a distinctly odd choice for a young, unmarried girl to make.

'I met the lady herself going into Nicholls's for some new dress lengths. D'you know, she has *thirty* completely new outfits every single year!'

'Such extravagance!' Mrs Kitto exclaimed, running a steward's eye over the rest of the canteen and linen.

Roseanne, who thought at first that her mother was ironically including Liston Court in the comment, realized she wasn't. 'I don't know,' she said. 'With a figure like hers, she probably gets three dresses out of one length.'

'I know. I could kill her!' Annette parodied a tigress in mime. 'Anyway, I gave her your invitation – said sorry for the short notice, et cetera – and she said she and Dawson will be delighted to attend.'

'Then I'm certainly coming,' Roseanne interjected. 'Don't ask Stephen, though. He's still their gatekeeper.'

'Good,' her mother said abstractedly. 'I hope you two young ladies aren't thinking to have your luncheon here. We got no time for they capers today, my lovers.'

Annette consulted her watch. 'Well,' she said as she tucked it back in her bodice, 'let's get Vosper Scawen to take us to the Angel. They say the new cook there is very good.'

But when they were halfway up Church Street hill Roseanne said, 'Could we just go on our own and not bother Vosper?'

'Why ever not?' Annette asked. 'He's such fun and always knows the latest on everything.'

'Even so, I'd just . . . rather not.'

So they went to the private dining room at the Angel, instead. Annette was rather surly about it until an intriguing thought struck her; 'I say, you haven't fallen out with Vosper, have you?'

Roseanne replied that she'd rather not talk about it.

Annette, more miffed than ever, sat and scratched the deep beeswax polish with one of her fingernails. 'What a wind,' she remarked listlessly. 'It could be quite a gale by tonight.'

Roseanne sighed. 'If you must know, it's me who's avoiding Vosper.'

'Ah!' Annette waited for more.

'For the sake of peace and harmony. I know it sounds absurd but for weeks now Jane's been behaving as if

. . . well, as if she can't trust either of us out of her sight. When I go home this evening there'll be a regular catechism from her. Where did I go? Who did I see? What did we talk about? What did we do? She'll make me account for every single minute.'

'Jane?' Annette seemed incredulous. 'It doesn't sound like her at all.'

'It's not exactly an inquisition. I mean, it's all very friendly. Suppose I tell her I met Mrs Tresidder. She'll say oh yes, such a nice lady, and did I know that old Mr Tresidder used to be . . . et cetera, et cetera. And there'll be quite a long conversation about the Tresidders. And then a little silence. And then she'll say, "And what did you do next, my dear?" And on we'll go again. And if I ever say I happened to run into Vosper . . . whew!' She fanned her face dramatically.

Annette shook her head as if she could still hardly believe it. 'Poor you!' she ventured. 'It must make life extremely awkward at times.'

'It does. I don't think I can go on living there for much longer.'

'I don't blame you.' Annette touched her arm gently. 'I'm sorry I was so brusque when you said let's not go and see Vosper. I had no idea.'

Beth Davey brought their soup. 'Mark Bodilly's in the dining room,' she said primly. 'Buying drinks all round.'

Annette chuckled and, when they were alone again, said, 'The Dawsons gave us a bill at sight yesterday, so Bodilly can afford it.'

'He's still Bodilly, then?' Roseanne commented drily. 'What's your excuse this time? He's no longer a servant of the estate.'

'Do *you* want to know every minute of *my* day now?' Annette asked with jocular iciness. Then, more briskly,

'But we didn't finish talking about your little difficulty. Or big difficulty.' She grinned knowingly. 'Is this going to be Stephen's lucky year after all?'

Roseanne gave a trapped sort of shrug and took her first sip of soup. It was good. 'Just what I needed,' she said with relish.

Annette stopped smiling. 'Seriously, Zan. Why not? He worships you. He adores Jake. And he hasn't the faintest designs on your money. Any sensible woman would give a year off her life for such a man.'

'I know! I said, didn't I: I'm a fool!'

'You put it even more strongly. I can only agree.'

'But the fact is, I don't love him, and I could never pretend I did.'

Annette, relishing her soup, remarked casually, 'I think he's aware of that, my dear. He's not blind. He'd quite accept it. You wouldn't need to pretend.'

'And I don't believe he loves me, either.'

That shocked Annette. Her jaw dropped and she exclaimed, 'How can you possibly say such a thing? He worships the ground you walk on. He always has done — long before that day he asked you to Ram-Buck Fair.'

Roseanne looked at her scornfully, not thinking it worth a reply.

'It's true,' the other insisted.

'He surely never told you.'

'He didn't need to. I remember the very day. We were driving into Penzance, to Trengwainton. I think it was the birthday of one of the Bolitho girls. Anyway, that doesn't matter. But as we went past that triangular field, where the lane goes up into Breage from the main road — you know it?'

Roseanne smiled ruefully. 'Every rod, pole, and perch.'

'It was summer. Very hot. We were both sweltering in our party clothes. And you were standing out there, turning the hay. And your arms were bare and you had your skirts hitched up to your knees, and you looked so . . . *wonderful*, just standing there, resting on your pitchfork, watching us go by.'

Prompted by so much detail Roseanne found she could recall the precise occasion, six or seven years ago. She must have been about eighteen — which meant that Annette could have been only fourteen.

'And I saw Stephen's eyes as he caught sight of you — they almost fell out of his head.'

'Oh yes!' Roseanne mocked.

'You know what I mean. He couldn't take them off you. "Is that Roseanne Kitto?" he asked, and I told him yes. And he just went on staring at you until you passed out of sight. And he's never so much as looked at another woman since, so now tell me he doesn't love you!'

'It's still not me, Netty. That wasn't *me* he saw there.'

'But I know it *was* you,' Annette protested.

'Yes, of course it was me. I'm only saying he didn't see it. Can't you understand? You said it yourself. There he was, all in his best bib and tucker, stuck in an oven on wheels, and he looked out the window and saw a bare-armed country girl having a bit of a rest. Ruth amid the alien corn — that's what he saw. He's in love with the simple life, and that's what I am to him: part of the simple life.'

'You're wrong.' Annette rapped the table to emphasize the point. 'You couldn't be more wrong, believe me.'

'Well, I think I'm right — and that's all about it, I suppose.'

Annette took a few spoonfuls of soup in thoughtful

silence. 'If,' she said at last, 'if you thought he really was in love with *you*, would it make a difference?'

Roseanne wanted to say no, but even as she rehearsed the denial in her mind it sounded false; Annette would see it at once. She hesitated so long that her silence was answer enough. 'In any case,' she blurted out in her anxiety to undo the damage, 'I think I still love Mark.'

Annette froze. 'You can't,' she almost whispered.

'I know.' Roseanne could not look her in the eye now. 'It's . . . awful. Stupid. I hate myself for it. But there it is. I've never been able to get over him.'

'No!' Annette shook her head slowly; her voice was that of an automaton. 'I mean you *can't*.'

'Why not?' Roseanne was more puzzled than annoyed at the assertion. Their eyes met.

'Can't you guess?' Annette asked.

There was a sudden, dreadful hollowness where Roseanne's innards had been. 'Oh no,' she whispered.

Annette nodded miserably. 'I hate myself for it, too – if that's any consolation. Not a day passes but I ask myself: 'How *can* you! How is it possible to have such feelings for a creature like that!'

'Yes!' Roseanne echoed fervently.

'I mean he's so . . . utterly . . .'

'Yes!'

'And he's got no . . . he hasn't the slightest . . .'

'Not a scrap!'

'And as for understanding how a woman feels! Or needs . . . or . . .'

'I know!'

'I can't even talk to him.'

'Nor me,' Roseanne agreed. 'Say three words . . .'

'. . . and he jumps down your throat. And if you cross him in anything . . .'

'. . . he just flies off the handle. You don't even need

to cross him. And he thinks he's the spider's ankles. And all women have to faint at the sight of him. D'you know, when Stephen asked me to Ram-Buck that time, the mighty Mr Bodilly commanded me not to go! He thought I'd break my word, just like that! Just because *he* said no.'

'I know. And he won't give you credit for anything. *I* sold Montpelier, not him — well, you saw me do it. But d'you think he'll allow that I had the slightest part in the transaction?'

'Not him! I'll bet he's down there now, bragging about it to all his cronies.' She closed her eyes and shook her head at the ineffable mystery of everything. Blindly she groped across the table, feeling for Annette's hand. Annette met her halfway. 'Oh, Zan,' she sighed. 'What are we going to do?'

'Nothing!' Roseanne said stoutly. 'Well, you're free to do what you like, of course. But for my part, I'll do absolutely nothing. And it'll just get smaller and smaller and one day it'll wake up dead.'

'Just so!' Annette put both her hands round Roseanne's. 'I certainly don't intend to do anything about it — except, like you, just let it run its course and die. Let's make a promise, eh?'

Roseanne joined her free hand to the other three. Firm, reassuring squeeze answered firm, reassuring squeeze as the two women smiled, and stared each other straight in the eye, and secretly wondered which would be the first to break such solemn vows.

44

Roseanne had a room of her own at Liston Court, which she used occasionally, if there were a ball or dinner in Helston, say, and the tedious homeward journey through Gweek and Mawnan Smith would have crowned the evening in the same way as a bag of wet kitchen scraps would crown a cheerful fire. Since Annette's return from foreign parts, it had become 'sort of' her room, too – in the sense that it was available to her for occasions like this. Naturally, she did most of her dressing at home; Liston Court was reserved for the 'finishing touches'.

'I call them that,' she said, 'because if my father saw them, he'd finish with me for good.'

They consisted of the faintest blush of peach-coloured powder on her cheeks and brow, the barely perceptible assistance of jeweller's rouge upon her lips, and a dab or two of eau-de-cologne.

On the evening of the hastily convened ball to welcome the new owners of Montpelier to the district she arrived especially early and took particular care over her finishing touches. Even so, the result did not please her. 'It's not fair,' she told her reflection in the glass. 'If I were just a little darker, I could add some colouring to my eyebrows and no one would notice.'

'If you were a little darker,' Roseanne pointed out, 'you wouldn't need to.'

'I know. That's what's so unfair. D'you think they'd notice if I did?'

'They' were the censorious legions of married ladies who would mark an unmarried sister down severely for such cheating — whose every trick they knew, since they had all done it in their time.

Roseanne pretended to take the question seriously. 'Perhaps if you hitched your skirts above your knees,' she suggested, 'they might not notice. Not your eyebrows, anyway.'

'Ha ha!' Annette sneered. 'They all paint themselves, anyway. It's so hypocritical.'

'Yes, but no one's awarding them marks for Simple Purity any longer. Can I try a little of your powder?'

'Ooh!' Annette stared at her in surprise. 'Ooh! Ooh! What's here, then? Roseanne Kitto wearing powder!'

'I just thought I'd try the look of it.' She reached for the puff.

'I'll do it.' Annette got there first. 'Take a deep breath and breathe out slowly through your nose. Close your eyes.'

When it was done, Roseanne inspected the result and giggled.

'Don't your lips look pale now,' Annette remarked lightly.

When that was rectified there was more giggling and then Roseanne said, 'I wonder what *he'll* be wearing. A bright silk cummerbund, I'll bet.'

'Who?' Annette asked.

'Edward Dawson, of course. The guest of honour. He still hasn't recognized you, I suppose? From Vienna.'

'Vienna?' Annette echoed in bewilderment.

'Yes, you remember. The first day they came to look at . . .'

'Oh, Venice!' Annette laughed at Roseanne's understandable error.

'But you said Vienna.'

'Did I? No, I couldn't have. I've never been there in my life. I certainly meant to say Vienna.' She laughed and thumped the table. 'I mean Venice! Oh dear, now I shall muddle them up forever. No, I saw him in . . . Venice — there! — when I was staying with the Vyvyans. They rented a palace on the Lido . . .'

'Yes, I remember all that from your letters. I knew you'd been to *Venice*.'

'Well, there you are, then.' Annette's laugh now sought to bury the whole misunderstanding.

'But then,' Roseanne persisted, 'why would it matter if he had recognized you? I thought the whole point was that he'd seen you somewhere where you weren't supposed to be — namely, Vienna.'

Annette's puzzlement only deepened at this. Then she gave a weak laugh. 'It just shows, doesn't it, how two people can hold the same conversation and come away with two entirely different impressions of it.'

'But you were terrified!' Roseanne insisted, trying to keep her voice calm. 'You ran away! Down to the stable yard! And then I pointed out . . .'

'Yes, yes, yes,' Annette interrupted. 'I know all that. I haven't forgotten that. But the reason I was afraid he'd recognize me was that the lady on his arm when I saw him in Vienna was not the lady he handed down from the carriage at Montpelier.'

'Venice.'

'Ye-es!' Annette replied tendentiously, as if Roseanne had been especially obtuse until now but had finally seen the light. 'And the lady on his arm in Venice was introduced to everyone as his wife. Everyone called her . . . S-Signora Dawson.'

Roseanne was sure she'd fluffed the title because the word on the tip of her tongue was not Signora but Frau. Then she remembered Annette had said she'd never heard Edward Dawson's name, anyway. 'Ah,' she said, giving a reassuring smile. 'Well, I'm glad we've got *that* cleared up at last.'

'Yes!' Annette plucked at the flowers in her garland and then laughed. 'Good heavens! All this time you've been thinking I went to Vienna without telling anyone!'

Roseanne pinned a small posy of violets to her corsage, the first of the season. 'That was the impression you gave, my lover,' she said off-handedly. 'This colour doesn't go, does it.'

'You want something bright red with it,' Annette advised, rummaging through the box and coming up with a dark-green ribbon, the colour of the violet leaves, with a fine scarlet stripe in it. 'Try that.'

She held it beside the posy and they agreed it would help. As Annette tied it into the posy she giggled again and said, 'What did you suppose I *did* in Vienna, eh? An incandescent week with a dashing young cavalry officer? An Archduke with sixteen quarterings? Or' – her voice went all sepulchral, to indicate the impossible horror of the thought – 'an Italian waiter with big, soulful eyes?'

Roseanne decided that the Italian waiter was the most – indeed only – likely candidate. 'Of course not,' she said. 'I was sure you went for the music. Talking of which . . .' She held up a finger, for, at that very instant, as if her words had been a cue, the band started tuning up downstairs.

Arm in arm, they went out to the grand staircase and began a stately descent to the festivities below. 'I'll tell you what he'll be wearing,' Annette said, closing her eyes and pretending to be clairvoyant, plucking images from the air: 'A dark caramel cummerbund with thin black horizontal stripes.'

'And Tamara?'

'Tamara!' The name could still raise a chuckle; it was even better than Araminta. 'She'll be in a pale blue silk with a tiny floral print. But I'm cheating, because I saw her choose it.'

'And she's had it made up *already*?'

'Two of her maids are dressmakers. They do nothing else. Just imagine! They're probably asleep now — for the first time in two days. We have no idea how the really-really rich live, do we — down here.'

'But I think we're all going to learn,' Roseanne replied, remembering how Tamara Dawson had blundered into every conversation they'd had that day; she was not the sort of woman to trim her sails to the local winds.

By the time they reached the bottom of the stairs the band was playing, a light background music — airs from George Moore and Gilbert and Sullivan. The dances would come later. There was already quite a crowd, people who knew that the talk at Liston Court was always rewarding, in every sense of the word, and were determined not to miss any of it. The Scawens turned up at that moment. Roseanne took Jane upstairs to use her room rather than having to mingle with the generality of guests in the principal bedroom. Annette went off with Ralph Lang to join a group of youngsters impatient for the dancing to begin.

'Now that wouldn't have happened when I was a girl,' Jane said. 'The young ladies would have been . . .' She paused a moment, one hand on the banister rail. 'In fact, I remember a ball in this very house, in old Liggat's time. And we girls had to gather over there and there was an absolute *picquet* of chaperones between us and the gentlemen.'

'There still is, if you look carefully,' Roseanne commented. 'Not between them, but not too far away.'

Jane went on staring at the group. 'A thousand candles,' she said as she resumed the ascent. 'That's what Liggat had that night. Oh, it was . . . such an occasion! I can't begin to tell you.'

When they reached the half-way landing and passed out of general view, Roseanne said, 'You remember what I told you about Annette and Edward Dawson and Vienna? Well now she's changed her tune completely. She says she meant Venice all along, not Vienna. Of course, we all know she was in Venice, so it's no scandal.'

'Ho ho!' Jane bit her lips and arched her eyebrows in merriment. 'Why did she cut and run at the sight of him then?'

They arrived at the first-floor landing. Roseanne took her arm to guide her to her room, though she knew the way well enough by now. 'Oh, she's thought it all out. Butter wouldn't melt on that tongue! She says the woman that Dawson introduced all round as his wife *wasn't* Tamara! And that's why she ran.'

'Better and better,' Jane exclaimed. 'Aren't we awful!'

'As if we'd care what she did in Vienna! Or in Venice. It's the way she thinks she's bamboozled me — as if I'm just some country *put*! That's what gets my goat.'

'My my!' Jane was surprised at her vehemence. 'What d'you propose doing next?'

Roseanne laughed and made light of it now. 'Oh, just tease her a bit, that's all.'

In fact, Jane had, as usual, put her finger on it. Roseanne would do precisely nothing with this new discovery — not even tease Annette about it. For as soon as she had overcome her initial surprise at the explana-

tion and her resentment at Annette for supposing it had
duped her, she did not give a hoot whether the woman
had or had not been to Vienna — with or without an
Italian waiter or an Austrian cavalry officer . . . or the
King of Timbuctoo. Such affairs (and even such
affaires) were part of the almighty ennui of other
people's lives; she wanted no part in them — not even
at the trivial level she had just indulged in with Jane.

Why had she bothered to speak at all, then, she asked
herself. Out of convention, she decided. Because it was
expected of her. Because that was part of the price to
pay for moving in society.

The sooner she got away from it all, the better, then
— some place where she could ignore the world and the
world could return the compliment and leave her in
peace.

Jane became brisk, too, throwing her mantle on the
bedspread and saying they must be quick for she didn't
want to miss what she was sure would be Tamara
Dawson's grand entrance.

And it was a grand entrance, too. There are some
people who seem to carry around their own personal
limelight. Whenever they enter a room, heads turn and
the volume of chatter dwindles for a moment. When
they speak, though the thoughts may be nonsense —
as they often are — the utterance acquires a gravity that
a regius professor might envy. And even in their repose,
the air about them has an aura that compels attention.
The Dawsons were of that tribe.

The invitation had been for eight; they arrived at a
quarter past, on the very borderline between fashionably
late and downright rude. The naphtha flares in the
portico seemed to burn a little brighter as they descended
from their brougham, and a personal breeze, or invisible
zephyr, bore her mantilla behind her to create a most

striking line. Her sylph's figure seemed to double the width of the door as she swept within — breasting waves of envy from women who could remember negotiating that same entrance, hip by hip by bustle. She was, as Annette had said, in the pale blue silk with floral print. Behind her — indeed, framing her in that moment of her entry — was the sober black of her husband's evening dress. As she moved forward, Roseanne saw he was wearing a caramel-coloured cummerbund with a fine black horizontal stripe.

'Dear Mrs Kitto!' Tamara exclaimed. 'How very, very kind you are to invite us to your little *soirée*!'

'Good of 'ee to come, my lover.' Mary Kitto beamed as she turned to her husband and said, 'Frank, you never met missis, did 'ee.'

Like an after thought, Stephen slipped through the door behind them. He glanced about, spotted Roseanne, and came to her at once. 'Cadged a lift with them,' he explained. 'She's a bit overdressed, don't you think? You're looking splendid.'

Taking both comments together, Roseanne wasn't altogether sure that the second was a compliment; but she thanked him as if it were. 'You could have brushed this coat a bit better,' she grumbled. 'And look at your hat! Oh, come on upstairs and we'll make you presentable.'

Annette, at her elbow, whispered in her ear, 'There's one sure way to stop him shaming you like this.'

'Roseanne, dear,' her mother said as they passed, 'will you take Mrs Dawson up and show her what's where? Good evening, Stephen.'

'Good evening, Mrs Kitto. It was good of you to invite me.'

'Did I? Oh well, you're welcome all the same.'

Stephen pulled a face at Roseanne as the three of them

370

started upstairs. 'I thought the invitation went astray in the post,' he explained.

'We seem fated to travel about in tandem, Mr Morvah,' Tamara commented.

'You can drive a cow,' he replied, 'and lead a horse. But a pig walks with you.'

Roseanne gasped and turned to see how the woman took this insult, jocular though it was in intention. To her surprise, Tamara Dawson laughed and shook her head, much as to say that he was incorrigible. What strange relationship had sprung up between them she wondered, and in so short a time. 'Well, there's no doubting which is the pig, Mrs Dawson,' she said coldly. 'I'm only bringing him up to get his coat brushed.'

Tamara smiled at her. 'I knew there must be some reason, Miss Kitto.'

Stephen was left at the bedroom door; a moment later it opened a crack through which Roseanne poked her hand, waggling a clothes brush. 'I don't want to see a speck,' she told him as she closed it again.

She asked Tamara if there was anything she required.

'Yes, come here,' was the reply. Then 'sit down.' Then: 'That was sly of you — letting me think Jake was your baby, and you all unmarried.'

Roseanne smiled and tried not to.

Then Tamara smiled, too. 'But I know why you did it. I was not myself that day. I had expected to hate Cornwall, hate Montpelier, hate everything down here. And I fell in love with it all at first sight.'

It was such a wildly improbable explanation that Roseanne began to wonder in earnest why the Dawsons had, in fact, settled in so remote a part of the country. Until now it had been a matter of the mildest curiosity with her.

'And that annoyed me so much,' she went on, 'that

371

I blurted out a number of foolish things. So your gentle reproof was well taken. Will you call on me at Montpelier? Without a particular invitation?'

Roseanne found herself imagining a conversation in which dear, trusting Stephen blurted out his feelings for her and Lady Bountiful here had promised to do what she could to help; so here she was, offering all the covering fire a pair of ardent lovers might need. The trouble was, a small voice in Roseanne's own mind was already urging, 'Why not?'

She replied that she would be delighted to take up such an amiable invitation.

Stephen passed muster and the three of them returned to the ball. On the way down Tamara said, 'You must be very proud of your parents, Miss Kitto. What a formidable woman your mother is! I first met her at Mrs Lanyon's where she quite overawed me.'

Stephen claimed the first dance, a measured gavotte; conversation was only intermittently possible, in those moments when the steps brought them together, but they managed well enough.

'Can you imagine anything overawing that one?' Roseanne asked first.

'I was thinking the same,' he replied. 'But why did she say it?'

'Because she imagines *I* am overawed by my mother, perhaps? To put the pair of us in the same boat. She's certainly trying to ingratiate herself with me for some reason. The day I first met her I told her Jake was my little boy.'

'I know.' He laughed. 'I put her right about that. She was furious!'

'Well there was no sign of it tonight. She was sugar and spice and all things nice. But why? Why me? Has she said anything to you about me?'

372

'Not much. She asks a lot about Annette. And Bodilly — she can't stand the sight of him. Is he coming tonight, by the way?'

'I have no idea,' Roseanne lied. 'I'm surprised *you're* here, actually.'

He gave her waist a little squeeze. 'Duty calls! I'm the temporary Society Correspondent of the *News* — seeing that the regular chap couldn't get an invitation.'

The music stopped and he bowed to her. They chatted a while longer.

'I'm surprised they don't give both jobs to you anyway,' she said.

He nodded. 'I do have the entrée to more places than poor old Stevens.'

'I don't mean that,' she told him. 'I mean it's the same thing, Nature and Society. They're the same. Feathering your own nest? Snouts in the trough? Don't you think?'

He laughed and went in search of his next partner. He left a small emptiness within her. He was a very comforting man to be with — reliable yet never dull.

'Why not?' the little voice asked again.

But another asked, 'Why?'

And between them was the old silence.

45

Edward Dawson claimed the military two-step with Roseanne; he proved as suave and elegant a dancer as anyone might have guessed from merely looking at him – supple of body, lithe on his feet. Roseanne found herself doing steps she had never learned, simply because he led so well. After a turn or two he complimented her on her nimbleness. His words afforded the chance, probably her only chance, to raise the topic that was uppermost in her mind.

After assuring him it was only because he led so well that she was able to dance at all, she went on, 'I hope you won't think it too personal if I say how much I admire your cummerbund, Mr Dawson.'

He allowed that it was one of the finest he'd ever possessed.

'Viennese, isn't it?' she remarked.

He missed the beat but swiftly caught up again. 'Why yes. But how clever of you to know that, Miss Kitto! How did you do it, pray?'

Courage failed her. 'Well,' she confessed, 'I must admit it wasn't me who saw it. Miss Morvah told me she was sure it was Viennese and I didn't see how she could possibly know – so I was just . . . fishing, really.'

'Ah!' To Roseanne's disappointment he relaxed. If the combination of Vienna and Annette meant anything to him, it was obviously nothing to fear; but more likely

374

it meant nothing at all. 'I bought it on my last visit there,' he went on. 'A sweltering day in August. Not the sort of day on which to buy any kind of apparel. But there it was in the window — too beautiful to resist.'

Roseanne said she could quite believe it.

After a short silence he asked, 'Has Miss Morvah ever been to Vienna, then?'

'I don't believe so,' Roseanne replied. 'Venice, yes — but that's quite a way away, isn't it.'

'Quite a way.' He chuckled.

'But she has a flair for clothing, as you must have noticed.' She would have said more, probing him for responses to her mentions of Annette, but he interrupted: 'Indeed I have, Miss Kitto. See here though, let's not waste the dance in talking of her. Tell me about yourself. My wife says you've adopted an orphan boy?'

'Jake,' she said fondly. 'He's the apple of my eye.'

'If he was the wiry little lad playing badminton on the day of our arrival at Montpelier, I don't blame you. But it was a brave thing to do, all the same.'

His voice had a warm, dark resonance that she found most soothing; yet it had a mercurial quality, too, as if he were constantly poised for either laughter or seriousness. And he never revealed one of those two qualities without retaining a hint of the other — so that merely to listen to him was to feel stretched between two opposite emotional possibilities. It made her wish she already enjoyed a closer friendship with him than their mere acquaintanceship, for that would be the only way to reduce the tension. 'Because of not being married, you mean?' she said.

'Just so.' He gave a little laugh. 'Why, I don't believe *you* think it was courageous at all!'

'I don't believe I thought anything, one way or the

other, Mr Dawson. You only think about things if you feel you have a choice, don't you find?'

After a pause he said, 'No, I don't, as it happens. How interesting! If I find myself trapped in a situation where I have no choice of action, then I think about it a great deal. On the other hand, thought is a grand excuse for never acting at all. I believe I'd never have had the courage to do what you did – and just see what I'd have missed!'

Their eyes met. Until then she had thought they were playing with each other in the manner of most such conversations – saying things as a kind of test, making statements neither would dream of holding against the other when the music stopped. But now she saw in his expression such a sadness, such an awareness of opportunities lost, never to be repeated, that it threw her into confusion. She knew she ought to have said something to the effect that bringing up a boy was like taming a savage; instead she found herself racking her brains for words to comfort him. 'I'm sure most people would be surprised to hear you, Mr Dawson, speaking of missing *anything* in life,' she said.

'Perhaps,' he replied offhandedly. 'Yes . . . regrets are always vain, aren't they.' It was a conventional response to what he must have seen as a conventional way of ending their conversation – though such had not been her intention.

Now she felt acutely disappointed, as if she had let him down. He had offered her an opening, a chance to say something significant, and she had retreated into the sort of phrases you could pluck out of any old book on etiquette. She felt unworthy of the trust he'd accorded her . . . inadequate to the challenge of his fine, sensitive mind. The dance was suddenly interminable.

Then, to her surprise, he gave a groan of frustration.

'Oh, these winter balls,' he exclaimed. 'I love them and I hate them! They introduce us to new people, interesting people, and yet they deny us any possibility for a true meeting of minds. I trust you won't think *me* too personal now, Miss Kitto, if I say I hope you will call upon us at any time – you and little Jake – without waiting for an At Home or any more formal occasion. Will you do that?'

He had timed it perfectly, for the music was entering its final coda. All Roseanne needed do was thank him and say how delighted she and Jake would be. He returned her to her party with a smile and a flourish that sent several envious glances in her direction.

Interesting! He found her interesting! She glowed at the thought; but there was no one she could tell.

'What did you talk about?' Annette asked.

'Oh,' Roseanne said airily, hiding her smile, 'this and that . . . Jake, Montpelier . . . Vienna.'

'You didn't!' Annette was horrified.

'Why ever not?'

'Oh, well, no reason at all, of course. All the same . . .' She consulted he programme and her face fell. 'I've got him down for the next dance after this,' she said glumly.

46

The dance after the next was supposed to be a polka though it was slow enough to be a schottische. Dawson was at Annette's side before the strains of the first bar. 'It's so pleasant to meet you, Miss Morvah, without being constrained to talk of roofs and drains,' he said as soon as he whisked her away. 'I was beginning to wonder where life's rich panoply had gone. I see it was lurking here at Liston Court all the while. I must say, the Kittos know how to manage an affair like this. Yet I understand he began life as a stonemason.'

'He was always just that little bit different,' Annette replied. 'My father called him *Mister* Kitto — which he never did any other working man, to my knowledge.'

'I can believe it. Look at him there, now!'

As they turned and turned, Annette saw Roseanne's father standing among a group of men near the door. Dawson asked her who they all were and what they did.

She rattled them off, as many as she knew, thinking it would be a way to keep him off the one subject that was uppermost in her mind: 'Hamill Oliver — he's one of the Troys of Pallas House. He doesn't do much except drink and talk his head off about Cornish history. The bald . . . the gentleman with the shiny head is Judge Callaghan of Trelowarren. And the one next to him is Squire Pellew of Skewjack. The Pellews bought the lands that used to belong to Montpelier.'

'Yes, I know him. We've met already. And the dark, Spanish-looking fellow next to him?'

'That's Daniel Jago. He owns a boatbuilding yard at Ponsharden, between Falmouth and Penryn — also, five or six Channel coasters that trade between Europe and here. He's another one who's come up in the world lately. It's said that Mrs Scawen put some of her money behind him.'

'She seems to have a bottomless purse.'

'I believe her husband is a very shrewd manager of funds.'

'Ah! A man to bear in mind, then.'

'He's the one standing talking with Daniel Jago. And the third man there's name is . . .'

'Enough,' Dawson said, 'or I shan't remember one of them. My point is, they're men of substance by the sound of it — every one. Yet would any stranger, looking at that group, be in the slightest doubt as to which man dominated it?' He smiled at her. 'That sort of thing fascinates me, doesn't it you?'

'Yes,' she enthused. 'Why d'you suppose it is?'

It occurred to her that if he and Roseanne had been talking about Vienna, then it must have been he who raised the subject. Roseanne would never have dared. So now, by indulging in all this boring talk of how wonderful Frank Kitto was, he was merely playing cat and mouse with her. He would surely spring his surprise upon her before the music stopped. The dance, which had barely begun, already seemed interminable.

'It's in our stars,' he replied. 'Or bred in the bone. Don't you think he may have passed something of it on to his daughter? She's a fairly remarkable woman in her own right. She tells me you've been to Venice, by the way?'

So there it was at last!

Annette responded angrily: 'She had no right to tell you any such . . . ah – did you say Venice?'

'Yes.'

'Ah.' She grinned sheepishly. 'Ah! Yes, indeed, she's quite right. I have. I was there in the summer.'

He gave a baffled laugh. 'I don't understand.'

'Oh . . .' Annette's tone suggested it was all too tedious for words. 'Its just that Miss Kitto confuses Venice with Vienna. She's mentioned to several people that I went to Vienna – which, of course, I never did! But you know how difficult a canard like that is to stop once it gains any circulation. That's why I flew off the handle like that. I owe her an apology – and you, too, come to think of it. What were you saying? Venice – yes . . . beautiful city! Such a shame it's falling to pieces, literally before our eyes! You know it, of course.'

He nodded. 'My mother-in-law owns a place there. It's funny you should ask, in fact, because we, too, were there this summer. And the moment I saw you at Montpelier, I felt sure we'd met before, somewhere. Could it possibly have been Venice? It must have been. Where were you staying, may I ask?'

'Where is your mother-in-law's place?'

'Beside the Canal Foscari, off the Grand Canal – d'you know it?'

'Oh well, the Vyvyans' place is in the next canal down. Barnabas.' She laughed with relief. 'That must be it! We probably sailed, or gondola-ed, past each other practically every day. Isn't it a small world!'

'Indeed. I might know your aunt, too.'

'I doubt it. They don't go about at all.' She gave a sigh of relief. 'Well, I'm glad that's all sorted out. To be candid, Mr Dawson, I, too, was almost certain I'd seen you somewhere before. I said so to Miss Kitto the moment we saw you draw up with Mr Bodilly. Is he here tonight, by the way?'

For an answer, Edward Dawson simply nodded and directed his eyes across the ballroom floor. She turned and saw him at once — dancing with Roseanne.

47

Roseanne determined she would hold no conversation with Mark except in direct answer to a direct question; it seemed the best way to avoid an unseemly public argument. He, perhaps because he knew it would annoy her – or perhaps because he was such a rotten dancer – simply whispered, 'One ... two ... one ... two ...' half through his lips, half through his nose. To make matters worse, his counting hardly ever coincided with the actual music. At last she could stand no more of it; she broke her resolve and said, 'This is torment for both of us. Let's go and get a glass of punch.'

He was off like a slipped whippet, leaving her to trail in his wake. She passed her father he beamed at her and said, 'Going on, maid?'

'No!' she laughed. 'Going off.'

When she arrived at the buffet, Mark was already holding a glass for her, filled to the brim. She tipped half of it back in the bowl and thanked him. 'I can't abide dancing, anyway,' he said.

'Why d'you come, then?'

'Because I was invited.'

'Oh, it's as easy as that, is it?'

'What is?'

She shook her head. 'Never mind. Don't let's fall out now.' She smiled at him sweetly. 'And of course, you've not needed to go dancing much these last four years, have you!'

He stared at her coldly and then, with the air of one who has tried his damnedest to be pleasant, and failed through no fault of his own, he became brisk and businesslike instead. 'Your father says you're looking out for a farm.'

She almost choked on her drink. 'He what?'

'That's what he told me. He said you wanted to buy a farm.'

She stared toward the door but her father was out of sight around the corner. 'I see,' she said drily. 'Does he think he can kill it that way?'

'What way? Damme to hell, woman, what are you ranting on about? He just said did I know of any farm coming up on the market?'

'He'll try and rush me into it now. That's his trick, eh? "Going on, maid? What? Haven't 'ee bought that farm yet? My dear life, you'll be in your box before the deeds are signed . . ." That'll be his game now. Just to make me think twice about the whole thing.' She laughed again as a new strategy occurred to her. 'Well, I can go better than that! *Do* you know of a farm coming up soon?'

He smiled at last, the smile of a magician who knows his new trick will truly amaze. 'Of all the farms in West Penwith, which would you like most?'

'You know my answer to that. We talked about it often enough, once upon a time.'

'Just say its name. 'Tis in Breage parish, I'll tell 'ee that.'

'Penbro?' Her heart skipped a beat. 'Oh, Mark! Don't say Penbro's for sale.'

He shook his head, but continued to smile. 'Better than Penbro.'

'But there's nowhere better than Penbro — not in Breage parish.'

'There soon will be. 'Tis near Penbro . . . across the valley, where it do get the early sun . . . good drainage . . .' He went on handing out clues until she exploded: 'Wheal Fortune!'

His smile turned to one of triumph. 'Now the mine is closed for good, the old miller's house — Barney Hoskin's old place. . .'

'Who owns that land?' she interrupted him.

'Rogers in Penrose. They don't hardly want it now the minerals are all gone. They got no other land within three miles of there, so they're going to sell it off with about sixty acres.'

'Oh yes!' She was slipping into the buyer's seat already. 'Sixty acres of old halvans, arsenic, and mine tailings! And the biggest hole in the ground west of Truro! How much are they paying for some fool to take it off their hands?'

'Sixty acres of arable,' he continued calmly, 'plus only fourteen acres of wasted land — where you could still run a dozen sows if you had a mind. Or whatever lucky farmer gets it.'

Now, indeed, her heart began to race. She had to force herself to remain calm . . . *will* her hand not to tremble as she sipped her punch. 'But the fields are all grown in,' she complained.

'Nice and fallow.'

'Nice and thorny! Nice and furzey! And what about all they old miners in cabins and hovels down by the blind adit opposite Sethnoe?'

'All gone,' he assured her. 'When Scott's closed, and then Grankum, they all upped and off to Mexico.'

'Leaving a fine old mess behind them.'

'Well . . .' His casual tone and wandering gaze

suggested he'd already given her up as a serious buyer. 'There's plenty will take it, mess or no mess.'

'With milk gone below fourpence? And barley too low to harvest? And Harry Mitchell told me he couldn't get a farthing a head for his cabbage last week. Rogers will be lucky to get a single offer, I should think.'

'There's one born every minute, they say,' he told her lightly.

'Mind you, if he was to cut back the furze and thorns and mend a few gates and till the fields to show what they're made of, he might have a chance.'

'So you're definitely not interested?'

She was silent a moment and then said, 'I was meaning to call on old Mrs Rapson, up Scott's. I could look at the place, I suppose. Just in passing, like. No harm in looking.'

'No harm in looking.' He cocked an ear. 'What tune is that?'

'Now that *is* a polka,' she told him.

'Is that the second of the set?'

She consulted her programme. 'It must be.'

'I'm supposed to be dancing with Miss Morvah,' he said lugubriously.

Roseanne, who had noticed Annette wandering around a moment earlier, sought in the direction she had taken. 'There she is,' she said and called out her name.

'I must have walked straight past you,' Annette said as she joined them; then, to Mark, 'Aren't you supposed to be dancing with me?'

'Don't!' Roseanne warned her. 'Stay and have some punch for your toes' sake. He's awful.'

Mark nodded in happy confirmation and filled a glass for her; she returned none of it to the bowl.

'Isn't Mr Dawson a *divine* dancer,' she murmured.

'Oh, and guess what! He clearly remembers seeing me in Venice this summer. His mother-in-law lives on the next canal from the Vyvyans' place.'

'Mystery solved,' Roseanne said cheerfully. 'Or that one, anyway. There's still the *other* mystery − the young lady he took to Vienna.'

'Yes,' Annette agreed, apparently only half listening.

'I'll love you and leave you, then.' Roseanne set down her glass and wandered off. A footman took it up at once and added it to the tray for the scullery.

Annette eyed Mark speculatively and then said, 'Was she on her latest hobby horse?'

'What's that?' he asked cautiously.

'This farm business.'

His expression turned to mild surprise. 'Has she talked to you about it?' The possibility pleased him and his tone became conspiratorial. 'How serious is she?'

'She hasn't said a word to me, but her father's made no secret of it.' She smiled. 'I know his game.'

'So does she. She thinks he wants to laugh her out of it.'

That made Annette laugh. 'Quite the reverse! He's so eager, he'd even put up the money himself.'

He shook his head in disbelief. 'How would a sensible fellow like him go and do a thing like that?'

'Can't you guess? Knowing Roseanne, he's sure she'd bite off more than she could chew. So you tell me: what is a woman on her own going to do when she finds she can't manage so many acres?'

A slow grin spread over Mark's face. 'Why, he's so clever as a troacher!' He laughed.

'She'd set her sights at *you* then, right enough,' Annette added, as if she knew she was stating the obvious but was only doing so to round off the story neatly.

It stopped him in mid-guffaw. 'Me? She can't abide me. We can't say words to each other without scratching and ramping.'

She shook her head pityingly. 'And you think that's because she dislikes you? My dear man! How little you understand women.'

He laughed ruefully. 'I'll own up to that fast enough.'

'But why so alarmed, in any case?' she persisted. 'It's obviously what you wanted all this time. It's what you've been working for, isn't it? A wife with a nice farm as her dowry, and a bit put by, and better prospects every year that passes.'

'Working for it?' he asked incredulously. 'Damme to hell, maid, how d'you make that out, then?' Her chuckle suggested anyone could see through such a shallow protestation. 'But why else did you choose the profession you're in? Surely because it needs no capital, no machinery, no particular premises — something you can drop at the first wave of a wedding ring. Wasn't that your reason?'

He shook his head in amazement that she could have misread his intentions as badly as that.

'And why,' she looked about them and lowered her voice, 'why did you go to such extraordinary lengths *not* to become entangled with another sweetheart? Surely it was to keep yourself available to answer the call when it came?'

Seeing him about to explode she put a finger to his lips and said urgently, 'Forgive me if I've misunderstood you, Mark — but I'm sure I'm not the only one who's followed such a logical train of thought to its logical conclusion. Just you think about it.'

He did. A cunning glint shone in his eye. 'I suppose there's worse fates,' he mused. 'A hundred-acre farm facing south, with a good, cut-granite farmhouse . . .'

His voice tailed off as he saw the look of disappointment in her eye. 'How?' he asked.

'It's sad,' she told him. 'A hundred acre farm — is that really the limit of your ambition?'

He scratched the lobe of his ear. 'There was a time when I'd have laughed at the folly of it — to dare to think I might own ten acres, never mind a hundred.'

She shrugged, much as to say it was no business of hers, but . . . 'I just thought you had more in you than that, Mark. A thousand acres is more your style, I'd have said. Why break your back on a single measly farm when you could live in style by doing the one thing at which you truly excel: *managing*! You could manage a dozen farms. There's no one in the whole of West Penwith can hold a candle to you when it comes to that.'

'Well!' he exclaimed, scratching his chin. Then he laughed. 'But 'tis all castles in the air, maid! A thousand acres! Why, there's only one estate of that size hereabouts and that's . . .' He fell to silence, unable to take his eyes off her as the full significance of her words struck him.

'Yes,' she said, 'just think about that, too.'

48

Roseanne paid her intended visit to Mrs Rapson at Scott's the following Monday, the first in November; the old widow's husband had been coachman to the Vyvyans, the former owners of Trevivian manor. She had begged a few young holm plants — as holly was called in those parts — from the garden of the old coach house, 'just to remember the place', she said.

'In other words, to get a free hedge out of me,' Jane commented.

'Noblesse oblige,' Vosper said.

Actually, it was an easy wish to satisfy since they pulled up several dozen volunteer hollies every year. Roseanne offered to take them to the old lady, and Jane, who had learned of her interest in Wheal Fortune from Annette, pretended not to know why her young companion was so keen — for Mrs Rapson could talk all four legs off a donkey once she got going.

The old woman was thrilled with the plants, couldn't thank Roseanne enough for her kindness, begged her and Jake to come in and 'sup a bit damson wine'. And that was only the beginning.

It was Jake's impatience that finally silenced the old lady. After she had expressed her gratitude, and told the tale of Mrs Snell's latest *accouchement*, and the scandal about Jenny, Mrs Treloar's eldest, and what they said about the new vicar in Goldsithney, and why

Hubert Jenkins's milk went sour last Thursday . . . Jake asked petulantly, 'When are we going to see Wheal Fortune, Mummy?'

Roseanne laughed awkwardly and explained that she'd told the lad all about the deserted quarry and the rusting machinery that was just lying about the place . . . but the old one was not taken in. Even if that *had* been Roseanne's only purpose, that fertile brain would have transformed her at once into a committed purchaser of the now available farm.

'I 'speck they'll put that place up for sale now, wouldn't you,' she said. 'Who owns it, I wonder? Duke of Leeds, is it?'

Roseanne agreed that it probably was. She knew for certain that it wasn't part of Skyburriowe.

'And they ought to plough the fields and mend the gates,' Jake put in.

After that, old Mrs Rapson couldn't wait to get them out of the house.

The direct lane to Wheal Fortune ran along the valley side, a good half-mile from the ridge, whose name was Carnmeal Downs; nonetheless, Roseanne set off to go the long way round, over Carnmeal, rather than feed Mrs Rapson's suspicions. They hadn't covered half a furlong before Roseanne nudged Jake and pointed at the road behind them. The old widow was already scurrying off in bonnet and shawl, down the road through Scott's, off to the village shop in Carleen to announce to the world that Miss Kitto was going to buy Wheal Fortune farm for four hundred and twenty-seven pounds — or whatever genuine-sounding price occurred to her evergreen imagination.

Actually, Roseanne thought, four hundred and twenty-seven would be about the mark. She had just over a thousand on deposit and in consols; she could buy the farm, stock it with a good herd — a dozen milkers, say, and a bull of her own — and still have enough to survive the first year without debt.

Jake couldn't sit still. He wanted leap down and run ahead of the pony. He wanted to stay and ask a dozen questions, the same dozen he'd asked a dozen times before. Can I milk the cows? Can I feed the calves? Can I keep one for myself? Can I hit the cows like they do in the market? Can Courtenay come over so we can I hit the cows together? . . .

Now he was actually at the farm, he began with a new variation: 'Where does our land begin, Mummy?'

They were on the track that ran south across the highest part of Carnmeal, from Poldown to the valley at the foot of Breage hill. She pointed out the fields in turn, beginning with the five small ones that lined the track to their left. 'That one there looks like it's got a bad patch running through it, see? Hardly anything growing there, only a few whisht old stems of Great King Harry. That's what we're keeping our eyes peeled for today, my bird. All the bad things we can say about the place.'

'But why?'

'So we can make them abate their price. We don't want to pay more for it when we could easily pay less, do we.'

He grinned at her cunning. She turned her attention to the fields on their right, where the land sloped gently down toward the stream. 'This big one's part of the farm, too, I should think. Now what can we see wrong with that? Let's get out and have a bit of a walk, shall we.'

But they remained in the gig until they reached the far end of the field, where the track wound its way among the wastes of the former mine — acre after acre of barren rock and dust. Here and there along its outer fringes were the first colonies of furze and cotoneaster. Where the puddled clay held enough water, there was marram and sedge, as well. 'Not even a goat could thrive there,' she commented.

Jake agreed. 'But if we planted some grass, he could. And then I could look after him, couldn't I?'

'Along with the ducks and the fowls and the pigs and the calves? Why not, my lover!'

They tried to lift what had once been a gate into the large field, but it came apart in their hands. 'Now let's see how many bad things you can find to say about this field,' she challenged him.

'It's all furze and brambles,' he sneered.

'True, but four men with hooks and eevils could clear the lot in a week — that's less than two pounds in wages. They're not going to knock much off the price for that, are they. Look again.' With the toe of her boot she scrabbled aside some grass to reveal a stone, which she pushed aside. Before it came to rest it unearthed two others.

'Stone,' he said.

'Good lad! Very smart. Now tell me — how long will it take those same four men to pick this field clean after they've cleared the furze and brambles?'

He picked up one of the stones and hurled it at a magpie. Now that he looked he saw the ground littered with rocks of every size, from pebbles to boulders he couldn't even budge. 'Years,' he said.

She laughed. 'Now you're getting the idea! In fact, I think it'd take a month or six weeks, spread over the summer. But we'll *say* it's going to take years.'

He bit his lip guiltily and grinned at her.

'It's not really a fib,' she assured him. 'It's the way you have to be in business.'

They picked their way, as well as the furze permitted, to the farther hedge and glanced over it to inspect the two smaller fields beyond. 'Not nearly so stony,' he said in a disappointed tone. She explained that they didn't actually *want* it to be stony, 'Only if it is, we'll make the most of the fact.'

Below the big field were three others, bordering on the lane they could have taken from Mrs Rapson's. But, as there were four more fields to look at on the downhill side of the lane, they went back and brought the gig around.

'Who lives there, Mummy?' Jake pointed at a straggly row of one-room shanties beside the stunted oak where they tethered the pony. 'That's not the farmhouse, is it?'

She thought of teasing him, saying of course it was, and what was wrong with it, and wouldn't he like to live there . . . but the disappointment in his question was so intense, she hadn't the heart. 'Nobody lives there. Not any more. When the mines closed, they all went to America.'

He brightened at the news. 'Will those houses be ours then? Can I have one for my very own?'

'If we buy the place.' She saw the wonder in his eyes and cautioned him: 'That's still a very big *if* my lad.'

The former tenants of those hovels must have run their goats in the lower fields, for they were almost clean of the sort of regrowth that had claimed the rest of the farm. 'We could plough and seed these before Christmas,' she said. 'And if the winter's not too harsh, we'd get a bite off it before Easter.'

'Will we have a plough like Mr Brierly — that you can just turn upside down at the end of each furrow?'

'I expect so, dear.' She bent and lifted a sod of the turf, picking the soil out of its roots and rubbing it

393

between her fingers. 'Oh, this farm is just ready to come back to life,' she exclaimed.

When they returned to the gig, Jake ran off to explore the abandoned hovels. But she caught up with him after only a few strides and yanked him back by the collar. He was about to howl his protest when he saw her face. 'I want to show you something,' she said grimly, 'much more interesting than those old shacks.'

They passed an island of fertility on the downhill side of the lane — six green acres divided into three fields. 'Aren't we going to look at them?' he asked.

'We'll look at the bottom one first. The thing I want to show you is on the way to it.'

After a couple of hundred yards she turned off downhill, along a sandy track that wound a serpentine path among heaps of waste rock and clay. As they turned the first corner she stared to their left, frowned, and drew to a halt. 'That looks interesting,' she told him as they jumped down.

'What?' he asked in disgust. 'Just a heap of old sand? I want to go back to my houses.'

'It's not just a heap of sand. It's all this, too.' She stamped her foot on the ground. 'We're walking on it. How deep is it, I wonder?'

They went to the farther edge, where the terrain dipped sharply to a second winding trail, this one leading down to the ore-washing plant down by the stream — whose waters had, indeed, powered the whole process.

'It must be twenty feet thick,' she exclaimed in delight.

'Is that good?' he asked.

'It's all the sand we could ever want for all the new building we could ever hope to do. This is the waste from the buddles and vanning tables down there. They couldn't put it in the stream, see. They had to bring it up here and dump it. Well, that's worth a tidy penny to us, so we'll just pretend we haven't seen it. And now' − she grasped him by the hand − 'this is what I want to show you, young fellow my lad.'

She hurried him back the way they had come, past the gig, and into a wilderness of jagged stone on the farther side of the sandy trail. They scrambled to the top of a ridge, where she immediately tightened her grip on him.

'Is it a volcano?' he asked excitedly. It looked just like the picture called *Inside the Cone of Mt Etna* in Mr Scawen's library.

'Something every bit as dangerous,' she assured him. 'Now don't you dare move. Just watch this − and listen!'

She released him and rolled the largest boulder she could manage to the top of the ridge. There she gave it the strongest push of which her arms were capable. It clanked and rattled down the shaly bank and almost came to a halt on the narrow strip of bare spoil between the foot of the bank and what Jake had taken to be the throat of the volcano. For a moment it teetered on the edge, and then it fell from sight.

What followed was the most awe-inspiring sound Jake had ever heard − a deep, cavernous, rumbling as the rock plummeted into the bowels of the abandoned mine. It struck the walls of the shaft as it went, bringing down more great stones in its wake. The adit, naturally, opened into the stream below, whose level was some twenty-two fathoms below the top of the shaft. It took only three seconds for the rock to fall − moments in which the very air shuddered at its reverberation; and when it struck the water, followed by the further hundredweights it had dislodged on its way down, the

395

tumultuous splash, which rang on and on into the deathly silence above, was the most blood-curdling of all.

Jake's eyes glowed with admiration at the stupendous power his mother had unleashed, just by rolling a stone down to the edge of that hole. His glance took in the hundreds and thousands of stones as yet unrolled and he began to measure his future in hours of happy fun, sending one after another of them crashing down to make that terrifying, booming splash at the bottom. Then his mother spoiled it all by putting her eyes close to his and saying, 'Now just imagine that was you! Down there alone in the cold and the dark, drowning to death even if you weren't killed on the way down.'

He put his arm about her neck and hugged her tight, shivering at the very thought. 'I'll tie myself with rope,' he promised.

'You'll do no such thing. This is called the Blueborough shaft and there are six other shafts like that on this farm, some of them even deeper. There's another one just over that next ridge, see? Some of them you wouldn't even know they were there before you fell right down them. So unless you promise me now, promise me absolutely faithfully, cross your heart and hope to die, that you'll never, ever stray off the lane when you're out on your own, we'll go home now and forget we ever thought of buying the place. Promise?'

It was one of those rare moments when you could actually see a little bit of the child die and fall away, and a little bit of the potential man show through the scar. 'Promise,' he echoed in a tone more resigned than resentful. Then he grinned. 'Let's roll one more, eh?'

49

When they were standing in the twenty-first and last field of the farm, Roseanne asked Jake how many there were altogether, more as a tease than a test, for she thought he could not possibly remember. But he closed his eyes and she saw his fingers bending and straightening in turn. 'Twenty-one,' he said at last, 'and five gardens.'

'Five?' she echoed dubiously.

'Yes. Three at the house — two in front, and one at the back — and one in the field with all the stones and thorns, and one in the field beside my cottages.'

My cottages! she thought.

'Where the hedges stick out like that.' He drew three sides of a rectangle in the air.

'Oh, were they gardens? I thought they were the field next door, just sticking out a bit.'

'No. I looked over the hedge. They're little gardens — no houses, though.'

The advantages of being small, of having boundless energy — and a curiosity to match! 'You're going to be a great help, I can see,' she told him. 'Let's go and look at the house — if we can break our way in through all those brambles.'

'It's like a shoe, isn't it,' he said, slipping his hand into hers. 'And we're in the toe of it now. This field is like the big toe.'

She did not have the sort of mind that automatically mapped the world about her; she thought in sequences. Perhaps that was why he had spotted the gardens out on the farm — which she had seen merely as parts of fields that lay in the future half of their inspection tour. But he was right about the overall shape of the place. Vosper had brought home the big twenty-five inch Ordnance Survey sheets covering the farm; casting her memory back she saw, in her mind's eye, something very shoelike as its outline.

'The first fields we saw were the heel,' he said, thinking her silence was caused by doubt. 'Then the bit where the old mine is — all that rock and mess — that's where the shoe goes up off the ground. What d'you call that bit?'

'The arch. Yes, I can see it now, my bird. It is very like a shoe. The farmhouse is where the ball of the big toe would be. And this lane is like the line between the big toe and the others. Very good! Perhaps we'll change the name from Wheal Fortune to Jake's Foot Farm.'

'I like Wheal Fortune,' he said as he helped her over a broken bit of hedge, down into the lane.

'So do I — though don't even whisper it to anyone. The more I see of it, the better I like it. I don't think it's going to take much to get these fields back into order, though they look terrible now.'

'Ho ho!' came a cry from behind them. 'Trespassing, eh! Caught in the act!'

They turned to see Annette, labouring up the steepest part of the lane. 'Whew!' she exclaimed when she had almost caught up. 'You'll need a good Percheron or Suffolk punch to haul water up *this* hill every day!' She panted heavily after every few words. 'You're not really thinking of buying the place are you?'

398

'I thought there'd be no harm in looking at it while I was here,' Roseanne said offhandedly. 'But you're right. It's very dispiriting. The sheer amount of work to be done before you could even run a plough through it! We haven't seen the house yet.'

Annette, somewhat recovered, leaned down to ask, 'And what does Jake think of it, then?'

Roseanne gave his hand a surreptitious squeeze and he knew this was a test of his discretion. 'You should see one field over there!' he replied. 'The stones and the furze and things! It'll take years.'

Annette laughed. 'I can see you've been furthering his education for the real world, Zan.'

'No harm in that.'

'Indeed, no. Personally, I think anyone who took this place ought to be certified and dragged off to the loonybin. The only good thing about it is the name.'

Jake could not resist telling her: 'We're going to call it Jake's Foot Farm.'

Roseanne explained the origin of the joke and wondered what it would be in Cornish. 'What's foot?' she asked.

Annette thought about it. 'All Cornish names are about hilltops,' she complained. 'Carn-this, Tre-that, Bray-something, Menna-something . . . they're all hills and mountains. Jake, I suppose, would be Jago. And Nance is valley. You could call it Nancejago. Or Coombejago. Coombe is valley, too. That's the best I can do. You ought to ask Hamill Oliver of Pallas. He'd tell you eight hundred Cornish words for foot.'

'Jago,' Jake said speculatively and then skipped ahead of them up the lane, repeating the name as a one-word song.

'He's already decided we must buy the place, just so that he can become landlord of those derelict cabins beyond Blueborough,' Roseanne explained, by way of insurance — just in case the lad's enthusiasm ran away with him in Annette's hearing.

'Landlord, eh!' she responded. 'You *have* been working at his education.'

The farmyard had a sharp dip in the middle before rising, equally steeply, to a two-storey barn, about thirty paces in from the gate. One of the barn walls projected at shoulder height and curved up toward the lane, creating a little mowie at the top end of the yard. Just inside the gate, to the left, was stabling for two horses, backed by a byre for three or four cows; both stood lean-to — or foreanenst, as they say in Cornwall — the farmhouse proper.

'Built by a man!' Roseanne said in disgust.

Annette laughed. 'What, in particular, gives it away?'

Roseanne pointed at the dip in the middle of the yard. 'Imagine four hours of a good Cornish downpour on that yard — after a dozen cows have stood there twice a day, everyday, at milking time! Where's all that water and you-know-what going to collect, eh?' She opened the gate and led them into the yard. 'See!' She pointed out a brown tideline along the side of the house. 'And I bet I know what we'll find indoors, too.'

The backdoor was in two halves — an epps door, as it was known locally. They had to set the upper half carefully on the lower, for it hung by a single, rusting hinge. Inside they found themselves in a long, narrow scullery built foreanenst the house proper. Immediately facing them was another, more ancient back door, which led down one step into the kitchen.

'There!' Roseanne exclaimed the moment they were inside. 'Just as I thought.' She tapped the toe of her boot on the flagstone floor, where, once again, there were tide marks of dung-stained water everywhere.

'This kitchen is awash every time there's a heavy rain.'

Annette put a hand to her ear and chuckled. 'I can hear them — the echoes of ten thousand ghostly arguments. Can't you?'

Jake, not realizing she was joking, shook his head and looked about in slight apprehension. Ghosts!

'Of course you can,' she assured him. 'Just listen. The wife is saying, "This place isn't fit for pigs . . . how am I expected to keep it clean and sweet when it keeps flooding all the time?" And her husband is saying, "Damme to hell, woman, you do love to hear yourself talk! Talk, talk, talk! You think a man's got nothing better to do than build drains night and day! What's a bit of water, anyway? Water never hurt anyone." Can you hear them now?'

Though she bent to ask the question of Jake, her eyes were on Roseanne — who knew very well which man of their acquaintance she was parodying. Nor was it such a wild parody, either. 'First thing we'll do,' she told the lad, 'is tank the whole wall on that side of the house.' Then she remembered to add — '*if* we lose our wits and buy this place.'

They explored the rest of the house, which had six rooms and a dairy, plus the scullery. The kitchen and dairy ran the full width of the house at the back. The front half was divided into two smaller rooms: a sitting room with a fireplace and an unheated parlour; in between was a narrow, creaking staircase that led up to a tiny, unlighted landing. The three upstairs bedrooms exactly matched the layout below — a large one at the head of the stairs, over the kitchen, and two smaller ones in front, one of which could be reached only by going through the other.

'There's a dilemma,' Annette said. 'The best bedroom — the warmest one, anyway, over the kitchen — has no dressing room. And the one *with* a dressing room will be absolutely freezing in the winter.'

'Dressing room!' Roseanne echoed scornfully. 'You've got some funny ideas of life on a farm, Miss Morvah.'

The ceilings needed new plaster. The best thing to do with the walls would be to scrape off all the old paper and distemper and start again. The floorboards creaked and dipped. There was a pail half-filled with rainwater in one corner of the cold bedroom . . . not to mention heavy soot-stains over the mantelpiece, where rain had come down the chimney and soaked through the wall . . . and none of the windows opened . . . All in all, it was what one might expect of a house that had been used as a mine office for as long as anyone could remember and had then stood vacant for the best part of a year.

They went into the dairy last of all. There Roseanne wiped a fastidious finger along the wall and fetched down a cloud of fungal efflorescence. Annette nudged her and pointed at the tiny window which looked out into the yard. Through the cobweb festoons Roseanne saw the burly figure of Mark Bodilly, striding toward the back door. It occurred to her to wonder whether he and Annette were in cahoots. Was she the advance party, sent out to scout her, Roseanne's, opinion before he launched the main attack?

'Poor fellow,' she murmured. 'There are houses going down Porthleven, bigger than this − new, dry houses with good drains − for fifty pounds.'

They heard him almost demolish the epps door as he came into the scullery.

'They'll have to give this place away, won't they, Mummy?' Jake said as Mark burst open the second door and stepped down into the kitchen.

'What?' He had a most convincing line in outrage. 'Give it away? This house was built by a *miller*, my boy! And millers don't skimp theirselves when it do come to comfort. A hundred pounds would still be giving it away.'

Roseanne kept her eye on Annette, watching for any collusive signal between them. She saw none.

'Morning, maids,' Mark said belatedly. 'Had a good look around, have 'ee?'

'Nothing good about it,' Roseanne grumbled. 'Discouraging is more what I'd call it . . .' And she ran through a list of all the defects they had noted, leaving the matter of the drainage until last.

But Jake beat her to it. 'And look at the way the rain comes in from the yard,' he chimed in as his mother's anti-eulogy drew to its close. The toe of his boot pointed to several dried-up pools of dung among the ill-fitting flags.

Mark laughed. 'That's only because there's been no woman of the house to mop it up, boy. You should see it when there's people living here — clean as a new pin, then!'

Jake, unwilling to argue with someone so positive, glanced uncertainly at the two women. Roseanne stepped in: 'But who would *want* to mop up buckets of water off the yard every time it rains?'

''Tin't every time,' he assured her.

'Often enough,' she replied, darting her eyes at the proof beneath their feet.

'Gusson, damme, woman,' he sneered. 'What's a bit of old water on the floor? Water never hurt anyone!'

50

When Wheal Fortune went under the hammer it failed
to meet its reserve, which, though not disclosed, must
have been more than £440, which was Roseanne's final
bid on that day. There was only one against her, a
farmer from Porkellis, some of whose lands were being
encroached upon by the expansion of the local mine.
The general lack of interest in the place sent a small
shiver through local landowning society, but it made it
easier for the Penrose Estate to accept Roseanne's
private-treaty bid of £455 after the failure at auction.
Vosper, who handled the conveyance, broke all records
to assist her, so that she would be able to take possession
in time for the spring ploughing. She finally moved in
on Tuesday, the second day of February, 1875.

The first thing she and Jake did, even before they put
a foot indoors, was turn half a dozen breeding sows and
a young boar into the large, stony field up at Carnmeal.
The pigs, the waggon, and the horse were the only
possessions they brought with them to Wheal Fortune
that day — apart from a few overnight things. After
the usual forays that all animals make in new territory,
the pigs soon settled down to grazing and grubbing for
roots. It made Jake wince to see their snouts, which
looked so soft and sensitive, churning up the soil and
thrusting aside the stones as if they were made of
cardboard. He pushed a stick in the ground and tried

to imitate the action, but he couldn't even budge it. The only other thing he'd seen as powerful as those snouts was an iron bar fixed vertically to a steamroller and dragged behind it to tear up the road surface when they laid the drains in Helston.

When they had marvelled long enough at the power of those seven wrinkly snouts, they took the wagon down to the Blueborough fields and brought back two half-good gates; Jake brought the rusted back of an old stove out of 'his' cottages; and with these they managed to stop up the entrance fairly stoutly, even against pigs. 'This is *not* how we intend to continue,' she promised him – privately wondering how long it would be before she got round to hanging proper gates everywhere. She repeated the assertion an hour later when they stepped back and surveyed, with shamefaced pride, a shelter of straw bales and canvas where the pigs could huddle at night. It was almost a replica of the old milking parlour up in Breage – the sort of building she had sworn never to allow on any place of her own, in the days when 'a place of her own' had been no more than the wildest dream.

'Heigh-ho!' she sighed as she turned her back on the sight. Jake, however, seemed reluctant to leave the place. He kept touching the straw bales and running his hand down the sailcloth.

'D'you remember?' she asked incredulously.

'I sort of seem to,' he said, joining her.

'Perhaps you were older than we thought. I can't remember anything back before I was four. There was a big shipwreck on Loe Bar and I can just remember that – eighteen fifty-three.'

They scaled the 'gate' and, hand in hand, returned across the wasteland to the farmhouse, leading the horse and wagon to avoid the worst of the ruts. 'I'll cut some wood for the fire,' he said. 'There's a saw in the barn, and a criss-cross thing to put the wood on.'

She told him it was called a horse. She also warned him to be careful with the saw. He stared at her with a weary resignation. That was another memory from her childhood – the boring way grown-ups were always telling you to be careful . . . and how she'd vowed never to do it to any of her own. It was a day for breaking old resolutions.

When they arrived back at the farmhouse, they found both Stephen and Mark leaning on the gate, staring into the yard. They stood as far apart as possible without quite crowding the gateposts, and they were talking about all the things that needed doing before Wheal Fortune would even begin to be habitable, let alone profitable; it was a competition to say how crazy Roseanne was, without actually mentioning the fact.

'I brought they keys for 'ee,' Mark told her.

'Where are all your things?' Stephen asked. 'I came to help you move in.'

'What keys?' she asked. 'There's not a lock in the whole house. I only brought our bedding and a box of things for the kitchen. That house is so damp it's a wonder it's not alive with mushrooms. I'm going to keep fires going for a week before we move in. Has Harvey delivered our coal yet? I ordered two tons.'

Mark opened the gate for her. 'There used to be a lock on the front door. 'Tis lying on the windowsill in the parlour – and that's the key for it.' He held it up like some kind of talisman before handing it to her.

She stuffed it in her overcoat pocket and went down into the byre, where she had arranged for the coal to be delivered. 'Nothing!' she exclaimed. 'You can't trust anybody.'

Stephen joined her. 'What can I do? I came prepared

to carry furniture and things.' He pointed vaguely at his clothes, which were old and shabby.

'Bless you,' she said abstractedly. 'If you could stable the horse and carry that box indoors? And then Jake's going to saw up some wood in the barn. There's a heap of small wood in the mowie. If you could take the big knife and trim it for him?' And she could not avoid adding, 'Be careful with it, mind!'

Jake gave a groan and led Stephen out to the mowie.

'You going back up Breage, are you?' she asked Mark. 'You could ask Harvey if he's coming sometime before next year with that coal.'

He cleared his throat awkwardly. 'I don't live up Breage no more,' he muttered.

'Oh?' She pricked up her ears. 'Since when is that?'

'Since last Saturday, really. I do lodge with Trevoses, the millers, down St Johns in Helston.'

'That poky little two-room cottage at the bottom of their garden?' she asked. 'That's a bit of a come-down, isn't it?'

''Tis only somewhere to sleep and keep my clothes,' he replied, matching her belligerence. 'I do eat all I want up the Angel or the Blue Anchor.'

'Oh!' She feigned surprise. 'You're actually going to sleep in *these* lodgings, then! That'll make a change. Fall out with the old widow, did you?'

He turned on his heel and strode away.

'Mark!' she called after him, annoyed with herself for going so far.

He stopped but did not turn round. 'What?' he barked.

She waited for him to face her. When he did not, she just said, 'Nothing!' and went indoors to set the fire in the range. His inability to converse like any normal human being annoyed her more than ever.

From the moment the first small flame caught at the kindling it was clear that there was not the faintest suck of a draught in the firebox. The stove might as well have been no chimney at all. Soon the kitchen was full of smoke. She failed to open the window and staggered outside, coughing heavily. It began to rain.

There was nothing for it, however; they had to have a fire. She got an old, rather rickety ladder from the byre and put it to the chimney, which was on the gable end. It reached to within three feet of the pot. There was an old besom by the back door; its twigs were rotten but the handle was stout enough. She carried it up with her. The first ten feet were fine; after that she began to realize that the house was a lot higher than it looked from ground level . . . and the ladder a great deal more rickety. The rain started falling in stair rods.

She made it to the roof, somehow, and saw that the problem was as she had suspected. Crows — generations of them, probably — had filled the flue with twigs. She tried poking them down with the besom handle but they were much too tightly packed. Her father had told her once of the day they unblocked a chimney at Antron and hauled out two full cartloads of twigs; but this could hardly be as bad as that. If she could just get one small hole poked right through it — any sort of an airway at all . . .

There was one spot where the twigs gave a little. She poked harder. It was definitely a bit springy there. She gave it one final shove, hardest of all, and it yielded. And so did the rung of the ladder on which she was standing. The other foot, resting on the very edge of the slate roof, which was by now streaming with water, had no grip at all. The next thing she felt was a sharp crack on the side of her jaw, where it struck the broken rung. How she managed to hold on, she never knew.

The crack made a kaleidoscope of her sense of space and time — and of smell, too. There was a most peculiar smell in her nostrils, like the smell of freshly exposed rock after blasting.

Sights, sounds, smells — the whole universe of sensations — reeled about her, and yet through it all some self-preserving imp within her made her clutch at the next rung down and hold it like grim death until the shattered world began to reassemble itself. And then there was the awareness of pain, from the side of her face, from her left hip, where it had struck the ladder, and from her shoulderblades, where they had wrenched in breaking her fall. Now she was shivering like an aspen leaf. She was also soaked to the skin, despite her thick coat.

Gingerly she went back down the ladder, testing each rung before she trusted it with her full weight. Now her chief emotion was anger — a towering rage at her own folly. Chiefly she was trying to suppress the memory that just for a moment up there she had felt the question forming in her mind: is it all worth it?

When at last she reached the ground she forced herself to ignore the protests of jaw, shoulders, and hip and walk up to the mowie in search of a long green withy, which she would need for the next stage of clearing the chimney — assuming she had, somehow, poked a small airway through the blockage.

Stephen poked his head out of the barn door as she passed. 'Got a kettle going yet?' he asked hopefully. 'Two men dying of thirst here.'

'Won't be a minute,' she assured him. 'I've just got to clear the chimney.'

As she passed him on her way back, withy in hand, he said, 'From the inside, I hope? No foolish games up ladders.'

'As if I would!' she sneered.

She left the withy by the back door a moment, while she went round the house, took the ladder, and threw it over the nearest hedge.

Inside, once she took off her sodden overcoat, movement was easier. The sharpness of the pain was subsiding into an overall ache. With a little lamp oil to ease the threads she was able to remove the screws that held the door of the chimney cleaning trap, which was located just below the point where the stove pipe was mortared into the much older flue. Then a little more lamp oil on a rag tied to the top of the withy . . . a match . . . a flame . . . and she was ready to go.

Gingerly she pushed the burning rag through the trap door. To her relief, the flame remained vertical − so there was live air above it. Slowly she pushed the withy up, up, up . . . until it touched some obstruction. Then, praying it was the bottom edge of the twigs and not some badly aligned flue pipe, she held the withy still and waited. There was no sound from up there − no crackling as the tinder-dry wood at the bottom of the heap caught fire. Perhaps it wasn't tinder-dry. After all, nothing else in this damnable house was! Her arms were aching from holding the one awkward position before she had the first sign that anything was happening up there. Three tiny cinders, glowing brightly from their fall, shot past the opening. Two more followed, one of which hit the withy and ricocheted out into the room; she had to jump backward to avoid having her dress singed.

Then she heard it − a muted roar like a wind devil running through a valley full of trees. She just got the trap door back in time, before a great shower of burning twigs came hurtling down the flue. It landed in the stove and set fire to the remains of the kindling, which had

410

expired for lack of a draught. A moment later the other two were at the back door. 'Are you all right?' Stephen asked anxiously.

'Why shouldn't I be?' she replied.

'It's Guy Fawkes Night out here, come and look.'

Like a woman who has better things to do but who also knows the importance of humouring the menfolk she hunched herself under her sodden coat and went out to join them.

It was, indeed, a pyromaniac display. The chimneypot was gushing sparks like a volcano, and giving out a roar like distant cannon. Poking up from the middle of it all was the charring stump of the besom handle. She glanced guiltily at Stephen and saw that he had just noticed it, too. His glance went at once to the nook where the besom had been which also informed her how familiar he had made himself with the place lately and then at her.

'Very pretty!' She turned to go back indoors. 'It won't burn long, don't worry.' It was, in any case, a perfect day for a chimney fire.

She filled the kettle at the tap, which was connected to a rainwater kieve outside the house, and set it on the hob, which was already too warm to touch with comfort. She returned to the back door, where Stephen and Jake were still admiring the display. 'If you've nothing else on hand at the moment,' she told them, 'you could bring me what wood you've sawn. This fire's hungry.'

Moments later they returned with armfuls of logs, their bark glistening wet even from so short a run across the yard. She pushed the kettle aside and lifted out the plate so as to throw the wood directly into the fire. It was now drawing so well that neither flames nor smoke came out into the room. She replaced the kettle over

411

the open hole, to make it boil the quicker. 'You might as well stay now. Tea'll be ready in half a shake. Is that all the wood you've managed to cut?'

'Is it?' Stephen asked with rhetorical sarcasm. 'I never knew anyone who could saw wood like this young fellow.'

'I am very good,' Jake agreed.

'He just goes on and on. Never pauses for a rest. I don't know how he does it. You'll have wood for a week before he's done.'

'He's going to be my greatest help, aren't you.' Roseanne tried to put an arm about him but he squirmed away from her.

'What's that on your jaw?' Stephen asked.

She rubbed it as if it must be dirt, forcing herself not to wince. 'Soot, I expect.'

'Oh yes? And if I went round to the byre, would I find the ladder there? Mysteriously wet?'

The singing of the kettle almost drowned his inquisition. 'At least I got the fire going,' she pointed out.

'That would have been a great comfort to us, I'm sure. Just what one needs after scraping people up off the ground.' He smiled at Jake to assure him this was just grown-up banter, but she could hear the seriousness when he went on, 'How am I ever going to know a peaceful moment with you and Jake all alone out here, and no better sense than that?'

'We won't be all alone. Lorna Verrigoe's going to start living in as soon as she can settle . . .'

'You know what I mean.'

She nodded. 'I'll take more care in future.'

But he had not finished. 'And I don't like the idea of that boar running around loose up there at Carnmeal. Jake told me about it. That creature should be penned up here with a rigged male and have the sows and gilts brought to him.'

She wrapped her hand in a cloth and put it to the handle of the kettle. Why would it not *boil*? She was silent so long that he had to prompt her. 'Well?'

'Well what?'

'You know what. The boar.'

'Listen,' she replied crossly. 'If it was Vosper Scawen or Ben Ambrose or any other *man* friend of yours starting to farm here, and he put the boar out with the sows — would you even dream of talking to him like this? It's only because I'm a woman, isn't it!'

He went and sat on an empty tea chest, giving her arm a consoling squeeze as he passed. 'You know why,' he told her. 'And you know it has nothing to do with that.'

'Anyway, I haven't got anywhere here to pen him. He needs a house and a little yard to run in.'

The kettle boiled at last. Gratefully she snatched it up and poured the lively water over the tea leaves.

But he was relentless. 'You could build one foreanenst the barn. In fact, you could build two — use the second for a farrowing pen. And then build a glasshouse parallel to the barn wall, and that would close off the yard from the back garden — which is something you're going to have to do in any case.'

'Listen!' she almost shouted. 'Whose farm is this? Mine or yours?'

He raised his hands in surrender. 'Sorry, old thing. Deeply sorry. Won't say another word — except this: I've lost count of the number of times people have come to me, people not a million miles from this very room, saying, "Why don't you write about such-and-such or do a piece on so-and-so in that column of yours?" And I don't remember huffing and puffing and saying whose column is it?' He smiled sweetly. 'But then — it could be that I am a great deal more confident in my chosen profession than . . . certain other folk are in theirs.'

'You!' She stabbed a finger toward him, half amused, half angry. 'You're worse than Mark Bodilly, d'you know that. If he finds a sore point, he'll pick away at it for ever and a day. But *you* — you'll make the point sore before you even start. Anyway, where have you learned so much about farming all of a sudden? How to manage boars . . . farrowing pens . . . all that?'

He smiled again. 'One of the advantages of having half a dozen tenant farmers, don't you know. One has every reason to go about . . . talk to them . . . one picks up all sorts of things.'

'Including cattle plague and swine fever, I shouldn't wonder. Well I don't want you bringing them here, thank you very much. And perhaps you'll go back to your pig tutor and ask him if he ever heard of a boar becoming temperamentally unreliable before the age of six — especially if he's running free with half a dozen sows!'

He bowed his head and murmured, 'This is how one learns.'

She clenched her fists, turned to Jake, and said in a strangled tone, 'I could easily kill him.'

Jake saw his chance. 'What's a rigged male?' he asked.

'Well,' she said, turning bright pink, 'I think this tea is ready. Get the cups and things out of that box, there's a good boy.'

While Jake obeyed she risked a glance at Stephen and found him whistling soundlessly, staring at the ceiling.

But the lad who would saw away in the barn until his arm dropped off was not one to give up so easily;

he repeated the question the moment he had set out the 'cups and things'.

'And the heavycake and fuggan,' Roseanne reminded him.

Now, however, he stood his ground, saying he wanted to know.

'He'll tell you,' Roseanne replied as she started pouring the tea.

'It's very easy.' Stephen was as unruffled as you'd wish. 'You know those two lumps the boar has below his tail? Well, that's why the butchers don't sell boar's meat. No one would buy it. Those lumps give out something that makes the meat taste horrid. So, when the little boar pigs are very young, we take a knife to them and *rig* them − cut those lumps right out. We only leave them in if we want to breed from the boar, because you can't breed from a rig. There! That's clear enough, isn't it?'

Jake turned to his mother and said, in a slightly sad tone, 'See? He does know some things you don't, Mummy.'

'Talk is cheap,' she replied grimly. 'Ask him if *he's* ever actually taken a knife to a baby boar like that.'

And now it was Stephen's turn to be shocked − for the implication clearly was not only that she had done so but that she intended doing it again with her own stock.

However, before he could protest, she gave a little cry and leaped away from the spot where she was standing. 'Oh,'she pursed her lips and shook with fury while she rejected a dozen unsuitable expletives. '*Rabbet* it!'

For where she had been standing was a rising pool of a dirty brown hue.

'It's only a bit of water,' Jake assured her.

She rounded on him. 'If you ever dare say such a thing again, I'll drown you in it.' She threw up her hands in despair. 'What is the point of trying to dry out this house when *that* happens every time it rains!'

Stephen passed her teacup, which she accepted with grateful resignation. 'We clearly can't live here until we've tanked that wall out against the yard. The question is where *do* we stay? Would there be a room for us at the Queen's Arms, I wonder?' She ducked her head to look out at the sky. 'It'll be dark early today. I think we'll hitch up the horse again and go up to Breage now — as soon as we've had our tea.'

'Or.' Stephen said slowly.

'Yes?' she prompted.

'I was only thinking . . .'

'Yes?'

'Old Widow Delamere may have a room to let now.'

51

May Delamere was at first too taken aback to make any response at all; she just stood at her garden gate, where Roseanne and Jake had surprised her, and stared from one to the other. Either this was a request of monumental impudence or it arose out of a naivety too large to comprehend. Or . . . it slowly dawned on her as she stared into the eyes of the young woman, there might just be a third possibility. For those eyes were troubled; and this simple request for lodgings was — perhaps even unknown to the woman herself — an entreaty for something deeper and less easily stated.

May distrusted instincts, especially in a woman. For proof of their dire consequences, she only had to think back to the one that had driven her to take in Mark Bodilly. And yet she could not help feeling that the urge to say yes to Miss Kitto's request was somewhat different. A profoundly instinctual woman herself, she did not reason it to the obvious conclusion that, whereas, in the earlier case, it was she who wanted something of Bodilly, now it was the other party who needed something of her. But some faint — perhaps instinctual! — awareness of that difference now moved her from indignant rejection to a feeble, 'Well, I . . . simply don't know, Miss Kitto. I mean, why here? Why me?'

Roseanne, who had staked all the emotion that

remained to her at the end of this rather fraught day, had no reserves to sustain an answer. She simply mumbled an apology, said it had been an error, and turned dispiritedly away. Jake, who had rarely seen her like this, looked from one woman to the other in dismay; if Widow Delamere had rooms and they needed a room, where was the difficulty?

'Wait!' May called after they had gone a few paces. She drew a deep breath. 'Of course I have rooms. And of course you can stay here. After all, as you say, it's only until your own house has been made habitable . . .'

Jake skipped back to the gate, an act that overcame the last of his mother's hesitation. She took their bag off the wagon, told the horse she'd be back in a shake, and returned to Mrs Delamere. 'It is very kind of you,' she said.

'I was only so surprised you chose me,' the other said. 'I'm sure you understand why.'

Roseanne nodded. 'I did think of it, and then I thought if you let your life be swayed by everything like that, you soon wouldn't be able to put your nose out doors.'

'There's something to be said for that,' May agreed, though she thought it an astonishing statement for its combination of bluntness and ambiguity. 'I'll just show you the rooms. I think you'll find them very comfortable.'

'Jake sleeps in with me,' she explained. 'We'd only need the one room.'

'Well, there's a nice little parlour where you may sit of an evening and the boy can do his lessons. I hope you're an attentive scholar, boy!' she added severely as she peered down at him. 'You'll be going to the same school where your mother used to be teacher, you know.'

'Yes ma'am.' Jake was savouring the smell of a strange house. Every house he went into had a different one. This one smelled of rushes — the sort of smell you got off rushwork furniture, slightly damp in an outhouse. Trevivian smelled of lavender, which the maids put in the beeswax. Wheal Fortune was just plain damp and earth at the moment, except the barn, which was mouldy straw and oats. He wondered how many houses you'd have to visit before you ran out of different smells, and where were the two nearest houses that had the same smell?

'It's five shillings a week if you only want breakfast or seven and six with dinner. And . . .' she was about to say 'halfprice for the boy' but prudence changed it to '. . . what sort of appetite do you enjoy, eh, boy?'

'Hearty, ma'am,' Jake allowed.

'Well, I'll abate a shilling off either price for him.'

Roseanne said it sounded most reasonable. May explained at once that it was only a token. People had told her she could charge much more. She didn't need the money at all, really, but it was a way to meet people . . . lonely widows often went a bit strange, living on their own . . .

The bedroom was to the front of the annexe, the parlour to the rear. The moment Roseanne saw the large feather bed — Mark's bed these four years past — she began to have doubts. Was it too late now to back out? She just managed to stop herself from commenting that it didn't look like a man's room at all, with all the chintz and frills and the floral wallpaper.

It was too late. Hadn't she said it herself — if you carry on in that fashion, you soon wouldn't be able to go outdoors? 'It's lovely!' she exclaimed. 'I'm sure it'll be a wrench to leave when the time comes.'

Even that comment had overtones.

After she had stabled the horse she went back to their rooms and found Jake in the parlour, staring out at the fields behind the house. Their outlines were just discernible in the gathering gloom. 'Is that . . .?' he asked.

She gripped his shoulders from behind and pulled him against her. 'Yes,' she said. 'I've shown you the place before.'

Well-meaning friends had advised her to keep the lad in complete ignorance of his past, but too many people in that nasty, interfering world out there were aware of the truth to make such secrecy possible.

She knew what Jake was thinking: it was one thing to glance at the place in passing, but quite another to live on top of it, even for only a week or two. But the thought was too cosmic for him to find the words. She wondered if she should tell him that field was also the place where Mark Bodilly had first kissed her, when she was fourteen and he fifteen . . . and all the associations the place had for her? If he said something, she would; but without a prompt from him, she had no cause to lay such information between them.

Actually, she wondered in that easeful silence that so often enveloped them, what associations *did* the place hold for her now, after so many years? She tested herself for emotions of any kind and found very few. It was almost as if it had all happened to some other little girl; or it was like something she'd read about in those childhood tales that linger with you for ever. Was it a sign that she was at last 'getting over' Mark? She was always on the lookout for such hopeful evidence – and always damping down her hope by saying she'd not be free of him until they could converse in a normal, pleasant way, like two civilized beings.

And, she added to herself a moment later, when she

could turn down a bed that had been 'his' for years without thinking twice about it!

They dined early and, in the circumstances, without dressing. Then Jake raced into bed for his one big everyday treat: an hour with a good storybook. His present favourite was *Alice in Wonderland*. Roseanne hauled him out again, made him clean his teeth properly, wash his ears properly, say his prayers properly — and add a new one for the success of Wheal Fortune. Only then did she notice that *Alice* lay unopened on the chair at his bedside. She tilted the spine of his book and read, *Oliver Twist*.

'I got it down from Mrs Delamere's bookshelf,' he told her. 'She said I could.'

'But how many times have you read it already?' she asked. He shrugged, unwilling to admit it must be at least half a dozen. 'I like it,' he remarked.

'Why?'

He shrugged again, impatient for her to go.

'Well,' she said, 'when the wick burns down to there . . .' She drew an imaginary line across the candle.

'Ye-es,' he replied wearily.

There was a hesitant knock at the door. It was May Delamere. 'I was just wondering, Miss Kitto,' she said, 'shall I get one of the maids to light the fire in your parlour? Or I've a nice blaze going downstairs if you'd like a little game of cards?'

They decided on two-handed whist. May thought of remarking that Mr Bodilly had been adept at that particular game, but decided it was a mite too direct an opening for what she suspected was on the young woman's mind. She unfolded the card table and shuffled the pack; Roseanne went on standing by the mantelpiece, leaning against it, staring down into the flames.

'You must be exhausted,' May remarked sympathetically. 'And such a disappointment, too − the rain
pouring in like that. Mr Delamere always said one
should be able to pick a house up in a giant pair of
tweezers and dunk it in a vast tank of water − to test
it before one buys it, you know.'

Roseanne chuckled at the notion and came to join
her. 'Oh, I knew all about it, even before the auction.
One can see tide marks from previous floodings. But
the speed of it was rather surprising. Mind you, it was
a ferocious downpour.'

May, who had hardly exchanged a dozen words with
Roseanne since the Kittos had left Breage, was still taken
aback at the woman's linguistic rise in the world, in
parallel with the increase in her fortune. It made her
wonder what potential queens of society lay buried
inside the other village girls − even her own servants.
Perhaps not queens but . . . ladies in waiting? Not a
thought to send one lightly to sleep!

She became aware that Roseanne had spoken; she
apologized and asked her to repeat it. Roseanne, who
had, in fact, said, '*Your* house is dry as a bone, I'm
glad to see,' before biting her tongue off replied, 'Oh
. . . nothing. I was just dreading the thought of having
to go and ask my father to send some men to deal with
the problem. He'll crow over me for months.'

'Ah!' Mrs Delamere's tone implied that one had to
learn to take the rough with the smooth. As she dealt
their hands she said, 'I was wondering what I'd have
said if any of my daughters − I have four, as I'm sure
you know − if one of them had come to me and said
she wanted to be a farmer. Not marry a farmer, but be
one. It is a very courageous step, I believe.'

Roseanne made a glum face. 'I'm just wondering if
it isn't a most foolhardy one, too. Mrs Scawen once said

422

to me, the trouble with making a new garden is that no matter what season you begin, you always find you ought to have begun the season before it. It's exactly the same with a farm, only ten times greater.'

'Yes.' May spoke offhandedly as she sorted her hand. 'Actually I didn't quite mean it in that way. You cut for trumps.'

'Spades,' Roseanne said. 'What way did you mean it?'

'I meant, you know, being a woman . . . farming on your own.'

May Delamere proved a careless player, far more interested in the conversation than in wringing the greatest number of points out of the chance fall of the cards. She allowed Roseanne to short-suit herself in diamonds and then take all the court cards in that suit with lowish trumps; after that, it seemed to Roseanne a breach of good manners to play with her usual competitive eagerness. Then she, too, concentrated more on their conversation.

'Still,' May said, picking up what was now an earlier thread, 'you're no stranger to the bold, unconventional act.'

Roseanne laughed reluctantly and said it wasn't by choice. 'I mean, I never wake up in the morning and think what can I do today to shock the neighbours. When I took Jake in — it was Christmas, if you recall . . .'

'I do, indeed! A Christmas we'll never forget!'

'I only meant it to be for those few days. Who could take an orphan of that age and drop him at the workhouse door on Christmas Eve? But there was never an actual moment when I said I'll keep him for ever and ever. It just sort of crept up on me.'

'I can't imagine bringing up a boy on my own. I had

to rear four girls, as you may know, which was bad enough — but somehow more natural. But don't you think he's going to need a father?'

'There'll always be men about him,' Roseanne said defensively. 'I'll have three or four on the farm, for a start.'

'Labourers,' May said with disdain. 'If he's to be a gentleman, there are things he can only learn from another gentleman. I mean, *you* could hardly . . . you know what I mean.'

Roseanne thought ruefully of the 'rig' incident that very afternoon — what a mess she'd have made of it, *did* make of it — and how naturally Stephen had passed it off.

'Don't for one moment imagine I'm criticizing you, my dear,' May continued. 'But, as a woman with at least two daughters of about your age — what would that be, may I ask? Twenty-four?'

'Twenty-five,' was the most Roseanne would admit to. She noted the wellbred arch of surprise it produced in the other's eyebrows.

'Well, well! I'm really just curious to know how you're going to face these delicate little problems.'

'I'm not a confirmed spinster, you know,' Roseanne complained. 'I'm not saying Jake will never have a father.'

'Ah!' May beamed. 'I'm delighted to hear it. Speaking as a mother of daughters myself, you understand. And I promise you, I'll pry no more. Dear me! You *are* chalking up the points, aren't you!'

Her words left Roseanne feeling as if it were she who had cut the older woman off in their conversation, almost snubbed her. In fact, and rather to her surprise, she found she had quite enjoyed opening up her thoughts to Mrs Delamere. Jane had become so awkward lately, what with her ridiculous suspicions that Vosper had been paying her too much attention. Her mother was robustly dismissive: 'We reared you well enough not to disgrace us, my bird, and you're old enough to know your own mind.' That was her line. And with Annette you never felt your secrets were safe. Not that she'd blurt them out to all the world, nor even to another living soul; they'd be safe enough in that respect. But you always had the feeling she was storing them up and would one day make use of them for her own purposes — not crudely, like a kind of blackmail, but to help her manipulate your feelings and get her own way.

Really, there was no one else she could talk to now. For a time she'd had hopes of Tamara Dawson, who always spoke so scornfully of the polite conventions, and who would have no interest in emotional manipulations of the Annette Morvah variety, but she'd decided the woman was too scatterbrained. She'd probably take a passionate interest in the business for two weeks and then simply drop it in favour of something else.

After a few more hands, played to the accompaniment of third-party gossip of a kind that any two people might indulge in, Roseanne remarked, quite casually, 'I'm sure everyone thinks I'm trying to *prove* something by taking on Wheal Fortune.'

'And aren't you?' May asked avidly, and in genuine surprise.

'Not a bit. I just realized that I can't go on living with the Scawens for ever . . .'

'Well, of course, I don't know what arrangements there might have been between you and Jane Scawen, but I'm sure you've been an enormous encouragement and support to her.'

'Ye-es,' Roseanne allowed. 'And they were to me, of course. You said about Jake needing a father, well, Vosper was *like* a father to him. He treated him just as severely, and just as lovingly, as he did Trevanion or Courtenay. But that's what I mean, you see. I was living a lie at Trevivian. They made it so easy for me never to have to decide anything about my own life.' She gave a little laugh. 'We used to go down and collect limpets for the shell grottoes, and I often used to think how like me they were. You know the way, when you try and dislodge them, how they absolutely *shrink* against the rock and cling like grim death? I used to think, *I know, little fellow, I know just how it feels!* So I had to make a clean break before Jake and I just got too . . . encrusted.'

'Yes,' May replied, 'I can see all that. But still – buying a whole farm! It's a bit like that man who burned down the entire pigsty just to enjoy one meal of roast pig, don't you think?'

Roseanne shook her head, not really comprehending the comparison. 'I couldn't possibly live at Liston Court. Not that I've fallen out with my parents, you understand. But . . . well, could *you* have lived congenially with a daughter of twenty-six?' The words were out before she could recall them. 'As I will be next birthday,' she added.

'There were other choices,' May hinted delicately.

'Take a cottage on my own? I'd just rattle around all the time and go quietly mad. I even thought of taking up my old place at the school. Or any school. And that's when I remembered why I gave it up the first time round – to work on my father's few acres. And how stupid everyone thought I was at the time!' She chuckled. 'I prefer to believe that all the stupid things we do in life are really a preparation for the one great sensible decision that grows out of them.'

'Ah!' May's eyes twinkled. 'So you believe that buying Wheal Fortune was the one great sensible decision of your life.'

Roseanne gave a deep sigh of satisfaction and said, 'Yes!'

'Then it is. That's all that need be said about it.' May wondered if the woman had even noticed that the single most obvious choice — obvious to any other female in the kingdom — had simply not occurred to her and that, in turn, caused her to wonder how, faced with so vast a difference in outlook between them, she might make her aware of it.

Roseanne went upstairs at that point, to see if Jake had obeyed her instructions. The wick had burned to its appointed level but the lad was already fast asleep. She took the book from his limp fingers and laid it on his bedside chair. Then she pulled the eiderdown over his shoulders, straightened an unruly lock of hair, and gazed in adoration at his impish face.

'You don't need a father yet,' she told him silently. 'But when you do . . . when you do . . . I promise!'

May Delamere must have harked back to that conversation, in her mind, while waiting for Roseanne to return, for her opening words were, 'Apropos fathers and so forth — what about the boy's *real* father? The brute who murdered his mother? The police never caught him, I suppose?'

Roseanne shook her head. 'Not to my knowledge. I sometimes have nightmares about that face.'

'Oh, so you did see his face? I thought at the time . . .'

'I don't know whether I did or I didn't. Perhaps I just invented it, because a faceless murderer is even worse, somehow. If I did see him, it was only for a second or so — and it was a full week before the murder, so I didn't even attach much importance to it. I just found Jake wandering in the road and took him back into the field to find his mother. I was more shocked to see *her*, in fact, Mary Williams. She was at school here in the village with me. How does a happy, homely little girl like that turn into . . . something that makes the flesh crawl?'

'All too easily,' May commented.

'*And* produce a little dazzler like Jake! It's beyond me.'

'You've done that, my dear. But for you he'd either be dead or in the reformatory by now.'

'No.' Roseanne shook her head. 'He was bright as a new penny from the day I took him in.'

May caught the fanatic gleam in the woman's eye and let the matter drop; as far as she was concerned, the boy was a boy — muddy boots, sly habits, warts and all.

She poured two glasses of port and set Roseanne's before her with the words, 'A sovereign remedy against fatigue, my dear. Sometimes one can be too exhausted even to sleep, I find.'

Roseanne, who had never needed any excuse to take a glass of anything — other than that she enjoyed it — accepted gratefully. She took a sip and then said, 'I hope you don't mind me saying this, but you're quite different from what I imagined, Mrs Delamere.'

'Indeed?' the other asked in surprise.

'Yes. I thought I'd find you very prim, very correct, rather conventional. I never suspected . . .' She gave a disarming smile and left the rest unspoken though not precisely unsaid.

The older woman's mind began to race. This, she suspected, was going to be a moment that would dictate much of what passed in the weeks ahead between her and this astonishing young woman, who could come out with 'sledgehammers' like that as if they were part of normal social intercourse. How should she respond? Alternatives flickered through her mind:

'Prim? Come come, my dear! We both have every reason to know I am not *that*!' Too crude. Too direct.

'Correct, eh?' Give a knowing laugh — not vulgar, you understand, but a light, insouciant tinkle. 'Well!' Better. But still too close to the point and too soon. Nothing of that tonight.

Then she saw the right response to give.

'Conventional, eh?' she echoed. 'You mean serve the meals, take the fee, and not poke my nose into your affairs. Well, I can do that, if it's what you really want.'

Roseanne toasted her with her glass and took another sip. 'You couldn't,' she said with a grin.

52

Frank Kitto's first visit to Wheal Fortune since Roseanne bought it came at her request. She wanted him to advise her on providing proper drainage to the yard. At first he was rather jovial about it, remembering his own good opinion of the place from his previous visit. He stared at the palimpsest of tide marks on the wall and laughed as men are wont to laugh at the gullibility of women. But when he saw the state of the house indoors, the smile faded somewhat; and the more he looked about him, the longer his face grew.

'I should have come afore now,' he murmured. 'I said you'd make a caunch of this on your own, but your mother said to leave you make whatever you wanted.' He shook his head in consternation.

The fact that he was more perturbed than angry, the fact that he was not taking this golden opportunity to crow over her, worried her more than anything. 'Listen,' she said, 'this place will be a success. You may set your mind to rest on that. I admit it's going to take a bit longer than I expected – and it'll be a lot harder than I thought. We can't all make our fortune in just three or four years. The only reason I asked you up here today was to see if you'd lend me a gang to put in one little drain. That's all.' Almost inaudibly she added, 'And one or two other little things.'

At least it made him laugh. He told her he'd never

heard small print spoken so beautifully before. 'What sort of drain do 'ee want then?' he asked.

'Ah!' She was well prepared for that, at least, and she went on to show him how she wanted a very wide trench dug out of the yard, against the wall of the dairy and to a depth below the floor level inside. Most of it would then be filled with a slate-walled tank built hard against the dairywall. That would take the rainwater off the roof. The rest of the trench, now reduced to a narrow width, would be bottomed out with land drains and covered over with large stones. The drains would lead through the byre and stables, then to an open trench through the front garden. . . .

All the while she spoke she saw her father looking for flaws in her idea. When he found none he stared at her suspiciously. 'Who you been talking to?' he asked.

'No one,' she replied. '*You* — for the past twenty years.'

He swelled with pride and tried not to. Fingering his gold collar stud, he told her it might work and they'd have to see. 'And what about all that small print?' he went on. 'That "one or two other little things"?'

She described the two sties up against the barn, and the glasshouse that would close off the yard — omitting to say where the idea came from. And then they walked the rest of the farm. She pointed out the half dozen or so abandoned mine shafts, each of which she wanted ringed by a dry-stone wall, 'With the top layer mortared,' she added, 'because the first thing Jake and his friends will do is throw stones down the shaft to hear them thunder and splash.' Then there were new gates . . . all the hedges needed cutting back and repairing with fresh stone . . . she wanted to get the old water wheel going again to pump water up to the farm . . .

'Make a nice little water-garden?' he suggested.

She told him she'd leave that sort of thing to the Scawens for the present. 'It'll be a year or two before we have a garden of any kind here,' she said. 'If we can't eat it, feed it, or burn it, we shan't grow it.'

It took the best part of the morning to complete the tour. As he left the place he wondered how he could possibly feel more hopeful than dispirited. And yet he did. If he had simply walked around the fields without Roseanne at his side, he would have come away convinced that Wheal Fortune was a mockery of a farm down to its very name; he would have set her chances of making a go of the place at nil − and he would have taken a horsewhip to Mark Bodilly for allowing her to buy it at all. Yet somehow, when you heard her talking about it − describing what she was going to do this season . . . what she was going to leave for next − she made you feel not only that it was all quite possible but that she was the one to do it.

What gave him most confidence of all was that she did not just airily say, 'We'll clear out all that hedge and patch the gaps.' Instead, she'd tell you, 'There's two days' work for a couple of good men there and a week to follow for a mason and boy.' And she'd tell you where the nearest stone was, too. One thing was certain: The men he sent to do the work were not going to know a single idle moment. He even began to select one or two could do with a lesson in the meaning of labour.

'She's our daughter,' he told Mary when he got back home.

53

Both May Delamere and Roseanne knew they forgathered of an evening to talk, and yet the ritual of the cards was still, for some reason, necessary. The dithering between this card and that, the gathering of tricks, the small exclamations of joy or chagrin — all of these allowed pauses for thought that would otherwise have been awkward; and they gave scope for those subtler hesitations that allow a conversation to be diverted without seeming effort.

'I keep thinking,' Roseanne commented one evening, 'that as soon as I've got this or that item finished, then I can really say I've begun. I used to think that, once the yard was properly drained and we could dry out the house . . . well, that would be a milestone. But it's no more than a two-minute wonder. We brought a great kieve of water up from the river and floshed it over the yard — and two minutes later there's a pretty little stream running down through the front garden — and not a drop in the house. And that's it! Triumph over!'

'But a satisfaction, surely?' May pointed out.

'A *moment* of satisfaction. Then you start to notice that the doors are all warped. They scrape the floor. The floor needs new linoleum. *Everything* needs new paint. The banisters wobble. There are several rotten floorboards upstairs.'

'Well, you know you're welcome to stay here as long

as you wish, my dear.' May interrupted their hand to unlock the tantalus and take out the port — a little ritual that was getting earlier and earlier each evening, Roseanne noticed. Not that she grumbled; one needed a nice, silky drink like that to relax one after the rigours of the day.

'You're more than kind,' she replied. 'I know we're trespassing on your goodness, though you never make us feel . . .'

'Trespassing! Good heavens, girl, these are some of the most exciting times I ever remember.' She set a good half tumbler down before Roseanne. 'I confess I thought you were more than half insane when you first described this project, but now I can't wait to hear all about it each evening. You've really turned the village upside down, I suppose you realize? Everyone was predicting disaster — Mrs Haynes, Miss Martin, Mrs Deakin . . . they all swore you'd come a cropper.'

Roseanne glowed at the news, which *was* news to her. 'And what are they saying now?' she asked.

'Oh, they shrug their shoulders and say, "Well, she's a Kitto." That seems to explain everything.' After a pause she added — as if the thought had only just struck her — 'Actually, I believe their greatest disappointment is that you didn't throw in the sponge and get married. I remember Mrs Willoughby saying to me, the day after you came to Vinery House, she said, "I give that gel three weeks," she said. And I said to her, "Three weeks for what, Mrs Willoughby?" and she said, "Three weeks to throw in the sponge, Mrs Delamere. Then she'll have to choose . . . a husband!" That's what she said to me.'

May had intended to say, 'choose between Morvah and Bodilly,' but her nerve failed at the last. She looked to see whether Roseanne took up the hint nonetheless.

434

Roseanne supped a good mouthful of port and savoured it awhile. This was the moment she had seen coming for several evenings past. May had got so close to it on several occasions — laying down these casual invitations so gently they could be taken up or dropped without offence. There seemed no point in letting them lie any longer. 'It's a shocking thing to say,' she confessed, 'but I'm beginning to wonder whether I'm the marrying kind. Or whether I need to marry at all. What do you think?'

'I think the rest of this hand is mine.' May laid down an unbeatable run of trumps. 'Not often I can do that,' she said as she marked up the score. She left the cards disordered between them and went on, 'I know what I *ought* to think my dear, and I know what I ought to tell you: such thoughts are folly. Marriage is a woman's purpose in life — apart from a few golden exceptions like Miss Nightingale and Jane Austen. But they are the exceptions that prove the rule. Incidentally, I never understood that saying, did you? How can an exception *prove* a rule — except by failing? And one certainly can't say those two women failed! Sorry, am I rambling again?'

Roseanne laughed and said, 'Not yet. I'll tell you when you start. And I'll tell you another woman I'd put in the same class — Mrs Moore of Lanfear. I hardly know the woman. I mean I know her by sight. But I remember one day when I was a little girl, about nine or ten, and a party of us went down Praa for a swim, and when we came back it was evening, and you remember how she used to drive home from Penzance in that gig with a thoroughbred between the shafts and a great sign down the side of it saying "Rosewarne's Ales" . . .'

May chuckled. 'Yes, and she'd blow that old bugle to let everyone at Lanfear know she was near — and the whole of Germoe parish besides!'

'Well, on that particular evening we heard her coming up behind us, and we turned round, and there she was – standing up on the driving board like Boadicea, I thought, because we'd just done Boadicea in school. She had the setting sun behind her and her hair was all flying free and all on fire. And she had that look in her eye and that smile on her face which said *that's* the way to enjoy life! And us girls just looked at each other after she'd gone by, and none of us said a word, but we all just knew. They say all little boys want to be engine drivers when they grow up. Well, we knew what we wanted to be! I've never forgotten that.'

'Plainly!' May herself was overawed at the power of the other's memory.

Roseanne laughed as she recalled something else. 'I told Jane Scawen that tale once and she gave me ever such a funny look. She asked if I'd been talking to Vosper about it and had he put me up to telling her. Of course, I had no idea what she was talking about but it turned out that on the very day she and her father arrived in Cornwall, which must have been about a year after the incident I described, almost exactly the same thing happened to her, except that she was about twenty. But she had the same feeling. That was the life to aim at. Be free!'

'But both of them married,' May pointed out delicately.

Roseanne nodded at this unhappy flaw in her apparent chain of reasoning. 'But they married the men of their choice, not the men the world had marked down for them. In fact, wasn't Jane supposed to marry your son-in-law, Richard Vyvyan?'

May ignored this attempt to deflect her. 'And who do you feel the world has marked down for you?' she asked.

Roseanne took a mere sip of port; it was beginning to relax her rather too much, she felt. She drew a deep breath and then said, 'Well . . . obviously Mark Bodilly, for one.'

'And?'

'Stephen Morvah. I don't know whether the *world* has him marked down for me, but *he* certainly has.'

'Has he actually proposed to you' May asked cautiously, knowing that this was the point where the conversation would either end abruptly or . . . take a most interesting turn.

'Years ago,' Roseanne told her.

'But not recently?'

Roseanne's smile was slightly naughty. 'He's smart enough to realize that saying no can become a habit too deeply ingrained to break.'

May laughed, slightly against her will. 'Oh, Miss Kitto! I don't know! You really are the most surprising mixture of . . .'

'Of what?'

She shrugged. 'Wisdom so profound it quite shakes one, and . . . I don't know. A lovely sort of innocence. I can see your difficulty so clearly.'

Roseanne pulled a face. 'Which is more than I can, Mrs Delamere.'

'I quite believe you there! Your difficulty is that — for at least two men in this county — you are far and away the most fascinating, delightful, and utterly mysterious woman they know. They can't . . . it's like a magic spell you've cast. They can't break it.' She laughed with a savagery that was far from humorous. 'I can just imagine how that must *gall* the great Mark Bodilly — who lives in constant surprise that women are nowhere listed in *The Probate and Valuer's Handbook of Prices*.'

The sudden intensity of her spleen and the venom of her outburst rocked Roseanne for a moment; but that part of her mind which remained forever cool and observant told her that never would such a moment occur again between them. 'I know!' she said sympathetically. 'The number of times I've been within an ace of killing that man! Only last week — after he said he'd never come near me or talk to me again — and he meant it — and I said good riddance to bad rubbish — and I meant it, too — he found some cause to drop by Wheal Fortune. . . . something to do with the mineral rights. And we went out on the old mine workings and . . . well, it's a long, dull tale — not a word of which would surprise *you*, I'm sure — but the long and the short of it was we happened to be standing within a few feet of one of the old mineshafts and I caught myself thinking, *If I gave him a little push, who'd ever know?* There now! I was *that* close to doing it, too.'

May simply stared at her, open-jawed.

'We always end up shouting at each other, screaming at the tops of our voices. And yet' — her voice softened — 'I think about him a lot. Not all the time but quite a lot. He imagines he's such a man and really he's just like a little child.'

May felt a tingling behind her eyelids and took a grip of herself. 'I know,' she murmured.

'I feel I must protect him — not that I really want to but that I must. I feel he needs me but he just won't admit it. Anyway, I can't ever bring myself to finally say that's it! Goodbye! Over and done with!' She laughed dourly. 'That's not true. The truth is, I say it every week, but it doesn't help. And really I think I love Stephen Morvah much more. In fact, I don't believe I love Mark at all. It's just that our lives are so . . .

we've always been so . . . you know what I mean.'

May fought with the tear that was insisting on forming behind her eyelid. 'I know,' she repeated.

'And while all that's going on . . .' She tapped her breastbone. 'How can I honourably do anything to encourage poor Stephen? Not that he *needs* encouragement, mind. But I know that if I gave in and married Stephen, Mark would go off in a grand fit of pique and marry someone else, completely unsuitable – the more unsuitable the better – just to teach me.' She gave another grim laugh. 'And I'd hate her for ever and ever.'

May nodded and the unbidden tear rolled down her cheek at last. It had not been the conversation she had bargained for.

54

One of the gilts was in pig when Roseanne bought them, though she had not known it at the time — and nor, she suspected, had the farmer who let them go. For a while she had thought that one was barren but then her increasing girth was enough to explain why she and Samson, as Jake had named the boar, took only the politest interest in each another. Then one Sunday morning in early May Jake came running home from Carnmeal in great excitement, with Tess, the new farm dog yapping at his heels; he said that the fat gilt was lying down and making funny noises and he was sure she was going to farrow.

Roseanne told him it was very unlikely to be so quick, but she put up her coat and went out to see for herself. They kept only one milch cow at that time, just for the house. It was Jake's job to milk her and put her out before he had his breakfast and went off to school; but on Sundays he could linger in the fields, look at his snares, inspect his cottages, and do all the other things that helped compensate for the loss of his erstwhile family at Trevivian. And that was how he had noticed the gilt.

There was no need to point out her location to his mother. The morning was still early and a heavy overnight dew made everything chill and humid; the steam that rose from where the creature lay was visible even from the gate.

'It's a blessing we've got Sampson in his pen at last,' she said as they crossed the field. 'They get very protective and aggressive at a time like this.'

'Even though the piglets aren't his,' Jake commented.

She let that pass. She had been ten before one of the other girls had told her the secret about boars and bulls and sows and cows; by then she'd even seen a bull serving a cow — and still she found the story difficult to accept. And not until she was fourteen had she been able to believe it of humans, too. She wondered what Jake had been hearing on the fringes of those sniggering groups up there in the school playground.

'The dog had better stay out of this,' she said and, turning to Tess, ordered, 'down!'

The creature looked as if it had committed every crime in the calendar and slunk to the earth, watching her intently and waiting for the words that would bring release.

Gingerly, mother and son approached the edge of the little clearing among the furze from which all the steam was arising. 'Well!' Roseanne exclaimed in surprise.

'She is! I told you! She is!' he cried excitedly until she told him to keep his voice down.

Actually, of all voices his was the least likely to disturb the pigs. He had spent hours up in the field 'herding the swine', as he called it. He said they were far more human than cows or horses or any of the other animals on the farm — the way they quarrelled and squealed and played nasty tricks on each other. He said they were the only animals apart from a dog that could smile.

The gilt was lying on her side, grunting with the regularity of a clock. Three of her litter were already born and the fourth was halfway out; two were sucking away as if they had been starved all week; the third was fighting with its halfborn sibling, who was giving as good as he got despite the fact that his back legs were still in the birth canal. 'Amazing,' Roseanne murmured.

They watched for half an hour or so while a further three were born, making seven in all. Tess was allowed into the circle by then; she lay with her head between her paws and made little encouraging whimpers.

'One widden,' Roseanne commented. 'It doesn't look as if he'll live.'

The runt was being chased off every teat he tried; he never got more than one or two sucks before one of his brothers or sisters decided his teat was better than theirs and chased him off it.

'It's not fair,' Jake complained. 'She's got eight teats, which is plenty to go round, and they just don't let him have one for himself. Why pick on him?'

'As you said,' she reminded him, 'they are almost human. Want to hand-rear him yourself, do you? That's his only chance.'

His eyes gleamed. 'And he can be mine? And he won't have to go to the butcher's?'

'We'll rig him and he can be Sampson's running mate. We'll send the fellow that's with him now off as a porker.'

The sow squealed as one of her sharp-toothed litter sucked too avidly.

'Come on,' Roseanne said. 'I think that's the lot. We'll take them back to the farm with us.' And she sent him to fetch an empty sack she had stuck in the hedge against just such an eventuality.

When the piglets were doing more fighting than sucking, Roseanne pulled them off their mother and passed them behind her to Jake, who popped them in the sack. Such a squealing and complaining they never heard! Jake put the widden inside the front of his shirt,

442

where it settled contentedly and sought for a nipple. 'I got no milk for 'ee!' he told it, then sniggered and looked guiltily at his mother, who just shook her head wearily and glanced at the sky.

The gilt complained a little but they talked to her all the way to the gate, by which time she seemed to realize that whatever was in progress, it involved no theft.

Another gilt, a sister to the anxious new mother, stood at the gate and did not budge as they approached. 'Come us on, old girl!' Jake cried in perfect imitation of Henry Kitchen, one of the Wheal Fortune labourers.

Still the gilt did not move. Roseanne was alert at once. 'Put your hand on her back,' she said.

Curious, he obeyed. The gilt grunted a couple of times and lowered her head.

'Oh dear,' Roseanne sighed.

'Is she ill?' he asked.

She chuckled. 'If it's an ailment, it's easy cured. I think she wants to spend a little time with Mister Sampson. She must have slipped last time. We'd better bring her along with us.'

He said very little all the way in to the yard — mostly about what a wonderful foster mother he was going to be to Mr Gladstone, as he immediately christened his widden. She wondered which of her labourers voted Tory — or would do so, if Gladstone had his way. She also wondered what Jake was really thinking; she knew her remarks about the gilt and Sampson had not, like almost everything else she said, simply gone in one ear and out of the other.

The wind was southerly, straight up the valley, so Sampson got a whiff of his latest mistress the moment they entered the yard gate; by the time they reached the sties, his jaws were white with lather and he was trembling. The sow, by contrast, simply stood her ground outside the pen and cocked an ear; occasionally she grunted in response to her mate-to-be.

Roseanne settled the piglets in fresh straw and ensured that their mother had room to stand and move without trampling them before she turned her attention to the by now demented creature next door.

'Go back, go back, go back!' she cried, hitting him with impassive strength, completely devoid of malice. Angrily he chased his present running mate indoors. Roseanne quickly opened the gate of the pen and pushed the gilt inside. 'Don't sit on the wall like that,' she told Jake. 'Never let your hands or feet hang inside a boar's pen. I know you think he's a friendly young thing, but they can turn on you in half no time.'

He heard her with only half an ear. The behaviour of the two animals was utterly absorbing. Sampson came bounding out again, heedless of the possibility that he might face yet another rain of blows from Roseanne's stick. He put his snout under the gilt's chin and chucked her a couple of times.

She grunted.

He got his snout under the pit of her foreleg and chucked her again.

She grunted.

His jaw shivered. He chomped and grunted back at her. Flecks of foam fell among the straw. He got his snout just in front of her hind knee and gave an enormous chuck that turned her a quarter circle, side on to the two spectators.

She grunted.

'Cor!' Jake exclaimed.

Sampson went back to her head and chucked her a few more times with his snout; when all she did was grunt and hold her ground, he trotted to her derriere and mounted her without further subtleties of courtship.

Even before his forelegs had found a steady purchase on her haunches that extraordinary corkscrew organ beneath his belly was making spiral stabs indiscriminately at anything between her tails and heels.

'What's *that*?' Jake asked in amazement.

'What d'you think it is,' she replied flatly.

He stared at it, mouth agape.

Sampson found his mark then and settled to the business, which lasted all of ten seconds. Apart from the occasional shifting of their back hooves, there was no movement of any kind; he did not thrust like a dog on a bitch. He might have been any fat old farmer enjoying a contemplative lean on a gate. Just when he finished there was a barely perceptible tightening of his hind quarters and a kind of shivery sigh in his throat.

As he pulled away there was a small after-spurt into the straw beneath her belly. He snaffled it up in passing and then went to chuck her about the head a time or two more.

'What was all that for?' Jake asked. She drew a deep breath and tried to think what Stephen would say. 'That's how boars and sows make piglets,' she said. 'He's just given her . . . the quickening, to make the piglets start growing inside her, see?'

He wrinkled his nose and said with hesitant disgust, 'Not . . . weewee?'

So he had made that much of a connection. 'No,' she replied, amazed at how easy it was once you bit the bullet. 'It's a liquid that comes from those lumps under his bottom. You remember Uncle Stephen said you couldn't breed from a boar unless it had those? Now you know why.'

'Was that what he ate up, from the straw?'

Now she wrinkled her nose. 'Yes.'

Sampson, seeing that the gilt stood her ground still,

even when he chucked her quite fiercely, mounted her once more.

'He's not going to waste it, see?' Jake said earnestly. 'That bit he licked up. He's going to put that inside her, too.'

She laughed so much she had to go and lean against the barn wall for support. He stared at her, uncertain whether to be wounded or proud. 'Oh Jake!' she exclaimed when she could speak again. 'I don't know what you'll be when you grow up, but one thing you'll certainly qualify for, and that's a farmer!'

55

By June the farmhouse was as dry as any place in Cornwall ever would be; certainly it would take an Old Testament deluge to flood the kitchen after those new drains had been put in. Now it was as if the walls and floors began to breathe again — and in doing so they started to shed the damage of the years, often in the form of substantial chunks of plaster. Her father's men wanted to hack it all off and start again, but Roseanne was farmer enough not to spend a penny on the house if it could go toward a pig or a plough; so they simply patched it and covered it with fresh distemper. ''Tisn't but a cottage, anyway,' she said contemptuously.

They also drove new pine wedges beneath the stair treads so that each ascent no longer brought forth the shrieks of the damned. Even the one-holer, which was in the lower front garden, discreetly hidden behind an elder bush, had a lick of fresh paint and a new latch; you were no longer forced to sit with one foot hard against the door and sing at the top of your voice. In short, all Roseanne's superficial reasons for remaining at Vinery House had evaporated, most of them quite literally.

She moved into Wheal Fortune without ceremony on the first of that month, a Thursday. In the morning Jake walked his mere halfmile to school knowing that from then on he would have to trudge more than three times the distance, morning and evening — and down and up two of the steepest hills in West Penwith into the bargain.

By then the farm had a dozen cows in milk, two of them with calves, which Roseanne was now starting to wean. And there were four beside who would calve down over the next two months, to give a good yield through the winter, when prices were higher. On the flush of summer grass the milkers filled three churns a day, which one of the men carried into the St John's Dairy in Helston. It was a handy arrangement because he could also pick up whatever the farm needed in the way of seed, parts, or hardware, and all without making a special journey.

As to the other livestock, there were the pigs, of course, and a couple of dozen geese being fattened for Christmas. And there were six dozen pullets in lay, yielding around thirty dozen eggs a week. That was the Sunday-night chore — cleaning and buttering the eggs, ready to be carried into market on the Monday. The milk earned some eight guineas a week; the eggs added another five shillings or so. The wages of the three labourers, Henry Kitchen, Willie Turner, and George Blight, came to thirty-six shillings. Roseanne's new housekeeper, Lorna Verrigoe, who lived-in, and slept in the front bedroom over the cold parlour, got fifteen pounds a year and the right to all the lard, which was worth another ten or so. And the total housekeeping budget was around twenty-four shillings a week. So in the summer months there was a weekly cash surplus amounting to over four pounds. To be sure, it would turn into a deficit of around six pounds when the bulk of the herd went dry and the pullets moulted. But that was the inevitable way of things in farming. And in any case, there was other income, apart from milk and eggs.

The ten yearling calves she'd be selling each year would bring in over a hundred; and there would be between forty and fifty fat pigs at around seven pounds apiece. Barring accidents, disease, and acts of God, she should do very well out of the place. She decided to sow no cash crops for at least the first year, concentrating instead on getting the land in good heart after its long neglect.

The sows had made a splendid job of rooting up the large, stony field. Roseanne moved them to the other fields at Carnmeal and set about reclaiming that first pasture. The larger infestations of furze, which the animals hadn't gobbled up, were soon pulled out with a horse and chains. They dragged them all to the centre of the field, where they piled them into a huge bonfire for Midsummer Day, which that year fell on a Wednesday. There was a local tradition of lighting a beacon on Trigonning Hill on that day. Some said it went back to the time of the Armada, when the men of Breage had been the first to sight the Spaniards and to touch off the chain of warning beacons that had sent Sir Francis Drake scurrying for his set of bowls. 'And this year we'll have an extra beacon to outshine them all,' Roseanne promised Jake.

When Annette heard of it she said they couldn't possibly waste such a splendid bonfire; they must hold an alfresco ball and roast an ox or something. When she put the idea to the Dawsons, Tamara said, 'of course,' and immediately ordered an ox from her butcher. Jake caught the general infection and invited his entire class to come along for the fun. And so Roseanne, who wanted nothing better than to be left in peace to pick stones and plough, found herself up to her neck in arrangements for the jollification of the entire parish — and, when her mother got word of it, of a goodly portion of Helston, besides.

Luckily the weather was all in her favour. In fact, the eve of the great day was so balmy that Roseanne and Jake carried their feather bed and sheets down to the orchard, spread them out on some oilcloth, and slept beneath the stars. Jake woke at two to find himself staring directly into the eyes of an inquisitive fox, not three feet away; at that magical hour it seemed so natural a sight that all he did was turn over, snuggle into his mother's big, warm body, and go straight back to sleep. The dawn chorus woke them at five. It was the only chill hour of the day and they went gratefully in to stoke up the fire and make some tea before starting the milking.

'Do I *have* to go to school today?' Jake grizzled. 'Someone ought to stay here and guard the fire in case those rough boys from Carleen come and try to light it.'

It amused Roseanne to reflect that, had Mary Williams lived, Jake himself would probably be one of those same 'rough boys' who now aroused his scorn. 'Of course you can stop home if you mind,' she told him − greatly to his surprise. 'What are you doing at school today?' He pulled a face. 'English kings. Dividing with a carry. And something about pro-something.'

'Pronouns?'

'Yes.'

'Well, if you think you can do without all that learning, you stay home and chase away the rough boys of Carleen. It'll be good practice for chasing the crows off the corn − which is all you'll be fit for when you grow up if you neglect your schooling now. But *you* decide.'

He knew all along that her apparent liberality had been too good to be true. 'Just one day wouldn't hurt,' he wheedled.

'Tell you what,' she said. 'I'll drive a bargain with you. You tell me all the pronouns and I'll let you off school for the day.'

He stared around the kitchen. 'Table?' he suggested. 'Chair? They're nouns, anyway.'

'I'll give you one more,' she said sweetly. 'School!'

Later, the milking done and a good breakfast swelling his ribs, he set off disconsolately down the lane. She stood at the gate, automatically counting the chickens with one eye and watching him with the other. He was so forlorn that she almost relented. After all, how many days had she missed school at his age, when some crisis on their smallholding demanded it? And what harm had it really done? When had she ever needed to rattle off the kings and queens of England? She was on the point of calling him back when she saw his whole demeanour change between one step and the next; suddenly he was skipping down the lane. Plainly he had just remembered an exciting reason for going to school after all. How impossible it was, she thought, ever to know other people and what was truly going on in their minds.

She carried the milk to Helston that morning because she wanted to get two or three barrels of ale from the Blue Anchor — an errand that would only put temptation in Henry Kitchen's way; also her mother said she had a nice blue dress she didn't want any more and it would suit her daughter perfectly.

She called at Liston Court, intending only to try on the dress and, if it suited, hasten back home. But when she found her father there, too, and staying for luncheon as well, it was a rare enough event to make her stay and join them. He was in good spirits, having just won the contract to remetal the road between Redruth and Bissoe.

'Bissoe!' she exclaimed. 'How are they laying new

451

roads to Bissoe? It's no bigger than Wheal Fortune —
and no one's laying new roads up my way.'

''Tis the mining, see,' he replied. 'There's mines all
the way down that Devoran valley, from Carharrack
right down Perranarworthal, and they've destroyed the
roads. They're all to be remetalled so we shall have a
busy year, I'm hoping.'

'That's seventeen contracts we're now working on,'
her mother chimed in.

'From repairs at Mousehole harbour to new arches
up Truro Infirmary,' he went on. 'We got seven traction
engines now, and that's three more than the Board of
Works . . .'

The statistics of success poured from him in an
unending stream. Yet he was not smug about it. He
produced each new one with an air of slight surprise,
as if his joy were tinged with bewilderment, too.
Roseanne could not tell whether they were boasting or
delivering a report to their principal shareholder.

'That reminds me,' she said. 'Jake wants a ride on
a steam engine. He saw one of ours going past the school
up Breage last week.'

'Repairs to the Porthleven — Rinsey road,' he confirmed. 'We bid too low for that because Hubert Moyle
got new teeth and I misheard what he whispered to me.'

'Anyway, Jake would like a ride on one.'

'Tell 'ee what, maid,' her father said. 'After tonight,
when you've got that field all burned off, I'll put a steam
plough up there and Jake can stoke and help turn the
shares at the headland. Birthday present for the little
cooze.'

'But it's not his birthday,' she objected.

He grinned. 'How do you know?'

The uncertainty over his age and date of birth stirred
ancient memories in her. 'Bissoe!' she said again.

'That's where I told Sergeant Evans that Mary Williams's aunty or mother lived. I don't know how the name came to me. I was never there in my life.' She gave an involuntary shudder.

'Someone walk on your grave?' her mother asked.

'No, I just remembered that man who was with Mary that time. I don't suppose he was Jake's father. Not to go by his looks, anyway.' Then she laughed and told them how the boy had tried to get off school that morning.

She returned to Wheal Fortune rather later than she had intended, oppressed with a dread of all that remained to be done still. But when she arrived at the field, she found it bustling with workers, paid and voluntary. Tamara Dawson had assumed entire responsibility for the ox roast; she was there already, supervising her own four labourers, who were digging the fire pit. Annette had similarly taken on the rest of the victualling. She arrived just after Roseanne, bringing four trestle tables from Skyburriowe, complete with fading and mildewed tablecloths. 'Seeing as it'll be almost dark . . .' she began to explain.

But Roseanne cut her short, saying she wouldn't have bothered with cloths at all. 'There'll be enough beer, anyway,' she added. 'I didn't know you were bringing some, too.'

'Rosewarne's best.' Annette pulled a face at the sight of all eight barrels — her five and Roseanne's three — side by side. 'Still, it's only once a year — and it's a long walk home for most of them.'

Stephen turned up then with the dishes and cutlery, some of it from Skyburriowe, the rest from the church hall. 'I had to tell them we're insured for breakages,' he said, 'but I kept my fingers crossed while I was speaking.'

'That's what we'll all have to do,' Roseanne told him.

Tamara came over and begged for some beer for her gallant pit-diggers; but she seemed in no hurry to get back to them with it, preferring to stay and flirt with Stephen, who played up to her with a hapless zeal that shocked the other two women.

Jake returned from school at four. He ran across the field to his mother shouting, 'I-you-he-she-it-we-you-they. So there!'

'What's that?' she asked solemnly. 'The kings and queens of England?'

He drew back a fist as if he'd hit her, laughing and snorting with alternate breaths. She caught him by the wrists and they pretended to wrestle.

Standing a little way off, Annette murmured to her brother, 'Did you ever see the like of those two?'

He stared at her, mildly surprised. 'They always go on like that.'

'I know. That's what I mean.'

Tamara, who had overheard her, turned and nodded to show that she knew what Annette was talking about.

Roseanne pushed Jake's hands down at last. 'Time for milking,' she said in her businesslike voice.

'I'll do it today,' Stephen volunteered. 'Where are they? Still in the field beyond Jake's Row?' That was the name they had given the derelict cabins between the Blueborough fields and the blind adit. He was ready for an argument with her but, perhaps because she saw it in his eye, she merely smiled and thanked him. 'Jake'll tend you,' she said.

'No, I will,' Annette volunteered. Then, turning a little pale, 'You don't have to throw them turnips or anything at this time of year, do you?'

'Just linseed cake.' Roseanne grinned devilishly;

then, relenting, she added, 'Jake'll come in and do it, don't worry.'

'I'll help Stephen drive them in at least.'

'It's easy, Aunt Netty,' Jake told her. 'If they give more than half the pail or if they're big in calf, they get the big scoop full. Otherwise the small scoop. And the one with the white face doesn't get any.'

'Poor thing — why not?' Annette grasped her brother's arm and started propelling him toward the gate.

'Because she's only just gone dry.' Jake was amazed at her ignorance.

'You don't mind, do you?' Annette asked Roseanne as she passed. 'Two free workers!'

'Free!' Roseanne grinned sarcastically. 'It'll be a two-hour wonder.'

'Now this,' Tamara exclaimed, 'is something I just have to see!' She skipped until she caught up with them and then she took Stephen's other arm. 'If Edward comes,' she called back to Roseanne, 'tell him I'm being Marie Antoinette.'

Jake gazed up into his mother's eyes, saw the enigmatic smile on her face, and asked, 'What?'

'What, indeed!' she echoed. 'What do they imagine they look like! Did you ever see three such farm hands? The two on the outside, anyway. I think you'd better slip in to the yard in about half an hour, just to be sure all's well, eh?'

'Stephen can milk all right,' he assured her.

'That's a thing I meant to ask,' she said. 'Why have you taken to calling him just Stephen lately?'

'Because he said he didn't want me to call him uncle any more.' He pulled a face. 'Old Ma Wilkins, she doesn't like it.' She was his teacher at Breage school.

455

'She doesn't like you calling Uncle Stephen, Stephen? How does she know?'

He pulled the same face in an even more exaggerated form. 'Because when we did possessive pronouns today, Harry Everett said, "My father's a postman." And I couldn't say that, so I said, "My Stephen Morvah's an author,' instead. And she told me to say, "Mr Stephen Morvah's an author." And I said there's no possessive pronoun in that. And she said to stand in the corner.'

He wished he hadn't started to tell this story; his mother almost always took Old Ma Wilkins's side. But now all she did was look into his eyes, tousle his hair, and murmur, 'Out of the mouths of babes and sucklings, eh?'

56

'Isn't this fun!' Tamara cried. 'One understands exactly why Marie Antoinette was so excited by all that dairymaid business. I mean, just look at them! Aren't they *darlings*! So placid and uncomplaining.' She raised her stick and brought it down on the nearest rump with a resounding thwack. The young heifer, being lowest in the pecking order and therefore unable to move forward, left the lane and ran off into the croft. 'It'll come on behind us, I expect,' she said, unabashed. 'They don't like to be parted from the herd.'

'Yes, they are almost human.' Stephen spoke as if supporting her argument.

She bridled. 'I'm sure *I* don't wish to be part of *any* herd, thank you very much.'

He turned and looked her up and down, taking in every fashionable frill and furbelow. All he said was, 'Oh?'

Annette laughed.

'I don't mean in matters of dress,' Tamara responded tetchily. Then, to Annette, 'Goodness, how frivolous men are sometimes! I'm talking about much more serious things — opinions . . . one's whole approach to life. I'm sure I'm no part of the herd in that respect. Goodness, how many people do you know who would tolerate a gatekeeper like *that* wretch?'

'Dear Tamara!' Stephen murmured. 'I'm sure that,

in the quarters where these things count, you are pricked down for sainthood. You are already beatified, you know? Why, only yesterday I heard two ladies of our acquaintance refer to you as "that blessed Tamara Dawson". So there you are.'

'Oh, he's impossible!' She recruited Annette's support directly by taking her arm.

'Not at all,' Annette assured her. 'And I'll tell you why: he's one of those ignorant wise-men who believe you win arguments by using words.'

Tamara frowned, stared at her, and then chuckled uncertainly. 'How right you are,' she observed.

Annette put a finger to her lips and said, 'Ssh!'

One of the cows arched her back and voided herself of a thin, green gallon. Stephen, more alert than his companions, leaped in front and shielded them as best he could. 'Placid, uncomplaining . . . and extremely agricultural,' he remarked.

Behind them the stray heifer mooed; they stood aside to let her pass and rejoin her sisters, which she did with a wary eye and a sudden dart of speed. 'See!' Tamara sounded slightly amazed that her prediction had, in fact, proved correct.

The women had to lift their skirts to negotiate the lake of green.

Annette decided on a frontal assault. 'Does Mr Dawson really not mind the way you two go on?' she asked.

Stephen laughed; Tamara's grip on her arm tightened momentarily. 'How we go *on*?' she ventured, as if she had no idea what the words meant.

Annette was not deflected. 'Is it a plot between you to stir Roseanne Kitto to some kind of response? Because I can tell you now — it won't work.'

Stephen did not laugh this time; Tamara's grip

tightened still further. Annette had guessed right – not that there was some deliberate and coolly hatched scheme between them to 'do something' about Roseanne, but that the subject was never far from their minds and that each, in his or her way, was eager to discuss it.

Eager . . . yet mindful of the conventions, too.

'She is our hostess today,' Tamara noted.

'I'm sure the entire human herd would agree with you there,' Annette replied.

Stephen laughed again; it was Tamara who took the plunge: 'Why d'you say it won't work, dear? I mean – as it happens – there's no such *plot* between us, but even so . . . supposing? Why wouldn't it work?'

'Because Roseanne Kitto is one of those rather odd women who hasn't the first notion of jealousy.'

She would have said more but Tamara butted in: 'Don't you want to see your brother settled?'

'What I want has nothing to do with it. I also *want* ten thou' a year. I want Cornwall to have the same climate as southern Italy. But we have to deal with things as they are. And Roseanne just isn't . . .'

'Do I get a say?' Stephen asked mildly.

'No. You stay out of this,' his sister said sharply – and with an intention not entirely jocular.

'Oh, very well!' He jogged a few steps away into the croft, to prevent part of the herd from trying its luck up where the old calciner had once stood.

'*Not* feel jealousy?' Tamara echoed. 'There's no such woman. It can only mean she has no deep feelings for him either way.'

'I can still hear you,' Stephen warned.

'You're supposed to,' Annette told him. Then, to Tamara: 'No, forgive me, but that's not right. It took me a long time to grasp it, but that's how she's been

459

able to go on in such an independent way for the past four or five years.'

'Mind you . . .' Tamara now took the opposite line. 'Four or five years is quite a normal period for an engagement. Most of my friends . . .'

'Not when both suitors are already well set up in life.'

Tamara stared in surprise toward Stephen and blurted out, '*Him*?' Then she considered the matter and added, 'I suppose so. Anyway . . .?'

'The key to the whole business is Jake, of course. And now Wheal Fortune, too. While Roseanne has them to plan for, care for . . . to exhaust all her energies – what need has she of a husband?'

Tamara, for once, said nothing.

'I actually saw it happening,' Annette went on; her tone implied that she could kick herself for being so blind at the time. 'I was at her side when that little cuckoo came straying out into the road. I saw that glint in her eye. He was an absolute godsend – the answer to all her prayers. And, fool that I was, I actually aided and abetted her design to keep him at all costs.'

'Why was that foolish?' Tamara asked.

The sharp twist of Stephen's head showed that he, too, did not follow that part of her argument.

'You can rejoin us,' she told him magnanimously, 'as long as you promise to take the matter seriously and not go all coy. Or godlike-aloof, which is the same thing with you.'

Actually she had no choice, for the road narrowed at that point, where it bridged the open-cast part of the old mine, dividing it in two. 'Why was it foolish?' he echoed.

'Because all *I* wanted was for you and her to be married. I knew *she'd* never want Skyburriowe. And I knew you wouldn't, either, as long as she didn't.'

'How could you possibly know such a thing?' he asked incredulously. 'What were you? Only eighteen. How could you know that?'

'Because I asked her. Not then, but later. After I returned from my Grand Tour.'

The reply brought the others to a momentary halt. 'You didn't!' he said.

'Not directly, of course. What d'you take me for?' Her exasperated eyes recruited Tamara's sympathy. 'We spoke about her parents' sudden rise in the world . . . Liston Court and all that. And I asked her if *she* could live in a grand house, too.'

'And she denied it?'

Annette sighed again. 'She didn't — now you listen to this, brother, dear — she hadn't the faintest notion what I was talking about. Of course, she knew what the actual *words* meant: "Could you live in a grand house . . . liveried servants . . . et cetera." But she couldn't even begin to match them with her own aspirations. I might as well have asked if she wouldn't have preferred being born Chinese. Or five centuries ago. Something utterly . . . pfft!' Her hands waved about, pushing the topic to the outer limits of relevance. 'She treated it as *that* sort of question. Now d'you see?'

'Fascinating!' Tamara murmured.

Stephen was torn between two contradictory emotions. The bluff, manly response was to scoff at these subtleties; but even as he felt the laughter rising to his throat, something deeper within him warned that his sister was edging toward a truth that had eluded him all these years — that if he could just keep his seat on this bumpy ride through alien territory, he'd glimpse it, too. 'Are you saying that, since most women marry for a home and children,' he began . . .

'Children!' Tamara interrupted with a contemptuous

461

snort. Unconsciously she ran a self-satisfied hand down the line of her belly, as if to quieten some alarm in that region at the very mention of the word. Annette began to despair of them both; but rather than cut her brother off, she took his half-spoken question as a new beginning. 'Yes,' she said, 'even at that superficial level of wanting a home and children, Jake and Wheal Fortune fit the bill.'

'Superficial?' His tone was miffed.

The words began to marshal themselves in her mind. She heard herself asking him *why* most women desired nothing more than a home and family? And why, on the contrary, did the women in those novels he read so avidly (and now reviewed for the journals, too) . . . why did they emphatically *not* want such confinement — never mind a series of confinements within it! But even as the words rang in her mind's ear, her mind's *eye* could already see the blank incomprehension in his gaze. Indeed, she doubted that even Tamara Dawson would really grasp what she was saying.

'I'm sorry,' she said meekly. 'I shouldn't have said superficial.'

'What did you mean by it?' he pressed.

'Immediate. Yes, that's the word I should have used. Perhaps it's better not to inquire too deeply into anyone's profounder motives. Jake and Wheal Fortune satisfy all her immediate needs. But, to go back to what I was saying earlier, I *thought*, you see, that Roseanne Kitto, saddled with a ready-made two-year-old boy, wouldn't delay two months in equipping him with a ready-made father, as well. How mistaken I was!'

Tamara screwed her face up, almost in pain. 'Why are you telling us all this?' she asked. 'We were having such fun, too.'

'Because,' Annette replied wearily, 'I have this terrible

462

intimation that we are at some kind of watershed now. If we let this situation persist just a few months more, it'll . . . I mean . . .' The words she so desperately needed deserted her. She turned to Stephen. 'D'you remember that time, that awful day, when we missed the train to Plymouth? When the carriage cast a tyre? D'you remember how we all piled out and ran along the road above the station? And we could see the train standing there, and hear the doors banging, and the guard blowing his whistle — and we shouted at them to stop and they didn't hear us?'

He laughed at the memory. 'And standing on the platform with the perspiration running off our brows, and seeing the guard's van just a vanishing speck on the curve at Penzance Green!'

She neither laughed nor smiled. 'That's the feeling I have about all this business now.'

57

Jake, being a thorough sort of lad, first reconnoitred the fields to make sure that one or two cows had not been left behind. Then, being a thorough sort of landlord, too, he made a small detour to survey his properties. That was how he came to see the well-dressed gentleman standing at the top of the path that led down to the blind adit. He went to tell him he'd missed his way to the bonfire and to direct him there. And that was the last anyone saw of Jake for some time.

His absence went unremarked until gone seven that evening, when some of his school friends began to arrive. 'Jake's a long time with the cows,' Roseanne remarked to Annette as they counted the last of the tumblers on to the tables. 'I hope they're all right.'

'What d'you mean?' she asked. 'A long time with the cows?'

'Didn't he come in and drive them back to the fields for you?'

Annette shook her head. 'We never saw him at all.'

'But surely . . .?' A little knot of alarm twisted in her innards. 'About half an hour after you started milking? Didn't he come in?'

Annette shook her head. 'We finished the milking and put them back ourselves.'

'Did you see him then? Out in the fields, perhaps?'

Another shake of the head.

'The devil!' Roseanne swore. 'He promised me he'd see everything was going smoothly for you.'

'Well, so it did. You don't think . . .'

'What?' Roseanne asked sharply.

'I was just wondering if he slipped up to Breage to bring his cronies down here. Perhaps they're up to some skylark on the way?'

'I wouldn't put it past him.' Slightly mollified, Roseanne went off to accost those of Jake's friends who had arrived, asking each in turn whether he or she had seen him. The unvarying negative of their responses, however, revived her misgivings.

The mine shafts were, of course, her first thought. Despite all her warnings and prohibitions – *and* the new walls she had erected around the four that were most easily accessible – she could just imagine him going across Sethnoe's fields to Breage, gathering his closest friends, and bringing them back the same way . . . and just happening to stop for a stone-throwing contest near one or other of those dreadful holes. She knew very well that, if something unthinkable had indeed, happened, the first thing the lads would do would be to come running to the nearest grown-up. Yet somehow it did nothing to allay her fears, which now lay beyond the balm of reason.

She had just received the tenth negative response to her increasingly agitated question when Mark Bodilly turned up. 'You look some cabbed about,' he commented jovially while he was still several yards away; but as he drew closer he saw her distress and became serious at once. She explained her worries and asked if he'd investigate the four worst shafts – the two at Blueborough, the one below the farmhouse and the one near the calciner. Stephen, who had heard the story from Annette, joined them at that moment, in time to overhear the last part of her request to Mark. He said he'd take the Blueborough shaft if Bodilly did the other two. They both assured her that nothing serious could have befallen Jake; at the very worst he'd torn his clothes and was waiting for the crowds to distract her so that he could sneak in and change.

It didn't sound like Jake, but she allowed herself to be soothed and, putting the bravest face she could on things, went to play the hostess as best she could.

Half an hour later they returned with the dubiously good news that none of the ground around any of those four shafts was freshly disturbed. They then volunteered to go off and search all the fields, as well as the two shafts up at Carnmeal, which were deep in furze and thorns and which she had considered unapproachable, even by inquisitive lads of eight.

It took them the most wretched hour of her life to draw yet another blank. With every minute that brought no good news from them, her own imagination served bad in its place, so that she was beside herself with anguish by the time they returned. She pressed them with questions. Had they gone in such and such a field? Did they look in the two little gardens? Had they gone back to the house? Was the boar in his pen?

They would have resented the catechism if they had not known that she was not so much looking for dereliction in them as for one small chink of hope in the situation in general.

'But a boy just cannot vanish off the face of the earth,' she insisted. 'He must be lying injured or unconscious somewhere. Did you go all up the valley? Did you look along the river banks?'

At last she had found one part of the parish they had overlooked. They set off once more, glad to have something to do, rather than stand around and just worry. By now, word of Jake's disappearance had spread and half a dozen men volunteered to join them; more would have gone but the valley was too narrow to permit more than eight or so to go abreast. A dozen could have held hands all the way — except that the twists of the river and the marshes and hillocks would have prohibited it.

Roseanne tried her best to entertain and be comforted by those who stayed behind, greeting fresh arrivals with a brave smile, and agreeing with one and all that, yes, one just couldn't say what lads that age would get up to. When she had taken as much of it as she could stand she went to Annette and said, 'There's one place I'm sure they won't look at, because unless you know it's there you could walk straight past it. The blind adit, just down the valley from Jake's Row. I'll just slip down there and see for myself. I'll bet that's where he is. He's played there a lot lately. He calls it Robinson Crusoe's cave.'

'Shall I come, too?'

'No, you stay and keep everyone jolly.'

Annette pulled a face. 'Thank you very much!'

Roseanne squeezed her arm. 'For me?'

Annette kissed her and murmured, 'I hope you're right.'

And that was the last anyone saw of Roseanne for some considerable time.

Except Annette, of course.

58

Annette recognized the man the moment she saw him, despite the fact that he now had the dress and bearing of a gentleman. His hatchet face and receding brows were etched deeply enough in her memory to override any such disguise. In fact, she recognized him in a second sense, too — and now it was *because* of that fine plumage; she couldn't put a name to him but she was sure she had seen him somewhere before. They had met socially, though many years ago — when she was a child perhaps.

However, notwithstanding that little puzzle, there could be no doubting his present intentions. Jake's disappearance, followed by Roseanne's could only mean that he had returned to Breage bent on dealing with the only two respectable and reliable witnesses to his crime of almost five years ago. Jake had been mere bait to entice them but she was certain he'd share whatever fate was intended for Roseanne and her.

She shivered to realize how she had almost walked into the trap — a bonus for which he could not have planned. With a tracker's skill, honed down her Peeping Tomasina years, she had trailed Roseanne into the valley, keeping quite close until they came to the open ground near Jake's Row. There she had been forced to wait until Roseanne had reached the spinney, which was below the last cabin in the row, almost at the marshes by the river. Then, remembering that the blind adit Roseanne had mentioned was a hundred yards or so to the right, upstream a little, she cut diagonally across the fields, hoping to save time. She had been on the point of climbing the hedge at the foot of the lower field, immediately above the blind adit, when Hatchet Face had appeared. His bare head was immediately below her, a mere six feet away. Not recognizing him then, she had almost taken him for one of the searchers and was on the point of asking if they had had any luck when he moved into profile — and turned her blood to ice.

He was looking for the search party, who were still more than half a mile away down the valley; but he could hear them calling to one another and their increasing proximity plainly alarmed him. She fought for breath, she fought to remain still, not moving a muscle, while he made a slow survey of the opposite slopes, the only area from which the blind adit was visible, except for the immediate valley bottom, which was plainly deserted at the moment. In none of the fields was there any sign of another soul. The nearest visible house was over half a mile away, up the valley to the north, at Trew; Sethnoe, an equal distance in the opposite direction, was hidden by a belt of elms. Apart from the searchers, then, everything was in his favour.

He now continued his survey along the Wheal Fortune side. Annette, a veteran of this kind of situation, knew that as long as she kept still behind the furze, which was just beginning to colonize the top of the hedge, she was virtually indetectable; yet when his eyes reached that spot and seemed, for a moment, to dwell directly in hers, it cost all her nerve not to run screaming for help across the fields. A moment later, however, his gaze had passed on. Now he was eyeing the spinney and anxiously kneading his lower lip between finger and thumb.

When he had surveyed the full circle he bent double and crept forward into the very bottom of the valley, among the brambles and rushes that bordered the little river. He was obviously trying to spot the search party. From his demeanour she guessed they were still out of sight, for he stood and strode purposefully back toward her, down into the valley that led to the mouth of the adit.

The moment he was out of sight she faced the choice between withdrawing and waiting. If she withdrew she could retrace her path across the fields, dash along the lane above Blueborough, which was beyond the spinney and Jake's Row from here, and then down over the old halvans to alert the search party — except that, by the time she had done all that, they would be almost here, anyway. She tried putting herself in Hatchet Face's position. He must have gone up to Wheal Fortune to reconnoitre his attack, thinking there'd be only a single woman and a boy to deal with once the farm hands had gone home. When he found that both his witnesses were there — and when Jake accidentally volunteered himself as decoy — it must have seemed too good a chance to ignore; within half an hour he'd have dealt with all three of them. He cannot have expected so much time to have elapsed before one of them noticed Jake's absence. Now, with the search party drawing ever-closer, he was certain to be discovered in the adit. Roseanne, in her agitation to be doing something, had been quite wrong about that; even the most casual searchers could not have passed it by unseen.

Like Hatchet Face, Annette now made a survey of the valley, and, like him, too, she decided that the spinney offered better concealment — indeed, the only concealment possible in the circumstances.

Sure enough he reappeared at that instant carrying

Roseanne's body over his shoulder. For one awful moment Annette thought she was already dead. There was a large area of blood, matting her hair, colouring her neck, and staining the right shoulder of her dress. Her hands and feet were trussed with cord and her mouth was gagged with a handkerchief, also tied with cord. In fact, events soon proved she was not even unconscious. She must have been shamming, waiting for some such moment as this; for she suddenly straightened up until she was rigidly horizontal across his shoulders, and then she collapsed, bringing her boots down hard against his hip. He gave out a curse and fell into a patch of nettles. She immediately tried to squirm and roll down the valleyside toward the river, struggling frantically with her bonds as she went.

But he swiftly recovered and, a moment later, was standing over her, kicking her anywhere he could until she again lay still and passive. Then he picked her up and threw her into a thorn bush. Annette had to stuff her fist in her mouth to prevent herself from crying out; even so she almost bit through the skin of her knuckle in her anguish. 'You do that once more,' the man cried, 'and I'll throw you in every thorn we pass.' He dragged her out, bleeding afresh from a dozen or more cuts and scratches.

The moment he had her over his shoulders again Annette climbed through the hedge. The risk of discovery was dwindling, for even if the fellow did spot her now, he could hardly drop Roseanne, who had just proved her ability to escape, given half a chance. With the searchers drawing ever nearer, he could hardly risk that. For the same reason he couldn't spare the time to return with her on his shoulders. Annette's main aim was to release Jake, who, she felt sure, must be lying in the adit, trussed like his mother.

She tore her dress in going through the hedge but paid it no heed. She stumbled and rolled down the steep bank into the valley of the adit. At least there she was out of sight of Hatchet Face. Winded and a little dazed she picked herself up and called out softly, 'Jake?'

There was no response, not even the sounds the boy might make in struggling with his bonds. Fearing the worst again, yet encouraging herself with the memory that last time she had been proved wrong, she stepped into the dank stone passage with its clay-mud floor — the home, it seemed, of a myriad mosquitoes. Outside, magnified by the horn-shaped mouth of the cave, a blackbird sang a song of incongruous cheer.

'Jake?'

Again there was no reply, no sound of a struggle. Somewhere down the far end she heard the steady *plink!* . . . *plink!* of water dripping into a pool. A moment later, as her eyes adapted to the gloom, she could see it all clearly — the whole cave to its far end, which was a mere twelve paces away. It was devoid of life of any kind, except for two ferns at the edge of the pool where the water was dripping so relentlessly. But the adit proved to have a small chamber, hollowed out to one side. She had to wait for her eyes to grow completely accustomed to the dark before she could assure herself that it, too, was empty. All the while, a chilling sense of her own vulnerability grew within her.

The moment she knew there was no point in further exploration here she ran out into the now blinding light of day and straight down into the valley. There she tore off the rest of her mutilated skirt and waved it with all her might, shouting for help at the top of her voice.

But the breeze was southerly, up the valley, and her shrill treble was borne away toward Trew and Carleen. What made it all the more frustrating was that she could see them now, quite clearly. But their eyes were down, searching under every shrub, into every clump of reeds, and behind every heap of mine waste. She leaped up and down, waving the remnant of her skirt for all she was worth, cursing their blindness.

And then a shadow darkened her immediate skyline and she found herself staring into the pitiless eyes of Hatchet Face himself, not six paces from her. She stooped, picked up a stone, and hurled it at him with all her might. It broke three of his teeth and split his lip. It even sent him reeling to the ground for a moment. But it did not stop him from retaliating; it only made him all the more vengeful, if that were possible.

59

Roseanne was kicked so nearly unconscious by her tormentor that the thorns, tearing at her bare arms and face served, if anything, to revive her; she hardly felt the pain of them then. She almost passed out again when the fellow threw her over the broken wall into the spinney and then grasped her by the hair to drag her deep into the undergrowth. She tried to think of Jake and what the man had told her in that smarmy, gloating voice of his all the while he had trussed her like a chicken. It couldn't be true. There was no mineshaft down in this part of the valley; the nearest ones were surely up at Blueborough — and he couldn't have got within a furlong of them without being noticed, even on an ordinary day, let alone today, with so many dozens around. No, it couldn't possibly be true.

The trouble was, she had never actually explored the spinney. It looked so impenetrable from the outside, and was, moreover, so choked with ancient rubbish thrown into it by the onetime occupants of Jake's Row that she had contented herself with surveying its boundary wall and assuring herself it presented no great hazard to the cattle; if the pigs got in there, they could look after themselves. So there just might be an ancient shaft in the heart of it.

A moment later all doubts as to its existence were

resolved — when he picked her up and threw her over its edge. There was no hesitation, no pause for a final gloating jeer from him — just a push and she was falling. In that split second as she went over the wall their eyes met. She had never seen a gaze so cold, so devoid of feeling as his.

The cry that rose to her throat was one long shriek of anguish. The gag reduced it to an inarticulate howl but it rang clear as a bell in the chambers of her mind: *Mark*! Time was strangely distorted in that fall. What the clock would measure with a single tick, her mind, knowing itself to be at the moment of death, stretched to a point where measurement itself became meaningless.

All she could think of was Mark. The idea of him . . . more than the idea, the living presence of him filled her and the enveloping darkness that now pressed all about her. She watched the green twilight of the mouth of the shaft as it dwindled with sluggish unreality and no other thought occurred to her than that he was out there where she would never be again. She would never feel his touch again, nor hear his voice again, nor see the shape of him. If a mortal creature still on the right side of death, can feel the slightest intimation of what it means to be sentenced to the outermost darkness of Hell, Roseanne felt it then. It was her last thought before she hit the side of the shaft.

And her first thought *after* that moment of contact was that it had been surprisingly gentle. And the green oval above was still surprisingly large. And she hadn't simply struck the wall of the shaft and bounced off again, she was still actually sliding down it. Half sliding, half rolling, spinning and turning in . . . in what? It wasn't rock and gravel, anyway — though her body, torn and bruised as it was, might not have been swift to appreciate the difference. But this was . . . well, it felt like tea leaves or leaf mould or something.

Was there a bend in the shaft? It was not impossible. In fact, very few of the more ancient shafts in Cornish tin mines were vertical. Before the age of steam, miners preferred to follow the lode, which generally sloped down at between sixty and eighty degrees. This could be one of those.

Of course, you could die from a fall even down a sixty-degree shaft, but it wasn't as absolutely certain as when the shaft was vertical. Especially if the site had been abandoned for some time and there were one or two . . .

Indeed there were. She struck one just at that moment — the stem of a volunteer sapling, imperfectly rooted in the thinly lodged detritus of all those idle years. It did not hold but it braked her perilous slide into the utter darkness of the pit. And now she and the jetsam in which the little tree had grown were all moving down together, piling yet more before them, gathering up loose rock, old saucepans, broken bedsteads, frayed cable, rusted chains . . . everything that had been cast over the rim down the years and that happened to have come to rest in that section of the shaft.

At the time, of course, she had no idea she owed her salvation to such a rich variety of objects, but her ears were filled with the slithering, clanking, rumbling of what was clearly quite an assortment of rubbish. She came to rest at last against something very soft, indeed. Soft and large, larger than herself. It took a long moment for her eyes to grow accustomed to the dark but when they did, she could see the unmistakable pattern of stripes, broad navy blue and pale grey, of mattress ticking. In her overwrought state, tears fought with hysterical laughter at the realization that, having

476

been hurled to certain death down an unknown, unmarked mine shaft, she was now, less than half a minute later, lying in something close to comfort on a feather mattress.

Not an old mattress, either. That was a bit of a puzzle. She was just considering the implications of this discovery when the mattress itself *moved*.

60

Annette, too was hurled unceremoniously over the wall of the spinney. But, not being tied hand and foot, and now beginning to revive from the terrible beating Hatchet Face had given her on the bank of the river, she immediately rose on all fours and scuttled away; the density of the vegetation made it impossible to stand. But he was swiftly over the wall and even more swiftly after her. She did not realize what she had done, of course, until the path gave out at the rim of a mine shaft — which was where he caught up with her. In her panic she had merely followed the most inviting avenue of escape, which was the one he had already beaten twice that afternoon. He laughed and told her how obliging she was to save him the chore of dragging her there. She struggled like a demon to escape once more though, pitted against his strength and agility, she knew it was hopeless.

The sight of her, half undressed and racing on hands and knees ahead of him, had already inflamed his lust; her struggles merely heated them further, to the point where not even his own instinct for self preservation could hold him back. He threw up her petticoats and was fighting for penetration when her hand found a large rock just small enough to hold. He was on the very brink of his goal when she brought it down with all her might on the back of his head.

He grunted. His eyes almost fell from their sockets. There was blood. And suddenly he weighed a ton.

A moment later she was standing above him, shivering with fright, hardly able to focus her eyes . . . possessed with a loathing and anger beyond anything she had ever experienced. She stared at the rock, which was still, somehow, in her hand. Her only thought was to wonder how on earth she had managed to lift it. Now it took both hands and all her remaining strength to raise it again and send it hurtling down upon him. She had meant to break his skull in but missed. She heard the crack of several ribs and saw blood ooze into the corner of his mouth.

It was the last thing she saw before, in reaction to that mighty effort, she lost her balance and fell over the low wall that surrounded the shaft. Desperately she reached for some handhold, found one of the stones in the wall, and clung to it for dear life. And fortunately it held. Her feet scrabbled in the loose bank that sloped almost vertically away beneath her. Then she felt the sand, or cob, falling into her hair and down her face. It could only be coming from beneath the stone that was now her only purchase on life.

It moved. Before it could fall she made a desperate lunge to transfer her grip to its neighbour − and missed. A moment later she was sliding and slithering down the slope and, like Roseanne some fifteen minutes earlier, wondering why she was not falling through free space. She wondered, too, whether this were not the ultimate trick of the Evil Fairy who plainly ruled this day − offering her the glimmer of a hope that would, at last, prove a cruel illusion.

There were saplings of ash and oak all about her, some as thick as her wrist. She grabbed at any that she saw in time. Most of them came away and joined her downward plunge; some held, though she was sliding too fast to keep her grip, especially with her hands all slimy from the leaf mould and wet earth. But whether they held or whether they gave, each of them helped brake her descent until she and the debris beneath her were moving slowly enough for the natural cohesion of rock mould, gravel, rubbish, and clay to bring all but the loosest garbage to a halt. What finally held her was something soft and large — larger than herself.

And she realized as she lay there trying to recover her breath, it was *moving*!

'Aunt Netty?' said a piping little treble out of the darkness behind her.

'Jake?' she gasped incredulously.

'Yes. Don't move.'

'Jake?' She still couldn't believe it.

'Yes. And me, too.' That was Roseanne. 'Do as he says. Don't move.'

'Where are you?'

'Below you, the other side of the mattress. There's a bit of timber — pretty rotten — wedged across the shaft here. I'm leaning on the slope with my feet against it. And it's our last hope, because the shaft dips almost vertical beyond it.'

'How d'you know?'

'For God's sake! Does it matter now? Jake told me. He's explored this shaft with a rope. We just have to wait here and keep as still as we can . . . and pray they'll think to come looking for us in the spinney. Where's that man?'

'I killed him — I hope. Where's Jake?'

He touched the back of her arm at that moment. 'Don't move,' he repeated his mother's warning, even more urgently. 'Did he tie you up? I can untie you if he did.'

'No, I'm all right. Did your mother say something about a rope?'

'It's up in one of my cottages,' he answered ruefully. 'But listen. There are some old steps here, cut into the rock. I cleared them away up near the top, and if . . .'

'Today?' she asked incredulously.

'No! Just now and then. Other boys and me. We've been going down on the rope and clearing them. They're not in the middle. They're at the side, over there. But if I can clear the bottom ones here, we can get out.

'No, Jake,' his mother said sharply. 'You're not to risk it. If you slip, there'll be nothing to stop you. Can't you *see* the edge of it there?'

Annette risked a peep under her forearm and, though Roseanne was out of sight beyond the mattress, she could just discern the slightly paler black of the sloping floor against the absolute black of the chasm beyond. 'Don't risk it, Jake dear,' she said, adding her entreaty to those of his mother. But he insisted it was their only chance. No one would hear them up there, even if they all three cried out at the tops of their voices. If he could get out and bring the others back with ropes . . . He begged her to scrabble around for an old billhook or the end of a spade or something. More to prevent him from carrying out his design than anything, Roseanne suggested that they should at least try calling out; if it didn't work . . . she never actually made the promise but she implied he could try clearing the steps as he wished.

'I tore my dress getting through the hedge,' Annette added. 'And I managed to leave a bit on the path to the spinney without Hatchet Face noticing it. If they see it, they'll surely come here.'

It was a forlorn enough hope in all conscience but

she managed to keep her awareness of it out of her voice.

'One, two, three . . .' Roseanne said.

'He-e-e-lp!' they screamed as loud as they could.

Absolute silence greeted the effort.

'Again,' Roseanne said.

Ten times they called, and ten times more, until their throats were sore enough to bring tears to their eyes and even Roseanne had to admit that Jake was right. Their voices might carry well enough to the top of the shaft but by then the walls would have absorbed and deflected so much of the volume that a man would have to be standing stock still and not more than twenty yards away before he'd hear it.

However, it took another five minutes for her to agree that Jake's idea of digging out the old staircase offered their best, and possibly their only, hope of emerging alive. Annette began to scrabble about her, searching for anything that might serve as a digging implement. She found an old hand hoe, the perfect thing for the job, and was just giving a cry of triumph when the mattress began to slide away from her.

'No!' she cried. 'Please God, no!' And she broke her fingernails and lost the hoe in a desperate attempt to halt the slide. She had a terrifying vision of pushing Roseanne off the rotten timber — and then following her into the void.

Roseanne, however, crawled hastily to one side and reached up the slope for the slightest handhold — anything on which to grip if the timber followed all the other rubbish that had gone over the edge. That there was water rather than solid rock at the bottom was no consolation. The thunderous and almost continuous splashing as rock, earth, uprooted saplings, and old bits

482

of scrap iron went raining into it was the most chilling sound she had ever heard.

And then the timber did, indeed, give way. It slithered down the last yard of the slope to the very rim, where the shaft turned as near-vertical as made no difference. It teetered on the edge and then slid over. But a foot or so into the chasm it lodged again, now at an angle of about thirty degrees. It must have yielded very near its end; that, plus the fact that the shaft narrowed at the point where it turned vertical, helped it lodge again – though how firmly was anyone's guess.

At least, for the moment, it held tight enough to support both Roseanne and Annette – and, a moment or two later, Jake, who slid to a halt with one foot on a shoulder of each. And there they froze while the thundering and splashing below them persisted for an eternity, chilling their blood and sapping what little hope remained.

'For heaven's sake nobody move,' Roseanne whispered vehemently when the reverberations of the fall had subsided enough to allow the others to hear her. 'We mustn't move or cry out. We'll just have to lie here and wait.'

'And pray,' Annette added.

61

At the top of the shaft Hatchet Face groaned, stirred
. . . and subsided back into unconsciousness. Down in
the valley the searchers drew ever closer. At last they
reached the broad, marshy stretch where the
bottommost Blueborough field ended and the spinney
below Jake's Row began. Shortly after that one of them
cried out, 'Well, I'll go to hell!'

'What?' asked those nearest him. He pointed to
Annette's torn skirt lying in the path on the northern
edge of the spinney. 'Was the boy wearing blue?' he
asked Stephen.

Mark joined them. The moment he saw it, he called
out, 'That's your sister's, surely!' And he led the
scramble to reach it first.

When he was several yards off his goal he shouted,
'Blood! By God, if anyone's harmed her! . . .'

'The old blind adit!' Stephen cried. He was staring
at the hedge above it, where the first torn part of
her dress was fluttering from a thorn bush. There
was another mad dash to reach the cave – a dozen
or so thundering pairs of feet that completely
obliterated all trace of what had happened there that
afternoon.

'Annette?' Stephen called into the dark mouth of the
adit. They held their breath but were rewarded with
nothing beyond the steady *plink! plink!* of dripping

water. Mark raced in, struck his head on a rock overhang, and, gritting his teeth against the pain, blundered on into every corner, feeling blindly with hands and feet for any sign of her.

'Nothing,' he called out as he emerged again.

'God, your forehead, man!' Stephen said. 'You should have that seen to.'

He ignored the advice. 'Walker!' he shouted to one of the searchers. 'Any sign of footprints on that path by 'ee, there?'

The man was, as it happened, standing ten paces or so beyond the most northerly point that either of the women or Hatchet Face had trodden that afternoon. 'Not a trace,' he replied after a careful scrutiny. 'But something's rolled in those nettles — and the rushes below them by the look of it.'

Several men ran to investigate, now taking care to tread only where there was no sign of disturbance. 'There's been a struggle here, all right,' one of them called.

'Which way did they go?' Mark called, coming down to join them.

Despite the most diligent search they could find no clear footprint, though there were plentiful signs of tracks toward both the spinney and the blind adit. Mark looked back at the thorn in the hedge above the cave, where the scrap of blue cloth still fluttered. 'Whoever attacked her took her that way,' he declared, 'out along the lane to Scott's.'

They all ran back to the valley, scrambled up its sides and crawled through the hole Annette had pioneered earlier. Stephen alone remained at that point, looking more closely at the torn scrap of material.

First he tried to pull it down the slope, but it would not yield. The thorns gave a little and then clutched it tight. Next he tried pulling it the other way, up toward the field. It came free of the thorns at once.

'Oy!' he called after the retreating searchers.

They stopped and faced him.

'This was torn as she went down, not up,' he shouted.

They stood their ground and stared uncertainly at him.

'How d'you know?' Mark asked impatiently.

'Come here and I'll show you.'

Mark waved a dismissive hand at him. 'We're wasting time. They've gone out past Scott's. No doubt of it. We can see the track through the grass.'

Nothing Stephen shouted at their retreating backs would make them halt again.

He weighed the piece of cloth in his hand and then stared at the spot where the rest of her dress had been found. And then at the spinney.

It was so dense and impenetrable − so obviously not the place where anyone would accidentally stray − that, so far, they had not given it a thought. But these signs of violence surely changed all that? Now it was clearly the place where an attacker might choose to hide from his pursuers − or, he hardly dared frame the thought − hide the evidence of his crime.

He raced back down the side of the gully and then up the path to the lower edge of the spinney. There a quick examination of the wall showed that someone had, indeed, scrambled over it quite recently. He quickly followed the spoor. The path that anyone would have to take was clear − even without the disturbance to the leaf mould, the broken undergrowth, and the living twigs that were snapped and bent. The disturbance to the leaf mould was most ominous of all for it suggested that something − or someone − had been dragged this way.

A moment later he came across Hatchet Face, still unconscious and bleeding. His first thought, naturally, was that this poor fellow, too, was a victim of whatever assailant had torn his sister's dress like that. He rose to his full height, stuck his fingers in his mouth, and gave the loudest whistle he could. He followed it with several more before he heard the first faint cry from the path across the fields 'What?' — very faint and only just managing to carry downwind and through the dense stand of trees.

'Here!' he shouted. 'Come quick!'

He bent and tried to make Hatchet Face more comfortable. To judge by his dress he was a gentleman. Probably he had witnessed the attack and had gone to Annette's rescue. 'Never mind, old chap,' he said soothingly, 'We'll soon have you comfortable again. He loosened the man's cravat, and made sure his tongue was not blocking his throat . . . and all the other things one is taught to do when people fall off horses or have a fit in the street. 'If only you could tell us where the blighters went with my sister!' Like Annette he had the feeling he had met the man before.

And that was when he heard the cries for help — very faint and far away. They were coming from . . . well, it seemed impossible, but they were coming from somewhere above his head. He had once heard people shouting from a hot-air balloon and it had sounded just like that.

He rose and stared up through the branches, ducking and walking to augment the tiny glimpses of the sky they offered. So convinced was he of their direction that it took several more cries to show him that he was wrong by almost a hundred and eighty degrees. But the moment he stuck his head over the edge of the shaft — whose very existence he had not, until then, suspected

— he was no longer in any doubt but that the calls came from down there.

It was all too sudden for him to be aware of much emotion. 'Annette?' he shouted down into the blackness, surprising himself at the matter-of-factness of it all.

'Ye-e-es!' There was no doubting the relief in the long-drawn-out word.

'Where are you? How far down? I can't see a thing.'

'We can see you. Two hundred yards? Three hundred? I don't know. Listen. There's a rope in one of the cabins in Jake's Row. Go and get it.'

'Who's we? Is Roseanne with you?'

'Yes. And Jake. We're safe enough for the moment. But don't waste time!'

'Are you alone?' That was Roseanne's voice.

'The others are coming,' he assured her. In fact, he could hear them scrambling through the undergrowth behind him now. 'Hold on,' he called down before he turned to face the other searchers. 'Don't come near this edge,' he warned. 'My sister's fallen down there. She's stuck on some sort of ledge. It seems to slope away, not fall sheer.'

'Like Carnmeal main-engine shaft,' one of the other commented.

'A bit steeper than that,' he told him. 'Miss Kitto's down there, too. And the boy.'

'Oh hell!' Mark exploded angrily. 'What do they want to go falling down there for? Trying to rescue the boy, I dare say. How didn't they leave it to we?' Then he noticed Hatchet Face. 'Who's that?' he asked.

The man groaned and stirred once more. Now they saw that his flies were undone. Even without that prompting Stephen had already been having second thoughts about this supposed gentleman. What with the two women and the boy down the mineshaft . . . the marks of a struggle all round . . . the open fly buttons – it was starting to paint an altogether different picture. 'I think,' he said, 'we'd better truss him up until we know more of what happened.'

Mark went straight to the fellow, lifted him by the lapels, and bawled at him, 'What have you done, you filthy bastard?'

Stephen pulled him off. 'We don't know, man,' he said. 'We can't be sure.'

But Mark was rifling the fellow's pockets now. 'Cord!' he said triumphantly, pulling out a hank of it. 'I don't need more evidence than this.' And heedless of the man's wounds, which were still oozing blood, he began trussing him like a Christmas goose.

Stephen asked one of the others to go and fetch the length of rope from the cabins. The path was now so broken open that the man was able to walk out, almost fully upright, snapping the odd branch as he went. Within minutes he was back, carrying the rope in a loop over his shoulder. By then Mark was having a furious argument with Roseanne.

He wanted to tie the rope around himself and let the others lower him to wherever they were stuck. She shouted back that he'd dislodge so much on the way that he'd sweep them off their precarious perch and send them all plunging to their deaths. The only safe thing was to send the rope down and let all three of them hold on to it while they went for three more ropes – one each. Then they could haul all three of them up together and none of them would be at risk from falling debris. 'Which we will be if you just try to get one of us,' she yelled. 'Or if you try to come down yourself.'

Stephen sent a party out to bring all the rope they could gather – from the farm, from neighbours . . .

anywhere they could find it. Then he and the remaining men managed to persuade Mark of the good sense of Roseanne's warnings. Between them they set about trying to lower the rope without dislodging anything and sending it crashing down upon them.

Half an hour later they had to admit it was hopeless. The rope was too light to go all the way. They tried shaking it like a snake and looping it like a lariat; but the best of their efforts brought it no nearer than a tantalizing twenty yards of the three who were waiting for it so desperately down there.

By then, with the evening drawing on, the foraging party had returned with more rope and several burly neighbours. Among them, too, was Frank Kitto, who assumed charge at once. He took one look at the low, crumbling wall around the shaft and set two men to demolishing it very carefully, stone by stone. He made them stand at the edge and pull each stone off, passing it back between their legs like rugby players in a loose scrum with the ball.

A search of the spinney produced several makeshift implements — an old ploughshare, a broken shovel, half a carriage spring — which they could use for scraping back the loose cob and gravel from around the larger stones. He sent another party to look for a fallen tree trunk, which they could set at the edge of the shaft once the wall had gone; it would take the bite of the ropes without risking the dislodgement of any debris around the rim.

Then Mark made the exciting discovery that there were footsteps cut into the rock at one side of the shaft. 'Let me go down there,' he begged Frank. 'Tie the lightest rope round me and I'll draw three heavier ones after me. There's no better way to get them down.'

At first Frank would not hear of it, but then Stephen

told him the trouble they'd had in getting the first rope down all the way. 'And it's the light one,' he pointed out. 'With those others we'll risk dislodging things all the way.'

Frank went to the side of the shaft and studied the steps. Now that he came to look at them more closely, they were freshly cleaned and quite well cut. Perhaps . . . if they went all the way? One of the miners told him that those steps used to be the only way in and out of Wheal Fortune mine, before the open-cast began and before there was a winding engine up on the Trelissick shaft. Men – and women and children, too – used to carry a hundredweight of ore up ladders in the shaft and then crawl up the slope by means of those steps. 'That's "the *easy* pitch", they used to call 'n,' he added. 'But I can't understand how he's so clean after all this time. That shaft haven't been used in five years.'

Frank looked at Hatchet Face, who was showing signs of reviving. 'There's a lot we can't understand about all this.' Then he peered at him more attentively. 'Here,' he said, 'I do know this bugger.'

'I thought the same,' the miner chipped in. 'That's Major Dumont's eldest boy, isn't it? Percy. I thought he was dead.'

'So he is,' said a third. 'I heard the major say so hisself.'

Stephen called down to Roseanne, asking her if she could see any steps in the rock away to their right. She shouted back the briefest necessary explanation – adding that Jake said that if a man was on a rope he could use the steps fairly well even beyond the point where they were no longer cleaned off.

That decided it. They tied what was called a 'captain's hitch' around Mark's chest and lashed the ends of three stout ropes to the thinner one that held him, leaving both his hands free to steady himself and to avoid accidentally dislodging anything large and loose. 'I'm starting down,' he called into the black of the shaft.

'Don't go away!' Stephen added. It was the first moment anyone had felt able to joke.

62

Though the first fifty steps had been hacked clean by Jake and his friends, they were the slowest of Mark's descent. It was not only that he had to let his feet grow accustomed to the steps, he also had to devise some method of signalling when he wanted to go faster or slower. And then there was the problem of the three heavier ropes, which constantly threatened to start small avalanches of debris as they were fed out into the shaft. This last difficulty was solved when the men paying them out moved round to the opposite side of the mouth — what was effectively the roof of the steeply sloping tunnel. In that way they kept the ropes off the floor until the very last reach of the descent, by which time the chance was negligible that a small slide might trigger a greater one.

By now the place was thronged with able-bodied men from half a dozen parishes. They came with axes, saws, litters, tarpaulins, blankets, storm lanterns . . . all the paraphernalia of a full-scale mine rescue, in which they were, sadly, well practised. There was a small stone quarry down near the stop gate on the Breage turnpike; from there they brought a six-man winch. It took more than two dozen of them to haul it into the ruins of the spinney and set it up at the mouth of the shaft. There was no time to drive ground anchors so they lashed its trestle legs to two tree trunks on which they piled all the loose stone they could gather. Others set up a pair of limelights to shine directly down the shaft; and they also hung naphtha flares from the branches of the few remaining trees. That special sense of cooperation which grips all mining communities in moments of crisis was almost palpable among the men who were there that night; not a moment of Mark's descent was wasted in futile or ill-directed effort. By the time he reached the bottom of the steps, everything at the shaft head was as ready as could possibly be.

Then began the most nerve-wracking period of all, while he worked his way along the rim — which was only a matter of three or four paces — and tied them securely with the heavier ropes. The press of bodies around the mouth of the shaft grew so dangerous that Frank ordered back all but the men on the ropes, the light, and the windlass; he himself then kept up a running commentary to prevent their creeping up again.

Dr Moore, veteran of many a mining disaster, arrived at that moment. They led him straight to Percy Dumont (if indeed, that were Hatchet Face's true identity), who was lashed to a tree some six paces from the edge of the shaft. The doctor was appalled to see any man treated so, no matter what crime he was alleged to have committed. They released him then and laid him on a stretcher. He was obviously in no condition to escape. Dr Moore himself doubted the fellow would even survive when he saw the wound in his skull.

'Give them one rope each to hold,' Frank shouted down the shaft. 'Then tie them fast one at a time.'

Mark held up a hand to show he understood. 'Can I stand on that timber?' he asked Annette.

'No!' the three of them shouted back in alarmed unison. 'Just give us the ropes for God's sake!' Roseanne added.

'You can't tie them yourselves, surely,' he said, feeling with his boot among the thick layer of rubbish that hung poised on the rim.

Roseanne closed her eyes and mouthed a silent prayer. 'I'll kill him, I swear it,' she whispered to Jake at her side. 'Give. Us. The. Ropes!' she shouted, making a fresh sentence of each word.

''Tis no use,' he told them. 'I can't find rock nowhere here. I shall have to go on hands and knees.'

'Then do as Roseanne says,' Annette cried. 'You can't keep the ropes in your hands and crawl. Throw them to me. I'll pass the other two theirs.'

Reluctantly he did as she bade — so reluctantly, in fact, that the ropes fell a little short of her reach. She made a lunge for them and managed to grab two — but the force of her movement caused the loosely wedged timber to slip another foot or so on the wall behind Mark, which the limelight now revealed to be oozing wet and covered in a grey, frilly species of slime.

The three of them gave out cries of terror, which carried to the mouth of the shaft. 'What happened?' Frank called down. 'Are 'ee all right?'

'It's still moving,' Jake cried. His chin was now level with the rim and he was scrabbling desperately in the debris above it for some kind of hold.

'Here!' Annette passed him one of the ropes and then gave the other to Roseanne.

'Have you got one?' Roseanne asked, holding — though not exactly accepting — it.

Mark put the third rope in Annette's hands at that moment.

'It *is* still slipping,' Annette cried, trying not to panic.

'Haul yourselves up!' Mark shouted at them.

'Get the boy . . . take the boy,' they screamed back at him.

The movement of the ropes across the shaft had dislodged some of the loosened rubbish, which was now pouring down upon them, filling their eyes and mouths as soon as they opened them.

And inexorably, inch by inch, the rotten timber slid down the wall to their right.

Miraculously, there was a hiatus in the petty avalanche of debris.

'The boy!' Roseanne and Annette shouted again, and in even greater panic. 'Get hold of Jake!'

'What's going on down there?' came Frank's cry from far above.

All three of them were now scrabbling at the rim and clutching their ropes for their very lives. Roseanne, holding on with her left arm only, was doing her best to help Jake with her right — and shouting curses at Mark for his hesitancy. One slip, one unlucky collision with a heavier piece of garbage and that would be the end of it for all of them.

Roseanne hazarded her own life by letting go of the rope entirely, in order to lift Jake toward Mark. For a moment their eyes met. She saw a man in the torment of hell. Forces he could not resist now impelled him to ignore the boy and reach down to pull Annette to safety first. She resisted, of course, but his anger was so fierce that she submitted swiftly and let him bend two or three turns of the rope around her. Only then did he turn to the rescue of Jake.

By now the boy was more than half over the rim, but his balance there was extremely precarious. 'Get my mother,' he said tersely, pulling himself up the slope, clear of the rim, to let Mark go behind. Annette was already half a dozen paces up the slope, watching the scene with her heart in her mouth. Thank God Roseanne at least had the rope round her left arm again.

The leaf mould and soil happened to be particularly thick where she was struggling to get over the rim. Despite all her efforts she had been unable to haul even one knee upon it. Her wet hands, too, kept slipping on the rope so that for every temporary inch she gained she seemed to lose a permanent two. And the timber was now slipping so fast that the rim was already level with her chest; soon only her head would be showing above the edge.

Slithering and stumbling among the detritus, Mark reached her at last. He just managed to get a grip on her upper arm when the timber finally gave way and went plummeting down into the dark. The massive reverberations it gave out as it cannoned off first one side, then the other, breaking off tons of rock and shale at each impact, was terrifying beyond anything in that long evening of terrors. And then came the tumultuous splash as it hit the water that drowned the shaft; the last echoes of that were more chilling still.

Roseanne clutched desperately at the rope in her left hand and at Mark's forearm with her right; but she felt the strength ebbing from her and knew she would never be able to pull herself up now.

'Mummy!' Jake cried in anguish.

Annette reached out and grabbed him to her. 'Don't get in the way now,' she told him. And together they watched as Mark, with one long, superhuman effort, pulled an exhausted Roseanne up and over the edge to safety.

Or to comparative safety, for, paradoxically enough, her greatest moment of danger came in one careless moment after she lay panting in the soft earth at the bottom of the slope. He released his grip in order to put the first twist of rope around her — and she let go of it for the same reason. And at that moment the mass of rubbish beneath her began to slide . . .

Again he caught her in the nick of time. And now he hauled her up and did not let go until she was wedged on the slope above him, with her boots against his legs. He stood his ground, bracing himself against any further movement, while Jake and Annette helped her get several turns of rope around her.

'For the love of God!' came Frank's tormented cry from above. 'What is happening?'

'All right!' Mark called back. 'We're all right now. Just let me see to their ropes and you can start to haul.'

'Did you say *wait* or *haul*?' came the shout.

'Wait!' the four of them yelled back.

Mark inspected them in turn, putting two half-hitches in the loose end of each rope. Roseanne was last. Their eyes met. The accusation in hers was terrible to see; he could not hold her gaze.

When he was satisfied they were secure he had to step over Jake's rope and under Annette's to untangle himself.

Jake giggled. 'Like maypole dancing,' he said.

The women's laughter bordered on hysteria. It was so impossibly wonderful merely to be standing upright again and to know that, no matter what happened now – even if they fell in a swoon – they were no longer in mortal danger.

'Haul away!' Mark shouted at the top of his voice.

They must have been waiting to hear it, straining at the winch, for the ropes went taut immediately and they had to trot a pace or two not to be dragged off their feet.

'I can stand!' Jake cried. 'Look, I can stand nearly lying down!'

An extraordinary light-headedness came over them, abetted by the unreality of their posture, for, like the

boy, they discovered that the best — indeed, only —
way to proceed was to lie back against the rope, making
a right angle with the slope and walk as if it were level
ground. And, thanks to the six burly winders, heaving
and sweating above, the effort required of them was,
if anything, less than it would have been on the flattest
of planes.

'I wonder if they started the dancing without us?'
Annette asked.

Mark remained silent but the other two laughed
immoderately. Their mood was now so febrile that if
one of them had said, 'Shorn hoggets made ten shillings
up Truro last week,' they would have thought it the
funniest thing ever.

'I'm hungry,' Jake giggled.

'I'm thirsty,' Roseanne said. 'Oh for a cup of tea!'

'I could eat an ox,' Annette told them.

That, too, was uproarious.

Mark alone kept his peace and stared grimly at the
twin lights above, which were getting farther apart by
the second.

When they had covered two thirds of the way their
hysteria settled and memories of an impossibly remote
afternoon and evening began to return.

'Was that man dead?' Annette asked Mark suddenly.

'Percy Dumont?' he replied.

'Of course!' she exclaimed. 'I knew I'd seen him
before. Major Dumont's son! Is he dead?'

'No. Concussed and hurted, but not dead.'

'Damn!'

'Nettie!' Roseanne was shocked.

Unrepentant, Annette stared across at her. 'What?'
she asked truculently.

'It's a shocking thing to say of anyone.' And when
Jake looked away, to see how his Aunt Nettie responded

499

to this rebuke, Roseanne pointed at the boy and begged with her eyes for the subject to be dropped.

'You're right,' Annette agreed, but with little conviction. 'It's not Christian.' She smiled down at Jake. 'And we were so close to Judgement ourselves, too. We should remember that.'

'I'm hungry,' he repeated — which explains why all four of them were laughing at the moment they emerged into the relief and bustle of what had, only hours earlier, been a dense, almost impenetrable patch of scrub.

'Father!' Roseanne flung herself into Frank's embrace, not even waiting for her ropes to be untied.

Tamara, too, was standing between the winch and the edge of the shaft, holding ready, like an apron, the larger remnant of Annette's torn skirt. Although her petticoats, mired and stained beyond recognition, covered her limbs to within inches of the ground, it would have mortified her not to have them more respectably covered. She hugged her saviour like a long-lost sister.

Stephen took up Jake, who clung to him like a leech, unable to utter a word for once. Then Mrs Kitto scooped him away and bore him proudly on her arms through three turns of a delirious jig.

When they had shrugged off the ropes, Mark took Annette in his arms. For a long moment neither could speak, but she felt the tenseness in his muscles. He was shivering all over — and so, she realized, was she. 'I'm sorry,' he murmured. 'I had no choice. I couldn't lose you. I couldn't lose you . . .' And she dissolved in tears at last, blubbing, 'I know . . . I know . . .'

Stephen and Roseanne stood a moment face to face, hands linked, gazing deep into each other's eyes. Neither said a word. Then she threw herself into his arms and hugged him with all her strength; and still neither of them spoke. But what could words have added to the touch of their bodies and the passion with which they clung together then?

Again it was Mary Kitto who broke up the tableau, claiming her turn to hug her daughter. By now the others were mingling and shaking hands and squeezing arms and patting backs and thanking one and all who had played a part in the rescue.

And only then — such was the measure of her emotional exhaustion — did Roseanne begin to wonder who was seeing to Jake.

The two limelights, still bathing the maw of the shaft with their intense radiance, created a zone of correspondingly intense dark in the immediate area behind them. Farther off, the kindlier light of the naphtha flares picked out the general mass of people, who were standing at a respectful distance. Still in her mother's embrace, and staring over her shoulder, Roseanne searched among them for a sign of the boy. But he was nowhere to be seen. 'Where's Jake?' she asked, beginning to feel the first twinge of renewed alarm.

Her mother squeezed her even tighter. 'He'll be all right,' she said. 'He was only now with me. Doctor Moore is tending him, I shouldn't wonder.'

In speaking this reassurance she turned them through a half-circle, leaving Roseanne facing the shaft again.

And at that moment there was a sudden flurry and commotion at the rim of it. Men who had been coiling the ropes and preparing to dowse the limelights dropped what they were doing and ran to the very edge, staring down with that special kind of paralysis that strikes into crowds when faced with death or some kindred misfortune. A terrible fear seized her.

'Jake!' she cried, struggling out of her mother's embrace and running to the knot of men.

But Stephen intercepted her, grasping her arm and pointing toward the edge of the crowd. 'He's there, look. It's all right.'

And so he was. Half obscured in the shadows, the boy stood with his hands in his pockets, a respectful distance from the edge of danger, staring intently into that limelight opening. The two of them hastened to him and squatted, one each side. He had the most curious little smile on his lips.

'What happened?' Roseanne asked. 'What are you all looking at?'

He turned calmly to her, still wearing that smile, and said, 'Now Aunty Nettie will be happy.'

Roseanne frowned in bewilderment. 'Why?'

'Remember how angry she was when Uncle Mark told her that man wasn't dead?' He turned to Stephen, eyes agog, and added, 'She said *damn*!'

His air of self-satisfied nonchalance was very familiar to Roseanne by now. The hair rose on her neck. 'Jake?' she said slowly. It was utterly impossible, of course. And yet . . .

'What?' He faced her again, his eyes large and dark. Was there a hint of secret merriment there, too?

'How . . .?' she began. 'I mean, what . . .?'

Stephen rose to his feet, lifting Jake with him. She, perforce, rose, too. For a solemn moment they stared into each other's eyes and then, as if a single will now led them both, embraced again — this time with Jake between them.

A grand silence enveloped them, and the outer world might as well, at that moment — and for a long while after — have ceased to exist.

And Jake, happy again, threw his arms round the

.necks of what he now felt sure were his mother and his father. He drew them together until their three heads touched — united at long last, just as he had always wanted.

And Roseanne just stood there in utter amazement, hugging them both, feeling her body, which should be racked with pain and misgiving, consumed instead with the most extraordinary happiness.

Then, as the snake sheds its skin, she shed the final vestige of her loneliness and isolation. Not her tenderest, most loving, most intimate moments with Jake had prepared her for the warmth of that sudden bathing of love which seemed to pour from him and Stephen toward her now.

How long they stood there, locked in that three-way embrace, she neither knew nor cared. She wished it might go on for ever. In an indifferent world, racked with greed and strife, they formed a little human tent of joy.

It was the one home she had always desired. It was the only home she ever wanted now.

MALCOLM ROSS

**A rich West Country saga
in the bestselling tradition of POLDARK**

On a Far Wild Shore

Young, beautiful and newly widowed, Elizabeth Troy travels to her late husband's Cornish home hoping to find comfort in its fertile hills and valleys. But she is shocked to discover the vast, decaying acreage of Pallas is now solely her responsibility – a legacy as unexpected as it is unwelcome.

Elizabeth's plans for her inheritance provoke the bitter hostility of her sister-in-law, Morwenna, whose word has been law at Pallas for thirty years. To bring the troubled estate back to prosperity Elizabeth must look for help elsewhere. And there are many very willing to be more than a friend to the widow – David Troy, a poor relation whose sober exterior hides some disturbing secrets; Courtenay Rodda, the sensual newspaper proprietor; and James Troy, the rich and worldly wise American cousin who begins a thrilling but dangerous liaison with Elizabeth . . .

'The book is beautifully written, the characters depicted with a passionate realism that held me entranced. I simply loved it!' Patricia Wendorf, bestselling author of *Larksleve*.

FICTION   0 7472 3001 3   £4.99

MALCOLM ROSS

The compelling Cornish saga from the bestselling
author of A NOTORIOUS WOMAN

An Innocent Woman

Brought up by her unconventional mother amid the
crème de la crème of Paris, Jane Hervey is in for a shock
when she and her widowed father go to live in Cornwall.
Polite Victorian society is a minefield of petty
restrictions and Jane's wings are further clipped by the
tyrannical behaviour of Mr Hervey, who, though fond
of his daughter, treats her like a recalcitrant child.

Being a young woman with a substantial fortune, Jane
soon finds herself courted by many of the district's
eligible bachelors. Richard Vyvyan has her family's
approval; lawyer Vosper Scawen makes no secret of his
admiration; but it is the brooding good looks and
devil-may-care reputation of Daniel Jago that hold most
appeal for Jane. On the other hand, as she observes how
the ladies of her acquaintance endure the "burdens of
married life", she wonders whether she might not be
better off a spinster. There is also a growing mystery
about her mother – and about Jane's own true parentage.

Her attempt to unravel the truth and to fathom the
eternal enigma of relations between the sexes leads Jane
on a voyage of self-discovery that is to overturn her
entire world and all its values. At the end she can no
longer count herself . . . an innocent woman.

Malcolm Ross's other West Country sagas, ON A FAR WILD SHORE
and A NOTORIOUS WOMAN, are also available from Headline.

FICTION/SAGA   0 7472 3347 0   £4.50

A selection of bestsellers
from Headline

FICTION

PARAGON PLACE	Harry Bowling	£4.99 □
THE BAD PLACE	Dean R Koontz	£4.99 □
LIPSTICK ON HIS COLLAR	Elizabeth Villars	£4.50 □
CHEYNEY FOX	Roberta Latow	£4.99 □
RASCAL MONEY	Joseph Garber	£4.99 □
THE DAMASK DAYS	Evelyn Hood	£3.99 □
LOYALTIES	Gavin Esler	£4.50 □
MONSIEUR PAMPLEMOUSSE TAKES THE CURE	Michael Bond	£2.99 □

NON-FICTION

LOSE 7LBS IN 7 DAYS	Miriam Stoppard	£3.50 □
SEXUAL AWARENESS	B & E McCarthy	£4.99 □

SCIENCE FICTION AND FANTASY

FLY BY NIGHT	Jenny Jones	£4.99 □
PUPPETMASTER	Mike McQuay	£4.99 □

All Headline books are available at your local bookshop or newsagent, or can be ordered direct from the publisher. Just tick the titles you want and fill in the form below. Prices and availability subject to change without notice.

Headline Book Publishing PLC, Cash Sales Department, PO Box 11, Falmouth, Cornwall, TR10 9EN, England.

Please enclose a cheque or postal order to the value of the cover price and allow the following for postage and packing:
UK: 80p for the first book and 20p for each additional book ordered up to a maximum charge of £2.00
BFPO: 80p for the first book and 20p for each additional book
OVERSEAS & EIRE: £1.50 for the first book, £1.00 for the second book and 30p for each subsequent book.

Name ....

Address ....

....

....

There was never any doubt where Roseanne Kitto's future lay, least of all in her own mind. From her earliest teens she had been Mark Bodilly's girl. Then one day Stephen Morvah, the squire's son, far above her in social class, invites her to the local fair – a light-hearted jest that is to change all their lives.

Roseanne, torn between her two suitors, comes to wonder whether she is really in love with either. Her immediate way out of the quandary is both surprising and, by the standards of her time, shocking: she becomes 'a woman alone'.

The differing reactions of the two men – Mark passionately angry, Stephen passionately encouraging – do nothing to help her choose between them. She *knows* Stephen would be the better catch, but she *feels* life with Mark would always be richer, more exciting. Not until dramatic circumstances force one of the two into an action that utterly rules him out does Roseanne see the solution to her dilemma . . .

Malcolm Ross's other West Country sagas, ON A FAR WILD SHORE, A NOTORIOUS WOMAN and AN INNOCENT WOMAN are also available from Headline.

United Kingdom £4.99
*Australia $12.95

*=Recommended Price Only

ISBN 0-7472-3576-7

00499

HEADLINE
Fiction/Saga

9 780747 235767